GODS' WAR

....

SARAH MACKLIN

MVmedia, LLC
Fayetteville, GA

MVmedia, LLC
PO Box 143052
Fayetteville, GA 30214
www.mvmediaatl.ocm

Publisher's Note: This is a work of fiction. Names, characters, places, and incidents are a product of the author's imagination. Locales and public names are sometimes used for atmospheric purposes. Any resemblance to actual people, living or dead, or to businesses, companies, events, institutions, or locales is completely coincidental.

Cover art by Sean Hill

Ordering Information:
Quantity sales. Special discounts are available on quantity purchases by corporations, associations, and others. For details, contact the "Special Sales Department" at the address above.

Gods' War/ Sarah Macklin. -- 1st ed.
ISBN 979-8-9905120-9-2

Contents

To all my readers. Thanks for taking this journey with me.

Chapter One

The sea smelled of home. Prince Yutuuan held on to the railing of the ship, bracing himself against the waves. They were ever closer and he swore he caught the scent of Wiluru on the air. The smell of fresh white paint on the buildings. The salt crusted along the edge of the docks. The freshness of today's catch. How he'd missed it. He couldn't wait to walk through the winding streets of his city again. He truly couldn't wait to be home again.

Far above, the lookout called the alert for Wiluru. The warriors on deck cheered and he heard the faint cheers from the other ships in the fleet. Yutuuan squinted, trying with all his might to see the capital in the distance. But what he saw was a dark smudge rising up from the coast where Wiluru should be. He knew smoke when he saw it. Yutuuan took a breath. The war had begun.

"We must be ready to fight," came Naret's voice from his left.

Yutuuan glanced to his bodyguard before studying the horizon again. "They can't have breached the gate."

Naret didn't answer immediately. "It depends on how determined the emperor is on taking the city."

"Or how determined he is to get my sister back." He spat a curse into the wind. It was a blow to his pride as crown prince and as a warrior that he wasn't there to refuse the emperor's entry into Wiluru. Instead, his sister Izriamat was the one who'd faced him down. He was sure she took great satisfaction in finally getting a chance to refuse her husband. But still it should have been him. If there was fighting to be done for the city, it should have been him leading the charge. He was supposed to be leading Wiluru back to freedom.

He watched the clouds of smoke, thankful that at least they

weren't the dark gray of raging flames. He prayed to Yutuu that only a small part of the city burned and that most of the its people were safe. He prayed that Talekh was safe. As well as their child.

Yutuuan swallowed deeply. He was a father. Surely, by now she'd had the baby. His heart clenched. He'd left her alone through all of this and now she was in a city under siege. He turned from the railing and called to the magicians to put as much wind in the sails as possible. The command was quickly relayed to the rest of the fleet.

Yutuuan hurried below deck to his quarters. With an anxious focus he brought out his armor. Before he could struggle to put the cuirass on, Naret's deft fingers were helping with the straps.

"You must keep your wits about you," he said calmly. "I know you're worried about the people and your family, your *entire* family. But you can't help them if you don't focus." Naret gave a tug on the armor. Satisfied, he moved to armor himself.

Yutuuan took a moment to close his eyes and breath. He put his forehead against the wall of the cabin feeling the movement of the ship. Naret was right. Naret was always right. The thought made him smirk. One day he would be the one dispensing wisdom.

There was a knock, polite but firm, at the door. Yutuuan pulled it open, expecting to see the ship's captain or another crew member, but it was a young man he'd been trying to avoid this entire trip back.

"Prince Mikhra," he said, trying to keep his voice even. "Did you need something?"

"Will there be fighting?" he said carefully in the trade language. "I heard warriors speaking."

Yutuuan spared a glance at Naret, whose face was neutral as a stone. "Yes, it looks like there may be fighting," he responded in trade. "You should probably stay on the ship until it's safe."

"I can help. I am a warrior also."

He glanced back at Naret who was absolutely no help. "I don't think-"

"I use sword, whip, knife, and spear." He gave a shrug. "Mother did not care for me so I used my free time to train."

Yutuuan looked over the slightly younger man. He had a good frame like he'd been diligent about his physical training.

"Have you been in battle?"

The younger prince hesitated. "No. But-"

"Then stay on the ship until I send for you."

Yutuuan pushed past the prince, heading back topside, Naret on his heels. More warriors assembled, taking in the sight along the coast. The smoke was more distinct now, wafting over the ocean. Warriors talked as they braced themselves against the chopping waves. The aura on the boat shifted from the joy of returning home to the reality of preparing for battle.

By the time the fleet had arrived at Wiluru's port, it was clear the parts of the city nearest the great gates were on fire. But something was wrong. He could see the doors of homes higher up in the city had been painted, changing their usual sea blue to the deep gray of an ocean tempest. The color of a funeral. Something deep in his stomach turned. Seeing the painted doors wasn't anything out of the ordinary but there were so many. So, so many.

Yutuuan rushed off the ship, barely taking the time to give orders for the warriors to prepare to join the war. The streets were clear and he took every shortcut he'd learned in his younger days to cut a path to the palace. Surely the war hadn't turned in the Egan's favor. Surely the damage wasn't that bad. The plan he'd started with his siblings wasn't becoming a disaster. As he neared the palace, the air became hazy, the smoke twisting and turning in the sea breeze. He slowed his pace, holding an arm in front of his nose to ward off the fumes. He began to see warriors now, those who had clearly been in the fighting but were taking a rest from the battle.

The sounds of distant combat drifted up to him and as he climbed the palace stairs he paused. He could just make out the gates of the city, standing wide open. His heart dropped to his stomach. Great columns of smoke came from the surrounding area. He could make out none of the colors of Wiluru among the warriors scurrying at the top of the wall.

Yutuuan looked behind him to see Naret and a few of the captains staring at the sight as well. Some stood stoic while others looked on in shock.

"Naret, captains," he called out. "See to the front. I will be there shortly." The captains immediately took off but Naret lingered, giving him an unsure expression. "Go on. I'll be fine." His bodyguard gave him one last look and then followed the others.

The prince ran up the stairs. Palace guards greeted him somberly as he passed, most not wanting to meet his eyes. Yutuuan hurried, a terrible worry knotting up in his chest. He didn't stop until he reached the king and queen's wing where as soon as he entered their main hall and heard the echoes of weeping.

He followed the sound, coming out into the grand meeting room where his family had entertained relatives and held personal celebrations for countless generations. On a stone bench to the side was his mother, weeping bitterly into her hands and his younger sister trying to comfort her while she cried. But in the middle of the room a dais had been erected and on it was the body of his father.

Yutuuan moved forward on stone legs. The 99th king of Wiluru, his father, was, gone. And he had been away when it happened. He suddenly found himself at the side of the funerary display, staring into his father's pale face. White flowers surrounded him, contrasting with the gray-blue robes he'd been dressed in. The light from the awninged skylight illuminated his form, making him appear almost like a specter than his flesh and blood father.

"Mama," he called hoarsely.

His mother and sister jerked their heads up. The queen struggled to her feet, running to throw her arms around her son. Yutuuan braced his emotions as both of them crushed him, weeping freely. He tried to speak, give them some words of comfort but only a choked croak came out of his mouth. When he could, he led his mother back to the bench where she sat vigil over his father's body.

"When did it happen?" he managed to get out.

"Two days ago," Umakaal answered, her voice hoarse.

He looked back at his father, guilt crushing him. He should have been here. Perhaps if he'd pushed the magicians harder to speed their ships along, he could have made it in time. He could have told his father goodbye. That he would be a good king. That the kingdom would be safe. A sob erupted from him. He sunk down on the bench beside his mother and let his tears flow.

It was firmly late afternoon by the time he could compose himself.

"Where is Izriamat?" he asked, trying to will some strength into his voice.

His mother took a deep breath. "Your father banished her from the palace."

Over his mother's head, he could see his sister make a tight face. She caught his gaze out of the corner of her eye.

"I haven't seen her for days. Not since…" Her lips shut and pursed. "We'll talk later. I'll find you."

Yutuuan nodded, wondering what had Umakaal so disgusted. "Mama," he said taking the older woman's hands, "I have to go and speak with the commanders. I'll return as soon as I can."

"Yes, yes, the battle," she said absently. She raised his hand to kiss it and sent him on.

The hardest thing he'd ever done was pull himself away from that room. He tried to turn his mind to the fight for his city and his kingdom, but his mind kept returning to his father's body, prepared for his funeral. Naret was waiting for him just outside of the palace. The man didn't say a word but put a hand on his shoulder in solidarity.

The rest of the day Yutuuan spent getting abreast of the situation of the fight with the imperial forces. They'd taken over the part of the city nearest to the gate and several buildings had been torched as they fought to control more. One of the biggest struggles was keeping a horde of regular citizens back that were trying to fight that had been conscripted by his elder sister. He cursed at the news. What in the depths was she thinking? She was going to get people killed.

But what surprised him by far was the rumor that the emperor himself had been struck down. People had seen him at the first of the fighting. His war garments would have been unmistakable. But no one had seen him since. And no one knew if he was alive and retreated or possibly even dead. Yutuuan knew it was too much to hope for the latter. That snake had slithered away to heal if he was even hurt at all. But his absence at the front was puzzling.

By that night, battle had come to a welcomed stalemate and both sides pulled back to their held territories. While Yutuuan was eager to join the fight, he was glad that his people would get the chance to rest and regain their strength. He was reminded to do so himself when a servant brought him dinner and his stomach reminded him that he hadn't eaten since his light breakfast on the ship. Yutuuan sat down, all of the weight, sorrow, and decisions he'd have to make crashing down on him. He leaned over the table, resting his head in his hands.

"Yutu," came Umakaal's voice gently.

He snapped his head up, not sure if he'd drifted off or not.

"Little sister," he called, trying not to sound devastated. "Did you want to eat? I can have something brought."

"No, I've already had dinner." She came and sat in the other chair, gesturing for him to eat. "You asked where Izri was, right?"

"Yeah. Why wasn't she at the vigil?" he asked around a bite. "Isn't she back on the route to become high priest?"

Umakaal scowled deeply, folding her arms. "Yutu, she's been… off while you've been gone. Acting like she only answers to Yutuu. Putting an army of her followers together to fight the Ega. She has followers! They're fanatics. Believing that they'll be victorious because they truly believe in her and Yutuu. It's madness. And then-" She bit her lip, plainly debating on what to say next.

"I haven't told anyone this, all right." She gave him a pointed look and he nodded his agreement to secrecy. She lowered her voice. "Right after father collapsed, I was wandering the halls at night and saw her in the palace which was strange because father banished her. I followed her to the throne room and she sat on the throne. She sat on the throne like it was hers."

Yutuuan put his utensil down, sitting back. "You're kidding. Surely, she wouldn't show such disrespect?"

"She did. I couldn't believe it. I think…I think she's making plans."

"Izri wouldn't do that." He waved the idea away. "One for the priesthood. One for the throne. That's the way it's always been. She knows that."

"You should ask her if she still does." Umakaal stared at him, her face hard. "I'm not so sure of it. She's not the sister you left behind."

Yutuuan softened his expression. "Uma, I'll talk to her. Everything will be fine. I'm here now."

His sister stiffened. "Yes. You are," she said, words clipped. "Everything will be fine. Enjoy your meal, Yutu."

Before he could respond, she left, closing the door firmly behind her.

***

The sun began to rise as the raft with her father's body was set in the waves at the shore and Umakaal still had tears left to cry. This wasn't supposed to happen for years to come. This was supposed to be a grand affair with the whole city and attendees from all of the cities come to pay their respects for their departed king. Now only her mother, siblings and his brother, the high priest, stood as family to see him off. The military commanders were at the gate district. The majority of the priests were attending to the wounded. The citizenry was locked in their homes as ordered. The beach that should be full of people was nearly empty, the gentle sound of the waves overpowering.

Umakaal looked to her brother who stood to one side of their mother. He was dressed in fresh battle clothes, looking like a perfect prince and protector of Wiluru. Their mother wore a voluminous storm gray gown, her hair unbraided and free in the wind, the look of mourning that she would wear for a full month. Umakaal's hair was also free but it would be back in braids for the war soon enough.

If her brother put her back in her proper position.

She glanced at him again as their uncle took his place to begin the ceremony. Her brother would be king. The thought was unfathomable. It was like she'd been thrown into a future that was impossible. And if he were king, he would have to relinquish command of the army to her. She almost laughed bitterly. That was something she couldn't see happening. Not with her brother's love of battle. They'd probably have to tie him to the throne.

Thoughts of the throne brought her attention to her sister. Izriamat stood to her left, hair taken out of its small braids but still restrained in one large one. She stared out at the sea, hands clasped demurely before her, face perfect as if she hadn't shed one tear or lost one hour of sleep. Hate began to fill Umakaal. Pure abject hate. Even their uncle had put off his duties as high priest to come spend hours beside the body of his lost brother. Couldn't she spare the barest bit of time from her "holy" mission to pay respect to her own father?

"Umakaal," Yutuuan called softly.

She snapped her attention back to the ceremony, realizing they were waiting for her. The youngest, and therefore the one who'd spent the least amount of time from Yutuu's creation, was supposed to sing the departed to their last voyage. She stepped forward, swallowing. All she could see was the funerary raft, the attendants waiting to send him off, and the unforgiving sea beyond. She took a deep breath and began, praying for her voice not to crack, for it not to fail her. Her father deserved the best.

Her last note faded, dying prematurely in her throat, and she stepped back. The attendants waded into the water, pushing the raft through the waist high waves. The last man stayed on the shore, using his magic to coax the waters to carry the raft farther out to sea once the others released it. Umakaal watched, her eyes glued to her father's body until it was just a dot in the waves. Her uncle made the final words over the ceremony and with that her father was gone forever.

Her mother blew one last kiss toward the ocean and let Yutuuan lead her back toward the palace. Tears ran down Umakaal's face as she turned to leave but she caught sight of Izriamat again, the woman's face still dry and unmoved.

"Why weren't you there?" someone snarled and she suddenly realized it was her own voice. Izriamat looked to her as if surprised she was there. "We held vigil for *our father* and you weren't there. His eldest. His priest of a daughter. Did you love him at all?"

Izriamat looked only slightly hurt and Umakaal didn't miss the touch of pity.

"Of course I loved him, sister."

"You swear you can heal people." Her voice grew shriller, echoing off the high hills. "Why didn't you heal him? You could have saved him!"

"Uma," her mother called. "Don't. Not now."

"She could have and didn't."

Izriamat's lips drew together, hesitantly. She spoke lowly with a tone as if she were speaking to a child.

"Father made his choices and we all have to live with the result of our choices."

White hot rage exploded in Umakaal's head and she slapped her. When her sister fell to the sand there was a moment that she regretted not using restraint. Her sister wasn't a warrior after all. But it was burned up in the anger that had consumed her. "You bitch!" she shrieked, looming over her sister. "You fucking gods damned bitch! You chose to let him die! You think you're so holy that you can play with people's lives? With our father's life?"

Suddenly she was being restrained and pulled away. She struggled with whoever it was, trying to get to Izriamat, to get her hands on her. She didn't know what she was going to do, but by Yutuu and the entirety of the gods she would make her pay.

"Uma, stop it," came her brother's sharp tone. "I'm not telling you. I'm commanding you."

Umakaal froze. Her brother had never spoken with her that way, as if he weren't her brother at all. On the ground, Izriamat looked up at her, holding her cheek. The utter betrayal in her stare, the tears that only now seemed to be forming in the corners of her eyes, made Umakaal want to lunge at her again. But her brother, her commander, her future king, told her to stop.

Izriamat took a breath, face settling into neutrality, and stood up. She brushed herself off and left in the direction of the temple of Yutuu. She didn't look back. She didn't say a word to any of them. She merely left.

The moment Yutuuan's grip slackened, Umakaal wrenched

herself from it, marching off toward the palace. She could faintly hear her mother say, "Let her go," as she left. Umakaal jogged up the stairs, thankful for the emptiness of the city. Her tears burned hot trails down her cheeks. Her sister had become a heartless monster. The same sister who she'd been so happy to see on her return had allowed their father to die.

She barely acknowledged the palace guards as she climbed the front stairs. She paused at the top, looking out toward the gate and where the battle was taking place. Muted sounds of shouts and spells drifted up letting her know that aggressions were restarting. And she was here. She hoped Yutuuan allowed her onto the field soon. If she didn't hit something, she was sure she'd combust.

Umakaal had just made it to the personal area of the palace when she heard an unfamiliar voice.

"Excuse me, Princess Umakaal?"

She turned, a little more fiercely than she'd meant to, and was confronted with a man she'd never seen before. He was tall with golden brown skin and very wavy black hair. He had a lanky build and wore what looked like a richer version of the merchants' wear at the docks. A foreigner.

"Can I help you?" she asked tightly.

"I am sorry to come to you at such a terrible time. You have my deepest regrets for the loss of your father." He bowed lowly. "I wished to speak with you earlier but it was not arranged and everyone was so very busy. I am Prince Mikhra, son of the lakhem of Rahaban."

He didn't say anything else and she waited in confusion. "Yes. Very nice to meet you. Prince Mikhra, now is not a very good time." She started to walk off.

"Perhaps, you would like to speak on the matters that trouble you?" he called. "I hope to be a good councilor to you when we are married."

Umakaal stopped in her tracks. She turned on her heel, trying to keep the rage from showing on her face.

"What are you talking about?" she said slowly.

Mikhra blinked in confusion. "Did I not speak clearly enough? When we are married, I want to be a good advisor for you."

Her face worked through a myriad of emotions. "What do you mean 'when we are married'?"

"We are to be married. Your brother arranged it with my mother. It was in exchange for dealing with the forces attacking your border." He looked shocked. "Has he not spoken with you about it?"

Umakaal ground her teeth together. She was lucky her brother wasn't king yet because it would not be as high of a crime when she beat him to a pulp. She struggled to compose herself.

"No. No he hasn't."

"You… do not seem pleased by this news."

She released some of her anger. "I am only surprised. My brother usually consults me about matters of state in which I'll be involved."

Disappointment colored his thin face. "I am sorry to be the one to bring this news to you." It was clear that he was choosing his words carefully. "And I am sorry that my presence causes you…discomfort."

"You do not cause me discomfort," she snapped, her frustration and anger slipping through. "I do not like men. Do you understand? So when I married, I was hoping to choose a husband who would understand that."

He frowned in thought, clearly running over the words. His eyebrows rose with understanding then fell ever so slightly in disappointment.

"I see. In the future, I would hope that we can be at the least amicable to each other. Perhaps even friends." He gave her a small, sincere smile.

"I hope so," she ground out.

He bowed deeply. "Please, do not let me keep you from your duties. Once again, I am so sorry for your great loss."

"Thank you," she said quickly and walked off.

Her anger had cooled some but she was still in a mood. Her father was gone, her sister was a monster, and now her brother had bartered away the one choice she thought she'd get to make in her life. All she wanted to do now was go to her rooms and throw herself into Ladawi's arms, crying herself to unconsciousness.

***

Izriamat entered the palace through one of the private side entrances, not wanting to cause a stir at this time of night. The guards there were sympathetic to her and allowed her to enter despite her father's order barring her from the building. She moved through the halls quietly, her destination the throne room. She had questions that needed to be answered and that was the best place to seek them.

There were no guards at the door at this hour and she placed her hands on the carved wood reverently. How many times had she and Yutuuan sat just outside these doors as small children, eavesdropping on council meetings, the guards indulging the two oldest royal children. It seemed like entering here was stepping into another realm where the kingdom could be changed with mere words.

Now, she understood that it may be just another room, but words spoken here still changed the kingdom. And perhaps even lands beyond.

Izriamat stepped inside, crossing the long carpet that the council sat on either side of when a meeting was in session. She stopped before the throne, taking it in. The twists and curves of the fused and carved driftwood displayed the full expertise of Wiluruan craftspeople. She knelt on the carpet before it, hands in her lap. This throne had been occupied by so many generations of her forebearers it was hard to contemplate. Whoever sat on it now would have to have the fortitude to lead Wiluru through one of its hardest times.

She closed her eyes, pulling inward, to the part of her that was connected to her god. Guidance was what she needed at this moment. No, not guidance. Assurance. By Wiluruan tradition, it wasn't her place to take leadership. She, as the oldest, was meant to become the high priest to lead the kingdom spiritually as her brother would lead it from here. But these were not traditional times. Wiluru needed a strong leader, a leader who could bring it back to its former glory. Only she had known the horrors of the Ega. She had been in the heart of their cruelty. Only she knew how best to fight against them. And after they were once again free, she would see her kingdom restored.

Visions of the destruction of the Egan temples came to her. She stood before them as they were brought down brick by brick. She saw each and every Egan who fouled the kingdom with their presence chased out to return to their horrid country. Every single sign of the occupation would be washed from Wiluru and she would be free again. The thought brought her an elation that caused tears to come to her eyes.

She doubled over, overwhelmed and thankful to Yutuu for the vision of Wiluru's future. It was all the assurance she needed.

The doors opened behind her and she sat up, comporting herself. Footsteps approached quietly and she looked back to see her brother walking in. She granted him a smile. He would be so sad that he wouldn't rule but he would have to understand that it was for the best.

"Yutuuan, good evening."

"Izri," he said. There was a cautiousness to his voice. "I didn't expect to find you here. I thought you were staying at the temple." He sat down beside her.

"I had so many swirling thoughts about our father's death. I thought it might be best to meditate here."

He chuckled. "I suppose I had similar thoughts." He stared up at the throne for a moment. "It's strange to think we'll never see him sit on the throne again. We'll never hear his voice again. I always knew this day would come but I also never thought it would."

"Father was an old man for most of our lives. It was foolish for us to think we'd have him for much longer."

Yutuuan stared at her for a moment. She could see his face shifting subtly in various emotions before he looked back at the throne.

"So you can heal now," he said after some silence.

"I can," she said. Part of her felt a true question hang over them. Could she have healed their father? And part of her didn't want to answer him, didn't want to see the look of betrayal on her little brother's face.

Another weighted silence passed between them, with Yutuuan pointedly not looking in her direction. She had to wonder what was going through his mind. She didn't know him, not truly if she thought about it. He'd been a boy when she'd left, caught in that lanky awkward stage between child and man. Now he was grown, a military commander who'd seen combat and war. His experience in such matters would be invaluable. He obviously enjoyed his position. He could continue in it.

Yutuuan cleared his throat. "We will have to plan for my coronation. I'm hoping to have this battle finished soon and then we can go ahead, but it may have to be faster. I know uncle Munabis is high priest but I want you to do it. I'd like to have my sister's blessing." He turned toward her with that crooked smile of his. "It could be the sign of a new beginning."

Sadness started to creep in her, making her hesitate with an answer, but she pushed it away. She forced a smile to her lips. "When that day comes, I'll be happy to do it." It was the truth.

Yutuuan nodded, satisfied, and turned back toward the throne. He sighed. "Izri, there's something else I wanted to talk to you about. Your…people at the gate. We need them to leave. Can you call them back?"

Izriamat's face fell into neutrality. "No," she answered calmly.

He stared at her, confused. "Izri, they're in the way. We've had to spend time and people trying to save them from their own stupidity."

"They have chosen to defend their home," she snapped. "It isn't stupidity that drives them. It is faith. Perhaps you should have more of it."

Yutuuan's face set in a hard way she hadn't seen before. She truly didn't know him. She only knew the boy of seven years ago. "Sister, the warriors are here now. I need them gone. Tell your people to pull back."

"I will not."

"Tell them to pull back or I will have them removed. If they fight back, it won't be a gentle removal either."

She raised her chin. "If you remove those at the front, there are more that are willing to take their place. Yutuu has called them."

"I don't have time for you and your fanatics," he said, voice rising. "Do as I say. I will be your king."

"But you will never be higher than my god. Yutuu will see his kingdom freed and through his people, the people of true faith, it will be."

Yutuuan leaned back, mouth hanging slightly open. "This isn't a game, Izri."

"I am far more aware of that than you are."

Her brother was taken aback. "You'd really put regular people in real danger just to prove a point?"

"Of course you don't understand," she breathed out. "Yutuu has spoken to me. I heard him directly. It is time for Wiluru to be free and time for us to serve him and the other gods completely and faithfully. We can only win this as a people."

Yutuuan didn't respond. He stood, shaking his head, and began walking back to the doorway. "A forceful removal then."

Izriamat only sighed as she heard the door close behind her. He didn't understand. Uma didn't either. But they would in time.

Chapter Two

Everything was going to shit. Tutahmen looked at the head of Kolehem in the basket and tapped his fingers angrily on his worktable. The young commander's face was frozen in a scream of pure terror, lips pulled back like a beast frightened of the slaughter. He supposed that was appropriate. Not another sign of the force he'd sent into the Ibatu'bangi had been seen. Just Kolehem's severed and water rotted head. One could only assume the rest of the force lay in pieces across the jungle floor. An absolute waste.

He flicked his hand and the soldier that brought it in took the basket away. Tutahmen leaned forward, resting his elbows on the table. Everything was going to shit. Nsongo drowned in chaos, the city split between the areas the empire still controlled and the section the Nsongans had managed to push them out of completely. Bold bastards, these Nsongans. He hadn't been one of the ones foolish enough to think the fight had been beaten out of them. But he had thought them smart enough to not fight back anymore. He supposed with the dara that had surrendered dead, they'd decided to get back to their bullheaded warrior ways.

This rebellion could be put down easily if not for the monsters. While he was trying to muster his troops and form a counter offensive, his men were being picked off, dismembered one by one. They were growing scared of the night and that wouldn't do. He couldn't have the might of the Ega, the force that had taken down the proud and powerful Nsongo, frightened of the dark like children. These things would have to be found and killed as well.

He dragged a weary hand down his face. Could they be killed? He hadn't even seen one. They were huge, gray skinned beasts, claws like sickles. At least, that was the description he'd pieced together from the poor man who'd escaped the first expedition. He'd ask the Nsongans for what their people had seen but they weren't exactly on speaking terms at the moment. And all this caused by one man who'd pissed off the tiny people of the jungle.

Tutahmen slammed his fist on the table, the sound filling the room. Everything was going to shit. And he was the only one here to clean it up.

He took a calming breath and stood, leaving the room. His main servant came to him immediately. The woman must have heard his footsteps approach the hall.

"Did you need anything, general?" she said in her Nsongan accent.

"Let anyone who's looking for me know that I've gone to access the current battles." She bowed. "And you may keep to your own activities until I return." He could give her that bit of rest. She'd been a most dutiful servant since they'd taken her home as their main headquarters. Her own servants had fallen in line behind their mistress as soon as she surrendered. She deserved a reward. Perhaps he'd let her visit her children and grandchildren soon.

Soldiers saluted him as they went about their duties outside. He saluted in return, heading out into the city. It had been too long since he'd taken a personal assessment of the battle. Things were starting to grind to a halt with both sides holding their lines firmly. A way to break them again had to be found.

This part of the city was full of soldiers moving to and fro. He didn't worry about an escort. They were completely secure in this district. It was the heart of Egan power in Nsongo. There was no way that they could be overrun here. But there was the possibility of surrounding them.

Tutahmen's lips pulled into a tight line. Their only way of exit would then be the river and a small side gate. Neither ideal and both could be easily monitored and blocked. He should have thought that through but he thought the Nsongans had been dealt enough damage to not be able to strike back. He would never underestimate them again.

He made his way down toward the river. The sounds of battle wafted to him on the breeze, the shouts of his people mingling with the distinctive war cry of the south. He came to a spot where a group of officers gathered in a small square, talking strategy. One was the new commander of the Red Wings and Tutahmen felt a pang of pity for the man. To have to take over an infamous regiment after nearly half their forces had been killed in the jungle. He had a lot to accomplish.

The group saluted stiffly as he approached. "General Tutahmen," one of the men said, an older commander he remembered from the war. "We weren't expecting you."

"I decided to come and assess the situation for myself, Ketmekun. Have we regained any ground today on the riverside?"

The commanders looked to each other with a wariness he didn't like at all. Ketmekun, the senior of the group, spoke up. "We haven't unfortunately. In fact, we've barely kept the position we had yesterday." He hesitated again. "We lost more men during the night."

Another commander spoke up. "We found them just before first meal. What was left of their bodies was piled outside the front door of one of the barracks." He looked sick. "All of their heads were turned to face out in a ring around the remains."

"Sir," another commander began, "how are we going to combat these creatures *and* the Nsongans?"

Tutahmen cast his sharp gaze on the younger man. "I know that is not defeat I hear in your voice."

"No, sir," he stammered.

"We will have to be even more vigilant in the night. Ketmekun, select your best men. Archers especially. Make them a squad to hunt down these monsters. They come from the trees when they're in the forest. Perhaps here they might favor the roofs to make their attacks. No man who is not on active duty is to be outside during the night."

"Yes, sir," the commanders said in unison.

Tutahmen looked toward the river and the great, thick forest beyond. He prayed that fool Hotempkhar had died an excruciating death for causing all of this. It was his fault for angering the forest people and now monsters harried them. How in the world were they going to fight off creatures that no one ever saw coming?

I know that is not defeat I hear.

"Take down every door, every shutter that isn't necessary.

Turn our holdings into a fortress. If the Nsongans want a war, they'll have to learn how difficult a siege is." He looked to the roofs, eyes catching a shadow that was only a black winged bird. He schooled the panic that spiked within him. He would not succumb to fear of monsters. "Everyone will pitch in with the effort. Including myself." The other commanders seemed reluctant so he added. "Anyone caught slacking or shirking their duties will be left out as a sacrifice for the creatures."

"Yes, General," they said in unison.

"Good. As you were." The group saluted him and he returned the gesture.

As he walked away, taking in the surrounding area, his eyes kept flitting up at the roof. Tutahmen cursed himself. He was starting to jump at shadows. They were just plays of the light, the sun on a bird wing or a stray animal. However, what if the creatures were watching them even now? What if they were even working for the Nsongans? He paused. He hadn't heard of any Nsongan casualties since the killings started and the whole city would have known if they had. Those people made a racket when someone passed away. If the forest people and the Nsongans were in league then they had to find a way to neutralize one of the forces against them to win.

He looked up quickly as a shadow passed over him only to see a flock of birds. He breathed out his frustration. Damned nerves.

When he reached the compound headquarters, he stopped, taking in all the soldiers lounging about. Clearly, they had grown too lax during their occupation. The Nsongans would have to bleed again to learn their place in the empire and bleed they would.

"Get up you sorry group," he yelled out to the main courtyard. "We have work to do."

***

There were bodies in the street, arrows sticking out of them like porcupine quills. Efemu and his force hunkered down behind the makeshift barricades blocking the alleyways on one side of the wide thoroughfare. Across the way, the Ega forces had also walled off every side street and entrance. All attempts to cross the street and attack had been met with a shower of arrows or spears from the opposing faction. It was going to be a stalemate until either one side was depleted or someone was bold enough to make a full charge.

Efemu took a long swig from his waterskin, wiping his mouth on the back of his hand. Judging by the heat of the afternoon, they would probably get a heavy shower tonight. His lips twisted into a wry smile. At least it would rinse some of this dust and sweat off.

He looked up to the rear of the alley from where he sat as a small group of warriors arrived. The leader picked her way through the cramped quarters, saluting him.

"Commander Efemu, we scouted as far as the spice merchant row and it looks like the Ega have made a full perimeter around the area they've taken. And it looks like they're trying to take over piece by piece instead of a full offensive attack."

"Have the people been able to evacuate?" he asked.

She shook her head, braids swaying. "No way to tell. It didn't seem to be inhabited by anyone but the Ega, but they could have, well…" She made a noncommittal gesture, not wanting to speak the other possibility.

Efemu gave a sharp nod, not wanting to think of the possible slaughter of Nsongans. "Good job," he said. "Return to your regular positions." The group saluted and dispersed down other streets.

This was not how he wanted this battle to go. They enjoyed the element of surprise for quite a bit, picking out Egan strongholds and slaughtering the warriors inside. They'd made a good dent in the forces squatting in their city, especially with a force lost to the forest across the river. It was exhilarating. But he should have known their general would find his footing soon enough.

Tutahmen. He remembered that man from the war. He was a good strategist even if his warriors weren't nearly as fearsome as the Nsongans. But the Egan had numbers on their side. If things had been even, they wouldn't have stood a chance. But that was the past. This was now. Tutahmen had rallied his people to set up defenses and dig in to make parts of the city fully theirs. It had turned into a new war for the city, one they had to win or there might not be a Nsongo left this time.

A hand touched his shoulder. "Commander," said his second in command, Seri. "You've been up for two days. Pull back and get some rest. We have this."

Efemu ran a hand down his face, feeling the scruffy beard that was growing. He remembered when Barabi would have to remind him to rest as well. He reluctantly nodded, patting the woman on the shoulder.

The other warriors saluted him as he made his way away from the edge of battle. He could only give a halfhearted acknowledgment. Now that he didn't have to be on edge, weariness was crashing down on him. He would sell his station and all his possessions for a bath and a bed right now. He had half a mind to find Barabi before he collapsed onto a bedroll, to see how his love was doing. Barabi had been assigned a different commander for this conflict and it was the first time they'd been apart in war. But the man would be miffed at being distracted from his own post. Better to seek him out later.

Efemu walked back to the drink house they were using as a makeshift barracks. It wasn't the best accommodation but it was inside and safe. There was little more a warrior could ask for. He took a moment to speak with the injured at the rear of the room. He made sure all of their needs were being taken care of and tried his best to boost their morale with promises of good alcohol and a few jokes. He started to head upstairs to the room set aside for him when someone called his name.

He couldn't help the sigh as the runner hurried his way over. "What is it?" he said, defeated.

"Your father wishes to speak with you immediately," the younger man panted.

"Truly?" Efemu growled and regretted it when the other man flinched. He patted him on the shoulder. "My anger wasn't meant for you. Forgive me. Thank you for the message." The runner nodded and rushed on his way.

Efemu closed his eyes for a moment, struggling to compose himself. His father forced him and the warriors of this city into this conflict and now he wanted to interrupt his command. He snorted in frustration. Fine then. He turned away from the stairs and the sleep he so desperately wanted and headed back into the city.

The trek to the council building was a long and odd one. The streets of Nsongo, usually so lively, were quiet save for the distant sounds of conflict in the river district. War Minister Ngali led the offensive there and he was sure the battle was bloody. But in the heart of the city only the occasional stray dog wandered about. It was eerie.

He didn't have to ask where his father was within the council building. The man usually savored his new position as Great Dara in the main reception room with assistants waiting on his every word and command. Efemu entered the room keeping the look of contempt from his face as he set eyes on his father. The high priest turned leader of the southern lands sat on the ornate stool of the daraship. A trio of servants, including that acolyte he so favored, brought him food and reports. He was out of his usual priestly robes, wearing something more warrior class in rich blue. An absolute farce. A damned costume.

Efemu placed his fist over his heart, bowing slightly. "Father, you called for me?"

Erenemo turned a stern eye on his son. "Tell me of the battle."

"We have maintained our line on Western Way. The enemy has dug in and so far, we're at a stalemate. We're trying to find a weakness in their defenses but haven't so far."

"It's been nearly a week since you secured that area," Erenemo said, testy. "I would have thought that a commander with your experience would have made more headway by now."

Efemu held in a tired sigh. "The Ega have set up their area like a fortress. We can't just throw our men at it. We have to find a gap, a weakness."

"Find one." The statement was a hard command.

Efemu felt his left eye twitch. "We are trying to do so," he ground out.

"Trying isn't doing. If you were really taking this battle seriously, you would have routed more of the Ega out of the city by now."

"Father, war doesn't happen on our schedule. If you were a warrior, you would know this." It took him a moment before he realized he'd spoken his last comment aloud.

His father sat reed straight, indignation like lightning in his eyes. "Leave us," he snapped at the attendants. Erenemo stared him down as they shuffled out and Efemu didn't look away from the challenge. "Who do you think you're talking to, boy?"

"I haven't been a boy for a long time."

"I am your father and your Great Dara-"

"Temporary Great Dara."

"You will show me the proper respect and obey my commands." His father's voice had risen in the way it did when he used to chastise him as a child and Efemu didn't find himself in the least frightened.

Efemu blinked, letting the silence hang in the air. "Why aren't you speaking on this with War Minister Ngali? This is her army."

"Because you are the commander of this front and I would like to hear from your mouth why you have stopped advancing." He narrowed his eyes. "Now, I wonder if the reason is apathy or sheer obstinance."

Efemu stopped himself from going into a tirade. His father still thought him a child and a fool. Yes, he knew he wasn't the most brilliant man but he wasn't completely incapable. And he knew he was a damn good leader. "Father," he said mustering all the control in his tone that he could, "I will not spend my warriors' lives carelessly just because you say so. I will disobey you, I would have disobeyed Ashaki, and I would have disobeyed my uncle if it had come to it. These people are my family until they are released from my command and I take that responsibility to heart. So, we will work to find a way to break the Ega defense and it will happen in time. You'll just have to accept that."

"Obey or I will have you replaced with someone who will follow my orders."

He wanted to snap back at his father. This is why priests didn't become dara. Don't take your frustrations at not being a warrior out on these people. But he was too tired. The threat of taking away his command didn't stab him the way he thought it would. If he was demoted, so be it. It would only build his case as to why his father was unfit to be dara.

"If you feel that someone else would be better for this position, then I can't stop you, father," he said calmly. "But I know how to win a battle and that is what I'm going to do. Is there anything else?"

"Watch yourself, boy." Erenemo flicked his hand at him, an insulting dismissal.

Efemu bowed to his father and turned to leave. This was a waste of time, just like he'd known it was going to be. Gods, his father was having him long for the days of Ashaki's rule. At least she'd kept the city going and she would have plans in place for this battle. A shame she was poisoned. And by her own daughter. Truly a tragedy. He couldn't imagine hating his father that much, but a good punch in the stomach might be in order. Efemu chuckled as he walked back to the front to finally get some much needed rest.

***

Erenemo looked over the map of Nsongo, his fingers tapping in a quick rhythm. The beautifully detailed map took up most of the large table. Figurines representing their forces and that of the Ega were placed at different districts showing the progress they'd made in clearing out their enemy. Smaller pieces denoted places of battle. There was the force led by War Minister Ngali along the river. The fighting had been fierce there, slow but fierce, and he had no doubts that she would clean out that area soon.

There was the force at the Smelter District, where Egan forces were stationed to oversee the production of gold and other valuable metals. Commander Lambem was clearing them out building by building. Erenemo had made sure that Barabi was sent there to be strategist. He wanted that too-clever-by-far boy as far away from his son as possible. He was sure it was him who put these disobedient ideas in Efemu's head. Even this idea that Efemu could possibly be Great Dara. It was utter foolishness and Erenemo needed to squash it as soon as possible.

He glared at the figurine representing his son on the map and the line they'd yet to break. The Ega lay just over Western Way. How difficult could it be to find a way around their defenses? Buildings had back entrances and windows. There had to be something that the Ega had forgotten to protect. Even if there was an entrance that had but a handful of soldiers that was a sure way in. These people weren't nearly the warriors that the Nsongans were. They'd had superior numbers. Cut off from each other in the city they couldn't be nearly as successful.

He was brought back to his son's insolence. That boy had promised to disobey his orders. He'd talked back to him. This was not the son he'd raised. His Efemu had been a respectful, obedient, even delightfully rambunctious son. This Efemu was growing more insolent by the day and Erenemo was beginning to think that he would have to bring the boy to heel very soon.

A servant timidly knocked on the door to his office. Erenemo looked up impatiently. "What is it?"

"Great Dara," they said bowing, "You have a visitor. Dara Ngoli from Ofolubaru."

Erenemo stood. The dara herself. This was quite unusual. "Do you have her in a meeting room?"

"Yes, Great Dara. With food and drink."

"Good. Lead me to her."

The servant bowed again and took him through the halls of the council building to a room set up to receive important visitors. It opened up to a courtyard with a statue of the first Great Dara of Nsongo, a lanky man named Ogulo. In the statue's hands were Ogulo's favorite spear and shield chiseled in exquisite detail. Erenemo would have to have his own statue carved one day.

He found the eastern dara perched on a stool near the courtyard to take advantage of the breeze. She nervously sipped from a glass of wine. The food on the table was only barely nibbled on. She looked like a hastily cleaned up mess. Her clothes still sported the faintest marks of road dust and her hair, while still beautifully braided, was slightly unkempt toward the roots. Her two attendants or bodyguards or whatever they were didn't appear much better. They looked like they'd run all the way here and that would be an interesting tale to pull out of her.

She looked up, surprised at his approach, and immediately stood. "High priest Erenemo," she said with a deep and graceful bow. "I mean, Great Dara Erenemo. I am honored to be in your presence."

He took in her saccharine smile as she rose and gave her a less enthusiastic one. If he wanted his ass kissed, he had people for that. "Dara Ngoli, it is good to see you again. We missed your presence at my niece's funeral."

Her smile twitched. No, he wasn't going to let her forget the slight. "I apologize for not being there to show my respects for our transitioned Great Dara. There were many matters happening in my city that I could not be pulled away from. Which is why I have come to you now."

"Oh?" He motioned for her to take her seat and took the stool at the other side of the table. "Is that why you've appeared before me, barely cleaned up from the road, a trip that looks like it was arduous and hasty?" He wanted to test just how desperate this woman was. If he wanted to be officially installed as Great Dara, he would need the support of the daras of the other great cities. Having Ngoli owing him a debt would be very favorable.

Her smile faltered as the barb pricked her. This was a very prideful woman. She visibly forced herself to look pitiful.

"Yes. I and my most trusted bodyguards had to escape Ofolubaru rather quickly. There is a horrible woman, a witch who claims to be the speaker for the god of death who's taken over my city. She commands vultures and has two hyenas the size of a house that protect and fight for her. She's brought an army of common people into the city to squat there. They call her the Lady of Death. And she has an Egan assassin. She ran me from my own city, the city my father and grandfather ruled over as dara."

Erenemo stared at the woman. "So you're going to tell me that a witch with an army of vagabonds came into your city and you and all of your peacekeepers were run out?"

"She and her beasts killed so many of my peacekeepers that

there was nothing I could do. Please, Great Dara, I need your help."

"For what exactly?" Erenemo asked.

Dara Ngoli blinked. "To take back my city. I need forces, enough to put this rabble back in line." A poisonous tone had crept back into her tone. There was the young dara he remembered. "I want my city back. And…and I will be in your debt." She reached over the table, putting her hand gently on his and Erenemo had to resist pulling away. "You will have my utter loyalty, Great Dara."

He savored the way she said his title, with the utmost reverence. He patted her hand, slyly removing himself from her grasp. "I so far have only been voted in as temporary Great Dara. And I have engaged in a war against the Ega, to expel them from our lands. I will need the support of the great cities in order to have this position permanently. The council must see that there is no other choice and once I'm fully invested, I will free us from occupation."

"I see," she said hesitantly. "I will gladly speak on your behalf if I regain my city. I will even work to improve your standing in their eyes while I am in your city."

Erenemo grinned, feeling like a predator about to strike. "But I will need more than just your good words, my dear deposed dara." He poured himself a cup of the wine. "I will need your forces. I know that when the Ega occupied our area, you were very accommodating to them. I find it strange that your city had virtually no Ega military presence when all of the other cities did."

Her brown skin colored maroon. "I was doing what I could to protect my people."

"You were doing what you could to protect your coffers. I know the Ega of their capital love your carved goods as much as we do. Trade above loyalty to the people of the south, correct? And then there are other rumors about what you did to protect your city." Erenemo took a sip to let her wriggle in the net.

She gasped indignantly. "Those are no more than filthy rumors set out by my enemies. I make no secret of who my lovers are and I assure you they have never been one of the northerners."

"That is good to hear. So, back to forces lent to the cause of expelling the Ega."

The dara looked as if she were swallowing bile. "I will be more than willing to lend you my forces to eradicate the northern pests."

"Excellent." He stood and she did as well. "I assure you, Dara Ngoli, you will have your city back from this 'lady of death.' I'll even send one of my best commanders to head the force."

She bowed, stiffly. "Thank you, Great Dara. Your generosity is overwhelming."

He nodded and left the room, pleased. One of the daras who'd slighted Nsongo so greatly was now in his debt, utterly and completely. She'd let common ruffians and some wild witch run her away so she wasn't as mighty as she'd like to think.

He paused in the hall, thinking. He'd promised to send one of his best commanders to take care of this and that's exactly what he would do. Efemu needed to be knocked down a peg. Being pulled from the fight for his home, away from all of his comforts, was just what he needed. Then perhaps he'd learn the lesson his father had tried so hard to instill in him.

Erenemo bowed his head making a gesture of supplication to the gods. He'd have to thank them for this stroke of good fortune.

Chapter Three

Mgobe walked through the streets of Djelebe, sandals kicking up small clouds of gray dust that clung to the hem of his long robes. Ash floated in the air in sparse flecks, dancing in the breeze. The breeze also carried the smell of smoke from the barely put out fire. It twisted the large column of smoke, leaning it towards the edge of the city from its origin of the ruins of the great library. The governor dragged his eyes up towards the ruined building, a black scar among the other taller structures of the city. The sound of creaking and crumbling wood echoed faintly through the silence.

Thousands of students of all levels of knowledge made the pilgrimage here to study in the library's rooms. To learn of the history of this land long before the empire. To become masters of the magical arts. To become healers of great renown. And it had been his duty to oversee it and the city that serviced it.

He bent to the dirt road, grasping a handful of ash that had been the work of countless generations. He paused as he realized the scrap of a page was hidden in the ash. As he tried to gently uncurl it, it crumbled into pieces, blowing away with the rest of the ash in his hand. Mgobe felt tears prick the corners of his eyes. He was a failure. The one thing he had under his protection and he'd been too much of a coward to do so.

Now the library was gone.

It had burned for three days, spreading to nearby buildings before magicians were able to contain it and containing it was all they could do. The rest of the city had been spared thanks to their efforts. Yet, it was clear that embers still waited to rise back into flame. The closer the governor moved toward the ruins, the hotter it became, pulling beads of sweat from his head.

He passed a group of city guards cautiously picking through the rubble of one of the adjacent buildings. When the fire began to rage, not everyone had been able to evacuate. The flames consumed with an unearthly hunger, blazing with renewed vigor when it reached more fuel. These buildings, support areas for the library and other centers of teaching, collapsed a few hours after the fire began. Part of Mgobe wanted to tell the guards to give up their search. It was useless. If the people trapped weren't crushed when the building collapsed, they surely were cooked alive. But he couldn't tell these people to abandon the hope of finding even one survivor. If this were how they kept themselves together after such a tragedy, he wouldn't snatch it away.

Mgobe walked along the road that circled the Library despite the heat. He bowed in respect to the charred wood and over baked and broken bricks that lay scattered. He bowed to the Library that had stood for countless generations, to the untold centuries of knowledge held in books and scrolls that could never be replaced. He bowed to the lost life, the most precious treasure of Djelebe. All lost because of the emperor.

The governor ground his teeth at the thought of that selfish, evil man. That…tyrant. He'd stolen so many of Djelebe's promising and powerful magicians to force them to serve in his army, to force them to become monsters. Then he'd burned the library despite their protests. Despite their pleas that burning the library would be a loss of knowledge unfathomable. And he'd given the order anyway. Mgobe's hands pulled into tight fists. If he ever laid eyes on the emperor again, he wasn't sure he could restrain himself.

"Governor," a voice, cracked with age, called to him.

Mgobe looked to his left to see three scholars walking up. Their robes were streaked with soot and looked rumpled from days of continuous wear. He recognized the oldest of the men from his time studying at the library "Learned Kiteme," he began' trying to bring the dignity of his position into his voice. "How can I help you?"

The trio gathered close, one of them glancing about as if he were trying to make sure no one was around to listen. "Can you come with us? We have something to show you."

Mgobe nodded and followed the scholars through the gray streets. The people who bowed to him as he passed reflected the same haunted look in their eyes that he had and he wondered if the sadness would ever leave this place. He wasn't so sure.

The group reached a building on the far northwest side of the city, almost against the outer wall. It was a modest structure with three floors, its façade modestly decorated with the bright geometric shapes of Djelebe's style. They entered, heading up the red brick stairs to the third floor. The elder scholar paused before the wooden door.

"We wanted to be sure the soldiers were long gone before we showed you."

When he pushed the door open and Mgobe entered the governor nearly fell to his knees. Crowded on every wall from floor to ceiling were neatly stacked scrolls and books. The scent of aged paper and glue filled his nostrils. It took him back to his youth spent with his nose in a tome next to a stack of books tall enough to hide him should his responsibilities come to find him. Mgobe took tentative steps into the room, looking about, mouth open. He couldn't count how many works were here and while it was a mere fraction of what the Library had held, at least some of it had been saved.

"How is this possible?" he asked, turning back to the scholars.

One of the younger ones, a high scholar of nature magics by the cuff he wore on his wrist, answered. "We labored to get as many works as we could out when the call to burn the library went out. There were many of us stealing. We even used back passages when the burning started."

"There are more on the second floor," Kiteme added. "And in the basement."

The other scholar chimed in. "Some of the scholars left behind are beginning to look through the rubble to see if we can find other works that were spared." The hope in her eyes stirred something in Mgobe. "Even if they are in pieces, we might be able to put them back together. Perhaps copy them."

Mgobe took in the trio of dedicated scholars before him. He could do nothing but admire their bravery in the face of the destruction of their life's work. He bowed to them, deeply. "Thank you for saving our history."

Horns blew toward the eastern gate. Everyone's heads snapped toward the sound. Visitors were arriving. After exchanging confused glances, they hurried downstairs and to the streets, Mgobe taking the lead. By the time they'd gotten close to the main gates, his lungs burned and there was a nagging pain in his side.

Mgobe came to a stop. A small group of soldiers, a few on horseback, most on foot, were making their way into the city. Flags hung limp from the front flagbearer's pole. It flapped once in the wind, showing the imperial insignia clearly before falling slack once more. Mgobe forced himself to walk forward slowly, normally, unconcerned with seeing that symbol once again. He'd regained his breath enough by the time he stopped in front of the group.

"Governor Mgobe," the leader of the group said urgently. A bit too urgently. Almost like he was hiding distress. "We need your healers. Immediately. The emperor has been injured. Our healers have been able to keep him away from the other side but we need Djelebe's abilities."

The soldier's words fell away as Mgobe looked past him to the middle of the procession where four men held another aloft on a stretcher. He could just make out the figure resting on it. The emperor, the source of all his woes, had been delivered to him. He subtly looked around him. A gathering of city guards had gathered for the soldiers' arrival. To his rear, the scholars were still with him and a few were coming out to the main street to see the arrival. His people may not be warriors, but they were skilled in magical arts that these soldiers were not. He could practically feel the hatred of his people. They were ready and so was he.

Governor Mgobe took a breath. "Capture them."

***

Sept'ha sat in a quiet corner of Hetsaf's room, meditating. Her dreams had been troubled lately, her mood both irritated and elated. She felt as if there was something coming, something she needed to be doing. She tried to reach out to her goddess. Pray to her goddess? Call her? She didn't know how to do this. She was no priest. Met always came to her when she least expected it. Why couldn't she just show up when Sept'ha wanted her to?

That would actually be convenient.

Frustrated, she rose from the floor to seek out her conspirator in service to the goddess of war. The other servants in the halls didn't meet her eyes as she walked along. But she caught the disapproving frowns or smirks. Her reputation as Hetsaf's kept woman had spread across the palace. It rankled her that everyone thought of her as no more than a bed warmer but it was the best way she could think of to be close to the chancellor. She would just have to endure.

When she walked into Hetsaf's office, she found him hunched over his desk, reading a paper. His shoulders were tight and one of his hands gripped the edge of the desk. Sept'ha paused. It couldn't be good news. "Chancellor," she called.

Hetsaf looked up, clearly not realizing she was there. He motioned curtly for her to enter. She came to his side of the table, taking a side glance at the paper. All she managed to see was the name of a general she hadn't learned from Hetsaf. "Bad news?" she asked casually.

"News from the south," he said sourly. "The Nsongans have revolted."

Sept'ha froze then leaned over to read the message herself. It was true. Nsongo had revolted. The force that they'd sent into the forest to find the gold mines had been killed. They were now in a fight for the city. "So now we have a revolt in the west and south." She cursed. It had been more than enough to deal with when it was just the war at Wiluru and a simple peasants' revolt. The southerners were legendary warriors. She'd heard stories about them as a child. It was generally considered a miracle that the army even defeated them. The empire was on fire. Even Met couldn't want this much war.

"We don't have the troops to expend for this. An entire regiment is lost. What troops we still have here need to protect the capital." He turned an angry gaze her way, causing Sept'ha to take a step back. "Is this what your goddess wants? The empire to fall apart?"

She swore she could hear a distant laugh somewhere. "Met is the goddess of war," she responded. "This is her worship. Just because the empire is faced with war everywhere doesn't mean that we won't win. We have to be smart and have some faith."

Hetsaf grunted. "Tell your goddess that she could warn us before she upsets everything."

Sept'ha started to refute him, but part of her agreed. Met hadn't spoken with her in over a week. She hadn't had even the whiff of a vision of what the future might hold for them. But he didn't need to know that. "So what can we do to aid the forces at Nsongo? Do they need more supplies? More weapons?" She snapped her fingers. "What about the former priests? Most of them are magicians. Send them. I know they're still struggling since the emperor's decree. They can serve the empire just like they did before."

"Perhaps," he responded, finally sitting down. Sept'ha didn't miss that he still hadn't gotten her even a stool to sit on in here. "Unfortunately, the emperor placed me *and* the Great Royal Wife in charge in his absence. I'll have to ask *her* if she agrees with it as well."

"Do we really have to?" she asked quietly. Hetsaf glanced her way. She leaned in. "The Great Royal Wife is worried about taking care of her new child." The idea started forming as she spoke. "Perhaps…perhaps she'll turn over the decision making fully to you. I mean, forgive me but, she doesn't seem like she likes to think. I've known women like her. They happily let everyone else make the big decisions for them. I'm sure if you presented the idea to her, she'd agree to let you handle all of this. And then you can guide the empire properly." She paused, another statement on her tongue. "Until the emperor returns, of course."

Hetsaf didn't look at her, but he didn't respond immediately either and she knew he was taking in her suggestion. It truly would be better for everyone if Hetsaf took over running the empire. Not because he was a man, as he liked to think, but because he was smarter. The Great Royal Wife was typical of higher class women she'd met, thinking she was conniving when she was just petty and vengeful. The fact that the emperor thought she was worthy of ruling in his absence spoke volumes about his judgment.

"I will consider it fully," he said and that was as close to an enthusiastic agreement as she could hope for from him.

He started to hand her a small gathering of other messages to look over when another servant came in. They bowed deeply, presenting Hetsaf with a sealed scroll. "News from the north, Chancellor."

Hetsaf took it with a small nod, the servant quickly retreating. He popped the seal and started reading. His eyes moved over the report then shot back up to the top to read again. Sept'ha moved to read along with him and gasped. The emperor had been struck down at the battle for Wiluru. An arrow hit him near his heart and they rushed him to Djelebe for healing. He was unconscious when he was sent off. News from Djelebe should be coming soon.

She stood up, speechless. Hetsaf was quiet as well, still holding the message in his hands limply. She wasn't sure what to say to him. It was unclear how close he was to his half-brother and emperor. Was he upset on a familial level or an imperial one?

Hetsaf slowly stood, composing himself. "I must tell the Great Royal Wife," he said, making his way to the door. She didn't miss that he hadn't even glanced her way. "Read over the rest of my messages for today and summarize them for my return. This shouldn't take long." Before she could respond, he was gone.

Sept'ha watched the door for a moment before dropping down into his chair. She read the note again still not believing the news. The head of the empire had fallen in the war that he'd started. If ever there was a bad omen, this was it.

"You doubt my plans so easily?"

Sept'ha jerked her head up at the voice of her goddess. Her first thought was where were you but she caught herself before she spoke it. Met laughed deep in her throat, a rich sound holding the low notes of a growl. The goddess stood just inside of the doorway as tall and imposing as ever. Her cat-like eyes regarded Sept'ha with amusement. Sept'ha stood up to bow so quickly, she knocked Hetsaf's chair over. "Great Met," she said reverently.

"Take your seat, my servant. And relax. I don't begrudge you your thoughts." Met waited patiently as Sept'ha righted the chair. "I know you have concerns about the recent happenings." She quirked a perfect eyebrow on a perfect face.

Sept'ha took a moment, reviewing all of the concerns of her recent days. "My great goddess, I know that we were to incite war, but I don't know if the empire can sustain this. We don't have enough fighters to send everywhere."

"The empire may not be able to sustain this," Met responded with a shrug. "War is push and pull, give and take. There may be retreat one day so that a greater attack can be mounted another day. Patience, my servant."

"But what about the emperor? Wasn't he supposed to be the instrument of war for you?"

Met gave her that amused look again. "Your emperor was the spark to light the fire. The blaze is already burning brightly on its own. What do I need with the flint?"

Sept'ha sucked in a breath. Was the emperor going to die? "Who would run the empire? The heir isn't even old enough for a name."

"I think you can answer that question yourself, Sept'ha."

Her mouth snapped shut. Hetsaf was the one truly running the empire at the moment. "Are you suggesting a takeover?" Sept'ha whispered.

"The word is coup," Met whispered back.

Coup. She mouthed the word, testing its feel on her lips. Her mind started working. If the heir were too young, he would need someone to step in to rule until the day he was an adult. The empire would far more readily accept a man in that role. Certainly not the child's mother. The late emperor's half-brother would be a better choice. And he was the chancellor. That would make the transition easy. But the empress would surely protest. She looked up to Met, question on her lips.

"You can persuade her into her proper role. Make her trust you even more."

Sept'ha nodded. She knew that she could. The empress would be in the midst of her grief. Easy to manipulate. She stopped. She was already thinking as if the emperor had passed. "Will the emperor die?" she asked cautiously.

Met shrugged again, actually looking sorrowful. "That is not my purview. That is up to Fate and Death." She suddenly looked surprised and turned her attention away, a slight frown starting to grow. She turned back to Sept'ha, face calm. "But in case he does, or doesn't awake again, you must be prepared to assist your Hetsaf in steering this empire."

"Of course, my goddess. I will do all I can to the best of my abilities." Met suddenly looked away again, the frown returning. "Is something wrong?" Sept'ha asked.

"I must take care of something," the goddess answered distractedly and disappeared.

Sept'ha stared at the empty spot for a few moments, dumbfounded by the sudden departure. The uneasy feeling she'd had for the past week grew even more.

***

Arkole smoothed back the hair of her newest son, humming a low melody as he slept in her arms. He was tiny, so very tiny, and she felt that if she put him down, he would break. He was such a quiet child too. He barely cried like her daughters had, only bellowing if his needs weren't met after a time. But he looked at her with such inquisitive eyes, focusing on her face with such intensity. Arkole was utterly enamored with him.

A breeze came into the room from her balcony, rustling the gauzy curtains and the leaves of the potted plants. It caressed her cheek cooly and she looked out. Beyond the city and the far plains, far to the north, was her husband. She smiled. How Bakari would dote over his newest son. She was sure he wouldn't want to put him down either. He'd been such an attentive father with Kolehtun.

Her heart cracked just a bit and she fought back tears. Her dear, dear Kolehtun. She focused on her new son to combat the grief that threatened to consume her. He would have loved to have a brother after all these years and so many sisters. She could see them learning the sword and spear together, the elder acting as a mentor to the younger. They would plan for battle together and one day this one would advise his brother the emperor. But it wouldn't be. Her son yawned and hiccupped and she stroked his cheek. This little one would be emperor now and she would do everything in her power to make sure he survived until that day.

One of her servants quickly made her way to her seat, the swishing of her skirts the only sound she made. "My empress, Hetsaf is here to see you."

She couldn't help the deep eye roll. What did that bastard want? "Send him in," she said.

Arkole resettled her son as the chancellor entered the room. Hetsaf only nodded to her instead of bowing but she chose not to fight about it. "Empress," he said quietly.

She stiffened. He didn't have his usual look of scorn that he wore to speak with her. There was concern in his eyes. Her heart skipped a beat. "What is it?"

"The emperor has been injured in battle. An arrow to the chest. They're taking him to Djelebe in the hopes that he can be healed." Hetsaf paused. "He...he hasn't woken since his injury."

Time seemed to stop, the world fell away, and it was several moments before Arkole remembered to breathe. She felt panic tighten her chest uncomfortably. Her Bakari, injured. This wasn't supposed to happen. He was supposed to return from battle victorious to see his new son and heir. Their daughters were supposed to see their father again soon. This couldn't be.

"Surely, you're mistaken," she said shakily.

"The report from General Ikhem arrived just minutes ago," Hetsaf replied. "There hasn't been word from Djelebe yet."

"So we have no idea what condition my husband is in." She looked out towards the balcony, mind starting to go to terrible places. She shook her head. "Thank you for bringing this to me, Hetsaf."

He hesitated. "There is another matter I must discuss with you since the emperor placed you and I to lead in his absence. Nsongo has revolted."

"What?" she shouted. Her son squirmed, agitated in her arms and she rocked and cooed to him to keep him asleep. "What do you mean the southerners have revolted?" she hissed.

"Not the southerners. Just Nsongo." His brow furrowed in thought. "But we must put a stop to this before it spreads to the other cities."

Arkole wanted to howl. She didn't need this right now. She had a son to care for to make sure he grew up to be the future emperor. Her husband was in who knew what kind of state. Why did everything pile on her? "We must send forces to stop them," she said after a moment, still rocking her son.

"We don't have the forces, unless we sacrifice the capital's safety."

There was that tone again. That sour, self-righteous tone that said that he knew everything because he was a man. "What could possibly attack us here?" she said. "We're in the heart of the empire. There isn't a force that could reach us or do damage to us that isn't being fought by our army already." She leaned in to kiss her son who was settling back into a deep sleep.

"Weren't we just putting down riots right after the emperor left for the Pilgrimage? What if they happen again? Who will settle the city?"

"They won't. The people have learned their lesson."

Hetsaf didn't respond for a moment and she thought he was about to leave. "What if they haven't?" he asked, voice rising a bit. "What if they see fewer soldiers roaming the streets and see this as their chance to get their revenge on us for the emperor's decree? The people are still angry about it despite their recent quiet. We have to think with this possibility in mind."

"The people won't rebel," she said, looking at him sharply. "We made enough examples last time. We can afford to send troops."

"You deluded fool," he yelled.

The baby's cry filled the room. Arkole looked to her son in alarm then turned to the chancellor, venom in her gaze. "Get out," she snapped. "I need to attend to my son."

"Then I will attend to the empire. I'll leave you to your most important matters." He turned on his heel and stormed out.

Arkole blew out a breath. She tried to calm down her child, cooing to him and stroking his head. That man was an absolute ass. Her husband could be at the brink of death and he wants to burden her with troop numbers. The empire was secure. Metkara was secure. All he had to do was send the extra forces like she said and Nsongo would be crushed *again* in no time. Why was it so hard to understand?

After she'd finally calmed her baby and fed him a servant shuffled up to her, bowing. "Empress, that servant of Hetsaf is here. She says that she has a message for you."

"Send her in," Arkole told her, waving the other servants in the room out. She passed her son to his nursemaid who followed them.

As they left, Sept'ha came in. She held her head down meekly, a small collection of folded papers in her hands. She bowed low. "Empress. I have copies of a few of the messages the chancellor received recently. I'm sorry that I couldn't bring them to you sooner. He's had me quite busy."

Arkole motioned for the woman to stand. "I'm sure he has," she said with a frown. "Give them to me." She looked through the papers once Sept'ha handed them over. They were mostly about supplies being divided to the force at Wiluru and those that were already earmarked for the force stationed in Nsongo. The servant woman had even copied the message about the southern rebellion. Arkole nodded and set them aside to look through fully later. "Thank you, Sept'ha. I will see you rewarded for your work."

"It was my honor, empress." The woman hesitated. "I am sorry to hear of the emperor's injury."

Arkole was surprised at the woman's genuine pity. The feeling of helplessness started to rise up in her again but she locked it down. "Thank you for your concern, but he's strong. I know that he'll make a complete recovery and be back to the front in the north soon enough."

"Of course, empress. I have no doubt that he will."

The woman hesitated again and Arkole raised an eyebrow. Did this woman not understand when a conversation was over? She needed to get back to her son. "Yes?" she said, annoyance seeping into her tone.

Sept'ha bit her lip. "Forgive me, empress, but perhaps this is a bit much for you. I don't mean that you aren't fit to handle running the empire." She added the last bit hastily. "But your son needs extra care right now. And I know you're worried about the emperor. Perhaps you should let Hetsaf handle most of the running of the empire while you focus on your family. I can still bring you reports in case he gets out of line. I know that if I were in your situation, I would want to think about nothing but them."

"But you are not in my situation," Arkole responded. "And you will never be in anything close so you can't even begin to understand. Continue to bring me the reports he doesn't want to share with me. Focus on that." She let the command hang in the air.

Sept'ha stiffened, clearly stunned at the rebuke, but she bowed deeply. "I apologize, my empress." She quickly left.

Arkole watched her go then called for the nursemaid to bring her son back to her. That woman could never in a million ages understand what being in her position entailed. Focusing on her family and holding the empire together until her husband returned was the best way to do so.

Chapter Four

Efah walked around the palace of Ofolubaru, one to stretch her legs and secondly to try to learn this labyrinthine building. In her time being here she'd hardly gotten a chance to explore. There had been so much to do to get her people settled into the city. Many of them now stayed in the palace to the servants' dismay. Efah tried to talk to as many as would listen, assuring them that they were no threat and if they chose to leave there would be no ill will. They were even welcome to join Efah's people. They were ushering in a time of more equality than was had under their dara.

The people of the city proper had been an entirely different issue. Many of them left, taking their precious goods with them. The ones that stayed barricaded themselves in their homes, refusing to come out or even interact with any of the newcomers. The city guard was protecting the noble districts and she had no desire to force entry. Let them fend for themselves.

Then there were the merchants. Shops started closing the moment she brought her people in. They refused to sell to her, instead sneaking their wares to the nobles. That had been an easy fix. The farmers that lived outside the city dealt directly with her people when they came to market. And they paid better prices as well thanks to the dara's coffers. As far as the luxury merchants went, who needed such frivolities?

Her people were enjoying their new life, far better than they could have scraped together in the forest. The children could play safely and they rested comfortably out of the elements. Perhaps she could find someone willing to teach them reading. That would make a vast difference in all their lives.

Efah laughed as Usi and Nesa bounded up to her like the world's largest pups. She gave each of them a vigorous scratch on the neck in greeting. "What have you two been up to?" They nuzzled and pushed at her until she started walking again. "Okay, fine. Let's see what it is."

She came along the hall, allowing her familiars to prod her until she heard the familiar call of a vulture. She paused as she saw them circling out of a window, over what must be another courtyard. Efah quickened her pace until she found the arcade that opened to where the vultures congregated. They rested on the edge of the roof focused on her deity in the center.

Death looked off, still except for the slight movement of the feathers at the shoulders of his cape. She couldn't see his face as she approached but there was a tightness in the air. The vultures quietly squawked with each other as if in conversation. Death did not even greet her on her approach, staying completely un-moving.

Efah bowed when she reached his side. "My lord Death," she said.

Only then, and after a moment, did he slide his milky white eyes onto her. "My follower, we need to speak." His face, usu-ally so serene when he talked with her, was strained. There was a worry there that made her uneasy.

"Is…is there something wrong?" she asked.

"War is spreading. Even here unto the south. There is a fight for the seat of power. There are those who wish to point the spear of battle towards your city." He looked off again and she realized he was concentrating on the north.

"Is it the empire?" She swallowed hard. Was the empire com-ing to take back the city for Dara Ngoli? Were they so con-cerned about their possessions? Perhaps she should have killed that woman.

"No, it is not the empire that threatens this city but it does threaten the south still. The old aggressions haven't been put aside, Efah. People seek vengeance and they will have it no mat-ter the cost." He looked back to her. "There are other forces at play here, forces that should not be."

Now worry truly snaked its way through her heart. "I will do all I can to protect my followers, but we only have so many fighters. We've beaten back forces because of the forest but only barely. If we have to fight anyone in a real battle, I don't think we'll make it." She suddenly wished Newa was here and her heart ached.

49

"There are more ways to win than fighting. You are wise and faithful. Use all that you have been given and you will have victory in all that you face." He placed a hand on her shoulder and Efah felt her courage bolstered. "I am with you in all things."

She closed her eyes, bowing her head, and when she opened them, Death was gone. Efah looked around as the vultures began taking off, flying to perch on other parts of the city. She took a deep breath. War was in the south again. After so many years of peace, war was back. But had her life, or the lives of the people she was leading, ever been peaceful? She'd lost her entire family to sickness. Lost her home in her village to vicious rumors. She'd been taken in by graverobbers and carved out a place for herself in a gathering of thieves, cutthroats, and worse. The people that had come to surround her had survived horrors at the hands of the Ega and their own people. They finally found a little bit of calm, maybe even of happiness, here. She wouldn't let that be taken away from them.

Efah called for Nesi and Usa who had been lounging at the edge of the courtyard. They jumped to their feet immediately, padding after her as she left the area. All of their playfulness was gone. They had a more serious mood that reflected her own. Efah reached back to scratch them under the chin and let them know that things were fine. Usa gave a short laughing yip while her sister leaned into the affection.

She walked through the palace until she found the section that Newa's students were using to train. It was a huge room that seemed to have been a bedroom before their takeover. The furniture, including a massive bed, was pushed to the side of the room, the carpets rolled up and laying upright against the cream colored walls. They went through more advanced drills than he'd taught her and it pleased her that something of him was left behind. Leading them through the drills was one of his favored students. Ifisi, she thought was her name. The woman noticed her at the edge of the large room and called out that the lady of death was present. The entire class stopped and bowed to her.

"Please don't stop for me," she said, surprised by the sudden show of respect. "Continue your training. But, Ifisi, can I talk to you?"

The woman raised her eyebrows but set the class back to work and came over. She bowed deeply when she reached Efah's side. "I am here to serve you, Lady of Death."

"Thank you. You've taken to your role as Newa's replacement very well," she said looking over the students again.

Ifisi looked horrified. "I could never replace him."

"No, no," Efah laughed. "I only mean for now. For someone who wasn't a warrior before, you're doing very well." Ifisi relaxed and Efah found it funny that this woman who couldn't be more than a couple of years older than her cared so much about what she thought.

"My father was a warrior. He'd fought in the war. He would teach me things… when he wasn't drinking the horrors away." She looked aside for a moment, face shamed. "But he gave me a foundation."

Efah put a hand on her shoulder. "I'm sorry."

Ifisi paused. "Was there something I could do for you, my lady?" she asked as if it were a natural change in subject.

Efah went with it. No need to dwell in sorrow. "I'd like to continue my training." The woman looked to her surprised. "Newa was training me privately and I shouldn't stop just because he's…," the word caught in her throat. She swallowed. "Just because he's gone."

Ifisi nodded slowly. "My lady," she said lowering her voice, "it may not be my place to say so, but our teacher cared for you greatly. I know he'll do everything he can to come back as quickly as possible."

"Will tomorrow morning be all right to start?" Efah asked with a little too much urgency. It was all she could do to keep her voice from cracking.

"Of course, my lady," Ifisi answered, clearly taken aback. "I'm sorry if-"

"No, it's fine." Efah worked quickly to compose herself.

"Then tomorrow morning will be fine. You can meet me here after breakfast."

Efah nodded. "I look forward to it." She forced a smile on her face, trying to show that she hadn't been offended by Ifisi's comments. The woman nodded, still looking concerned, but returned to her class.

Efah fled the room, emotions swelling. She didn't think that she could miss someone so much. Newa had become so important to her life. It was so calming talking to him, even just walking with him in silence. He understood what it meant to be chosen. He understood her calling like no one else could. What was she going to do without her closest companion?

***

Newa dreamed of Efah. They lay in a field of high grass, arms outstretched, fingers touching just enough to intertwine. They watched the clouds and talked. He couldn't understand the words of their conversation but he understood their meaning. They spoke of any and everything and it satisfied him more than any good meal, than any righteous kill had ever done before. The feel of her fingers against his sent a sense of lightness through his body and he felt like he would float into the great void of the sky at any moment.

Then he awoke and the feeling turned to an aching longing. It took him a moment to realize where he was. No, not Ofolubaru. A low bed in a travel house in a tiny closet of a room. He sighed, putting an arm over his eyes to block out the light coming from the small slit of a window. And maybe sear the feeling and image of his dream into his memory.

Newa sat up with a growl. He was a lovesick pup. At his age. With a woman that had to be twenty years his junior. But Efah was everything to him. So being away from her voice, her smile, was torture.

Aggravated, he moved to a position to meditate, crossing his legs beneath him. He had a mission. Newa breathed evenly and slowly, pushing away all errant thoughts with each exhale. *I am the blade of justice*, he thought, beginning the mantra. *I am the blade of repentance. Wickedness shall be cleaved from this world by my hand. The unrepentant shall be ushered unto Death.*

Death.

The Lady of Death.

Efah.

His eyes shot open and he cursed aloud. How was he supposed to fulfill his mission if his mind kept wandering to her? He closed his eyes again. He skipped the mantra, focusing instead on his goal. There was a pretender out there, to the west, acting in the name of Gu'un, of Takiri. They had to be brought down for their heresy. The image of the man enveloped in black smoke, the symbol of Gu'un on his chest, came back to Newa and so did his hatred. His righteous hatred. It urged him to get going, to head out and complete the mission.

And then he would return to her.

Newa went out and found the bath, scrubbing off quickly before coming back to his room to prepare for today's leg of his journey. He ate in the common room, letting the travel house's keeper know that he was leaving. The old man asked him if he needed any supplies warily, eyes darting toward the handles of his swords. Newa told him no kindly, a gesture he wouldn't have thought to give just a few months ago. Then he would have relished the man's fear. How he had truly changed.

Outside was hot but thankfully a thick patchwork of clouds kept the full sun at bay. Several routes met at this crossroads and wagons pulled by bulls or horses made their way along them even this early. He closed his eyes for a moment, feeling the direction of the tug of his mission, and chose a road to follow. People stared at him as he walked, sickle like swords at his side, his obviously Egan clothing. Sure, they had travelers from the main empire all the time in the outskirts of the south, but those were merchants. He was certain that none of them had ever seen a priest of the Arakgu'un.

The thought made him pause. Was he even still a priest of the order? He'd abandoned their most core goals of actively bringing people to repentance by whatever means necessary. The thought of doing so again seemed shameful. So, no, he guessed he'd severed himself from his order. But was he still a priest? A resounding yes was his answer. What kind of priest was he? The question ran around his mind as he walked.

Around midmorning he slowed as he saw a small wagon on the side of the road. A wheel had split and the contents of the wagon were strewn about the grasses. A short, middle aged woman stood nearby, the rod to prod her bull in her hand. She waved it menacingly as she yelled at a young woman, a girl really, who worked to put the packages and jars back into the wagon. The girl strained as she tried to lift some of the items, the woman not caring that this task was obviously beyond the girl's strength.

"You'd better move faster than that!" she yelled. "I paid good money for you."

As Newa came closer, he took a good look at the girl. She was young, maybe early teens. Her hair was cut short and had dust in one side as if she'd taken a tumble when the wagon wheel had broken. Her clothes were rough spun cloth, barely better than the sacks she lifted. Her feet were bare and blistered as if she weren't used to being shoeless.

One of the sacks slipped out of the girl's hands. It dropped heavily to the ground, seam bursting spilling rice into the dry dirt.

"You clumsy, little bastard child," the woman snarled, raising the rod. She brought it down savagely, striking the girl across the back of the shoulders. The girl cried out, earning her another strike that landed across her back. "Now finish picking up those sacks."

Even from this distance, Newa could see the large red welts starting to form on the girl's exposed skin. "How can she work if you've injured her?" he asked, coming closer.

"Mind your own servants," the woman snapped before looking at him. Once she caught sight, she paused, taking in his appearance and weapons. "If you're a brigand, you'll find nothing but rice and jars of still fermenting jura."

"I'm not a brigand," he said. He looked over to the girl. She stared at him with wide, fearful eyes. "I didn't think the south dealt in slaves."

The older woman looked caught then had the decency to look abashed. "She is not a slave. She came to work for me. Her parents are beggars. Couldn't afford to take care of her."

Newa had been trained to notice the little tells of a liar but this woman's tells would be obvious in the dark. He sighed. "Girl," he called as gently as he could, "where are your parents?"

Fat tears started to form in her eyes, a true soul deep sorrow. "My mothers are dead."

"You little liar," the woman snarled, raising the rod again.

Newa caught her wrist, twisting it to a painful angle. The woman cried out, dropping her weapon. "Were you sold to this woman?" he asked the girl. She hesitated and he actually felt pity for her. "You can tell me the truth."

She looked from him to her obvious master. "Yes."

"Would you like to be free?" He tightened his grip on the woman's wrist and her knees buckled in pain.

The girl glanced back and forth again. "Yes."

He nodded and looked to the horrible woman trying in vain to work her way out of his grip. "Give her your shoes." The woman stared up at him in horror. Her lips parted in protest but his expression made her think otherwise. She stepped out of her sandals, kicking them at the girl.

Newa took the woman far to the side of the road while the girl slipped the sandals on. He twisted her arm behind her and pushed her down. The woman hit the ground hard, sliding a few inches. He turned his back on her as she recovered. He took several steps before he heard the sound of the woman running back up, the chase he was expecting. In one smooth movement, he unhooked one of his swords, turning to bring the blade up. She stopped just in time for it to only brush the soft skin of her neck.

He stared at her with deadly calm. "This girl is free and if you come after her again, I will send you on to be judged accordingly."

The woman's eyes flicked to the girl once and she backed away one terrified step at a time. When she was far enough away for Newa's liking, he replaced his sword at his belt. He turned and rejoined the girl at the side of the road.

"You're free," he said with a smile. "What's your name?"

"Masola," she said meekly.

"All right, Masola. I'll take you to the next town and you can find a place there." She looked at him very warily. "I won't hurt you. I swear. I have no desire to hurt a child and, I promise you, I have no desire for a child either. I swear on my deity Takiri."

"That's one of our gods," she said, looking at him with more confusion than fear now. "And you're Ega."

"I've come to learn that our gods are not so different."

"You're the enemy."

"I was," Newa said. His gaze started wandering back to the southeast. "But I am not anymore. I've fought for southerners, for people who've been mistreated just like you. And I want to help you. Will you let me travel with you?"

Masola looked down at the sandals reluctantly given to her, to her former master standing terrified in the high grass, and finally back to Newa. She put the sandals on. "Okay."

He smiled at her and began leading the way. "Good, let's go. I'm sure we have a bit of a journey before we can rest."

***

Eyes were watching him. Tekhamun knew it. They whispered about him when he wasn't looking, his whole group. Ever since Karatel's murder, no, his execution. People spoke of him in hushed tones. Their eyes darted away as soon as he brought his attention to them. Today was no different.

Tekhamun watched from a shaded doorway as the morning meal was being distributed to his followers. People gathered into small groups, happily greeting each other and chatting. Some quickly ate before getting to weapon practice. But he saw each and every time that they noticed him there, how they paused and looked away. How they brought their heads closer together in conspiracy as they talked. They judged him and part of him felt it was rightly so.

He hadn't wanted to kill Karatel. The man had been his very first follower, bringing his entire group on, suggesting the most fitting targets of iniquity for them to render judgment on. But he had let his grief cloud his mind. Pta's death was a great blow to him. He clearly loved the woman, but that was no cause to forget their important and holy mission. Karatel had blasphemed against the gods and against the mission. Tekhamun had no choice but to send him to Gu'un for true judgment. There was no other way.

The words rang hollow in his mind. Surely, he could have

56

saved him. No, it was the right thing to do. The two sides had been swirling in his head since they left Karatel's body in a field to rot. He prayed to Gu'un for guidance, for some sign that he'd gone down the right path. He desperately meditated, searching for something, anything, from his god. But he'd gotten nothing but the weak threads of guilt that continued to plague him. Tek-hamun's breathing had quickened and he took a few deep breaths to calm down. He couldn't fall apart. His people needed him.

Out of the corner of his eye, he saw someone approaching. He looked over, stiffening, as Hamena walked up to him, hold-ing a bowl of this morning's breakfast. Her hips swayed hypnot-ically and he had to tear his gaze away. His body threatened to react as the memory of sensations he'd never felt rose but he concentrated on his role as leader and priest.

"Good morning, Master Tekhamun," she purred.

He swallowed. Even her voice was like fingers up his spine. "Good morning, Hamena. I pray you're doing well today." She offered him the bowl but he put up his hand in refusal. "Moon has already brought me my meal."

Hamena nodded, taking up the spoon herself. "People are talking about what we're going to do next," she said after taking a bite. "They're worried after that last attack from the army. We lost quite a few people. They wonder if following you is going to get them killed."

"Those that died did so honorably," he said, a little affronted. "They will meet the gods. Do none of them have faith?"

She held up a hand as if to hold off his judgment. "There are many who follow you even more devotedly since our victory. I am one of them. But…there are still rumors. They say you are becoming ruthless, like an evil king. You killed one of your closest followers. Some are saying it's because he lost his faith and deserved to die. Others, once again not me, are saying it's because he challenged your power and you had to put him down."

Tekhamun was aghast. He would never. "Karatel blasphemed against our gods and our mission," he said, hurt. "There is only one punishment for that."

Hamena nodded in agreement. "Of course, master. I know you did the right thing. But if I can make a suggestion?" She looked to him with a pleading smile. He gave a quick nod, knot in his throat. "Perhaps you could talk to the people more. Show them who they're following and answer questions to put these nasty rumors to rest."

He looked out over the gathered assembly. Perhaps she was right. He needed to show that he was their leader, a leader who cared about them and their future both here and in the afterlife. "Your council is wise," he said, only glancing her way in the slightest. "I need to speak to my people."

With a quick nod, Tekhamun left the safety of the covered doorway and walked out into the square. He paused as several people noticed his approach but forced himself to continue. He stopped briefly by gathered groups to greet them and ask of their wellbeing. His people responded kindly asking after him as well, but he could feel the tense undercurrent. There were many that wanted to speak but were holding back. And everywhere he went, he could feel eyes on him.

He took his time and went throughout the city, speaking to his followers. All seemed pleased to see him but he could tell, they judged him. Hearing talking, he turned a corner to see two of his first followers in conversation. Mjobe and Netja spoke lowly, Netja's hands in constant motion as was his habit. They both stopped as soon as they noticed him. He greeted them and they in kind, but there was a distrust in their demeanor. There was wariness in their eyes. Tekhamun didn't speak on it but continued on to let them restart their discussion.

He hurried back to his rooms, breath quick, the utter feeling of defeat crushing him. His people were losing faith in him. His mission wouldn't succeed without them. He dropped down on his bed, sitting with his head in his hands. Why wouldn't Gu'un answer him? If ever he needed guidance, it was now.

Tekhamun slipped off his sandals to sit cross legged on his bed. He closed his eyes, trying to meditate. He needed to focus on his god harder. He recited the central tenets of his priesthood repeatedly, willing his mind to fall away from the concerns of this world.

Karatel's face came to the forefront. His expression was frozen in the horror that came with the realization of one's imminent death. Tekhamun could see his own blade, covered in the man's blood. How could he have let Karatel slip away? How could he have not seen him turning away from the right path? Guilt squeezed his chest and his eyes opened. He breathed deeply several times to calm himself.

He'd taken so many lives before. Why was this one so, so different? Karatel was a sinner just like the others. He deserved his fate. Tekhamun closed his eyes again. He focused on the image of Gu'un, in his strength and absolute wise judgment. He willed those attributes to be imbued in him so that he may be a true leader, sure of every step he took. At first, he felt nothing but he kept his mind focused. If he had to stay here all day until he felt his god's guidance then so be it.

His meditation was disturbed sometime later by an argument outside his door. Two women's voices talked back and forth with a sharp terseness. He recognized the breathy voice of Moon immediately. The second brought him fear. Hamena. He rose from his bed, walking to the door reluctantly.

"I bring him his meals every day," Moon said with firmness.

"Perhaps the master would like a change," Hamena countered with a viper's sweetness.

"This is *my* duty," Moon protested.

Tekhamun steeled himself and opened the door, cutting off the discussion. He pushed a smile onto his face, briefly taking in both women before settling his gaze on Moon. "Ah, Moon, I didn't realize it was lunchtime already. Please come in."

Moon pushed past Hamena, bringing in the meal, and closed the door in the woman's face. She set the plate and cup on the room's small table and stepped back. "Please be careful with the food, Master. It's still quite hot."

Tekhamun brought his stool up to the table. Moon, who usually left, still lingered nearby. He glanced up at her face and he noticed the uncertainty in her eye. "Go ahead and say what you're thinking," he sighed.

She rubbed one of her thick arms. "That woman. Hamena. You don't…desire her. Do you?"

"What?" He choked. "No, no not at all."

"Did she take advantage of you?" Moon asked dangerously.

"No," he gasped. He wrestled with the confession. "She made her intentions plain, yes. But I didn't refuse her. I had a moment of weakness."

Moon looked off, worrying her bottom lip. "I think she just wants to get your favor."

"I think you're right," he said looking into his lap. Gods, he was a fool.

"I...I didn't think priests had those kind of urges."

Tekhamun felt a lifetime of shame, a lifetime of being shunned and mocked by women, fall on him. "I am still a man," he said carefully. "I am dedicated to my god but I do still have urges. I suppose I am not strong enough to fight them off all the time."

To his surprise, Moon knelt down beside him. She looked up at him with the most concern anyone had ever shown him. Her bad eye watered slightly. "Master, if you ever feel you're not strong enough to fight off those urges, you can call me. I would do anything for you. Anything."

He breathed in, holding it. No one had ever been devoted to him. His own mother had hated him. She surprised him again by taking his hand in her battle calloused ones and kissed the palm gently. A sensation that he'd only felt once before surged through him, warming him throughout.

"Anything?" he breathed out.

Moon hesitated, looked aside shyly, then placed his hand on her full breast. His heart raced. She filled his whole hand and he squeezed slightly, feeling the softness through her shirt. His manhood responded, channeling the burning need to his mind. He licked his lips nervously.

"You would do this for me?"

"You are leading us on a righteous path. You are saving us from heresy." She pressed his hand firmly against her. "If this is another way I can show how thankful I am, then I'm glad to do it."

His manhood strained against the fabric of his robes. Tekhamun felt like he would explode right there. He tried to slide his hand under her tunic and she helped by lifting it up. Her torso held a handful of scars but it was the most glorious thing he'd ever seen. He trailed nervous fingers up her ribs until he could cup her, sighing hungrily.

With a ravenous growl he pressed his mouth to hers, pushing her awkwardly to the floor. His hands were a frantic web of movement, not knowing what to touch next. He was hard, so hard against her. Then next thing he knew, he was roughly pulling off her pants and freeing himself. They fumbled against each other until he entered, getting a small grunt of pain from her.

Tekhamun's mind was filled with nothing but need. He started a rough, wanton rhythm, mouth still on hers. He needed this, this union, this woman who had devoted herself to him. The rest may spread rumors about him. They may plot against him. But here he had true devotion, true loyalty, and he would drink in every drop of it.

Chapter Five

A heavy rain rolled in from the sea with the first light of the sun, dampening the fighting spirits of both the Ega and Wilu-ruan warriors. The invaders pulled back to the gate and the burned out buildings near it that they'd managed to take. A wall of infantrymen held their position, even in the rain, shields raised and hands ready to unsheathe their swords.

Yutuuan watched the distant line of enemies from a covered porch, thankful for a small break in the fighting. His warriors, while not at attention like the Ega, were still stationed at the edge of their side of the battlefield. He huffed. Battlefield. He was far more used to fighting at sea. This push and pull was not to his liking at all. Give him a grand decisive battle and be done with the affair. This was going to be a long conflict with most of the enemy forces still outside the city, waiting for their chance. That was fine. His warriors were anxious to meet them. He was anxious to kill more of them, enough to steal their courage and send them scrambling back to Metkara. Then he could finally turn his mind to more pressing matters.

Almost as a reflex, his gaze wandered away from the front to the rest of the city. He'd asked Umakaal to fortify the palace and he knew that she would do an exemplary job of it. He had an or-der put out for people to take refuge there and in the larger tem-ples just in case the fighting spread out beyond the gate. He hadn't made it mandatory and wondered if Talekh had chosen sanctuary or to hide in her apartment. He didn't want to think of her all alone in the city. Pregnant and alone. Pregnant with his child.

He looked up at the sky, watching the rain come down. He had to go to her.

Yutuuan turned to go back inside, heading up to the second floor. He and the other captains had taken this floor of the build-ing as their barracks and place of command. Naret looked up to him from where he sharpened his sword.

"Has the fighting begun again?" he asked, almost hopeful. Another of the captains turned his attention from the city map he studied.

The prince shook his head. "No. I need to head back to the palace. Captain Izgarim, you have command until I return." The captain stood and saluted him.

Naret got to his feet, sheathing his sword. "I'll come with you," he said tying it back to his belt.

"That's not necessary." He cursed himself. Did that sound suspicious? "The city is secure and the streets are nearly deserted."

Naret raised an eyebrow ever so slightly. "I insist."

"Very well," Yutuuan replied, shaking his head as if Naret was just being overprotective.

He avoided his bodyguard's scrutinizing stare as they went out into the back streets, donning their cloaks against the rain. They walked quickly toward the palace, Yutuuan running over every reason he could come up with to separate from Naret as soon as possible. Naret didn't say a word to him and he thought that he'd managed to fool the man until a simple statement was made.

"So, where are you really going?" Naret asked, walking nearer.

Yutuuan resisted a guilty grimace. "I have to see her." Naret didn't speak for a moment and Yutuuan was afraid he'd finally pushed his friend too far.

"So you shirk your duties as leader of this war."

"She is having my child, Naret," he pleaded. "She may have already had the baby. I can't abandon her."

"You're going to have to eventually. You can't just sneak off when you're king. What about your wife?"

Yutuuan sucked in a breath. "Luunja can never know. And I know I'll not be able to sneak off when I'm king. All the more reason for me to see her now. It could be the last time."

Naret stared straight ahead and he wished he could see the man's expression. "Fine."

"Thank you, Na-"

His bodyguard held his hand up, cutting him off. "At least

show your face at the palace so you won't be caught in a bold faced lie."

They headed to the palace, Yutuuan checking in on the palace guards and visiting with his mother for a moment. Then Naret helped him slip out of one of the private entrances. They took a winding route to the neighborhood Talekh had moved to, Yutuuan's steps growing more rushed the closer he grew. It was so quiet with no one on the streets. He felt extra exposed but the thought of seeing the only woman his heart desired pushing him on. Naret stayed back at a street corner when they saw the building, to both give them privacy and watch the area, and the prince headed in alone. Each step set Yutuuan's heart fluttering until he was finally at the entrance to the apartment Talekh had chosen to call home.

Yutuuan knocked on the door nervously. There was a rustling inside and he heard floorboards creaking as Talekh came near. "Who's there?" she asked sharply, rougher than he'd ever heard her.

He swallowed. "Me."

There was a moment when he wasn't sure if she'd open up to him, then the sound of items being moved and the door was flung wide. Talekh threw herself against him, wrapping her arms around him tightly. Yutuuan crushed her to him. He breathed in the scent of her hair, felt his fingers pressing into her soft flesh. They awkwardly moved into the apartment, closing the door behind them. He turned her face up to him, covering it with kisses. He could taste her tears on his lips and it pained him that he'd left her alone for so long.

Talekh reached her hands behind his neck, pulling him into a punishing kiss. "I missed you so much," she said in a moment to take a breath before kissing him again.

"I missed you too. I thought about you every day."

She brought up trembling fingers between their lips to stop the reunion. "You have to see your son."

All thought ceased in Yutuuan's mind as she led him by the hand to a second room. A bed was near one side and in the middle was a babe. His breath caught as they came near and she moved to scoop the baby into her arms. She spoke lowly to him and moved him so that Yutuuan could see his face clearly. He had Talekh's round jawline and darker complexion but definitely had his nose. Wavy jet black hair clung to his scalp and he stared up at Yutuuan with wide, dark eyes.

His heart swelled until he thought it would burst. There was nothing in the world more important to him at this moment than his son. He looked to Talekh, tears starting to sting his eyes. Nothing more important than his family. "How old is he?" he asked, trying to keep the emotion out of his voice.

"Just over a month. You're just in time to name him."

It took Yutuuan only a moment. "Taagreb," he said, thinking of his father.

She laughed. "Could you make it more obvious?"

Her question stung him for a moment, then he laughed. "I suppose it would be obvious," he said, a little embarrassed.

"But Taagreb would have been a good name." She reached up and touched his cheek, sorrow in her eyes. "Yutu, I'm so sorry about your father."

He put a hand over hers. "Thank you, Talekh. I wish I had been here. I wish I'd been here for you, for both of you." He ran a gentle hand over the baby's head.

"Would you like to hold him?" she asked.

Yutuuan paused. "Really?"

Talekh nodded and patiently handed their son to him, moving his arms and hands to hold the baby properly. He was shocked at how nearly weightless he was. Surely his sword weighed more. His son focused completely on him now, eyes roaming his face. "I'm your father," he whispered, completely in awe of this new human in his arms, a human he helped make. The baby gave him a toothless smile and Yutuuan knew he couldn't be happier.

Then his heart broke. His son was a bastard. He wouldn't become high priest as he should. He would never officially inherit anything. Yutuuan held the baby close, kissing him on the forehead. The son of his heart would have to grow up watching his siblings lead the kingdom while he waited in the shadows. "I'm so sorry," he said, voice choked with emotion. He looked to Talekh, perfect, loving Talekh. She deserved so much better. "I'm sorry to you too."

"Why?" she asked. "You've made me happier than I've ever been."

"I'm going to be king soon. I…I won't be able to see you as much." He choked. "If ever. I have a fiancé."

"What?" Her eyes were filled with panic. "When did this happen? Who is she?"

"The daughter of the governor of Asfara. I had to agree to it to have their support." He panicked when she still seemed concerned. "I don't love her. You are my heart."

She looked down to their son, her eyes concentrating on his face. "So, what will happen to us?"

Yutuuan felt as if he may shatter. "I will make sure you have the best life possible. You two will want for nothing."

"Except for you," she said, completing his thoughts.

He grabbed her hand, squeezing her fingers tight. "Talekh, I will find a way. I swear, I'll find a way for us to be together. You and this child mean more to me than my own life. I swear I won't abandon you."

Yutuuan leaned over, pressing a kiss to her lips, trying with this one gesture to prove his utter devotion and desperate, soul deep love for her. He would give anything to have her by his side in all things. If only he weren't the prince. If only he weren't the king. If only….

With painful reluctance, he pulled away from her. "I need to return to the battle," he said, handing off his son to her. The baby quietly protested being moved from a comfortable spot.

"Be safe," she said. "We need you."

Yutuuan nodded. He kissed her and the baby one last time and walked to the door. He couldn't help glancing back every other moment. Everything in him didn't want to leave, wanted to forget the war raging at the gate. But where would that leave his city, his people? He jogged down the steps, putting on his cloak again. He would have both his life's responsibilities and his life with Talekh and their son. He made a quick vow to his god and namesake. He would find a way to have both.

***

Umakaal watched Ladawi's slender fingers as she tied on her

armor. It was late and Umakaal was about to head out to serve her watch of the palace. While she was thankful to be restored to her former position, she'd rather be at the battle, serving her kingdom. Yutuuan promised that he would set her to her proper place once he was on the throne but she knew that wouldn't be until after the war. Now she was still stuck at the palace, watching the battle from afar.

Her face soured thinking about her brother. He'd arranged her marriage to some foreigner without her input or her permission. A quick word and he'd changed her life completely. What was he thinking? No, clearly he wasn't thinking. He sacrificed her for the country just as their father had sacrificed Izriamat years ago. She thought he thought better of her than that, that she was more than a doll to be shifted to and fro. Her mind shifted to all their time together, especially after Izriamat left. All she ever wanted to do was walk in her brother's footsteps. Now, for him to betray her, and like this, was enraging.

"Which one are you mad with?" Ladawi asked, adjusting one of Umakaal's bracers.

The princess snapped out of her thoughts. "Yutuuan," she grunted.

"I know you're still angry over the betrothal." She stepped back, looking Umakaal over. "It was going to happen sooner or later," she sighed. "That a man would come between us."

Umakaal took one of her lover's hands, looking down at her but Ladawi was avoiding her gaze. "No one will ever come between us. I love you."

Ladawi did look at her then. "I know that," she said with a smirk. "But you'll have to split your time now." Umakaal frowned. "You will. And you'll have to talk to him eventually and I know you've been avoiding him. Talk to him."

"You talk to him," she grumbled, feeling petulant.

Ladawi stood up and tapped her nose. "Don't be a child."

"I'm not being a child," she said, but took the whine out of her voice. "I'm not being a child. I don't want to talk to him. He's some foreign boy my brother dragged back here and dumped on me. Another thing my brother has dumped in my lap and I'm supposed to just deal with it. This is my life, Ladawi.

Our life." She put a hand to the other woman's cheek.

"But I am a servant and you are a princess. Our life was always going to be in the shadow of the life you'd have to live for the kingdom."

Umakaal saw the tears forming in Ladawi's eyes and pulled her close, crushing her in a hug. She blinked away her own tears. A marriage, the thing that would throw her life in a new direction, had always seemed so far off. It was an annoyance she would have to endure. Eventually. Now it stared her in the face.

"I'm not talking to him," she said lowly. "We can talk at the ceremony and when we have to bed each other."

Ladawi chuckled into her chest. "Do I still get to use him for children?"

Umakaal kissed her forehead. "Of course. And we'll raise our children together." She pulled back so she could tip Ladawi's face up. "I love you."

"I love you too."

She kissed her lover, savoring the soft fullness of her lips, trying to draw this moment out. Reluctantly, she pulled away slowly. Her touch lingered on Ladawi's arms, her hands, until she finally let go and left the room. She set off down the halls in a hurried march, putting as much distance between her and the enticing serenity of her bedroom.

There was a quiet tension in the palace. Servants only went about the most urgent business so those few who worked outside of the private quarters rushed through their duties. Virtually all of the palace guards were stationed at every entrance. Her brother had charged her with making the palace impenetrable and that's what she'd done. They'd taken in as many of the citizens as possible and they occupied the lower floors. She wished that she could take in more but there was only so much room. Many others sheltered in the city's various temples. The city was locked down as tightly as could be done.

And here she was, locked in as well.

The thought soured her mood even further as she approached the eastern courtyard. It looked out over that side of the city. The highest point in the palace, it gave them a perfect vantage point to view the gate. From here she could hear the muffled roar of fighting and even see the bright light of fire spells being thrown back and forth. If, in her worst fears, the enemy was able to break through their fighters, they would be able to see their approach and prepare. They just hoped it didn't come to that.

A couple of guards rushed up to her as she came into the courtyard. "What's going on?" she asked fearing the worst by their fraught faces.

"My princess," one began, "we've been trying to get him to leave but he won't. The foreign man your brother brought to the palace. He says he has to speak to you."

Umakaal looked past them to the table that served as her makeshift headquarters. Standing by it was her fiancée. She scowled deeply. "I'll take care of this."

The foreigner bowed as she came closer. "Good day, princess. I hope you are well today."

"Why are you here?" she snapped, a little louder than she'd intended.

"This was the only place I could think of that you would be. I did not want to invade your private rooms." He stood firmly, shoulders back. "We need to speak."

Umakaal stared at him, torn between shouting or laughing in disbelief. She looked to her guards, gesturing with her head to give them space. The guards glanced to each other warily but moved out of hearing distance. She folded her arms, cocking her head to the side. "Mikhra, right? If you haven't noticed, we're in the middle of a war for our independence. I don't have time for social meetings so that we can find common ground."

His brows furrowed. "I understand that Wiluru is at war. But I have not come for that kind of meeting. I understand that you are busy with your command." He paused, thinking over his next words. "I tried to tell your brother that I am a warrior and I am willing to fight. He told me to stay in the palace because I had not been in battle before. But this is to be my home. I cannot stand to the side if there is something I can do to help."

Umakaal had been ready to dismiss him outright, but his words gave her pause. It was clear her brother was thinking the same about her. She should be involved in the main fight. Command of the main forces would fall to her as soon as he took the crown. She should be involved. The sound of an explosion carried itself on the wind, causing everyone to look toward the battle. She looked back to Mikhra who was staring out to the distance, a subtle expression of longing on his face.

She sighed. "What weapons do you use?"

"Sword, spear, bow and arrow, and whip. I am a decent fighter with a knife."

Umakaal's eyebrows raised. Multi-talented. She quickly tamped down the inkling of respect she felt growing. "So what do you want from me? I can't send you to the battle. That's my brother's decision and clearly he doesn't think you can cut it."

"But you command the palace guard," he countered. "Allow me to join you here, as one of them. I am more than happy to serve under you. And it will give me a chance to see what sort of woman you are." He gave her a small smile, a slight upturn of his lips that was confident without being cocky and with the barest hint of flirtation.

Umakaal rolled her eyes. She could see people falling for his handsome smile and easy charm left and right. She called for one of the nearest guards. "Get the prince a set of armor. He wants to join us to defend the palace."

Mikhra bowed. "Thank you, my princess." He looked up through his lashes before standing.

Her breath caught for a moment. She nodded stiffly watching him go off with the guard briefly before staring pointedly away. She made herself take a deep breath, liking this foreign prince less and less.

***

There were so many people to heal. Izriamat looked over the crowd assembled in the street before the temple. They clung to the sides, some sitting against the rock walls, some unable to sit up so they made makeshift beds out of blankets and cushions taken from their homes. If they had a home. So many bore a hollow look as if they'd seen the worst horrors of the world and now they could see nothing else. Izriamat's heart ached for them.

She moved through the temple's courtyard first, healing what injuries she could. Deep wounds could be mended, infections drawn out. But what could she do for a missing eye or leg? The smallest pang of guilt stabbed her. This was her fault. Izriamat quickly chased the thought away. It was mandated by their patron deity that all of Wiluru fight for their freedom. It wasn't she that called them to the war. It was Yutuu himself and these people should be praised, not pitied.

She saw a young woman with a series of crude bandages wrapped around her head, starring off blankly. When she bent down to speak with her, there was no reaction. Another woman beside her spoke up.

"My lady, she was injured in the fight with the Ega. She hasn't spoken since. It's like she's gone."

Izriamat's heart broke for her. She nodded and placed her hands on either side of the young woman's head. "In the name of he of the deep waters who brought us to these sacred lands, return to us, my sister." She felt the holy magics flow through her, a sensation of pure euphoria that made her want to ignore the world and bask in it for the rest of her days. She concentrated on this woman's injury, on her mind. She willed the flesh to heal and after the power of Yutuu saturated them, they did. It took all of her concentration and by the time she'd finished, she felt a little drained.

The woman blinked after a moment, then looked up at Izriamat as if just registering where she was. Her eyes grew wide when she realized who she was looking at. "My princess," she gasped and did her best to bow.

Izriamat put a hand on her shoulder. "No need to bow. You are healed. Go and help our people in the best way that you can."

Tears began to flow freely down the woman's face. "Thank you, my princess. Thank you."

Izriamat stood. A wobble threatened her posture, but she stiffened her legs against it. As if drawn, Sami appeared at her side with water. "Perhaps you should take a rest, my princess."

"I am fine. I will rest in a bit. There are still people that need me." Izriamat looked farther down the street at all the people waiting and steeled her resolve. She would heal as many as possible until her strength gave out.

As she continued, another contingent of followers approached the temple. They looked dejected, some injured, some not, and they were flanked by soldiers on each side. Spears were held at positions that could easily be turned hostile and others had hands resting on the hilts of their swords. The soldiers' faces were set in an attempt to appear neutral but their annoyance showed through.

Izriamat made her way through the crowd, stopping just before the first of her followers that arrived. "What is going on?" she asked helping a limping man down to rest. She turned her fierce gaze on the nearest soldiers.

"Prince Yutuuan ordered these people to remove themselves from the battlefield," answered a female soldier flatly. "They refused so we were forced to remove them."

Izriamat's usually peaceful demeanor melted away. "How dare you treat my people like prisoners," she cried out. "They are the faithful of this kingdom."

The soldiers looked between each other, passing around guilt and confusion. Only one stood resolute. "They were in the way. Getting themselves killed and maimed while we save the kingdom. The prince commands that you keep your people here. This is his final warning."

Izriamat heard the thunderous rolling of the sea in her ears. "Tell my brother that he commands neither me nor my people. We bow only to the will of Yutuu and the gods. If he wishes to go against them, then it is his own soul he jeopardizes."

A few of the soldiers made gestures of supplication but others stared at her, shocked. The soldier that had spoken gawked. She regained her composure after a moment. "I will pass on your message." With a gesture, the group of soldiers turned and left.

Izriamat watched the soldiers march off, anger, betrayal, and disbelief swirling inside her. She had no idea that so many were so dismissive of the god they claimed to follow. So dismissive of her, the one called to execute his will in this kingdom. And the fact that it was her own brother who gave these orders appalled her. Didn't he understand that she didn't send these people into battle lightly? This was a holy war.

"My lady," called a hoarse voice to her left.

Izriamat turned, indignation still ablaze. She schooled her expression at the sight of the tall woman before her. She had a hawkish nose with cheekbones and a jawline like the edge of a sword. "Yes?"

The woman stood a little straighter as if mustering her courage. "I wanted to bring you good news. The netkoleh has been struck down. I did it myself."

Izriamat's world stopped, all sound around her muffled. She struggled to comprehend the words this woman had just uttered. "You did what?" she stammered.

"I struck the netkoleh down with an arrow. In the chest." Around them murmurs began. "His men took him off and I lost sight of him in the confusion of the battle but I saw him fall."

Izriamat stepped closer to the woman, looking her deeply in her eyes. The woman flinched ever so slightly but held her gaze. "What is your name?"

"Liisira, my lady." Her answer was unwavering.

"Liisira, you wouldn't lie to me to try to curry my favor, would you?"

The woman looked horrified at the thought. "No, my lady. I was at the gate when the empire broke through. The moment I spotted him, I knew I was chosen to make this blow against the empire and pay the netkoleh back for his blasphemous ways. I only did it to be of service to Yutuu."

A flood of emotions swept through Izriamat and she pulled the woman into a hug. Bakari had been struck down. He'd been taken off the field of battle and who knew what condition he was in. The enemy of her soul could be dying just beyond the wall. Or perhaps he was already dead. An arrow to the chest was a near sure way to die.

"We will write songs about your great feat," she said into Liisira's ear. Pulling back, she called out for all of the people around to hear. "The emperor lies injured, unable to continue his perverse war. The great warrior of the gods, Liisira, has felled our enemy. Yutuu be praised."

Cheers and praises went up from those who could and Izriamat hugged Liisira again. Her eyes looked toward the gate where her brother pushed her people out of their divine path. Yutuu had given this first victory and Yutuuan would see their god deliver many, many more.

Chapter Six

Efemu shoveled the meager rice porridge into his mouth, not bothering to register the taste. He'd forgotten how horrible breakfast was during battle. The cooks weren't anything like at his family compound and spices were generally reserved for dinner. It was the only time he had to admit, reluctantly, that he was a bit pampered. But food was food and he had to eat to keep going.

It was nearly the end of the week and he couldn't see a way to break the lines of the Ega. They'd literally made their section of the city a fortress. They'd blocked off all alleyways and boarded up all the windows, leaving only slits for their archers to fire through. It was like they'd pulled every piece of nonessential wood from the surrounding buildings to make the new fortifications. He had to admire their determination. It was a smart thing to do. But even in the most secure building, mice and insects managed to find a crack to crawl through. He just had to find that crack.

A couple of warriors came up to where he sat on a discarded bench outside the makeshift battle kitchen. A thin man jogged behind them, clutching a few sheets of paper to his chest. The warriors saluted him and the other man did a rough copy of the gesture. "What is it?" he asked, swallowing down a soggy bite.

"This carpenter thinks that he has an idea to help with the battle," said one warrior, a woman.

Efemu looked to the man, skepticism plain on his face. He sighed. "What is this idea?"

"I heard about how the enemy has built up walls on their side of the city," he started, flipping through his papers, "and it made me think of games my siblings and I would play where one would be the fortress and the others would be warriors trying to get in."

"Children's games. Really." Efemu glanced at the two warriors disapprovingly.

The carpenter looked a bit ashamed but pushed ahead. "When we who were trying to get in couldn't figure out a way to break the walls, we started using our slingshots to fire over the walls. We'd use small stones, half rotten fruit, anything that we could launch. So, I started drawing and I came up with this." He thrust one of the papers at Efemu who took it in one hand. "What if we made a large slingshot and used it to launch attacks at the enemy?"

Efemu looked at the drawing. Instead of a hastily scribbled idea it was a carefully drawn out picture of the contraption with notes surrounding it. The machine looked somewhere between a slingshot and a longbow. It would take a number of men to pull the twine back that would launch the projectile and had a hook that would hold the shot ready until they wished to release it. The carpenter flipped through his papers again before holding out another one to the commander. This one had one end like a spoon and the other had a weight. From the notes he saw that when the weight was risen and released, the spoon end would hurl the attack. Much like when he flung porridge at his cousins as a child.

He looked up to the carpenter. "This is brilliant." He put his bowl down and pointed to the counter-weight machine. "I like this one. Do you have any made?"

"Only a small model," he said crestfallen.

"Did it work?"

He perked back up. "Perfectly, Commander Efemu."

Efemu stared at the drawing, thinking of the possibilities. They could launch stones to break the impromptu walls down. Break in the windows. He stopped, a wicked smile spreading. If they covered those stones in pitch and set them on fire…

"How long would it take you to make a full sized one? One we could fit in one of the alleyways or on a roof?"

"If I can get help, maybe a week?"

"Bring the model and explain how it works to my captains. In the meantime, get whoever you can to help you build this. As soon as you can get it to us, bring it."

The carpenter stared at him, then bobbed his head respectfully. "I'll get to it right away."

Efemu endured the man's flood of thanks as the two warriors escorted him away. He was about to pick up his bowl to choke down the rest of his breakfast when he noticed an unfamiliar warrior walking down the street. He narrowed his eyes, concentrating on his face. Efemu thought he'd seen him briefly in a meeting with the other commanders or maybe he'd worked close to his contingent in the war. But he couldn't place a name with the face.

The man stopped short and saluted him. No full bow. Noted. "Commander Efemu, I'm Commander Beruluma. I've been sent to take command of this front. You've been reassigned."

Efemu swore he'd heard the man wrong. "I'm sorry?"

"Reassigned. Your father has a new mission for you." Beruluma handed over a rolled up piece of paper. The man looked neutral but Efemu could see the slight smugness hiding behind his eyes.

He unrolled the paper, reading over each line with growing anger. He was being taken from the fight to head a force to take back Ofolubaru. He crumpled it in his fist, throwing it at the other man's feet. "So you're to be my father's lackey here."

Beruluma scowled. "I am no one's lackey."

"Did my father hand pick you?" Efemu chuckled. "Let me guess. You thought this would be your chance to move higher."

"You speak dangerously."

Efemu stood to his full height, just enough to look down at him. "And you speak to a son of the line of Yundasha. Know your place." He could see the deliberation within the other man and waited until he came to the right decision. When there wasn't any sign of an altercation coming, Efemu pushed past him. "Hope you find loyalty to my father more rewarding than I did."

He couldn't speak to his fellow warriors as he picked up his weapons and left the district. He could barely focus as he made his way through Nsongo's streets. All he had was rage. He'd given his all to this city, to the whole south. He nearly died several times in the war. Now his father wanted to jerk him about as if he were just a piece on a game board.

He didn't bother to let himself be announced as he barged

into his father's meeting room. "Ofolubaru," he roared. "You snatch me away in the middle of battle to head east? How petty are you? All because I wouldn't kiss your ass, father?"

"You will lower your voice and remember who you're speaking to," his father said, voice flat.

Efemu growled in frustration. "You hide behind your new *temporary* status to get away with bullshit."

Erenemo looked unmoved by the disrespect. "The dara of Ofolubaru came to me, chased from her city by a witch. She's filled the city with paupers and other ne'er-do-wells. You will take an appropriately sized force and liberate her city."

"A witch," Efemu shouted. "You take me off the front for some rogue magician?"

His father sighed heavily as if Efemu were a petulant child. "Your force has already been chosen. They are prepared to leave tomorrow."

Efemu narrowed his eyes. "My force is at the front against the Ega district."

"You'll have a new one. Ngoli chose them so you know that you won't have brand new initiates."

"Is this how you plan to rule, father? You'll just get rid of anyone who doesn't bow down to you immediately?"

Erenemo went back to the books and papers he'd been combing over. "I expect the Ofolubaru to be taken back in a reasonable time." He glanced up at Efemu, dispassion in his eyes. "And I don't expect to see you until it is taken back." The dara of Nsongo motioned for him to leave, not looking up from his work.

A deluge of curses burned on Efemu's lips but he left them unsaid. He knew his father. No amount of yelling, no amount of insults no matter how foul was going to change his father's mind now. The old man's mind was set. *Bull headed old bastard.*

"Very well," Efemu said. He relaxed his shoulders and calmed his face. He forced himself into a bow that every vertebra resisted then left the room.

His anger sat within him like a flooded river, ready to crest its banks. He would be obedient. For now. Let his father get what he wanted. Let him think that he was the great war dara he'd never gotten the chance to be. And when it all came crashing down, Efemu would be there to bear smug witness.

***

General Tutahmen was finishing the last bites of a much savored dinner when someone cleared their throat in polite interruption. It had been a long day inspecting fortifications and personally making sure troops would be ready to fight at a moment's notice. He'd taken refuge in the building's smaller courtyard to have his meal. All he wanted to do was eat, wash the day off, and have his most loyal servant warm his bed. Now someone dared disturb a rare peaceful night.

"What is it?" he growled after swallowing.

"There is someone at the gate leading out of the city," came an attendant's voice. "It's a southern woman. She says she wants to speak to you personally."

Tutahmen rolled his eyes. Foolishness. He was constantly plagued by foolishness. "Bring her here."

"Yes, General."

He ate another bite trying to hang on to this feeling of peace for as long as possible. By the time he'd finished his food and drained his wine, the attendant was announcing that the woman was here. Tutahmen set his cup down and motioned over his shoulder for them to come near. He frowned, expecting an old woman here to beg for the release of her daughter or son from their service or other such nonsense, but when he looked to the woman that had come to speak with him his eyebrows shot up in surprise.

She grinned, slyly coquettish. "I'm honored to be in your presence, General," she said without bowing.

He looked behind him to the attendant still standing to wait for the woman. "Leave us." The man bobbed his head and quickly left. Tutahmen turned his attention back to the dara of Olofubaru. She was just as comely as the day he'd met her, beautiful dark brown skin and long, long braids with golden beads. Yet, there was a tiredness in her eyes that was undeniable. "What are you doing here?" He searched for her name but it was lost to him. "Nbasi?"

Her smile dropped. "Ngoli," she corrected him flatly.

As if he was supposed to remember. He'd met so many daras during the early days of the occupation. "Dara Ngoli. What are you doing in Nsongo?" His suspicions were starting to form a number of reasons.

"I came to the city because I have a bit of a problem." Her flirtatious tone returned. "I've been run out of my city by a horrible sorceress and her rag tag army. Some of my own people have turned on me."

He stared blankly. "And what am I supposed to do about that?"

"Well, I did come to ask the Great Dara for help but then I remembered that you had settled in here. You have so many men to fight for you. I'm sure you could defeat that horrid woman and her people in no time." She moved to stand closer to him and he could smell the faint scent of lilies.

"Ngoli, I have a battle here that I need to focus on. I thought you would have noticed since you had to sneak your way here through the back." He raised an eyebrow, expecting some sense from her.

Ngoli's lips pursed ever so slightly, but she turned the expression into a pout. "I understand that you have a battle, but if you were to help me get my city back, I would be most grateful. Don't you remember how grateful I was that you didn't burn my city?" She reached out to run a hand across his chest. "I can be that grateful again."

Memories of a series of nights celebrating the surrender of Ofolubaru by taking pleasure in its young and willing dara rose to mind. But those memories, while pleasant, were not enough to sway him. He stared at her again. "What's between your legs can be found in any noble compound or any common back alley so I am not so easily moved by the offer. If you wish for my help, you'd best come up with something more useful to me."

She pulled back, affronted. "I can lend you troops to help defeat the Nsongans."

"You'd actually turn on your own people completely?" He was genuinely surprised at her treacherous offer.

"You all still don't understand the south," she chuckled.

"Ofolubaru has been waiting for the chance to take the title of Great Dara from Nsongo for ages. They've held onto it for a perverse number of generations. The other great cities feel the same. And now with the last dara dead and the position being held by an old priest?" She leaned over, clicking her tongue in disapproval. "Things in the south aren't as stable as you would seem to believe."

Tutahmen ran her words back over. He didn't like to be ill informed but it appeared he was. He'd made too many assumptions about the southerners. If there was infighting, it could be exploited to quell this rebellion. "You still have forces in Ofolubaru, forces that are still loyal to you?"

"This woman has taken over the palace from me but I'm sure my peacekeepers within the city are still loyal."

"I can hear the unsurety in your voice."

"My people are loyal to me." She moved closer again, coming behind him to place her hands on his shoulders. "And wouldn't you like a dara that is more…pliable to the empire's wants?" she whispered in his ear. "I can be very pliable."

Tutahmen weighed his options. While Ngoli may not have the forces to turn the tide here, having a Great Dara more aligned with the empire's wants would be a boon. Also, he was growing tired of a lover that just endured his lust. Having one who responded and participated would be a welcome change. "I can make no promises of a date when I can spare the soldiers but we will see about returning your city to you."

"I am most grateful for your kindness, General."

She moved to take her hands off of his shoulders and he caught one of her hands. "Show me how grateful."

Ngoli came around to move the small table out of her way, smiled seductively at him, and lowered to her knees.

***

The compound was so quiet with Patya gone. Erenemo strolled through the halls of their private areas slowly, taking note of everything that she'd added since their marriage. He passed a statue of two dancing girls that she'd had commissioned in Ofolubaru for their fifth anniversary. Their smiling

faces stared out from the polished wood making him think
fondly of the moment that she'd revealed it. Patya had been so
proud, making him close his eyes as she led him to the spot.
He'd presented her with a pearl and gold necklace from Ama-
kari that covered her shoulders and draped nearly down to her
navel. She'd rewarded him by wearing nothing but the necklace
when he came to the bedroom that evening. Erenemo gave a
small chuckle. He was pretty sure Efemu was conceived that
night.

His lips tightened to a line at the thought of his son. The boy
better be considering his position and his loyalties on his trip. If
he thought this mission was an insult Erenemo could do worse
to him if he didn't fall in line. It pained him to have to be so unforgiving to his only progeny but lessons had to be learned.

He entered the reception room, the scent of the hearty breakfast wafting in on the morning breeze. It wasn't an extravagant
display. His guest wouldn't be swayed by that, but it was one
she might appreciate after being out in the fighting for the past
few weeks. Ngali was of the old and venerable line of Hembe.
She was used to finer things.

A servant ducked her head in the entrance. "Great Dara, War
Minister Ngali is here to see you."

"How is her demeanor?"

The servant hesitated. "Angry," she answered quickly.

Erenemo sighed and motioned for the woman to lead Ngali
in. Let her be angry. He put on his most pleasant and welcoming
smile as his guest entered.

Ngali was a tall woman, like her mother, with a gaze that
could whither fields of sorghum. She wore a black leather
eyepatch and hadn't bothered to change into a clean uniform before she came. Her hair sported the first streaks of gray and the
scar that extended above and below the eyepatch, almost to her
jaw, only added to her dominating presence. She was becoming
a living legend, her deeds in the war quickly rising her up to
War Minister, even bearing three children during the conflict
with the last directly after.

She saluted him and bowed, deeply and respectfully. "Great
Dara," she said. Her eyes flitted around the table and the

breakfast. The slight disapproval couldn't be missed.

"Ngali, sit. Eat," he said gesturing to a nearby stool. "I brought you here to speak on the battle."

The War Minister hesitated but she took her place at the table. A servant quickly came to pour her a cup of water. "What is it you wish to know?"

Erenemo almost chuckled. Every year she sounded more and more like her mother, the old blade. "Have some food, War Minister. I'm sure you could use a good meal." He waited as she eyed the food suspiciously, then piled some on a plate. "I wanted to speak about how much of the city had been taken back from the enemy."

Ngali took a bite, chewing thoughtfully, obviously weighing her response. "We are still at a stalemate. The Ega have dug in and we have yet to find a way in. However, we have found more of their bodies. Don't know who or what's doing it. Ghastly stuff."

"Really," he said, making sure he didn't show his concern. He'd been sure than starting this war anew would have appeased the Batu'bangi enough that they'd call off their monsters. It could only be a matter of time before they'd be set on the rest of Nsongo. They had to do more to cleanse their city of these outsiders. "Do we need more forces? We can call warriors from the surrounding smaller cities."

"It's not a matter of forces. They've created a walled city within our city. They wait at every possible entrance with spear wielders and archers perched on every building. They seem even more on guard at night. Probably because of the killings. Thankfully it only seems to be them getting killed."

"Yes, thankfully," he said taking a sip of his drink.

Ngali eyed him with that withering gaze. "You speak as if you know something, Great Dara." His title was sharp as a knife coming from her mouth.

Erenemo paused, not sure how much, or even if, he should tell her. But her narrowed eye showed she would not be satisfied until she received a satisfactory answer. He scowled back. "This goes no farther than us. Is that clear?" She nodded curtly. "There are creatures, sent by the Batu'bangi, against the Ega. They feel that we can't control the northerners well enough so they'll take revenge against them personally."

"The creatures from the deep forest," she breathed. "There are monsters roaming Nsongo in the night and you didn't see fit to tell anyone?"

Her voice had risen slightly and he shushed her. "It was my concern, alone."

"It is not your concern alone, priest."

"Great Dara."

"Whatever," she snapped. "I am War Minister. Anything that affects the safety of the city, the safety of the entire south, is my concern." She put her head in her hands for a moment then shot as scowl at him. "So we have no choice. Do nothing and invite the ire of Egans and the Batu'bangi or fight and just restart aggressions with the Egans."

"That magistrate put us in a bind. If we don't expel the Egans, we'll never see another speck of gold in the city again." She was looking at him as if it were all his fault and it grated on his soul. "So I need you to find a way to win this war as quickly as possible. Do whatever you have to."

"I am working as quickly as I can. This takes time."

He grunted. "Efemu gave me the same sorry excuse."

"Thank you for taking away one of my most experienced commanders," she said, rising from the table. "It's the kind of battle planning I would expect from someone who's never been on the field."

Erenemo was tired of this. He was tired of being treated as less than because he chose the path of a priest. He was tired of the looks of disdain whenever he tried to speak of battle. He was of the line of Yundasha. He was the brother of a great dara, son of a great dara, the grandson of one, and so on for generations. He had been surrounded by warriors his entire life. Who was she to talk down to him?

"I don't have time for your churlish behavior, Ngali. I have a council meeting soon." He waved her off.

The younger woman looked down her nose at him, chaffing at the dismissal. She moved toward the door but stopped. "When the council elects a true Great Dara, I'll be first in line to pay homage to the gods to thank them. Shouldn't be too much longer." She smirked and left the room.

Erenemo sat still as a stone, Ngali's last words echoing in his mind. Surely the council wasn't already seeking to replace him. They were in the middle of a conflict. They couldn't change leadership in the middle of it. It would be foolish. He rose, thinking of those old meddlers plotting against him and the more he thought of it the more his ire built until by the time he'd reached the council building, he was furious.

He was thankful that he was the first one to arrive. He took the ornate stool of his office that was at the rear of the room, pleased at the chance to look each one of these conspirators in the eye as they entered. He was going to stay Great Dara and they would have to tell him to his face if they didn't want him to be. Then he would just have to find better council members who'd follow his commands.

The first arrivals paused in the doorway when they saw him waiting for them. Oshala and Embalu, the two old commanders, came in, bowing before taking their seats. Whatever they'd been speaking on was suspended and Erenemo had a strong guess as to what that was. Soon the other members came in, all looking surprised and caught when they saw their leader already in attendance. The great dara had to wonder who were the instigators of this plan of replacing him. He'd place money on Oshala. He and that old bat had never gotten along.

Once perpetually late Hafulo meekly made his way in, Erenemo clapped his hands together, making everyone jump. "Let us begin this long overdue first meeting."

He let them go over the normal business of the city first. Gold, iron, and other currencies had to be tallied, conflict or not and while Nsongo was still in a good place, it was clear that the shortage of incoming gold had taken a toll. Their food and spices were still at acceptable levels. He threw out an idea of selling some of their surplus to fund the battle efforts but found the council reluctant to do so. He ordered it done anyway. The people would survive.

Once the banal items were completed and the council seemed ready to adjourn, he raised his voice. "There is one last piece of business I wanted to discuss with you all." The members glanced to each other in confusion but settled back into their seats. "It has come to my attention that you all are looking to re-place me as soon as possible and in the middle of a battle for the freedom of Nsongo." He chuckled disbelievingly. "Surely I must have heard wrong."

Another round of glances and Okepeli, the eldest member spoke. "Erenemo, I thought we established that your tenure as Great Dara was a temporary stopgap to prevent the other cities from taking the mantle. We've made it clear that we would come back to choosing a permanent dara sooner or later."

"But," Erenemo countered, holding up a finger, "that was be-fore we were in conflict with the Egans."

"Sounds suspiciously like you ordered the attack to keep your position for a little longer," Oshala grunted.

Erenemo kept himself from scowling at the old woman. "I called for the attack because it was what should have been done ages ago. Ashaki had been a coward, surrendering to them. We've licked our wounds long enough. It's time for us to re-mind these dogs who we are again."

"It is one thing to meet them on the battlefield," Embalu said, his bass voice rumbling across the room, "but it is completely different to be fighting within our own walls. We have the peo-ple to think about."

Oshala added, "My daughter tells me that the Ega have barri-caded themselves in the area they hold. Made a fortress. We still have people within that district, workers, merchants, even nobles who've been forced to serve them. Now they have captives. What of them, Great Dara?" His title was said in the same cut-ting way her daughter had earlier.

"We will free them."

"How?" asked Palia, youngest of the councilors.

"I'm sure Ngali will find a weakness in their defenses."

"Your brother would have been out there," Embalu said. No one nodded but everyone's face held the same stoic expression one makes to hold back their true feelings. "Ashaki would have been out there."

Erenemo's eyes flared with rage. Oshala, who had never been

a fan of his late niece, took the comment in consideration then nodded her agreement. The priest turned ruler of the city could hold his composure no longer. "While I am Great Dara, I will rule how I see fit. The Ega will finally be run out of this city and it will be because of my leadership. This meeting is over."

Everyone sat in silence for a moment, stunned. Then slowly, one by one, they rose to leave the room. Oshala gave him one last wrinkled smirk before exiting, adding more fuel to the fire of his anger. Erenemo was left alone, sitting on the stool of the office he had coveted since his father died, and knew he'd just made a grave mistake.

Chapter Seven

Beats of sweat rose on the emperor's temple, a perverse constellation catching the lights of the room. His breathing was a whisper heard only in the moments of silence between the healers' work. Mgobe entered the small room, noting the mingled smell of healing ointments, a long unwashed body, and injury. It didn't have the distinct scent of a stomach wound, the repulsive mix of rot and shit. He'd seen one of those wounds once, back in his days of study. A farmer had fallen on his sickle. The smell had stayed with him for days.

But this gods abandoned bastard before him reeked of the metals of blood with the faintest hint of puss. But it lacked the one note he was hoping for. The emperor did not smell of death.

Mgobe came closer, standing over the low bed the emperor rested on. How easily he could just smother the man. No incantations. No weapons. Just take the pillow behind his head and press it to his face until he stopped breathing. He'd never contemplated murder before but revenge made it an alluring choice.

"My governor," said one of the physicians timidly.

He suddenly noticed the focused attention of the others in the room. Mgobe's brow twitched out of his scowl. He relaxed hands that he hadn't realized had curled into claws. He took a deep breath until his chest ached, held it, then let it go between his teeth.

His wife's voice cut through the silence. "Leave us." While gentle, the command was clear. He didn't turn as her quiet footsteps approached. The physicians quickly filed out leaving them in silence. "Murder is not your nature," she said gently.

A wry chuckle escaped him. After all of their years of marriage she could tell his thoughts without even a look. "He deserves every horror I could possibly imagine."

"And so much more," his wife responded. "What will we do with him?"

Mgobe's shoulders sunk as the gravity of the situation settled on him. He'd captured the emperor. He'd made his city enemies of the entire empire. The might of the capital would fall on them and he wasn't sure the walls or their magicians could hold them off. "I'm not sure." He swallowed hard. "I didn't think much past his capture. Perhaps I should consult the council?"

His wife paused, staring down at the emperor but her eyes unfocused. "I would not presume to tell the governor what he should do on such an important matter."

"Adisa, I've always valued your opinion, no matter the subject. What are your thoughts?" He took her hand gently.

She didn't take her usual, thoughtful time to answer. "Either kill him or hold him hostage for when the axe of the empire eventually falls at our gate."

He gave her hand a squeeze. Both were reasonable paths. But neither felt right. And nothing was ever so cut and dry. He led his wife out of the room. "Continue to keep him alive," he told the waiting healers. "At least for now."

They returned to the governor's compound, Mgobe getting one of his lower secretaries to gather the council. Adisa sat beside him in the meeting room placing a supportive hand on his as they waited. The large round table was quickly set with refreshing drinks for the people that would assemble. The councilors trickled in one by one, ducking their heads in respect to their governor as they took their seats on the cushions around the low table. Mgobe greeted each of the men and women as they arrived, truly pleased to see them. He needed them more than ever.

He cleared his throat nervously once everyone was settled. "I want to thank you for assembling on such short notice. I assure you I wouldn't have asked for anything that wasn't highly important." He took a breath. "I need to decide what to do about the emperor." There were sharp intakes of breath and grimaces. Mgobe didn't miss a couple of sour looks among the group. "Speak your minds," he said preparing for the worst. "I know the capture was a shock."

The council glanced to each other before a man around Mgobe's age spoke up. "Governor, this was a rash decision.

What's going to happen to the city when the capital gets word of this? We've taken the emperor hostage. They've already burned the library. It would be nothing to them to burn Djelebe next."

"He deserves to suffer," said a woman in the blue robes of the elemental scholar school. A few looks of disapproval were thrown her way. She waved them off. "The deed is already done and I, for one, am glad it happened. He destroyed countless centuries of knowledge and history. I ran my hands through the ashes of my entire school of study. Those of you who work outside of the library cannot possibly understand how that feels."

"We understand, Sileh," said another woman kindly.

"You don't understand," Sileh snapped. "He took one of our librarians off to be a concubine." She looked to Mgobe, her face set in intense resolution. "If you choose to execute him, I wish to be there."

A few others nodded in agreement and Mgobe was shocked at their burning anger. A short man of about sixty, dressed in a city guard uniform cleared his throat. "If I may speak?" came his soft, even voice.

"Go ahead, Nkuro."

The guard captain leaned forward, steepling his fingers on the table. "We have a very valuable hostage at the moment. Valuable to the heart of the empire, the north, and even the south. We can use him to stay the capital's hand, but they may attack us in an attempt to rescue him. We could sell him to our distant cousins in the south, but they lay on the other side of the Ega. Such a plan would require a level of stealth we are not used to and an insane amount of divine favor. But the north? They're virtually at our doorstep and have an army. We offer them the emperor in exchange for protection. We could even offer them magicians to aide them in their effort."

Another scholar balked. "Haven't we had enough of our magicians kidnapped into war?"

Nkuro nodded, a concession. "We are in unprecedented times. We will have to do more to meet them. The guards train daily and with renewed determination since the great fire. We could train your magicians. Turn Djelebe into not just a city of scholars but warrior scholars."

His last words hung in the air. Mgobe sat back. None of them had ever thought they'd be called to war, to become warriors. This wasn't the ancient days. Djelebe had always been a neutral place. He swallowed. But with one rash decision he'd cast that neutrality aside. "Do you think our scholars would be willing to become warriors?" he asked his two councilors from the library.

Sileh and the other scholar looked at each other, hesitant. "I think," Sileh began, "that they will rise to the occasion if necessary."

The other man grimaced. "I'm not so sure."

"People are angry," Sileh countered. "I know the younger people especially want to do something about this. Many of their elders, family and not, within the library were conscripted when the emperor last came through. They'd want the chance to save them."

Mgobe nodded, taking in her words. "Nkuro, do you think it would be wise to train some of the regular people to be guards while some of our warriors are away?"

"We could do that, my governor."

"Excuse me, governor," cut in a man, the eldest in the room. He had a long white beard and still sported a full head of hair. "May I say a word?"

"Go ahead, Rofuma," Mgobe said.

"Whatever path we take, holding the emperor hostage, bartering him off, joining in this war, we will be in rebellion. What happens afterward?" He gestured about him as if encompassing the entire city. "We know what will happen if we lose this war. But what happens if we win? What happens to us after we've thrown off the empire?"

"We will finally be free," Adisa said quietly beside him.

Mgobe sipped thoughtfully from his cup. Freedom from the empire wasn't something he'd ever considered. There had been a time, long ago, when Djelebe was independent, ruled by scholar-warrior kings. Free to conduct their affairs and their studies in peace without worry of foreign interference. And wasn't a place to be free to contemplate and study the workings of the world what their great founder had traveled so far north to find?

91

He looked around the room at all of the people assembled here. They looked to him, waiting expectantly for his decision. "Then we'll finally be free." He motioned over an attending servant who also served as a scribe and messenger. "We will send a letter to Wiluru. We have a bargain for them."

***

It was an unusually cool day. Rains had come in overnight and their clouds still hung in the air blocking any warmth. Sept'ha followed Hetsaf at a distance as they walked through the city. The morning was quiet as well without many people wanting to navigate the puddles dotting the streets. As they left the more populated areas of the city and moved closer to the abandoned temple of Usirah, the area became completely empty. She looked around at the surrounding buildings as they walked, looking out for any nosy spectators who could report their travel. Some may not care but there were plenty who would be more than willing to make a few coins by reporting people going into a temple to the city guard. It was a chance they had to risk. They had a meeting to attend.

Sept'ha took off her cloak when she found her way inside through a side entrance. The temple was dark and had that dusty scent of a place that hadn't been inhabited in ages. She supposed no one had even dared squat inside after the emperor's cleansing of the temples. A safe night's sleep wasn't enough to risk being made an example, she guessed.

Using the light of the high windows, she navigated her way to the front, ending up inside the room just behind the public altar where the priests conducted their more sacred rituals. Hetsaf was already there, taking off his cloak and draping it over his arm. "Put your hood back up," he said quietly. "Their order doesn't allow women and I don't know how he'll react to you being here."

"I will be very curious as to why she's here," came a voice from a shadowed corner.

Sept'ha bit her lip to keep from screaming. A man in dark brown robes stepped out into the faint light. He was of medium height and build with a clean shaven head. He didn't walk with

92

the slightly bowed posture of a man of his age but moved with a grace that was unnerving. As he came closer, she caught the momentary glint of a sword at his side and she stood still. It was one thing to know of the Arakgu'un. It was another to be standing so close to one.

The older man bowed to Hetsaf who nodded in return. He then glanced toward Sept'ha and quirked an eyebrow. Hetsaf gestured to her offhandedly. "This is my assistant, Sept'ha. She is involved in everything I do."

She bowed and the man looked her over assessing. "I thought that we were meeting alone," he said.

"I didn't mention her in case you would decline the invitation. It was actually her idea for this."

The old man laughed, looking more like a jolly grandfather than assassin priest. "You let a woman into your plans?" he said. "From what I understand from the emperor, I thought you hated women."

Hetsaf bristled at the remark. "I do not *hate* women. I have no use for them." He huffed. "Antakhanan, we have a mission for your order."

"Oh, do you?" He seemed to light up.

"There is a rebellion in the west, a peasant uprising. They've managed to defeat the local guard and the small force I sent to subdue them." Hetsaf's face turned sour at the mentioning of the defeat. "I need some of your priests to go in and take care of their leaders. And I also may need members to head to the south. Nsongo has rebelled as well and getting rid of their current leaders would make things easier."

Antakhanan nodded, thinking. He turned to Sept'ha and she was shocked to suddenly be the focus of attention. "Was this truly your idea?"

"Yes," she answered. "The bulk of the military is in Wiluru. The force in the south has its hands full and we are stretched thin here. Throwing more men hasn't worked in the west. You can't beat a splinter out. You have to pull it out carefully."

"Or cut it when it gets too deep," he said, adding to her metaphor. The priest studied her again. "You are a smart young woman. Much smarter than most your age."

"So can we count on you?" Hetsaf asked.

"Of course," Antakhanan replied. "There is a priest I sent out months ago that I've yet to hear word from. I can let them know to search for him as well." The old priest eyed them with an amused yet suspicious eye. "As I understand, both the empress and you, Chancellor, were placed in charge in the emperor's absence. Is this an order from the both of you?"

"No," Hetsaf answered and Sept'ha cursed him for his honesty. Could he learn to be even slightly duplicitous?

"The empress is focused on her newest child," Sept'ha jumped in. "It may be some time before she is ready to take the reins of leadership again."

Antakhanan nodded again. "Very well. I will send groups out as soon as possible." He started to leave but made his way closer to Sept'ha and stopped. "There is something about you," he said conversationally. "Something different. You walk with authority. Who are you? Because you're not just a simple 'assistant'."

Hetsaf looked slightly alarmed, but Sept'ha stared back into his eyes. "I am the chosen of Met, here to set the empire on the right path." As if called, she felt the familiar touch of the leopard at her side. She let her fingers brush the top of its head while she kept her eyes on the priest.

His eyes widened and he took a few steps back. He watched the cat, amazement and the slightest bit of fear swirling in his eyes. "Pardon me for being so familiar," he said with a bow. "I didn't know I was in the presence of such a favored one." He looked over to Hetsaf. "I'm going to guess that you don't believe in all of this throwing off the gods as your brother does."

Hetsaf hesitated. He looked to her and she stared back, daring him to lie. He'd better make it clear what side he was on.

"I did, out of loyalty to him, but I've since changed my mind after meeting Sept'ha. She's made it very clear that the deities are real."

"Met wants the worship of warfare," Sept'ha said. "We will give it to her."

The old man seemed to take her in truly now. The slightly amused look he had for dealing with these two young people was gone and she could tell he was looking at them as equals in this conversation. "What of the emperor?"

The answer came to her lips as if from Met herself. "The emperor has served his purpose."

Both men looked to her in shock, but Antakhanan was the first to recover. He studied her eyes, searching for something and apparently found it. "Very well," he said. He reached down and put a hand out for the leopard who considered him and then looked away as if she were too good for the interaction. He chuckled. "She didn't growl at me so I'll take that as indifference. I'd rather that than hatred from the goddess of war."

Sept'ha stroked the leopard's head who purred. "I know your priests will fulfill their duty. This distraction in the west, especially, is taking away from the main conflicts."

The Arakgu'un glanced between them again, a knowing smile on his face. "The offenders will be sent to the judgment of the gods, my lady of war." He bowed to her, sparing a shallower bow towards Hetsaf and left the room.

Sept'ha was about to walk back out when the chancellor caught her arm. "You were supposed to observe, not speak in this meeting," he hissed at her.

She looked down to his hold on her arm, then at him. "We are in this together." She stressed the last word to make sure he understood. "We serve Met together. I'm not your servant when it comes to her will." The leopard, who had been silently at her side all this time, gave a short, warning growl. Hetsaf uncurled his fingers from her, stepping back with a wary glance toward her companion. Sept'ha rubbed her arm. "Gods, you do hate women."

"I do not hate women," he retorted, almost sullenly.

"We got what we wanted, right?" she asked moving to catch his gaze. "The rebels will be taken care of and the south will be unbalanced so we can destroy them with the army. So maybe, you should continue trusting me to do what my goddess sent me here to do?"

His lips twisted in a frown. "Fine," he said as if the capitulation was devastatingly bitter. "Let us return to the palace."

Sept'ha watched him as he left then rolled her eyes. Men.

***

Arkole meandered along the columned balcony to the east of the palace. Morning sunshine warmed her face, not quite the oppressive heat the day seemed to promise for later. She read through a series of papers in Sept'ha's careful writing. Below, in the courtyard, the delighted screams of her daughters could be heard, freshly released from their morning meal. The girls were so eager to see their newest brother when she visited them last night, but she'd been reluctant to let them get attached to him so early, before he even had a name. They could wait just a few more days until he was ready.

She spared a sad smile at her daughters' play, wishing Bakari was here. The baby's naming day approached and they should have already had one picked. A good name that showed he embodied the new hope of the empire. Something that would honor the future before him and those who went on before. She pushed aside the image of Kolehtun's face before it fully formed and her tears could consume her. She had to keep herself together. Bakari needed her to. This child was the future, she reminded herself.

Arkole turned back to the papers from Sept'ha. They were the normal reports that for some reason Hetsaf didn't deem her worthy to have. The southern rebellion continued on which concerned her. She thought the Nsongans hadn't any fight left in them after their surrender. But hostilities continued on. She flipped to another message. Hetsaf had sent a force to the peasant rebellion to the west. She read the missive twice, making sure she didn't miss anything. No great details as to what this force was, no numbers, and not even where he was pulling the forces from were given. Just that a force would be sent which should take care of the problem in short order.

She bristled at the thought of Hetsaf cleaning up the situation so tidily. She should be the one giving the orders to steer the empire. Was she not the Great Royal Wife? She knew Bakari and his wants better than he knew himself. She flipped through the papers again. There was no update as to his condition. Anger and worry tumbled over each other in her mind. It could simply be that there wasn't any news to report. However, she had a feeling that the true reason was that Sept'ha had overlooked the message or Hetsaf wanted to keep that information to himself. The selfish bastard.

Arkole called for one of her servants. The young woman hurried up to her, bowing meekly. "Fetch a scribe," she said folding the papers. "I need to send a message to Djelebe." The woman bobbed her head and rushed out. A smug smile pulled at Arkole's lips. If Hetsaf wouldn't give her the information she needed then she would find it out herself.

After a moment, another servant shuffled up to her. "Pardon me, empress, but second wife Nitiri is here to see you."

Arkole scowled, looking past the gauze curtains of the entrance to the balcony to where she was sure that woman was waiting. "Bring her out here," she spat. She turned away looking out over the courtyard as she heard the light footfalls approach.

"Empress," Nitiri called.

Arkole threw a glance over her shoulder, trying her best to look unconcerned at the intrusion. The younger woman's beautiful darker skinned face was tight with concern. In her arms she carried the son of Izriamat who rested his head against his foster mother's shoulder. Wonderful, two of the three people she couldn't stand in this palace. At least she'd left her disruptive son behind. Arkole turned back to watching her daughters, scowl returning. "Can I help you?" she said, voice tight.

"I just found out that our husband was injured." Nitiri came to stand beside her on the balcony and when Arkole glanced at her again, it was clear that she was close to tears. "I wish someone had told me earlier. Did the chancellor bring you the news?"

"He did."

Nitiri pursed her lips in a way that Arkole was sure Bakari loved. "Hetsaf doesn't tell me anything. I have to find out everything through servant gossip." She hesitated. "I…I don't like him. Every time I've run into him, he looks at me like a thing that shouldn't be here if he even acknowledges I'm there at all. Perhaps I shouldn't say this, but I don't trust him."

Arkole slowly turned toward her, looking over the young woman. That was one thing they could agree on. "Hetsaf is a bastard," she said. "He thinks himself higher than us because he's a man and the emperor's brother. If Bakari didn't order him to work with me for the good of the empire, I don't think he'd tell me anything either."

Nitiri adjusted her hold of the baby, looking over the balcony at the princesses. She frowned thoughtfully. "I don't think he has Bakari's best interests at heart if he's excluding us. And if he doesn't have Bakari's best interests, then he doesn't have the empire's best interests at heart either." She looked up to Arkole with those damned big, doe eyes.

Gods, this girl was right. Arkole glanced to the papers still folded in her hand. She should let her know. Bakari would want her to know, just as he'd planned for Izriamat to be involved in the running of the empire. But the very idea of treating this girl as her equal still sizzled along her skin. She closed her eyes. *For Bakari. Do it for Bakari.*

She handed over the papers and Nitiri took them cautiously. "Hetsaf's servant has been bringing me copies of the items that Hetsaf refuses to share with me. I can share them with you as well."

Nitiri read over them, worrying her bottom lip again. "So Hetsaf has been bringing you news of the empire," she began slowly. "You chose not to share them with me either."

Arkole was taken aback. "I assumed he was informing you as well," she fumbled.

The second wife took a breath, a sorrowful expression growing on her face. "Empress, I don't know why you don't like me. All I've done is try to be the best wife I could be to our husband. I even helped with the birth of your son. I want the best for everything Bakari cares about and that includes you. Why can't you do the same for me?"

Arkole felt slapped. She hated this girl. She couldn't deny it. Some young thing plucked out from the lesser wives and raised to be her near equal. This pleasing flirt, body hardly changed by children, who surely did every act that her husband wanted and more. But she'd done no more than she was meant to do. That's what the lesser wives and concubines were for. Bakari had seen something in her that made him want to pull her up from the rabble and she would, at the least, have to respect that.

"You're right," Arkole forced herself to say. "Bakari wanted you to be a full part of the empire. As the empress, I should have made sure you were included. I'll be sure to do that from now on."

This seemed to bring Nitiri some relief. "If Hetsaf doesn't want to work with us, then we'll have to work for the good of them empire without him. Together."

The girl smiled hopefully at her. Arkole felt the tiniest pang of guilt. It wouldn't hurt to have at least one true ally in this palace. "Yes," she began, returning the smile. "We will look out for the empire and each other."

Interlude

The room was dark, candles low, and the orchestrator of all of this chaos lay on a bed attended by a trio of healers. His soul held on by a frayed, thinning tendril skirting the other side of life. Death stood at the foot of the bed, white eyes taking in the emperor's form. He had known many mortals who'd unbalanced this land but none had done so in such a complete way in ages. He'd plucked far too many souls as of late and he feared that being able to pluck this one man's soul wouldn't be enough to stop the tide of dead.

"Will he be mine sooner or later?" he asked.

"He will be yours when it is his time," answered Fate. She sat at the head of the bed, unnoticed by the healers. Her long gray twists fell past her shoulders and her hands were held in her lap.

Another presence entered the small room. "What are you doing here?"

Death looked to War, brows drawing together. "I am not here to collect this man if that is your concern. It is not his time." Fate nodded once in confirmation.

War made her way to the side of the bed, moving with feline grace, never taking her eyes off of Death. "So you're going to wait until it is?"

"War, you have overstepped," he said, low voice rising.

"Oh, have I?" War put a hand to her heart.

"You are beginning to manipulate people and places that you shouldn't. Places that aren't your domain."

She scoffed. "And you choosing your little servant in the south isn't manipulation?"

Death bristled, his vulture feather mantle giving a small tremble. "You are becoming greedy. You'll have the entire land drowning in war which is unbalanced." His voice echoed in the room, the healers still going about their duties.

"We've had peace too long," War said with a growl. "I've been patient. While you may be content with quiet funerals and culling the spirits of those too long in this world, I've been starving for blood on the battlefield, for real worship. How could you deny me such?"

"You know this won't stand, War."

Fate added, "There is a time for everything. We all must wait our turn for our roles."

War looked to her ferally. "I have chosen and my time is now." Without another word her presence left.

Death looked to Fate who was watching the emperor. He scowled at this unwitting servant of War, this pawn happy to throw away the tranquility this land had finally achieved. He left the room to attend to the souls ready to be reaped from this unnecessary war.

Chapter Eight

The girl was sleeping peacefully and Newa was grateful. Her rest had been fitful while they were on the road. She tossed and turned, waking at every sound and calling weakly for her mothers. Of course that meant Newa hadn't gotten much sleep as well. While he was trained to sleep in short bursts when necessary, he'd gotten accustomed to at least four hour stints. Now that they were in an inn and safe he was thankful for a full night for both of them.

Newa sat up from his makeshift bed on the barely swept floor. He knocked the dirt and hay off of his robes in a futile attempt to look presentable. After a moment he gave up with a quiet chuckle. He was traveling. People expected you to look a little dusty. He looked across the small room to the bed where Masola slept. He almost hated to wake her up but he needed to be on his way and she needed to be placed somewhere safe.

He stretched and rose from his spot that blocked the door. Gently he reached down and shook her shoulder then instantly regretted it. Masola winced and woke with a panic, curling into a ball and throwing a hand out as if she were trying to fend off an attack.

"Masola," he called. "Masola, you're safe. No one's attacking you."

After a few more calls of her name, the girl slowly relaxed, turning to look at him. He felt sorry for her as he noticed the tears welling in her eyes. "Newa?" she croaked, sleep choking her voice.

He did his best to smile reassuringly. "Good morning. Did you sleep well?"

"I did." She uncurled, sucking in breaths with pain.

Just over the edge of her collar, he noticed the purple bruise that was healing. "I'm going to get us something to eat. Don't let anyone in while I'm gone, all right?" She nodded. "I promise

I won't be long."

At her second nod, he left. He made his way quickly down the left arm of the long, U-shaped hallway the travel rooms were located on. The large room that served as the common area was still quiet and mostly empty but a few travelers sat at the scattered tables. The room was filled with the scent of breakfast and his stomach twisted noisily. He hoped Masola had an appetite. He most certainly did.

"Excuse me," he said as he came up to the woman at the corner kitchen.

"Breakfast'll be ready in just a little while," she responded, not looking up from the large three legged pot she stirred. A host of fish cooked behind her.

"Do you know where I could get some salve? My niece took a tumble on the road."

The cook looked him up and down, seeing through the flimsy lie and disapproving of whatever truth she'd settled on. "There's a healer to the left and two streets up. You'll see the blue pots beside the door."

He thanked her and left. The healer wasn't hard to find and he paid for the small container of healing balm without hesitation. Newa paused, looking toward the sky. What was he doing? This wasn't his concern. His mission was all important. There were a thousand girls right now with similar situations and they were making their own way. She would do the same.

Masola was sitting on the bed when he returned with two bowls of porridge and a fish to split between them. She had drawn her knees up to her chin. She wrapped her arms around them as if they were the only thing anchoring her here. Newa took in the blank look on her face solemnly. He knew such a vacant stare. This girl was chased by ghosts, thoughts that consumed her in the quiet moments.

He placed one of the bowls in her line of sight, breaking the spell. "Eat," he said. She blinked but unfolded herself to take the food. Newa watched her until she began eating, then sat on the floor to begin his meal. He observed her carefully, reading every little movement. The girl must be hungry but she ate lethargically. Every swallow looked like a struggle. She wasn't sick and while she moved carefully because of her bruising it wasn't completely preventing her from moving properly. Guilt. Guilt weighed heavy on her.

"Tell me, Masola," he said after swallowing, "do you have any family you can go to?"

She looked up, a slight alarm in her eyes. There was the beginning of an answer on her lips, the first formation of a yes before she said, "Not anyone that would want to take me in."

A tempest of information stirred behind those words. He chose his next question carefully. Probe too deep and she would shut herself off from him. Like his subjects at the temple, he would have to slowly draw this confession out of her.

"I can tell that you were loved, Masola." Using her name made it less of an interrogation. "I've seen children that were discarded or neglected by their parents. They grow up half feral, gangly from malnourishment and jaded. I was one of them." She studied him slowly as if searching for the scrawny boy from the slums. He chuckled. "I grew up."

Masola stared into her bowl, poking at the porridge with her spoon. "I ran away."

"Because your mothers died?" he asked gently.

"No," she said shaking her head. "Mommy died in the war. Mama died…" Her voice caught with grief. A strangled gurgle of a cry escaped her and she sucked in a breath. "My Mama died because of me." Her sudden weeping came in hiccups as if it were too much to pour out at once.

Newa's senses as an assassin priest pricked along his skin. He hadn't planned on making this confessional yet here they were. Redirect. Calm her into a sense of safety. "I found a salve to help your bruising. Let me put it on for you."

Masola nodded, putting her bowl down and shyly lifted up her shirt in the back. Not the movements of a country girl. Too much modesty. Newa pulled out the small jar, applying it as gently as he could. He didn't try to speak to her now. Too much of a distraction and she would start to shut down again. He needed to keep her hovering just above the subject. He moved back when he was done, sure to stay where he could only see her back. "Is that better?" he asked just a hair more positive than

104

flat.

She lowered her shirt and nodded. "It feels much better." She paused. "Thank you."

Newa allowed another silence to pass until he could see the subject returning to her eyes. "What did you mean that your mother died because of you?"

Masola looked to him in shock. She stammered, the beginnings of sentences falling away from her lips. Newa stared at her, not cruelly, but with the firmness that expected a complete and truthful answer. It was only a shadow of the stare he usually gave his victims in the temple and she folded immediately. "I killed my Mama," she sobbed. "I…I poisoned her."

Newa sat frozen in place. "You poisoned your mother?"

"It was an accident. I was mad with her and I wanted to make her a little sick but…but I must have used too much and she died." Masola dissolved into incoherent weeping, burying her face in her hands.

Newa watched, for he was speechless. To murder one's parent. It was a crime that was unforgivable. His teachings as a priest spoke on it clearly. This girl should suffer the same fate as her mother and die in the same way. He had to poison her.

But Efah came to mind. He knew she would take the girl under her care and put her on the path to redemption. Perhaps even forgiveness. He swallowed difficultly, a war beginning inside him. It was his duty, his sacred duty, to rid the world of those most unforgivable. The girl had to be sent on. Yet as he sat watching the sobs violently shaking her body, he couldn't bring up the conviction to do so. He couldn't even bring himself to feign it. He was a dealer of death who didn't want to do so.

Newa rose from his position on the floor and sat on the bed beside her. "It was an accident," he said, trying to sound genuinely kind. "It wasn't in your heart to kill her."

He felt the weight of his old master's disapproval. The teachings of Gu'un were clear. The war in his heart paused. He didn't serve "Gu'un" anymore. He was a servant of Tikiri who served Death and Death was far more merciful than he'd been led to believe. Efah was proof of that. Death was change, she'd told him. He had to change.

Awkwardly, he put an arm around Masola's shoulders. "I can't make this sound any better. What you did was a horrible act. But you feel sorry for what you've done which means you are redeemable. You can become better than the deeds you've done." His words caught as the many faces of the people he'd tortured and killed over the years came to him. He suddenly felt a thread of connection with this girl.

She fell against him, crying harder into his chest. Newa stiffened uncomfortably, then slowly pulled her closer. He let her cry until she settled into quiet sniffs. He kept his silence not sure if it was the right time to break it.

"You're going to leave me here?" she asked. The question was plain without an iota of accusation.

"No." The answer came immediately despite his earlier plans. "You may travel with me until you want to leave. But I will make one thing perfectly clear. I'm on a dangerous mission. My god has sent me to kill a false priest that's leading people astray. You'll have to learn to fight if you come with me. I may not be able to protect you."

Masola sat very still, the room plunging into silence once again. Slowly she sat up enough to look up to him. "I want to come with you. I'll learn to fight and I'll help you any way I can. You saved me."

He patted her on the shoulder. "Very well. Eat your breakfast and we'll head out." He reached for his bowl on the floor and they both continued their meal. Newa couldn't help but steal glances at Masola as they ate. He would help her on her road to redemption. Perhaps, she was helping him on his as well.

***

Efemu had never been to Ofolubaru but part of him had to chuckle at its attempts at grandeur. Wide golden domes topped multistory buildings, a clear imitation of Nsongo. The walls rose higher than home, however. But he also didn't see the repairs from the war that discolored Nsongo's perimeter. None of Ofolubaru's great towers bared any signs of battle scars either. The grand eastern city seemed untouched and he would have to ask around to find out why.

He signaled for his force to halt, the command echoing down the column. His current second in command, a barely battle tested woman named Kehesi, came to his side. "Commander, should I have the force camp here?"

"No, Kehesi." He'd decided to be patient with her. It wasn't her fault she had been saddled with this mission. War Minister Ngali had sent him a letter hailing her attributes as a soldier, but Efemu hadn't seen anything yet to make him want to put his full trust in her. "We won't camp yet. However, fan them out so our enemy can see what they deal with. A gaggle of peasants against a trained force from the capital of the south. I don't think there's much of a contest, do you?"

"No, Commander, "she answered, brightening up.

"Then see to showing off our strength and choose two squad captains to accompany us to talk to them."

She saluted him, fist over heart, and started calling out orders. He watched her for a moment, wishing Barabi was here. That man had a way of giving orders that made you want to follow his every word. His heart drowned in longing, not just for Barabi's companionship but for his advice as well. Efemu scowled. He guessed he would have to suffer through this belittling mission on his own.

To her credit, Kehesi had their warriors in place sooner than he expected. With his small entourage, Efemu approached the gates of Ofolubaru. A quiet series of bird calls brought his attention up to the top of the city walls. He slowed his pace at the sight of vultures starting to assemble, staring down at them. As they got close enough to talk to the gate guards the birds stopped their squawking all at once, watching intently.

"Halt," said one of the guards, obviously terrified. "What is your business here?"

Efemu took one last glance at the ominous birds before turning his attention back to the guard. The man was short and held his spear unsure. This was not a true warrior and by the look of the others here none of them were. "I come to speak to the witch that's stolen the city from its rightful dara."

The guards bristled. "You will not speak of the Lady of Death like that," one ground out, grip tightening on his spear.

Lady of Death? So, these were fanatics. He hoped they would have the good sense not to fight back. As much as he loved a good battle, there was no honor in slaughtering those who weren't warriors. "Then I will speak with your Lady of Death," he said, raising his voice to make sure all the guards heard. "Tell her to come out and we can discuss the terms of her surrender."

There were uncertain glances between the guards, whispered words shared, then one ran back into the city. "They hold their weapons like farmers," Kehesi said with alarm. "I thought we'd at least face warriors from the war."

"This is the mission we've been sent on by the Great Dara," Efemu said, cutting the discussion short, "and we will fulfill it." Kehesi didn't respond but he could tell there was an uncomfortableness about her.

After some time, a small group of people came to the gate. Dressed all in black, they regarded Efemu and his group with contempt. The leader, a slender woman with long braids tied back, motioned for them to approach. "We'll lead you to the palace," she said, an oppressive country accent in her voice. "Our lady will speak with you."

Efemu followed, his group falling in behind him. The all black guards surrounded them, their leader up front. He took in everything as he walked, from the nearly empty streets to the vultures that came to watch their procession. He'd never seen so many congregate outside of a battlefield. A bad omen, Barabi would probably say. Efemu smirked. Omen or not, he was going to win this conflict and get back to Nsongo to his real work.

They arrived at Ofolubaru's great palace which had proper guards at the entrance in uniform. These guards showed no fear either but watched with a level of suspicion that garnered his respect. A thought rose to mind. If these were official palace guards had they turned traitor and what could make them follow some hedge witch? The vultures squawked quietly as if in response to him.

The inside of the palace was as quiet as the rest of the city and Efemu wondered where this army of vagabonds the ousted dara claimed was here. He saw other people in all black here and there staring at the procession with animosity. The main hallway looked as if nothing had happened. The decorations of gold, ivory, and the prized rare wood found only near Olofubaru were still in their places. Such valuable items he thought would surely have been looted, sold to merchants for any currency. The carpets remained unsoiled and in pristine condition. He frowned. Something wasn't right.

The leader of the black clad warriors reached to open an ornate set of doors. "You are about to stand before our leader and the avatar of Death himself," she said looking directly at him. "You will show her respect. I don't care if you are an Nsongan warrior."

Efemu let the subtle threat slide. "If she shows me respect, I'll do the same." The woman scowled at him but opened a door to lead them in.

The court room of the dara was an ornate affair, so different from Nsongo's which was utilitarian, meant for work not show. Columns raised up a high ceiling where carved wooden beams made a faux canopy. High windows were covered with complex lattice work. A raised dais sat in the middle of the room with a high backed throne and on it sat what must be the Lady of Death.

She was barely more than a girl in Efemu's eyes. Round faced with eyes that held too much knowledge. Her hair was braided halfway to let the rest free in a halo of an afro. She wore simple clothes, a basic dress in blue that seemed to be a bit too big for her. At her sides were two massive hyenas. One sat to her left, her hand petting it calmly. The other lay, head at her feet, as docile as a spoiled pet. Efemu stopped short and he heard Kehesi's sharp intake of breath.

This woman, this Lady of Death looked into his eyes and he felt…something. Authority. Power. It was overwhelming. He tore his eyes away from her, coming back to focus just above her head. At the bottom of his vision, he saw her give small smile.

"I'm going to guess you're the commander of this force."

Her accent was muddled and he couldn't place it. "I am Commander Efemu, of the line of Yundasha. I have been sent by the Great Dara, ruler of the entire south, to take the city back from you and your people." Recognizing his father's authority was bitter on his lips.

"Dara Ngoli ran to the Great Dara for help." This young woman sighed with a weariness beyond her years. "Did she tell you how she treated her people? Did she tell you how the poor of the city and the lands around it would rather scrape out a living in the forest than suffer under her rule? I gave her a chance to become a better ruler and she refused."

Efemu's eyebrows rose. "I suppose your powers over these beasts and birds made you feel you had the authority to oust her?"

This woman sat up; smile gone. Her hyenas reflected her pose, eyes now locked on him. Efemu's hand reflexively moved toward his sword and the beasts immediately growled lowly.

"I wouldn't do that if I were you. Usa and Nesi are very protective." She closed her eyes, taking a breath, then her smile returned. "What was your name again?" she asked far more kind.

His hand moved away from his sword but he was still suspicious of this change in demeanor. "Efemu."

"It's an honor to meet you, Efemu. I'm Efah. Would it be all right if we speak alone?"

Efemu looked back to his group. Kehesi and the others expressed unease in their posture. He turned back to Efah and she was whispering lovingly to her hyenas. They nuzzled up to her then padded out of the room reluctantly. She turned her attention back to him, smile still kind. He glanced around the room. "That will be fine."

Kehesi was at his elbow immediately. "Are you sure that's wise, commander?" she hissed. "What if she is a witch?"

Behind them, the leader of the warriors in black spoke up. "My lady, are you sure?"

"I will be fine," Efah replied. She gestured for them to leave the room. They took one last lingering stare at the warriors from Nsongo and exited.

Efemu glanced to Kehesi. "Go. I'll be fine." His second nodded hesitantly but ushered the other warriors out.

The Lady of Death rose from the throne and walked toward him. "This wasn't my idea," she said with a slightly embarrassed smile. "My followers felt that I should greet you in the throne room."

He was at a complete loss. This young woman had run a dara out of her own city. But there was something about her, something that still made him avoid looking in her eyes. He composed himself. "There is a force waiting outside the city to remove you and your people, by violence if necessary. If you surrender and leave, then there won't have to be any bloodshed."

"Commander Efemu, what lies did the dara spread about me?"

"I didn't come here to hold conversations with a witch."

"Look at me." The simple phrase was more an honest request than an order. Efemu steeled himself and did so. He wouldn't be afraid of this girl. The moment he did so he was caught. He felt her presence on him, around him. "You hold the string of betrayal in your heart. Someone close. Your father?"

Efemu stiffened, giving himself away. There was no possible way this woman was seeing into his mind. "That is beside the point."

She took a step closer, raising a hand hesitantly towards his chest. He moved to step back but she closed the distance, making contact. Efemu felt her spirit touching his, invading his. There was no other way to describe it. He could see Nsongo. He saw his father sitting on the stool that wasn't rightfully his. He looked distorted, face pulled into an unnatural frown. Black tendrils emitted from him, turning into pools of poison where they touched the ground and spread out. He felt his own hatred, burning so hot it turned into a bright light. Then he saw the battle for the city as warriors from both sides were shot and cut down. Finally, he saw the image of Barabi reaching out for him, bathed in a hazy light.

And then he was back.

Efemu stepped back, breathing hard and looking around at the details in the throne room trying to determine if this was real or still his vision. It had been a vision. It couldn't be anything else. His eyes finally settled on this small woman, this Efah, the Lady of Death.

"What did you do to me?" he asked raggedly.

"I read your soul, Efemu." Her face looked troubled. "So, your father is the Great Dara but you feel he poisons the position he has. That's a terrible feeling to keep bottled up inside you." Realization sprang up on her face. "He's the one who sent you here, isn't he? And you're supposed to be back at home, in the battle and with your love."

He felt his face heat at the mention of Barabi. "Witch," he spat, reaching for his sword.

"Efemu, you can't kill me." She set those large deep brown eyes on him, capturing his full attention and holding him with that aura of authority again. "I am the agent of Death itself. I was sent to bring about a new beginning for our people, free from the influence of the northerners. If I wanted to, I could pluck your life from your body before you had a chance to draw your sword." She took a breath, releasing her hold on him. "But I'm not going to because I think you have a larger part to play in freeing the south than you realize."

Efemu paused, his hand hovering over the grip of his sword. This woman, this witch or lady of death or whatever she claimed, spoke with such conviction that he struggled to find his contempt of her. She'd seen into his soul and read his life. "What do you mean?" he asked cautiously.

Efah stared off, in the direction of Nsongo. "When Death first called me into his service, I thought that I would just be ridding our people of the Ega. As time went on, I realized that I was here to rid the south of the rot inside as well." She turned back to him. "Death brings sorrow, but it can bring new beginnings too. It can bring much needed change, like a great tree falling in the forest gives the smaller saplings a chance to reach for the light."

Efemu felt his heart squeeze the tiniest bit. "And what if that great tree refuses to fall on its own?" he asked, not sure if he wanted an answer.

She looked off again then back to him, young face serious. "Then it must be cut down." Outside, the vultures called in agreement.

Chapter Nine

The oddest bird perched on the palace wall. Umakaal watched it as it moved from windowsill to windowsill before taking flight again. It wasn't the usual avians that flew along the coast. The way it flew, as if it were unsure in the ocean breezes, marked it as an inland bird. She watched it make a loop over the courtyard then fly over the palace and out of sight.

She turned her attention back to the papers on the planning table. Supplies had arrived from all the major cities and she was making sure they were distributed among the populace. If they could be taken care of by outside help then they could direct the bulk of Wiluru's supplies to the warriors. The Ega would have to stretch their supply lines to keep up this attack. Waiting them out wouldn't be a problem. She looked toward the gates and the fresh smoke from new fires. But having a way to break their spirits would be very welcome.

A shadow passed over her and she glanced up to see the weird bird again. It circled over the courtyard several times, each loop bringing it lower. It flew close enough that she could make out its true colors, brown with white tips and an odd blue about its throat. It was a pretty bird. Umakaal grunted. Poor thing was probably a lost pet if it was seeking out humans. It landed on the railing walking a little closer while peering at her curiously. That's when she noticed the small cylinder shaped pouch on a strap around its neck. It took a short flight to land on the table. It was almost the size of a small cat and moved along just as circumspectly. One of the guards moved to shoo it away but she stopped her.

The bird walked within arm's reach then bowed its head. With almost an air of pride, it lifted its head back up, presenting the pouch. Umakaal looked askance at her nearby officers who were just as befuddled as her. She reached out cautiously, opening the pouch and pulling out a tiny scroll. She began reading over the small, precisely written letters casually, then read again in earnest.

The note from Djelebe claimed to have the emperor in their custody. They were doing enough to keep him alive but wanted to trade him for Wiluru's help. Protection. Djelebe asked for protection and in exchange they could have their most hated enemy and the assistance of mages from the scholarly city.

Umakaal had to read it a third time just to believe its message. The emperor's life for Djelebe's protection. An easy agreement. She stopped herself. It wasn't her agreement to make. She reached out and stroked the back of the bird's head that coo-purred in return.

"I need to take this message to my brother," she said urgently.

Salutes were made as she left, quickly finding her way to the nearest exit and running along the streets toward the gate district. She found her brother just coming off of the front, blood splattered across his armor. He looked haggard and tired. His usually smooth face bore the start of a curly beard. Darkness surrounded his eyes. Umakaal was taken back looking at him. She'd never seen him in the midst of battle. He looked every bit the warrior she knew he was but seeing him now made all the difference.

"Brother," she called out.

Yutuuan raised his head, eyes searching before he found her. The cheerful smile that usually greeted her was absent. "What is it?" he asked, voice weary. He motioned for her to walk with him.

She fell in step, noting the smells of blood and smoke rising from his body. "Has the battle turned?"

"No, but it's picked up intensity. Is something the matter at the palace?" They entered a building a couple of streets over, weary warriors taking time to catch a meal here. Yutuuan only mustered a nod in response to their salutes.

"I have a message." She leaned closer to him, lowering her voice. "From Djelebe."

He only grunted at first, sitting down in the nearest chair. "Djelebe managed to get a message through?"

"Yes, they ask for our aide." She looked around but there was no one close enough to overhear her whisper. "In exchange, they're offering us the emperor." Yutuuan's hands paused over the ties of his greaves. "They say that he's near death but they're keeping him alive."

He held up his hand to silence her, glancing about. He waved for her to follow him and they went upstairs to a room at the far end of the building. He closed the door firmly behind him. "They took the emperor to Djelebe? I mean, it makes sense. They have the best healers. And the scholars took custody of him?"

Umakaal nodded vigorously. "They want our aide in protecting their city and they said they'd give us magicians to fight this war."

Her brother laughed, mirthlessly. "What did that jackal fucked bastard do to piss off the scholars?"

"So, are we going to take them up on their offer?" she asked. "Hanging the body of the emperor on the walls for all of the Ega to see would be devastating."

"Little sister, I never knew you to be so vindictive," he chuckled. She gave him a nonchalant shrug in response. "But we need to think on this. I want to gather the commanders and I want Izriamat here. This war is because of her, after all."

Umakaal groaned. "She's not a warrior or even a councilmember."

"This is her husband. Her hated husband, might I add. If anyone deserves to know that he may leave his flesh at any moment, it's her." He crossed the room, wooden floorboards creaking under his weight. Putting a hand on Umakaal's shoulder, he added, "And if I can give her the chance to plunge a knife through that bastard's heart, I'm going to do it."

Before she could make another protest, he left and she could hear him calling for people. So Umakaal waited. And fumed. And waited until all of the available commanders were assembled in the room and finally Izriamat glided her way in. The commanders eyed her with a mixture of annoyance, unease, and plain contempt. She wore that same damn aloof look she always had now and it irked Umakaal just as much as it irked her the last time she saw her. Izriamat's eyes turned her way briefly, her expression unreadable. The younger princess didn't bother hiding her hatred. Let her feel what she'd earned.

Yutuuan returned with the last commander. "We need to speak briefly on a message we received from Djelebe. They have the emperor. He's injured and they're keeping him alive just enough."

"Has Djelebe rebelled too?" one commander asked.

"It seems they have," he answered. "And they're willing to barter him for our assistance and protection. The question I present to you is what answer do we give them?"

There were glances around the room. Umakaal stepped forward. "I think that the obvious answer is yes, we will bring them under Wiluru's protection." She looked to the commanders. "If we have the emperor, if we show the enemy we have their great leader in our custody, think of how much that would affect them. Their regular soldiers might even flee the battlefield."

An older commander grunted. "Or it might fortify their resolve to burn the city down."

"How would they even get him to us?" asked another.

There was a small silence as people contemplated the question. Umakaal frowned, realizing she hadn't thought of the logistics of it. Naret cleared his throat gently, catching everyone's attention.

"There is one way," he said, deep voice rumbling. "The old western pass. It was one of the entrances to Wiluru before the gates were erected." He looked to Yutuuan. "It is part of the escape plan to get the royal family out of the city if leaving by sea was impossible."

"Is it even open after all this time?" a younger commander asked.

Naret blew out a breath. "I'm not sure, but I can't think of another way without them having to sail all the way around. They'll have to risk it. With their magicians, I'm sure they can manage it."

"Then it's settled." Everyone looked to Izriamat who stared at Yutuuan with a wild intensity. "We will instruct Djelebe to bring the emperor through the pass. Then we can execute him."

The group turned their attention to Yutuuan, Umakaal

scowling at their sister. "We haven't decided what to do with him," Yutuuan said firmly.

"What else does he deserve after all he's done? After all the Ega have done?" Izriamat looked around to each of the assembled. "They've subjugated us for centuries. They fouled our cities with their temples and false gods. They've made us pay for continued peace with the flesh of our princesses. With my flesh." Her voice cracked as she said her last words and she took a moment to take a breath. "That man represents every foul urge the empire has and we should make him suffer before he dies. His army should see that even he can be broken."

The room was stunned into silence. Umakaal took a slow look around the room, alarm growing as she saw agreement in some of the commanders' eyes. She locked her gaze on her brother, willing him to knock down Izriamat's rash decision. He needed to say something. Take control of the conversation. Yutuuan stood, eyes fixed on Izriamat, his face changing between uncertainty, pity, and outrage. "Perhaps we should ask the council first?" Umakaal offered, hoping to jolt her brother out of his thoughts.

"Yes," he said slowly, pulling his eyes back to the rest of the room. "I will send off the response to bring the emperor here but I'll speak with the council as soon as possible to decide what to do with him."

The majority of the room nodded or voiced their agreement. Izriamat's face melted into neutrality. Without a word, she swept from the room, not even looking Yutuuan's way. All eyes followed her before returning to the prince. "She'll be alright," he said, sounding more like he was trying to convince himself.

Naret's eyes caught Umakaal's for a moment, both of them sharing an uneasy stare. The princess looked back to her brother as he dismissed the meeting. He may be convincing himself that everything would work out, but she wasn't so sure and others were starting to see it as well.

***

Murmurs of confusion and anticipation drifted from the throne room. Izriamat listened carefully from the hallway just outside. All of her father's council members arrived shortly after her summons. She'd purposefully made the call to a meeting a vague one, leaving out that she was the one calling for it. These people were extensions of her father's beliefs for the most part. If they knew that she wanted to speak with them, she would arrive to an empty room.

One last member arrived, a stout older woman with a gnarled walking stick that was two hands taller than her. The guards let her in with a respectful nod and with that, the entire council was assembled. Izriamat came out from her viewpoint, half hidden behind a column. The guards looked at her wary as she approached. One made the sign of Yutuu, bowing his head and opening the door. His partner rushed to do the same though he made sure to give her as much space as possible. Izriamat smiled kindly to them and swept into the throne room.

The council looked up from their seats, some in utter shock, some outraged. An older man, even older than her father had been, rapped his cane on the floor angrily. "What is the meaning of this?" he creaked out. "This is a council meeting."

She passed by him, not looking any of them in the eye as she walked down the long rug and stood before the throne. "Yes. I called it," she said turning around. The gasps and cries of outrage were delicious. These were the same people that nodded along as her father banished her from her home in the palace. Let them feel a little outraged.

"Where is the queen?" a thin woman asked cautiously.

"She was not invited," she replied evenly. More sounds of outrage and a barrage of accusations. Izriamat sighed, so weary. "I have called you here today," she said loud enough to cut through the clamor, "because there are matters that need to be decided on for the kingdom."

"Your brother will be the king," the eldest member said. "It's his opinion that matters for what's best for the kingdom."

"My brother is consumed with the war effort and a most pressing matter has come to us. Djelebe has captured the emperor." She waited for a moment as the sounds of shock started and the news sunk in. "They've offered him to us in exchange for an alliance against the empire. My brother has decided to have them bring him here through an old trading pass. But the matter I wanted to bring to you is what do we do with him when he gets here?"

The council exchanged glances, all of them obviously struck numb by the news. A few moments passed before anyone could find their voice. A younger man, one that Izriamat didn't recognize, spoke first. "He would make an excellent hostage," he said, looking around the room for support.

Only a few members reluctantly nodded. "It also might raise the ire of the empire against us even more," countered another man. "They may feel they have to rescue him."

The eldest councilor looked up to her. "What did your brother say about the matter?"

Izriamat tried hard not to let her annoyance show. Her brother was busy. "He said he would consult you when he had time," she said. "With such an important matter, don't you think he should have already called you? He didn't even convene the council when the message arrived. Just his commanders."

This seemed to finally concern many of the councilors. There were even a few grunts of disapproval. "When did the message come?" one man asked.

"Yesterday. My brother managed to think of me when it arrived but didn't consult you all." She sighed. "Obviously, he is too occupied by the war. And rightly so. But this decision needs to be made as well."

The woman who'd spoken earlier leaned forward in her chair. "Princess, what is it you wish to have done with the emperor? He was your husband after all."

Something in her snapped. She wanted to yell, to tell this woman to never remind her of that fact ever again. But she held it in. She took a deep breath, pushing a smile onto her face. "I want him executed. Publicly."

The room could have been a painting for all of the movement that went on. A few members then sat back in their seats, another releasing a breath. "I think," the younger man said, "that would be for the best. For crimes against our kingdom and the gods. Such blasphemy can't go unpunished."

Izriamat looked at this young councilman with new eyes. He

appeared to be slightly older than her and she assumed he must be new. She gave him an appreciative smile. At least one person remembered the original crime this fiend had committed. "The emperor has committed the ultimate crime against the gods themselves. If we don't punish him for that, how can we call ourselves faithful followers?"

The doors opened, catching everyone's attention, and the queen mother stepped inside. She looked around the room, the lines around her mouth deepening in a frown. Her hair was pulled back in a barely restrained gray ponytail making it look like a storm cloud followed her. She made eye contact with each and every councilor before settling her attention on her daughter. "What is going on here?" she asked, voice calm.

Izriamat bowed to her mother, the others doing the same. "Mother, we're having a council meeting. I didn't-"

"Want to involve me," she finished.

"Mother, I-"

"Don't treat me like some old, addle witted woman. I am," she paused, "I was your father's chief councilor. I should have been the first to know of this meeting and be the one to lead it." Her mother quirked an accusing eyebrow. "I believe you're in the way of my seat."

Her mother walked up the ancient carpet stopping only when Izriamat didn't move out of her way. Izriamat locked eyes with her mother for only a moment, two monumental wills pushing against each other, then decided to allow her passage to her seat beside the throne. She schooled her annoyance. "We were speaking on what to do about the emperor when Djelebe delivers him."

The queen mother blinked in shock. "When did this happen? Why was I not informed?"

"None of the council was informed, mother," she said. "My brother didn't see fit to inform them yet. Or you." She let the words hang in the air.

The queen looked aside, the hurt on her face enough to pain Izriamat. Slightly. The older woman quickly regained her composure. "What has been the consensus so far?"

"There hasn't been one, your majesty," jumped in the eldest

councilman.

Izriamat stopped herself from scowling at him. "I feel the most prudent course of action is to execute him the moment he arrives."

"Izriamat," the queen mother started evenly, "I know that you would like revenge on him, and rightly so, but we need to think of what ripples our actions would cause."

Izriamat turned around the room, settling her attention back on her mother at the end. "Do you all think I'm asking for his execution because of what I went through? Do you all think I'm so hurt and selfish?"

"You were the one who taunted him into war at the gates," said a councilwoman.

She turned on the woman, venom in her eyes. "This man has decreed that we become godless heretics like himself. The gods themselves demand his life so that he may be judged accordingly."

"And you've heard from all of the gods yourself?" her mother asked.

The disbelief in her mother's voice stabbed her to her soul. The woman who'd given her her first lessons about how Yutuu had chosen them as a people would show her such disdain. She turned to her with sorrow filled eyes. "Mother, I speak with Yutuu all the time. He has chosen me. He has given me the power to heal his people. He has shown me the future of a free Wiluru, a Wiluru that has returned to her glory under his blessing. And I know, within every thread of my soul, that he wants the emperor to die."

There were a few grunts of astonishment but, to her satisfaction, they were tinged with agreement. The younger councilman spoke up next. "Your majesty," he said with a deferential bob of his head to the queen mother, "we may want to think of what will happen if we kill the emperor but should we not also think of what will happen if we go against the will of Yutuu?"

Several council members grimaced. Some made signs of supplication. Her mother's lips pulled into a tight line. "Then," she began, the words pulled from her, "we will execute him if it is Yutuu's will. But not immediately. And we will consult with

Prince Yutuuan, *our future king*, on when will be the best time to do so." She looked around the room. "Agreed?" The sounds of yeses rose up from the group. The queen mother's gaze fixed on Izriamat, the sternest she'd seen from the woman since her return.

Izriamat lowered her head. "I'm thankful that you've all come to the most appropriate decision. May Yutuu continue to guide you through the storms of life."

"Thank you, daughter," her mother responded tersely. "Council, if I may speak with you? Izriamat, you may return to your duties at the temple."

She wanted to laugh, but she bowed and made her way out of the room. Let her mother feel that she had control of the situation again. Izriamat, with Yutuu on her side, would guide the council on the right path through all of this. Soon, all would see that the path that their god had laid out for them and she would be the one leading them on it.

***

Yutuuan felt all the days of this war in his very bones. He dragged himself, Naret in step behind, to the private room he'd been given and began to take off his armor. If it weren't for his bodyguard, he would have probably collapsed at the front still giving orders on his way to the ground. For that alone, Naret had his eternal thanks. His fingers fumbled with the ties and he even needed assistance with that simple task.

"You can't keep pushing yourself this hard," Naret said, weariness creeping into his voice.

"I'm the grand commander. I have to-"

"You have to survive to command," the other man interrupted. "And to be king."

Yutuuan nodded. "Maybe you should be king. Clearly, you still have better sense than me."

Naret grunted but it was clearly+.30
. to cover a chuckle. "I would never want to be ruler if I were the last person left in Wiluru. However, if my king would like to give me a seat on the council and perhaps arrange a decent marriage for his longtime friend, I would be very grateful."

Yutuuan barked out a laugh. "Oh, now we're asking for favors?"

"It's the least you could do after I've put up with you," Naret said with a shrug.

The prince made a betrayed face as Naret set his armor to the side. Yutuuan would have like to even take a quick wash to get the grime of the day off of him, but his bed called to him. "Thank you for putting up with me," he said in all earnest as he sat down.

Naret headed toward the door. "It may be my job, but it is also my pleasure. I'm heading back to the front line. I'll fill you in when you wake."

Yutuuan nodded as he lay down and was vaguely aware of the sound of the door closing. His mind drifted immediately, bringing images of Talekh and her beautiful smile to mind. Her voice was pure honey in his dreams, a balm that led him to a deep restful sleep. The next thing he knew someone was calling his name.

The room was dark as he opened his eyes. Someone lit a lantern which illuminated the smiling face of Luunja staring down at him. "Yutuuan, good evening," she said.

He jumped, knocking his bad shoulder against the wall behind him. "Luunja, what are you doing here?"

"I brought you dinner." She backed up, leaning her slim frame against the room's table. She held up a plate containing an enticing display of roasted fowl and vegetables.

Yutuuan swung his legs over the side of the bed, shaking his head to knock off the last bits of sleep. He tried to avoid her gaze but she was watching him intensely. He came closer to get his dinner but when he reached for it, she pulled it away. He frowned at her and was surprised to find her smile gone. "Have you come to tease me or did you want something?" he said, mustering annoyance.

"We need to talk," she said flatly. She still held his plate just out of his reach.

A jolt of concern made him stand straighter. "What about?"

Luunja put the plate on the table beside him, gesturing for him to eat. As he glanced between the plate and her, she steepled her fingers, tapping the tips against her lips. "I know about your little lover."

Yutuuan's hand stopped over the plate. A thousand responses were born and died on his tongue. "What are you talking about?"

"Whoever this woman is you keep slipping out to see." She reached over and picked one of the vegetables off his plate and took a bite, chewing thoughtfully. "You put up a pretty good cover. Going to the palace and all of that. It's a shame you were seen leaving the palace and heading into the city."

"You were spying on me?"

"When my fiancé has moments were he wistfully looks toward the western districts, a woman starts to get suspicious." She finished the bite, making him wait for her next statement. "When he makes a point of ensuring everyone knows he'll be at the palace, she may start to wonder."

"I have business at the palace," he said, using irritation to cover his worry.

"But when one of my runners sees you heading out to the city, away from the battle, the docks, the temples, or any other place where it would be normal for you to go, let's just say suspicions get confirmed."

Yutuuan struggled to keep his heart from beating out of his chest. She couldn't find Talekh. He couldn't let her find out about his son. He summoned all of his charm bringing forth his most dashing smile. "Luunja, it's just a tryst," he said, leaning into his reputation. "I needed a distraction."

Luunja threw her head back and laughed. "You must think I'm one of those birds that titter every time you smile. You may have a reputation as a beguiler but you also have one as an enthusiastic warrior. Everyone knows how much you love battle. You wouldn't leave it for a fling so deep in the city. If you needed a distraction, I'm sure you could have found a very willing one amongst the servants in the palace. So don't try to work those shallow charms on me."

Yutuuan had never been so caught in his life. He struggled for a response knowing that with each passing moment his guilt was more confirmed. Luunja's smile turned cunning as he worked. He decided to put aside feigning innocence. "And what if I do have a dedicated mistress?"

She clicked her tongue. "I don't think my father would like to hear the news that you're dishonoring me already. He might tell the rest of our fleet to not come at all."

"Your father and I made a deal," he growled.

"Yes. You get your forces and I get you." Luunja turned to him, moving so they were barely a breath apart.

He stiffened as she put a hand to his chest, bringing her face close to his neck. "So, what do you want me to do about this?"

"Drop her." The demand hit him like a blow to the chest. "Whoever this little plaything is. I will be your queen and I won't have you traipsing around Wiluru, leaving bastards behind you. I want you all to myself."

A part of Yutuuan relaxed. She didn't know of his son. But he couldn't call off his relationship with Talekh any more than he could cut off his sword arm. Her hand moved down to his crotch and he grabbed her wrist. "I can't just leave her."

Luunja stared at him, her face a mixture of confusion and insult. "You don't have a choice. If you want Asfara's support, you'll do it."

Yutuuan looked away, to the direction of the western city where the love of his life and his first child waited for him. He took a deep breath. "I'll let her go," he said, gaze falling.

She raised his chin so he was forced to look into her eyes. "Promise me."

"I promise." The words tasted foul.

"Good," she said, cunning smile returning. "I need you to make this dedication to me official."

Yutuuan couldn't hide the defeat in his voice. "I swear, I will be faithful to you and only to you, my future queen. I will never have another."

Luunja pressed her body against his, kissing him fully on the lips. Her tongue teased him and he parted his lips to deepen it. She sighed when she finally pulled back. "I want this union consummated, Yutuuan," she said, moving her free hand to rub his manhood through his clothes. "And I want your best show."

Yutuuan couldn't see a way out of this. She pulled him into

another kiss and as their mouths entwined, his heart felt like it would seize up at any moment. Wrong. This was so wrong. Luunja put her arms around him and he returned the embrace. He tried to summon up the carefree attitude he'd had bedding so many women before but it was like trying to be a stranger. He moved his hands against her, feeling the curves of her body and every touch was a betrayal.

As he led his future wife to the room's bed, he cleared his mind of all thoughts of Talekh, of any thought. He closed his eyes as she stroked his manhood, coaxing it to erection. All he allowed himself to feel was base lust and they undressed each other, doing more to raise the other's arousal. Yutuuan did his best to pleasure her, using everything he'd learned from his dalliances with other women. Luunja writhed and moaned under his rhythm, wrapping her legs around his waist and running her fingers through his short curls. With each stroke his feeling of failure morphed into anger. Anger at being forced into this situation. Anger at Luunja's father for still playing games in the midst of war. Anger at himself for allowing himself to be caught, exposing his greatest secret.

He managed to come to a rough, forceful completion. A moment later, Luunja buried her own strangled cry into his shoulder. He tried to disentangle himself but she held on. "Even better than I dreamed of," she purred in his ear. "Next time I'll have to be the one in charge."

Yutuuan avoided looking her in the eyes and rose from the bed. As he redressed, desperately wanting to wash, Luunja languidly got up, slipping her arms around his waist. "I need to get back to the front," he said.

"Don't let me stop you." She went to gather her clothes.

Yutuuan dressed slowly, like his muscles had turned to stone and ground against each other with every movement. He worked to keep himself appearing calm, avoiding her gaze because if she saw his eyes she'd see his fury. He managed to compose himself until he closed the door behind him. His face fell into the deepest frown and he marched down the hallway.

Naret waited for him at the foot of the stairs, looking up with the barest hint of question in his expression. "Get me a messenger," he commanded. "I need to send Umakaal to Asfara. The governor needs to be reminded of his promise."

Chapter Ten

Erenemo slipped off his sandals and headed into the temple washroom. He stripped his robes off in the same order he'd done for over forty years. The ritualism was comforting. It brought him into the familiar state of mind to commune with the gods. It had been too long since he'd come here. Too long since he'd performed his duties as high priest. He stood as both priest and dara now and it was clear that one might have to be sacrificed.

He filled the nearby bucket with water from the room's pool, dowsing himself three times. He shivered from the cold as rivulets wound down his body. He wrapped his body in a fresh set of robes, sighing heavily. Erenemo paused a moment at the door. His temper had gotten the best of him lately. As much as he hated it, he needed the council on his side. He needed them to install him as Great Dara permanently and he didn't think blackmail and bribery would work this time.

But, damn it all, couldn't they see this was the best way? The other cities nipped at their heels like jackals at a lion's kill. Any show of weakness and another dara might declare themselves the Great Dara. They couldn't lose this. He couldn't let the title slip away from his family. He was the only heir of Yundasha left. His mind briefly went to his son. The only suitable heir of Yundasha left.

He made his way down the short hallway toward the innermost sanctuary. Only he and the keeper of the temple were allowed access to the space. The stone floor of the hall was swept and polished meticulously, without a single errant grain of sand or dust laying anywhere. It looked just as perfect as his last visit. He would have to make sure the keeper was rewarded for her diligent service.

Erenemo hesitated at the entrance of the inner sanctuary. The dark room lay just beyond, its many statuettes dimly lit by the room's one window. A host of earthenware candles waited for him to light and bring life to the room and the attention of the gods and Nsongo's collective ancestors. It was the same, unchanging room that he'd stepped in so many decades ago. But how he'd changed over those years.

He'd never intended to become high priest. Being the son of a dara, he'd spent his early childhood under the solid belief that he would become a great warrior like his father. Then he grew up. Any accomplishments were always overshadowed by his family. He lived his life being nothing more than the second son. He would never become dara and whatever feats he would do on the battlefield would always be compared to those of his brother. He decided that he would never live a life as second best. Whatever accolades he'd receive, he'd do so on his own. He threw off his warrior ways and entered the priesthood as a teen.

Erenemo worked tirelessly to rise within the ranks. High Priest was his only goal and now Great Dara was so close to being indisputably his. Patya had left him. Efemu was making it clear that he would be a thorn in his side. He would have to walk this path alone just as he always had.

He stepped into the inner sanctuary, bare feet warmed by the sand floor. He took his time to light the candles from left to right, then greeted all of the deities one by one. The small statues stood on a series of shelves arranged from the most important on the top and descending down. On the lowest shelf gathered a myriad of small dolls that represented the ancestors that witnessed all exchanges and reminded the gods of their promises.

With a grunt, he sat down before a small table. On it were three small bowls and two carved gourd containers. He poured their contents into the corresponding bowl, pushing it forward as a reverent offering to the assembly. One bowl of grain liquor and one of fresh milk obviously left by the keeper since she knew he was coming. The last bowl had no gourd but had a small knife on a cloth beside it. He picked it up, slicing the thumb of his right hand. He dripped his blood into the bowl until a small pool lay at the bottom then wrapped his injury with the waiting cloth.

Erenemo bowed over the bowls, sincere in his reverence. He settled into his seated position and focused not on the statues and the hypnotizing flames, but to the space between. He needed to reach the space beyond this world where one's spirit could be in the presence of the gods. He must open himself up. Pride made him reluctant to do so and he could hear the old high priest scolding him on his conceit. But, for once, he would do so. He would be an open vessel welcoming their divine council and help.

He concentrated on the figure of Bahali, eldest of the pantheon, creator of humankind, whose jurisdiction was wisdom among many others. Erenemo let his mind flow through the ethereal. He needed a clear path to expel the Ega from Nsongo. He needed to see how to sway the council to his side.

The gods remained silent.

Erenemo was tempted to rise out of sheer stubbornness. If he had to find his way alone then so be it. They could stay quiet. But he calmed his mind and focused on being receptive. He envisioned the pantheon, turning to each of them to try to figure out which one he should beseech on his behalf. He asked for his ancestors' help to direct him in the right direction.

A great crash caught his attention and the small table was suddenly knocked over. When he opened his eyes, he saw the figure of Ngema, goddess of war and wrath had toppled over, half landing on the table. The bowls of liquor and milk had spilled, their contents absorbing into the sand. Erenemo chewed back a curse and moved to pick up the figurine but stopped. The bowl of blood had spilled as well, directly onto Ngema's face. He came closer, inspecting. The liquid pooled in the carving, settling into the grooves of her feral smile.

Erenemo set the table back to rights placing the figurine on top of it. He stared at all the other divine representations looking off without a word. He bowed to Ngema. His path was war. That would bring everything into line. When he finished this war, everyone would see his brilliance and his seat would be secure. He thanked the goddess, squeezing fresh blood from his wounded finger and promising that there would be even more blood on her altar soon enough.

***

Nsongo suffered a steamy, humid night after a full day of rain. Tutahmen tugged at his armor thinking of his first time fighting in the southern lands. After a life on the plains of the empire proper, coming south was a slap in the face of thick air that made it hard to breathe. He spent most of his first campaign moist from his own sweat and longing to head back home. Now it seemed that he would spend the night reliving the same feelings.

The troops around him were nervous to be serving a night watch with their general at their side, but Tutahmen wanted to see how things went during the night for himself. He had to witness the normal routine that was leading his men to being picked off without notice. However it was being done, and whoever was doing it, would be discovered and he would put an end to it.

A shadow flitted overhead, catching the light of the torches in the area. He snapped his head up only to see one of the many black birds that plagued the city. He watched the roof pointedly but only saw the avian, now preening as if it hadn't set his nerves on edge.

"Did you see something, general?" the nearby commander asked, his voice barely covering his nervousness.

"I thought it did, but it was just a bird."

He took his focus away from the roof, looking around at the soldiers. They were all nervous, shaky. Eyes darted to roofs or at the far, shadowed corners of buildings. Their fear permeated the air. At the front of their defenses such paranoia couldn't be tolerated. Tutahmen came to the squad commander, tugging the man close by his breastplate. "Get these men working. Have them check the defenses so they're not looking for dangers that aren't there."

"Yes, sir. Immediately, sir." The man saluted and started giving orders.

Tutahmen made his way to each point in their defenses, making the men check every inch so they would have an objective to focus on. They'd made a tight perimeter to keep the Nsongans out but the killers were still getting in. Three grizzly bodies were found just this morning. They lay in the middle of a crossroad, bodies opened in almost artistic carnage. Ribcages broken and pointing skyward like teeth. Intestines laid out in what almost looked like a pattern. A few men who'd come on the scene wretched immediately and he couldn't blame them. Not truly. War could be gruesome. But this was a different level of disturbance. And whatever was doing it whittled them down each night.

You know what's doing it.

The general pushed the thought aside. He couldn't give in to the terror that came with acceptance of that. He would focus on his men, right here, right now. The possibility of monsters in the night couldn't be a concern. Possibilities were not facts and facts are what won wars.

He pulled two men from their duties to walk with him as he made a quick patrol. He checked on one of the front line buildings, making sure that they were ready to attack at a moment's notice and had everything they needed. If he had to send runners to other southern wings he would do so.

When they were in the streets again, he saw a shadow move around a corner of a nearby building. He hurried that way, the soldiers trailing behind him. When he turned the corner, he saw a figure alone in the narrow street. "Soldier," he called out, "you are to only travel in groups at night."

Caution rang out in his head and he caught his hand moving to his sword. The figure didn't move immediately and slowly, Tutahmen realized that the figure was too tall to be a man. It stood even straighter and at its legs another mass could be seen, hanging from one hand. The figure turned its head, eyes catching the light of a faraway torch. It wasn't the usual red or yellow of most animals, but an unnatural ghostly blue. The shine of long teeth appeared as the figure grinned. That was all he could call it. A grin.

Tutahmen's fingers closed around the grip of his sword, pulling it out a thumb's length. The quietest sound caught his ears, a quiet, deep rumble that had the same rhythm as laughing. A shiver ran up his spine. With his free hand he motioned for the other soldiers to be ready.

The creature didn't miss the direction and its smile widened just a hair before it shot down the street. Tutahmen was in immediate pursuit, drawing his sword free. He shouted the alarm as he went, straining his voice for as much volume as possible. The sound of the soldiers accompanying him echoed behind him. The general had no idea what they would do once they caught up to the creature, or even what they could do to such a murderer, but he would try to bring it down.

The thing ran swiftly for something of its size, ghosting around corners and moving down the narrow streets like a fish through water. It moved on all fours and as it ran, he could see small sparks trailing from its feet. He saw it cut around a corner into an alley that he happened to know was a dead end. Tutahmen forced his aging body to move faster. The thing couldn't get away. It was murdering his people. It was costing them this conflict.

When he made it to the alley, the creature was stopped at the wall that ended the alley. Three multistory buildings closed it in. He jogged to a halt, his accompanying men stumbling behind him. The moon shined down with just enough light for him to get a good look at the creature for just a moment. Taller than any man he'd seen and standing upright, it wore a gleaming covering of short, dark fur. Its eyes, glossy and dark, studied him in that moment, a mirth coming from them. Long curving claws, like daggers came from its hands and feet. The muzzle full of teeth grinned again.

"Follow if you can, enemy."

Tutahmen stood, so stunned at the ability of speech from this creature, that he didn't register the monster running straight up the wall for a moment. He cursed himself as he rushed forward. He shouldered in a nearby door, storming inside.

"There are intruders," he roared, frightening the unfortunate Nsongans living here. They scrambled out of his way. His knees protested with every flight of stairs, reminding him he wasn't the youthful soldier anymore. He ignored the gnawing pain and burning lungs. A door leading outside sat at the end of the hallway. He burst through and took another set of stairs to the roof, taking two at a time. The creature might have climbed down the other side of the building or even taken to another roof by now but he had to give chase.

Tutahmen jumped up to the roof, looking around frantically in the night. There was nothing at first as his eyes adjusted to the uneven light. His sword rested comfortably in his hand, at the ready in case the creature wished to surprise him. Then he saw the large shadow hulking near the far edge. It turned, grinning once, then leaped to the next building, landing and running with an agility a body that large had no business having.

He took a step forward then forced himself to give up the chase as he saw other shadows on other roofs. His sword grip slackened. There had to be at least six of them, all moving at in-human speed. He had believed the reports of monsters from the lone survivor of the jungle scouts. It was another to have the re-port confirmed and by his own eyes. His sword clattered to the roof. What were they to do against monsters?

Chapter Eleven

Silence, save the scratching of her reed pen, filled the office of the chancellor and Sept'ha enjoyed it to its fullest. It was rare that she could find a moment alone in here without his overbearing snide tones or cold demeanor. This was the peaceful afternoon that she needed. Before her on the table, a number of messages from the past few weeks spread out. Most were everyday missives, petitions for the emperor to do this and that. Some contained the tallies of supplies for the palace which Hetsaf also had to keep running. But two she pulled out as most important.

Sept'ha gathered a new piece of papyrus to begin copying. These messages were reports from the battle fronts. The fight for Wiluru was slowly expanding into the city. Building by building, their foothold grew. In the south, things were not so encouraging. Still locked in a stalemate with the Nsongans, they had gained nothing yet they still lost men. She read over the message again. No reason for losing them was noted, no poisonings, no disease, no accidents. They were just losing people. She'd have to bring this up with the chancellor.

She started copying the notes, getting the main points of the war on each front down for the empress. It had to contain enough to make it sound like the entire report when really it was just enough to keep that woman satiated. She blew out a breath at the thought of dealing with the Great Royal Wife again. The amount of petty, childish venom in that woman confounded her. Everything done for her had to be enough to stroke her ego. No wonder she and the emperor had gotten along so well. They went together better than a scarab and its dung ball.

"What are you doing?" Hetsaf snarled from the door.

"Copying messages for the empress," she replied without looking up.

By the time she did look up, he'd crossed the room, yanking her out of his chair by her upper arm. She yelped in pain, the reed falling from her hand. "Only I decide what that witch knows," he barked, his grip tightening. "How long has this been going on? Are you trying to undermine me all while saying you're helping?"

Sept'ha gritted her teeth against the pain. "Let me go," she ground out.

He shook her. "Answer me."

"Have you forgotten who I am?" She stared him down, meeting the poison in his gaze with her own.

It took him several moments to release his anger. Eventually his fingers peeled away from her arm, but he released her roughly, causing Sept'ha to stumble. "How long has this been happening?" he asked more calmly, yet there was still danger lurking in his tone.

Sept'ha rubbed her arm, looking daggers at the chancellor. "About a month now. I came up with the idea. We feed her enough information to keep her from barging into your office demanding answers."

He snatched up the paper she'd been writing, looking over the message. "You will let me see whatever you write for her before you take it. Is that clear?"

She resisted the urge to punch him although her right hand flexed dangerously. "Fine," she spat out. "You would think you'd be more grateful that I'm keeping her out of your hair." Hetsaf pushed past her, righting the chair before sitting in it. He riffled through the messages. Sept'ha frowned. No thank you was coming apparently.

Hetsaf looked through the papers again, frowning. "Was there any news from Djelebe?"

She pushed aside her anger towards him, settling on annoyance. "None."

"They should have some sort of update about the emperor by now," he said sitting back.

"Unless there is no update." She hesitated. "Or they're afraid of reporting an even worse situation."

He shook his head. "No, my brother is fine. As fine as one could be considering."

Sept'ha raised shocked eyebrows. She'd never heard him call

the emperor anything else but his title. She didn't miss the slight note of concern in his voice either. She leaned in a bit, lowering her voice. "We do have to consider the possibility," she said, thinking of Met's lack of concern about her greatest agent of chaos. "The emperor might die. We have to be prepared. You have to be prepared."

"To run this empire until Arkole's newest squalling babe comes of age. Yes, yes." He waved his hand dismissively.

"Or…." She let the possibilities hang in the air until he grasped at one.

He turned his head toward her, cautious thoughts forming behind his eyes. "Or… what?"

"Or… you do not turn it over to him. This will be in nearly twenty years. The empire will have grown used to you and your commands governing it. Will they want to suddenly see their stable and fruitful empire in the hands of a boy? The son of the heretic emperor? No, they won't." She stood up, mimicking a prideful stance. "But the man who took them back to the way the empire was supposed to be? That's who they'll clamor to follow."

Hetsaf's eyes darted around the room. "This is a ridiculous notion." He opened his mouth to speak again but closed it quickly, turning back to his papers.

Sept'ha leaned in close. "The man who was only supposed to sit in the shadow of the emperor would rule it himself. Not standing behind the throne but sitting upon it." Hetsaf didn't respond, didn't even glance at her, but sat still as stone and she knew she had his full attention. "Emperor Hetsaf."

He took in a breath and blew it out excruciatingly slow. "You must never speak those words again until it is true," he said in the barest whisper.

"I promise." She stood straight again, attentive servant once more. "I believe that Met has great plans for the both of us."

Hetsaf turned to look at her fully. His eyes studied her in a pensive way that she hadn't seen before. He frowned, looking away before coming back to meet her eyes. "Thank you," he said, his sincerity shocking her. "I promise I will not forget you when I ascend."

Sept'ha fumbled for a response. Graciousness wasn't a trait that she'd thought he possessed. "Perhaps, I could be chancellor?"

His face twisted in disgust. "Finish your message to the empress," he commanded, turning back to his work. Sept'ha chuckled and did so. There was her bastard of an accomplice.

***

Arkole disliked her husband's old office. It was stuffy and only had access to a small window that barely let in the breeze. But this was where he conducted business and that would be where she did it as well. She watched Nitiri as the younger woman moved along, running her fingers over old scrolls that Bakari had surely read over. Arkole wrinkled her nose for a moment. She thought of their husband so fondly yet barely knew him. It was a slavish devotion and Arkole was thankful that she'd never acted in such a way.

"I can't believe the fate of the empire was decided in such a small room," Nitiri said as she stopped to look at a scroll.

Arkole chuckled. "The fate of the empire was decided wherever the emperor was. This was just where he liked to read and think."

"You must have spent a lot of time with him here." Nitiri threw her a smile.

"Not too much time," she answered, unsure why the statement pricked her. "I had other duties." She began selecting a few scrolls from the shelves, more recent records of army numbers and supplies. "Come here. I want you to look at something."

Nitiri stopped her perusing and approached the wide table in the middle of the room where Arkole had set out the scrolls. Arkole set out the copied messages from Sept'ha as well. She looked across the table to her counterpart. "Do you understand the complete situation the empire is in?"

"I know the north is rebelling against the empire. That's why our husband is away to quell it."

Arkole nodded. "Yes, but there is also rebellion to the west and south." She handed the smuggled information to the young woman, watching as her eyebrows rose while reading it. "The west is a peasants' revolt. It should be easy to put down but it hasn't. I believe Hetsaf is holding back. I don't believe he takes such a threat seriously or he would have had them crushed by now."

The young woman looked up, concerned. She motioned for Nitiri to keep reading. "But the south presents a real problem. It took ten hard years of war to finally break them and we can't let them get free again. They need more men."

Nitiri put the messages down, face frowned in thought. "Why haven't we just sent them what they needed?"

"My thoughts exactly," Arkole said, thankful that at least *someone* saw things her way. She rolled out one of the scrolls. "I'm going to teach you about the empire today, Nitiri. How it works and how it should work and we will make sure that in Bakari's absence, it will still work as smoothly as when he was here."

Nitiri nodded, determined and eager. Arkole began showing her the army records, what wings were stationed where and their numbers. She knew these scrolls had been kept up to date by the palace scribes and their information, save a few recent changes, could be relied on. By the time they were through, they figured out that the city had more than enough men to send to the southern front. The Nsongans didn't have *that many* troops even if they did recklessly throw their women into battle as well.

Arkole, pleased at their final decision, called for the head of the Metkaran wing of the army, Commander Ikhantan. She hadn't ever met the man and wondered how he would take to being commanded by two women. She hoped, for his sake, that it was far better than Hetsaf's treatment. If he didn't show the proper respect, she would always find another who would.

She and Nitiri sat at one side of the table, Arkole's chair slightly higher, as the commander entered. He looked at both of them in confusion, then bowed deeply. "Great Royal Wife Arkole, it is an-"

"Empress Arkole," she corrected him.

"Empress Arkole," he stammered. "It is an honor to be called into your presence. And…" He turned his attention to Nitiri, eyebrow quirked in question.

"This is the emperor's Second Wife, Nitiri."

Both of his eyebrows shot up. He bowed to her as well. "Second Wife Nitiri. It is an honor."

"Thank you, commander," she said sweetly but far less bubbly than usual. Arkole had told her to keep a cooler demeanor.

"What may I do for you, great ladies? I have to admit that I'm slightly surprised not to see the chancellor here."

"The chancellor is attending to other matters," Arkole said firmly. "I called for you. I have a task for you and your force."

He looked at her face starting to twist with uncertainty. "Empress, I'm not sure what we could do for you."

Arkole passed a confident glance at Nitiri. "We have looked at the number of forces that we have here in the capital and have come to realize that there are more than enough to send south to quell the Nsongan's rebellion. I think sending about sixty percent of the force will do. Crush the southerners and they will be back to their post in no time."

The commander opened his mouth to speak but closed it. His lips drew into a thin line. "Empress," he said with utmost reverence, "It is not a matter of just throwing numbers at the southern problem. We have to assess what exactly is going on at the front. Adding more soldiers, more men, and animals to feed and keep up, may just make the situation worse. I think it would be wise to consult the chancellor on this matter."

Arkole's brow twitched. "The emperor has charged me, has charged both Nitiri and I to look after the wellbeing of the empire. Do you think that allowing a rebellion to continue is in the best interest of the empire? Do you think that showing people that you can disobey the emperor easily if you throw a large enough tantrum is in the best interest of the empire?" The commander didn't answer immediately, stoking her anger. "Well, do you?"

"No, my empress," he said lowering his head.

"Then send those forces."

Before he could answer, Hetsaf walked into the room, looking at a number of papers. All attention turned to him and he stopped mid step, realizing that people were in the room. His sharp eyes took in the commander, then Nitiri, finally resting on Arkole. His usual expression of contempt deepened. "What is going on here?" he asked, evenly.

"Nothing of your concern," Arkole hissed.

He looked back to the commander. "Commander, could you go to my office? We can have a discussion there."

"Yes, Chancellor," he said, giving a quick bow to him and the empresses before scurrying out of the room.

Arkole turned her full, heated attention on her enemy. "I was speaking with the commander."

"Concerning what?" the man asked dangerously.

"We were seeing to the southern rebellion," Nitiri piped up. "Since it appears you will not."

Arkole had never seen pure shock on Hetsaf's face before. He stared at Nitiri as if he'd never noticed the woman sitting there. "Who are you?" he asked, voice thick with disgust.

"I'm the emperor's second wife," she answered, slightly quieter.

Hetsaf looked her over slowly, like a man tallying up a wagon of grain. "So you're the one he raised up," he grumbled, the sneer on his face showing his teeth. He suddenly looked between both of them. His gaze settled on Arkole. "So you've found a co-conspirator. This is just pathetic. Even for you."

"I will make sure Bakari makes you pay for how you've treated me in his absence," Arkole snarled. She stopped, waving her hand in the air as if clearing it. "It doesn't matter. Commander Ikhantan has his orders from us. This Nsongan matter will be taken care of before year's end."

Hetsaf looked between them again, looked down at the scrolls and papers on the table, then started laughing. He started snatching the papers away, tucking scrolls under his arms. Arkole tried to stop him but he only evaded her hands. "I am running the kingdom. You two are caring for his children. I don't know why my brother allowed his manhood to choose who would be his voice."

"You would question the wisdom of our emperor?" Nitiri said, shooting to her feet.

He looked her up and down again. "My brother enjoys a

pretty face and wide hips. These aren't the qualifications to run an empire." He turned to leave.

"I suppose no woman would ever meet your qualifications," Arkole spat back.

Hetsaf paused, turning back just enough to see them. He looked almost thoughtful. "Most women no. You two, certainly not." He looked at Nitiri. "You would do well to separate yourself from her delusions of grandeur before she drags you down. Take care of your children. That's what you can do for the empire." Turning back sharply, he left, leaving Arkole with nothing but an empty table and seething hatred. Something had to be done about that man.

***

Sept'ha skirted around the other servants making their way from the eastern kitchen to bring food to their companions in this area of the castle. It was late for one of the nobles to be eating but everyone knew Hetsaf kept odd hours. They had to be ready to cook for him at any time and she had to be ready to retrieve it.

Her later excursions still put her in the direct line of the other servants' scorn and it was starting to wear on her more and more. She was not a bedwarmer. She was a strategist and a chosen of Met. A deep part of her wanted to let the leopard loose in the servants' hallways and see if they would still look down their noses at her then. She laughed to herself. Cruel, yes, but still amusing.

The kitchen was structured chaos when she arrived with bowls being piled on trays to be taken out as soon as they were filled. The heat of the room was oppressive with its large brick ovens at either side of the chamber. Long tables were set up in front of each cooking pot where the meals could be placed. The head cook saw her the moment she entered and looked around for someone to help her. His eyes found a small woman, tending to an oven's fire. "Imtaret," he called over the roar. "Fix the chancellor's food." He pointed sharply at a cooking fire and two large pots then at Sept'ha.

Sept'ha moved to the spot where she normally waited, a

place just off to the side of the main commotion of the kitchen. The woman shyly looked up at her, then went to her task. Sept'ha didn't recognize her at first, but then something seemed very familiar. "Could you get a plate for me as well?" she asked kindly. The woman paused, then nodded.

Sept'ha watched her. She felt like she knew that face from somewhere. The woman quickly placed the items for Hetsaf on a plate, handing it to her before fetching a bowl for the bread and lentil stew of the servant's meal. Sept'ha wanted to correct her but the woman was already almost trembling at the task. She didn't want to make her feel worse for making a mistake. "Do I know you?" she asked the woman as she was handed the bowl.

Imtaret didn't look up but backed away like she wanted to be back at her original task. "No, I don't think so."

Sept'ha nodded. Maybe she just looked like a familiar face. She took the meals with a thanks and headed back down the halls. Hetsaf sat at the table, head in his hand when she returned. She set the food down before him, placing hers at the other side. "Water or wine?" she asked, going to two pitchers she'd secured earlier.

"Wine, please," he answered wearily.

"You have to stop working at all hours of the day," she scolded, placing his cup down. She poured herself a cup of water.

"It would be easier if that woman would stop meddling in everything." He raised his head and began eating. "She tried to send troops to the south on her own. She'd even got that girl my brother raised as her minion."

Sept'ha froze, bread halfway to her mouth. "I didn't think the other wife was concerned with anything but her two children."

"She, apparently, wants to play at affairs of governance now." He angrily chewed on a bite of roasted fowl. "If I could send her back to the lesser harem, I would. Both of them are forgetting their place."

Sept'ha let the comment go unchallenged, resisting rolling her eyes. They ate in silence for a few moments. She chewed thoughtfully. Hetsaf was right even if he thought it for the wrong reasons. The empresses were forgetting their places. She had to think of a way to convince them to stay out of the way. She let out a small breath. That Arkole proved herself a difficult woman to manipulate. So prideful that anything that went against her view of things was an attack. She had to find a way around it.

Hetsaf began coughing and reached for his wine. She smirked at him. "Perhaps you should chew like a person," she said.

"No," he managed between coughs. "Just. Something. In my throat."

The cough continued and when he wheezed, she looked over, concerned. Sept'ha rose from her seat, patting him on the back. The coughs turned into more wheezing then morphed into gurgling sounds. Hetsaf's hand clutched his throat. She moved to where she could see his face. Veins bulged, his face growing red underneath his golden brown skin. She was about to ask if he was choking when she noticed the foam starting to gather on his lips. Hetsaf jerked and fell out of his chair to the floor.

Sept'ha ran to the hall, going to the main hallway. "Someone get a healer," she shouted at the top of her lungs not having to feign her panic. "Please, someone get a healer. It's the chancellor." She saw one servant farther down the hall nod quickly and run off. She gathered up her skirts and ran back to Hetsaf's room.

He was an unearthly shade of purple now. Red welts covered his throat where he'd clawed at it. His eyes fixed on her, an unsaid plea in them. She dropped to his side, placing her hand over his heart. She could feel it beating fast and erratically. Her own breath came in fits.

"Don't you die," she said. He couldn't die. All of this would be for nothing if he died. All of their planning, all of their designs for the empire, gone like the last spark of a flame.

He must fight this.

"Fight," she told Hetsaf, voice choked. She felt a warmth within her that quickly rose to the heat of a fire. Flames ran through her bones but no pain came with it. Beneath her hand, Hetsaf's heart began to slow. "Fight," she commanded. Her hand on his chest flexed as if to grip his body. She let some of the flames pass through her, allowed the glorious power that struggled to be contained, reach him.

Hetsaf took a strangled breath. Some of his color returned. Sept'ha worked, letting waves of the power of Met into him. Then she felt something. Something unnatural lurked in his body. She closed her eyes. An inky blackness branched through him, invading his blood. Poison. Her eyes locked on Hetsaf. "Fight."

His heart began beating faster under her divine coaching, an even rhythm but faster. Sweat formed in fine beads on his face. He managed to suck in another breath. His face twisted in pain and she couldn't tell if it was from struggling for breath or from the flaming power she was pouring into him. Either way, she needed him alive. This empire needed him alive.

She heard running footsteps down the hall and a servant led a healer into the room. Sept'ha moved back, gently pulling the power from the chancellor. The healer opened Hetsaf's eyes wider. "Poison," he said grimly, confirming her fears. He put his hands on Hetsaf's chest and began chanting a spell. A golden glow emanated from his hands, spreading out. After a moment, Hetsaf gasped, coughing again. The healer then placed a hand to the chancellor's throat and the coughing calmed.

Sept'ha made her way out of the room, leaning on the wall just outside. She placed a hand to her chest, trying to calm her own heart. She'd almost lost him. Someone had poisoned him. The thought sobered her shock. Someone had his food poisoned. Her mind snapped to the kitchen worker she'd never seen before. The shyness that surely wasn't shyness.

She rushed down the hall, the flames of anger on her now. The last servants out and about at this time of night gave her a wide berth as she walked. The rumblings of a growl vibrated in her throat.

"Where is she?" she roared when she reached the kitchens. The staff looked up in alarm from their cleaning. "Where is the woman who prepared the chancellor's food?"

The head of staff swallowed. "I think she went to relieve herself. It was a few minutes ago."

Sept'ha turned, stalking away. Her eyesight seemed to grow sharper as her anger grew. The hallways, which were so dim with most of the torches snuffed, appeared as clear as day. Each person she passed stood out in sharp detail. She made it to the nearest servant restroom, looking around, ready to unleash her holy anger on the woman, but no one was inside.

She backtracked, the growling becoming audible. She stopped on the path the woman would have to have taken to make it to the restrooms, concentrating. Scents came to her. The heady spices of the kitchen. The sharp notes of sweat. Then another scent cut through the others. It made her want to recoil. It was foul to her, not an offensive smell but not one she liked to the core of her soul. Sept'ha followed the scent.

She rushed along, knocking anyone who impeded her path out of the way. She went through several hallways until she reached ones that would lead outside. She quickened her pace, running to catch up. She turned a corner and saw a figure pulling a cloak out from behind a statue's base. The figure looked up and Sept'ha could make out the clear features of the woman from the kitchens. She ran toward the woman, who was now making her way toward a door that led outside.

Sept'ha caught her just before the woman's hand touched the door handle, grabbing her by the back of her collar and yanking her back. With a snarl she turned her, grabbed her by the throat, and slammed her against a wall. Blinding rage filled Sept'ha, fueling the fire within. She slid the woman up the wall, leaving her feet dangling. The smell of the foul substance was potent on the would be assassin. Her eyes stared down at Sept'ha, wide with terror. She tried to speak but the firm hand on her neck reduced it to strangled cries. Sept'ha wanted to rip this woman open. Snap her neck. Throw her down the hallway like the trash she was.

The feeling of a calm hand touched her shoulder and her anger abated, leaving her with a grim focus. She lowered the woman. "Come, we're going to have a little chat about how you almost killed the chancellor." Sept'ha caught her by her collar again and dragged her down the hallway.

Chapter Twelve

Mgobe read the letter from the empress and tore it into pieces, scattering it into the wind. Before him, the party to carry the emperor to Wiluru gathered, nearly ready to depart for the old western pass. Two handfuls of magicians of all the offensive arts were ready to stand guard with just as many city guards. Six healers surrounded the carried stretcher where the emperor's prone form lay, still unconscious, still so close to death that he could be tipped over at any moment. No healing efforts had been expended on him but those to keep him alive. What the Wiluruans chose to do with him once they'd delivered him was up to them.

"My husband."

Mgobe turned to his left to see his wife approaching with his children. He smiled and kissed each of them on the top of their heads, noting how little he had to bend over for his eldest two. He did his best to assuage the fears of his littlest ones, telling the older ones to be brave while he was gone. He left his farewell to his wife for last, taking her hands and giving her a lasting chaste kiss. "I will miss you dearly, Adisa," he said holding the sides of her face.

She placed her hands over his. "I have not slept alone since our wedding. How will I rest peacefully now?"

He kissed her again, guilt over leaving paining him. "I suppose we'll both have to find a way, my heart. But I will be back with you soon enough."

"You don't have to go," she pleaded. "Someone else can be our representative."

Mgobe looked back over the assembled party, eyes finally coming to rest on the emperor. "I couldn't trust such an important mission to anyone else. How can I call myself the leader of Djelebe if I can't even muster the courage to make this trip?" He kissed her one last time on the lips and forehead, then joined the middle of the party.

Most of the city gathered to see them off, singing an old song meant to invoke a speedy journey and fair weather to the travelers. Mgobe glanced back nearly constantly to see his family as they walked down the main street and out of the gate. His heart tightened as the party stepped out onto the plains, his family firmly out of view. When the sound of the city gates closing rang out, he flinched as if his way home was severed.

You will go back home, he scolded himself. He knew that he would. However, he'd never set foot out of the city before. The son of the late governor and grandson of the previous Master of Histories in the university, he had no reason to travel. All of his time had been spent learning all he could so that he could be a proper leader for the city. Now, as he looked out over the endless plains and the low, lonely mountains that interrupted the view he suddenly felt exposed, unprotected. Everything in him wanted to turn around and retreat to the safety of his home. But he took one look at the emperor and the promise that delivering that monster would rid them of the empire once and for all and his courage was bolstered once again. Mgobe drew himself up and settled into the pace of the journey.

The first few days proved uneventful. They set off on a smaller road, avoiding the main path that most travelers used. The small towns they moved through were surprised to see them, especially with an injured man in tow, but quick lies settled any curiosity. The man wanted to die in his hometown. He wished to see the ocean in case he didn't make it. Mgobe had no worry that anyone would recognize the emperor for what he was. In plain clothes and looking so frail, no one would mistake him for the leader of the empire.

After five days, the path they took began to head upwards. It grew rockier and they had to watch their step. The path the Wiluruans suggested they use was on an ancient map they only had half of because of the fire. He thanked the gods that they'd been able to find a copy at all. They would head up towards the highlands just outside of the northern kingdom, cutting through rough terrain. The end of the path was burnt and he only hoped that it would bring them close to Wiluru.

By the end of the day, as the sun began to set and Mgobe realized how high they'd gone, he and the guard captain called for a rest. Tall walls made of enormous boulders rose up on both sides. It gave a sense of protection and claustrophobia. The governor sat down roughly, thankful for the chance to rest his hurting feet. Fires were set up and food was prepared. Dried strips of meat, boiled to soften them, wasn't his ideal dinner but his stomach ached for sustenance.

It was just before he went to bed that he saw the eyes on the top of the rocks. Mgobe sat up straight as he saw movement in the small spaces between the boulders. "Something's out there," he shouted. "On the other side of the rocks."

A magician raised her hand, fast chanting a spell. A ball of light shot into the air, expanding into a tiny sun over their camp. Mgobe bit his lip against the scream that threatened to erupt from him. Now, with the area completely illuminated, dozens of creatures perched on the surrounding rocks, ready to pounce. They were the color of the stones with mottled patches mimicking natural weathering. They had small, almost human-like hands with jet black claws. Their faces protruded thin and pointed like a jackal with snarling teeth and large eyes. The beasts were no bigger than a large dog but he noticed the distinct extra folds of skin that indicated a glider.

Curses and screams erupted from the camp, the creatures launching themselves down. Chaos reigned. City guards hurried to take out weapons. Magicians began casting spells, cautious not to hit any of their party. Those who were not combatants grabbed makeshift weapons. Mgobe had nothing on him or even near him that would make do. He shielded his head and saw a large rock to the side of the neglected path, taking it up.

He heard the eerie clicking laugh that was the creatures' call in his ear and swung back. His rock connected with the side of one of their heads, sending it careening to the ground. Dazed, it scrambled, trying to get airborne. Mgobe rushed over, bashing its head in before it could recover. Another landed on his back and he felt its claws dig into him. Panicking, he twisted and jumped, trying to shake and pull it off before those teeth could find a target, dropping his weapon in the process. With much contorting, he grabbed a fistful of the animal's gliding flap, dragging it off of him. He yelled as the claws dragged away, leaving cuts across his back.

He looked up just in time to see one flying right at his head. He covered his face with his arms in a futile attempt to protect himself and luckily heard the swing of a sword, then the thud of a small body hit the ground. He peeked out to see one of the guards next to him, already cutting down another one. Mgobe didn't have time to thank the guard properly as another creature glided down for him. He scooped up his rock again, swinging until he'd killed it.

After what seemed like an eternity, the creatures lay dead at their feet. Mgobe approached one, rock still in hand in case it decided it wanted another chance at life. He'd never seen such an animal and had never even run across such a description in his studies. If it were any other time, he would want to have examples brought back to the university, to be dissected, stuffed, and studied. Now, all he wanted was to be away from them.

"Are you all right, governor?" one of the healers said coming up to him. She had a cut across her cheek but, as a typical healer, she was more concerned about the others around her.

He looked around at his party. They all seemed relatively fine. Some had taken injuries, bites, and claw marks, and were being healed while the magicians formed a protective ring around the emperor. He winced as he turned back to the healer. "I was clawed across the back." She nodded once and immediately began healing him.

"We need to move on," the leader of the guards called out. "The bodies will attract scavengers and I don't want to find out what feasts on these things."

A collective shudder went through the group but there were no complaints. Mgobe found himself no longer tired, his aching feet a distant memory. Magicians put up light spells. It might have given away their location, but they decided it was better to see another attack coming than be caught off guard again.

The next attacks were just as terrible. Over the next few days, they learned to be ready just after sunset because the creatures were coming. Mgobe had to wonder if this was why the pass was no longer taken. These creatures infested it and there seemed to be no end to them. One of the guards gave him a knife after the second night and the governor was finding himself quite the quick learner. But fighting for one's life created the necessity.

The path widened on those next days, looking more like the well-worn route of travelers instead of a path that happened to exist. They chose a place to rest for the night, weary from the anxiety. Mgobe sat against one of the stone walls, willing his heart to beat evenly. What was he thinking, coming on this journey? All that he'd provided the party was dead weight. He hadn't even provided true leadership. The commander of the guard had thankfully assumed that position.

He looked around the group as they began preparing for the night. They were weary, not just physically but in spirit as well. They needed to help them keep going. Something to let them know that this trip was still worth it. They needed a leader.

Mgobe pushed himself up, ignoring the protesting of his knees. He stopped with each of the guards and magicians, inquiring after their wellbeing and thanking them for their service so far. It truly had been them who'd kept the party safe. He turned to the healers who gathered near the emperor, working their magics to keep the man alive. If anyone didn't deserve to be on this trip, it was them.

He came to the side of one of the healers, a young woman who now sported a scar on her face from ear to the side of her mouth. He hid a grimace. She would have a stark reminder of the trip for the rest of her life. Mgobe cleared his throat, quietly. She looked up with a strained smile, wrinkling the scar. "How is he?" he asked, pointing his chin toward the emperor.

"He's the same," the young healer responded.

"We've had to heal a few wounds from the creatures, but he's still in an even condition," another healer added. "We've been doing our best to keep him…safe." They slid a venomous glance toward their patient.

Mgobe's face twisted with guilt. "I'm sorry," he said addressing all of the healers. "I know this has become a far more taxing journey than any of us imagined. I know that this is of little consolation to you, but you are doing Djelebe a great service. The city will be forever in your debt." He put a hand to his heart. "I will forever be in your debt."

Mgobe turned to the rest of the party. "To all of you, I am in your debt for taking on his task. If there is ever anything, anything at all that I can do for you, you have but to ask."

Murmured thanks sounded around the camp and Mgobe was relieved that they sounded sincere if exhausted. A slight weight lifted from him. He prayed that these people knew that he would be true to his word. He glanced at the healer with the scar. There was no price too high to repay them.

As if to punctuate his declaration, all around them the clicking laughter started. Whatever modicum of calm the camp had allowed itself was gone in an instant. Everyone took to action, gathering in the makeshift formation they'd worked out in haste. The healers surrounded the emperor, Mgobe taking his place with them. Magicians formed the next ring with the guards forming the outer perimeter. Mgobe unsheathed his knife, holding it in what he hoped was a defensive posture.

All eyes watched the tops of the rock walls, waiting for the inevitable attack. The governor's heart quickened at the sight of pairs of eyes peeking over the walls. Magicians readied themselves to cast. Warriors settled into combat positions.

Then a new sound rumbled through the area. It began low, like the groaning of boulder against boulder, then rose in pitch to a growl that vibrated the chest. The calls of the creatures ceased nearly at once. The few pairs of eyes vanished behind the walls, their calls sporadic and growing more and more distant.

A terrifying quiet fell on the area. Mgobe willed himself not to shake, to have at least a sliver of courage. Beside him he heard the deep ragged breaths of one of the healers. The sound reverberated through the area again and one of the wall's boulders groaned under a new weight. All eyes turned to the left and in the waning light of the sun, a new horror waited.

The hulking creature perched across two of the rocks, muscular body half as large as a rhinoceros. It had a face like a stunted baboon that emerged from a just too long neck. Two spider-like mandibles extended from the sides of the mouth, moving as if eager to stab into prey. It stared at them carefully, looking over their group. Mgobe swallowed the lump in his throat as he realized that was probably him.

"Fire!" the guard captain shouted. "Don't let it get close!"

Spells and arrows flew over their heads, engulfing the path in the sound of battle. Only a few spells hit the creature as it jumped down into the path, avoiding the others. It took one look at them to assess them again, then charged forward. Its speed surprised everyone, the creature making to the group before they had full time to process the attack. The soldiers at the front took the brunt of the attack, hacking and slashing to try to fend it off.

The creature dodged agilely. The guards' attacks connected with its hide multiple times but it barely cut though the thick muscle. A few archers managed to land hits, the arrows dangling from its body as if it didn't even know they were there.

The creature backed away from them suddenly, leaping up to the side of the wall, before landing with a loud thud within their circle. Magicians scrambled to get away from it. A healer screamed. More spells were cast, but the magicians could only do so much so close to their own people. The guards closed in to fight but it swiped at them with massive, blunted claws. In the midst of it all, the creature still looked around to assess the humans, still searching for a target, eyes finally locking on the emperor.

It burst forward from the soldiers, deep roar rumbling. Mgobe realized what it was doing at the same moment as the rest of his group. He ran from his position, pushing a healer out of the way as the creature barreled into him. He put up his left arm to protect himself. Pain exploded from that arm, radiating down his shoulder to his chest. All of his breath was knocked out of him and Mgobe realized his was on the ground, the creature's maw clamped firmly on his arm. The two spider mandibles stabbed down for him, but only managing more punctures on his arm.

He faintly heard the soldiers attacking the creatures from behind. There was shouting and screaming. His blood dripped down from his arm, soaking his shirt, and dripping hot and wet onto his stomach. He saw the creature turn its head as if it were going to tear his arm off and panic surged through him. Mgobe swung with his knife, stabbing for the creature's eye.

It howled, shaking the ground and pushing whatever breath Mgobe had recovered back out of him. The creature's teeth scraped off of him when it let go, leaving even deeper wounds on his arm. He cried out in pain, wanting nothing more but to lie there and die. He forced himself to look on the battle. Another archer had managed to take out the other eye. He could see bleeding wounds from spells and cuts along its underbelly. A soldier was down and stared at him, eyes unfocused. Mgobe could only pray that they would make it through this, that death would come to them another day, another time. They had to make it through this. Djelebe depended on them.

The creature shook off its attackers, making one last charge in Mgobe's direction. Snarling, stumbling, and dripping blood it ran. It wanted the emperor, the easiest meal to be had from all of them. But, as he locked eyes with it, he knew it was coming for him. It wanted revenge. Mgobe forced himself to sit up, bringing the knife up, hoping against hope that the beast's softer skin reached his neck. He stabbed, the blade sinking into the flesh. He yanked it out, stabbing again and again as the creature fell, half on him. He continued stabbing, taking out all of his fear and frustrations on it. The creature's blood flowed in steady streams, pooling under him.

Finally, a guard caught his wrist. "Governor, it's dead."

Mgobe blinked at him, not catching his words. He looked at the animal, limp, blood starting to lessen its flow. Then all of his own pain came crashing down as his adrenaline fled. The healers rushed in to tend to the injured, and those guards and magicians who could helped free him from under the beast. His head started to swim and the blurry image of a healer was the last thing he saw before he passed out.

Mgobe woke up sharply, mind still half under attack. He was sitting up against the stone wall, hands crossed in his lap. His left sleeve had been cut off and he could see the arm that the thing had mangled. A series of thick scars ran along it, dimpling where the creature's teeth had first punctured. The healers truly worked miracles.

Around him, the camp rested. The healers sat, some asleep. The magicians were doing their best to tend to those who needed it. Many of the guards sat as well, heads down. The man he'd seen on the ground lay to the side, one of the healers still tending to him. The beast lay to the far side of the group, a terrifying but, thankfully, still heap. Mgobe pushed himself up to stand.

All eyes turned to him. "Welcome back, governor," the guard captain said with a respectful nod.

He looked around, everyone waiting for his next words. "I know we're tired and wish for a full night's rest, but as soon as we're able, we must press on to a safer place to stop. Wiluru should just be a few days away." The group nodded, fully accepting of his command.

Chapter Thirteen

"Good. Again."

Newa oversaw Masola going through the fighting form. She used one of his longer knives, holding it in the reaper's stance, slicing in more of an arc, like a sickle. He watched her every move, looking for any inconsistencies, any weaknesses that could be exploited by an enemy. He popped her wrist with the long grass reed he'd plucked from the roadside. "Straighten your wrist," he said firmly. "Again." Masola didn't complain and began the drill over.

Newa was impressed with the girl. He warned her that his training would be hard but she hadn't shied away. In fact, she'd embraced it. To be fair, he wasn't being *quite* as hard as his teachers had been on him but he wouldn't disrespect her desire to train by being lenient.

They'd taken a moment in their trek to move off the road to practice, have lunch, then set off again. Newa walked around her, watching. "Remember to control your breathing. Control is your advantage over your foes. The normal people attack wildly, undisciplined. They hold the fear of death as they fight. You must not."

"I can't be afraid of death?" she asked.

He was proud of her for not stopping her dill but he popped her forearm anyway. "Questions later," he said. "No, you must not fear death because you are death. When you serve Gu-, when you serve Takiri, you become the blade that Death works through."

He saw her face work through several emotions and sighed. "Ask your question."

"Do we *have* to kill people *every* time?"

"No," he answered and motioned for her to come over to their packs. Now was a good time as any for lunch. He watched her as she approached. Her breathing was labored but she didn't pant. Good. If only his other initiates had this much dedication. "We do not have to kill everyone in every instance. Only when the situation requires it."

She reached in her pack, pulling out the waterskin he'd managed to get for her and took a long drink. She wiped her mouth, pensive. He frowned. "You do understand what I am, don't you?"

"Not exactly," she said slowly. "I know you're some sort of warrior, a mercenary maybe. But a very religious one. Maybe you came from a family of priests?" She shrugged.

Newa laughed heartily and retrieved their lunch. It was a mix of dried meat and fruit. "My father was a sandal maker and a drunkard. He made half decent shoes when he wasn't beating my mother or my siblings and me. I ran away from home at ten, living on the streets of Metkara until I was found by a member of the Arakgu'un. Have you ever heard of them?" She shook her head and he continued. "The Arakgu'un are priests who work as the blade of Gu'un who we Ega believe find and force the wicked to repent even if that means their deaths. In that way, we also work as assassins. If you want to learn from me, you want to learn the way of the assassin."

Masola tore off a bite of a dried fruit. "If it means no one will be able to hurt me again, then I'll be an assassin priest."

"You can't be Arakgu'un," he chuckled. "They don't allow women." She twisted her lips and he stopped himself from chuckling again. "Go ahead."

She frowned. "My mamas said that you Ega were backwards. They were right."

"In a lot of ways, I suppose we are." He gave her a small smile as he chewed on a bite. "But I'm teaching you, aren't I?"

She nodded. "Thank you, by the way. I am grateful. But I want to learn to fight to protect myself, not just kill people. I want to protect others, like you did for me."

Newa's throat felt like it was about to close up. "That is a noble goal," he said, trying to keep the emotion out of his voice. "It's an objective that I didn't learn until I came south and found the Lady of Death. She and her god showed me that there could be a different path."

Masola stared at him wide eyed. "Is *she* dead?"

"No," he said, slightly annoyed. "Eat your food so we can finish training." The girl held a hand up in mock defense but continued eating. Thankfully in silence.

They made a quick meal then returned to their makeshift training area. He had to admit he enjoyed teaching her. He took up the grass reed again. "Turtle stance," he called. Masola turned the blade around, crossing her arms in front of her, one protecting her upper chest, one protecting her stomach. Eventually she would graduate to two knives. But for the safety of a novice, for now, they would stick to one. "Horizon form," he called.

Masola went through the series of strikes. She moved slowly and Newa allowed it. He continued to correct her form, working her closer to perfection. Speed would come later.

He paused as he noticed movement on a faraway hill. There were three figures blurred by the heat, black clad and heading south. His mind immediately went to the comfort of being combat ready. "Masola, get your pack and hide in the grass just like we practiced," he said, not taking his eyes from the distant travelers. They dipped down behind another hill and only then did he look over. She stared at him, the fear of a child still in her. "Go. Now," he hissed.

Masola hurried into the tall grass with her things as he put on his pack. He returned to the road, taking half a step forward and halting. He held his pose, waiting for the trio to crest the nearest hill. He felt every heartbeat as the moments passed. His breaths grew deep, keeping in time with his heart. This meeting, if these were true Arakgu'un, would end in a fight. That much he knew. There was no explanation for him to be so far south without having left his duties. There was no explanation for them being so far south except to find him. Newa resisted reaching for his weapons and continued to wait.

The first sign of their heads appeared over the hill and Newa finished his stride, falling into a comfortable pace. By the time the trio reached the top of the hill he was almost up to it. There was no mistaking the gray-black robes of the Arakgu'un, the signature sickle-like swords at their sides. Their appearance matched his own although he was far more road worn. He stopped in the road, looking up in feigned surprise.

The other Arakgu'un came to a halt. One raised his eyebrows as he looked down at Newa. "Newa," he called. "I didn't think we'd actually find you down here."

"Well, here I am," Newa answered evenly. Telmet. He was sure the man had jumped at the chance to drag his possibly traitorous rival back for punishment. The other two men he recognized, but not enough to know their names.

"You never sent word back to the Hand," Telmet continued. "There was talk that you were dead."

"You would have liked that." Newa refused to hide his disdain. It ran both ways. But he couldn't help that their master, The Hand of Gu'un, had chosen him instead of Telmet as his protege.

"So," Telmet said, a hand coming to rest comfortably on his sword hilt, "have you shirked off your mission? Left the order?"

Newa sighed. There was no reason to lie. "I have a new mission. I am in the service of the Lady Efah, she who is the voice of Death himself. I am willingly and completely her servant just as my god Tikiri is servant to Death."

"Heresy," hissed one of the other men.

Telmet barked out a cruel laugh. "Are you trying to tell me that the 'best of us' wandered away to play dog for some deep south bitch?"

A pure, righteous rage sprang to life in Newa and he had to work to keep it under control. "You will not speak of the lady in such a fashion," he said, barely keeping his voice even.

"Did you finally get to slip between a woman's legs?" Telmet laughed. "How good were her treasures if they made you turn against the brotherhood? I've heard deep south women were as wild as the jungle."

Newa's hand freed one of his swords as if it acted on its own. *Calm down. Calm down.* But the anger he felt on Efah's behalf refused to be tamed. "Do not speak of her that way," he ground out.

The other men took out their swords, ready for the fight he'd known was coming. Telmet shook his head, all mirth and smugness gone. "If you want to be cut down for some heathen woman, I'll be glad to oblige you."

Newa freed his second sword, twirling it once out of habit. "I was trained personally by the Hand. You do not want this fight."

Telmet took up a stance, easing his way down the hill. "I've wanted it for a long time." Then he charged.

Newa stood his ground, taking in the situation. Telmet came straight for him along with the man to his right. The one to his left was moving away from the group as if to flank him. That man only had one sword out, so either a dagger or throwing knives would come from him. His instinct told him to move back, put a little distance between them to better control the battle, but he couldn't take the risk of them discovering Masola. So holding the low ground would have to be it.

He darted to the right, arcing to engage that priest. This man was younger than he and Telmet, probably faster too, but it meant that he lacked the extra years of training and experience. The priest sliced upward with one sword, holding the other to follow with a delayed attack. Newa countered the first blow upward, bringing his second sword down to block the other attack. It left him with the perfect space to headbutt the man in the bridge of the nose. The loud crunch was deeply satisfying and Newa kicked him away.

The expected slice from Telmet came down for his shoulder and he blocked just in time, allowing the one edgeless part of his blade to hit his shoulder. He flipped his second blade downward and caught Telmet's other blade before he could swing it properly. A flash of light from his left caught his eye. He jerked his left blade, pulling his old rival in the way just in time to block the thrown knife with his shoulder.

Another throwing knife glinted in the sunlight and Newa ducked, spinning with the move. He swung both blades in a low circle, making Telmet jump back. The priest with the broken nose was caught in the knee, forcing him to an awkward stop. Newa rose in a graceful crescent, both blades slicing the younger priest from crotch to hairline.

As the man screamed, blinded, Newa turned, blades up. Telmet's double blow collided into his weapons. The man was the same height as Newa but a hair bulkier. His added muscle bore down on Newa and he let him push him down slightly. He could feel the subtle shift in force and knew Telmet was trying to push him into a better position for their remaining brother. Newa caught the knife glint again and shifted his stance. Telmet's force made him slide down the edge of Newa's swords long enough for the knife to graze his already stabbed shoulder.

"Gods damn you," Telmet snarled. "I should have been the Hand's protege." He burst into a tempest of arcing strikes.

Newa blocked every blow, keeping light on his feet. More importantly, he moved to keep Telmet between him and the other priest. He could just see him, right over Telmet's shoulder, trying his best to move into position to throw again. Frustrated, the man ran wide to the right, free hand moving to take up his second sword. *Good.*

Newa let it appear his attention was pulled to the approaching priest for just a moment, enough to give Telmet an opening. The jealous, angry fool took it, making a wide slice for Newa's neck. Newa blocked it easily, ready to parry the next blow in time to engage the last man's sword.

But the man didn't have his sword in hand. Newa saw the long dagger flying toward him almost too late. He twisted, arching his back to let the dagger fly past. He winced as white hot pain sliced across his stomach.

Newa responded with a hard kick, catching Telmet in the torso. He stumbled back as Newa stood. Newa pulled back, making his way to the last priest. Now that he could see him closely, this one was much younger, maybe just over five years as a full priest. Newa switched to viper style, one sword held out behind him, trailing. He punished the man with his attacks, using only one blade. He had to overwhelm him. There were only moments before Telmet attacked.

He found his moment, knocking the other priest's blade wide before slicing his throat nearly to the spine. He turned, stomach on fire, to block the attack from his rear. He turned and attacked Telmet with every ounce of hatred. The wetness of his blood soaked his robe, making the cloth stick. He fought without honor or the proper back and forth, because as his master taught him, when your life was at stake honor was worthless.

He kicked Telmet's knee, making the joint pop loudly. Flipping the blade in his right hand, he hit the other man in the underside of his jaw with the butt of the handle while blocking a blow with the blade. Telmet sliced down with his other blade but it went wide. Newa leaped on the opportunity, slicing up and cutting the man's hand off. The move caused his wound to pull open more and he struggled not to recoil.

With all of his strength, he crossed his blades and cut for Telmet's neck. The priest's head toppled to the ground, face still working in shock. Newa stepped aside as the body fell. He made his way to the injured man who groped around blindly in abject pain.

"If you do make it back to the capital," he said, kicking the man onto his back, "tell the Hand I'm not coming back. I've found the truth."

He didn't wait for a response and moved away from the grisly scene. "Masola," he called, hand to stomach. The wound wasn't deep but it was bleeding freely. He dropped to his knees beside his pack. He started to search through the contents, but his hand began to shake as his battle high wore off. "Masola," he called again, laying on his back.

"I'm here." She appeared over him. Her eyes were shiny with unspent tears.

He tried to give her a smile but it was weak. "Look in my pack. You will find a small leather pouch with needle and thread. Can you sew?" He pulled aside the fabric of his robe showing the wound.

She grimaced. "Only a little."

"Well today you're going to learn how to sew a wound shut."

***

Efemu walked the halls of Ofolubaru's palace feeling out of place. This sort of useless opulence would never be found in Nsongo. They had their displays of wealth but it was mostly in the size of their noble compounds and the contents therein. For the place named the City of Gold, they didn't have nearly the display of the metal that Ofolubaru did. Their dara didn't even live in the compound where the major decisions of the city happened. Efemu frowned. If he had to live in a place like this, he'd be afraid of causing a mess every day.

He passed a courtyard where a large number of people gathered. He paused, watching for a moment. Families gathered under the various fruit trees having a meal. The smells of the cooked vegetables made him think of home and the meals he was missing with Barabi. Children ran about the garden freely. A pair of them stopped near the entrance to stare. He smiled and nodded, sending them scurrying to their families, laughing all the way.

Efemu moved on. This was the terrible group of vagrants that he was supposed to oust on behalf of the deposed dara. They weren't even warriors in the barest sense of the word. Parents, children, elders. All of whom had obviously just come out of desperate times. If their dara, who was supposed to be their protector and leader, lived like this while they scrapped for food, he could understand why they rose up against her. This new Lady proved herself a better dara already. Perhaps she would be willing to do so officially. It would be good to have one assured ally if he took the seat of Great Dara.

No, he reminded himself. *Not if, when.*

His hand went to his chest, to the spot over his heart where the Lady of Death touched him. She'd read his life, all of it, seen the deepest parts of him. And she hadn't exploited it. If he'd found out his enemy's weakness, he would have taken full advantage of it. Probably taken her hostage to make her people comply. She, instead, gave him advice.

What if the tree refuses to be uprooted?

Then it must be cut down.

Efemu took a moment in an alcove. Surely, she didn't mean to murder his father. Yes, he was furious with him. The man was petty, vengeful, and utterly unfit for the position he'd bribed his way into. He deserved to be striped of it. But murder? His father wasn't deserving of that. He was greedy, not evil.

Banishment was a possibility. Efemu shook his head. Let loose on the world, his father would surely find a way to be a problem later. Murder was looking increasingly like the most prudent outcome. Efemu sighed from deep in his soul. Either way, he would have to return to Nsongo to take action.

He left the alcove, finding his way to the front gates. The guards looked to him cautiously as he approached. "Let your lady know that I'm going to speak with my force," he said to one. "I'll return shortly."

He picked his way to the outer gate, only managing to get lost twice. He was surprised when he saw his commanders waiting just outside. They came alert when they noticed him, Kehesi saluting first, quickly followed by the others. "Commander, we're glad to see you."

"How was the meeting with the witch?" asked another vice-commander.

Efemu moved them away from the gate and the possibly eavesdropping guards. "She's not a witch. But...she says she's the voice of the god of Death."

His vice-commanders passed glances. "You don't believe her, do you?" another asked, a man with the patches of a beard.

"I do," he said slowly. "She has two great hyenas and an army of vultures at her command. The people flock to her."

Kehesi spoke up next. "What are your orders, Commander? Do you think we'll need the entire force to run them out of the city?"

"We're not running anyone out. We'll be returning to Nsongo shortly." He held his hand up against the protests and questions that started. "The people in there are just the poor looking for better conditions while their dara sat in a gold roofed palace. Their Lady of Death seems to have done more for them than anyone else cared to."

"But our mission from the Great Dara," the patchy bearded man ventured.

"It was a foolish errand. Any dara run out of their own city deserves to lose it." There was hesitation but they all nodded in agreement. "Ready the warriors. We'll move out tomorrow."

The other vice-commanders saluted and moved about immediately, but Kehesi hovered nearby. "Commander," she said, nervousness hanging about her. "Would you like to talk? You seem troubled."

Efemu looked to her, truly taking her in for the first time. She was barely older than he was when he entered the warrior's core. But there was an eagerness to please and an underlying need to prove herself. As his second, she would be the person he would talk over any concerns with. But she was placed here as part of a twisted punishment from his father. His face scrunched up in hesitation.

"I know that I'm newly your second," she added hastily, "and I know we haven't gotten to know each other very well on this mission, but I'm more than willing to be your loyal confidant." She looked away, a little shy, then brought her gaze back to his firmly. "I had the honor of following your command during the war. Your leadership, along with your second Barabi, brought us victory time and time again. Your fierceness in battle is unmatched. I am beyond honored to serve as your second now and you have my utter loyalty." She saluted him sharply, fist hitting her chest with a thump.

Efemu was taken aback by her open honesty. "Then I won't dishonor your loyalty by refusing your offer." He waved for her to walk with him.

They made their way along the perimeter of the city wall. He watched the guards at the top, waiting until they no longer patrolled to speak again. "When I met the woman in charge, she wasn't what I expected. She's young, maybe a year or two younger than you. But there is such a strong presence to her."

"And you believe that she's really the voice of Death?"

He glanced at Kehesi. The woman's face held no judgment, but there was a mix of trepidation and disbelief. "She touched me." His hand went to his heart again. "She saw into my mind, my soul. She saw what kind of man I am. She even saw my father and all I feel about him." He stopped, not wanting to speak on the rest of the conversation.

"What did she think of all of that?" Kehesi asked carefully.

He worried his bottom lip. "What I'm about to say stays with us." She nodded. "She agreed with me that my father can't be the Great Dara."

The younger woman's lips pulled into a grim line. 'There are many who would agree with you. We've heard the whispers that you were vying to take the position. I've spoken to a lot of other warriors and we would rather it be you. We remember your leadership in the war and with this new fight against the Ega flaring up, we want you to lead us to victory. I'm sure you'll find more support than you think among the warriors."

She looked off, back toward the force who were being spurred into activity. Her face turned bitter. "Besides, it should be a warrior on the stool of Nsongo. Not a soft priest."

Efemu hesitated. "My father won't give up that seat easily," he said, testing her.

"Then make him," she answered firmly. Her face immediately lightened and she looked panicked. "I don't mean to imply that you should attack your own father. Just make him see reason."

He barked out a laugh. "There's the more impossible task. I would have an easier time dragging him off the stool and throwing him out of the city."

"If that's what it takes," she said. "Nsongo needs a dara. A good one. I believe in you and many others do too."

Efemu let her words sit with him for a moment. "Thank you," he said. "For your honesty. I have a lot to think about."

Kehesi saluted again, heading off towards the camp. As he watched her go he felt like a fool. Why hadn't he thought of looking for his support within the warriors? If the majority of them supported him or even if a large number of them did, he could apply pressure to the council to vote for him. And with the backing of a woman who was the voice of a god? They couldn't deny him. He focused on the warriors beginning their departure preparations. His father had hoped this mission would be a humiliation. He smiled. It turned out to be the best boon he'd received in ages.

***

Governing felt like a flock of birds, many bodies moving toward the same destination but each member must work to keep the flock together. And Efah felt like the bird being left behind. She focused on the notes she'd scribbled down for their food supplies. She was trying to make the food distribution easier by dividing her people by the part of the palace that they'd settled. Those who had squatted anywhere would have to choose a section. She frowned at the thought of being tough with her own people. It might be distasteful but it would be for the best until they settled the matter of the incoming food.

Before her, a number of her people and converted palace guards moved supplies out of the main storehouse to divide into the palace. There were other rooms nearer to the various kitchens that could be used. Thanks to her new map, she knew where they were.

"My lady, you seem troubled."

Efah snapped out of her thoughts, looking up at the man next to her. He was a guard of middle age with a constellation of dark freckles down one side of his face, kind eyes, and full lips. His hair was pulled back in a thick ponytail of braids. "I'm just trying to make some decisions," she tried to say cheerily.

He nodded, glancing down at the paper in her hand. "Are you worried about the amount of food we have in the palace?"

Efah hesitated. She knew this man had to be one of the converts if he was here helping, but she was still wary. "Yes. These people have had a rough life. I want to make sure they never experience missing a meal again."

"Then you'll want to speak to the farmers who supply the city directly. They're not sure what to do with the news spreading that the dara abandoned the city." He tapped lightly on her paper, and she began writing. "You'll also want to speak directly with servants that remain, both us guards and the regular staff. If you want to ensure our loyalty, you'll want to see that we are paid."

She tried her best not to look overwhelmed but she knew she wasn't successful by his surprised expression. "Thank you," she said quietly. "What's your name?"

"Kembi."

"Thank you, Kembi."

He nodded with a small smile. He took half a step closer, lowering his voice. "You're not a noble at all, are you?"

"No, I am not," she answered, standing straighter.

"Neither am I, my lady. It seems that life has chosen to raise both of us up. I served as a peacekeeper in the inner court under the dara. The only people who had more access to her were her favorites. I know what it takes to keep this palace running and what I don't know, I can find the people who can tell you."

Efah stared at him for a moment. "Why are you helping me?" Despite her god's favor, her life had taught her not to trust too much of a good thing.

"You brought my brother back to me." Emotion threatened to choke his voice and he cleared his throat. "A man provoked a fight with him ten years ago. He won but the man died. The dara decided to have him executed and my brother ran into the forest. But you brought him back. Our parents get to see their youngest son again because of you. I will do anything to repay you."

She nodded, looking over her hastily written list of things to do and all of the activity going on around her. "I would truly appreciate your help, Kembi. In the future too, if you're willing. I think I'm going to need as much help as possible."

He gave her a deep bow; with the reverence she was sure normally went to his dara. "I would be honored."

Efah returned to her writing, asking questions of Kembi and happily taking down notes. She never expected to be a true leader of a city. She would have been perfectly happy to stay in the forest helping people just like her make a living out of what little life had given them. But she never thought she would be the voice of the god of Death either. Her life had completely changed for the better. But with far more complications.

She noticed Ifisi entering the room as she made another note. The woman had a pinched expression, more concerned than her usual serious face. "My lady," she said, bowing once she crossed the room.

"What is it?" Efah asked.

"That commander from Nsongo wants to speak with you again." She made a sour face as she delivered the message. "He's waiting outside."

"Very well. Take me to him." Efah nodded to Kembi with a smile and walked off with her self-appointed bodyguard.

Efemu was indeed standing just outside the room, far enough away from the entrance to give the people working enough room to maneuver unimpeded. He looked very serious, but there was an anxious energy about him. She smiled friendly when he noticed her approach. "Good afternoon, Commander Efemu,"

He bowed like it just occurred to him, rushed and awkward. "Lady Efah, thank you for taking time out of your day to speak with me."

She was grateful for his change in demeanor. She'd far rather to be on friendly terms. "What can I do for you?"

"I'd like you to return to Nsongo with me and my warriors. You could help me sway the opinion of the people to help me oust my father."

Efah blinked at him. "I…I can't leave my people. There's so much to be done."

"It won't be permanently. Just for the time it takes me to become the Great Dara. But before that, the Ega have to be run out of the city." He paused, looking aside as he contemplated his next words. "For several reasons."

His eyes flicked to Ifisi and she caught on. Efah looked back to her stalwart bodyguard. "Ifisi, could you give us some privacy."

Newa's student looked daggers at the commander but she bowed and retreated out of hearing distance. Efemu led her a little farther away from the bustling activity of the storeroom, checking to make sure no one was around before he spoke again. "Nsongo is caught in a vise. Months ago, the Ega murdered one of the Batu'bangi. They cut off the gold supply from the forest. Then my cousin was found dead and now my father has restarted aggression with the enemy. The other major cities know we're vulnerable and they're waiting for us to fall so that they can take the title of Great Dara for themselves."

Efah cursed quietly. "Then the Ega absolutely must leave." She stopped herself, allowing the clarity of her connection with Death's will to rise. "No, they must be destroyed. They must never want to return to the south again. There has been enough war. It's past time for peace." The vehemence of her last words surprised her, but she felt it in her spirit. The time for war was over. Peace had to be made.

"So will you come with us?" Efemu asked, hopefully.

"I must come with you. We will put an end to this and see a dara of peacetimes on the seat of Nsongo."

Chapter Fourteen

Umakaal jogged down the streets toward Wiluru's docks. Bobbing in the water waited The Winter Squall, the ship that would spirit her to Asfara. Ladawi had already boarded, making sure that she and her small retinue had everything they needed for their journey. Her second in the guard was in charge in her absence, Umakaal pressing on him the importance of the safety of her mother and all citizens under the palace's roof. She knew she didn't have to remind him but she needed to assuage her worry. This was her first time leaving home and the second time she'd had to turn her command to someone else. Her spirit wouldn't rest until she knew she wouldn't come back to ruin.

Umakaal took one glance back at her home. At least one bright spot existed on this trip. He would be there. His ridiculously pretty eyes and that damn smile would remain far behind in Wiluru. He was trying to charm her, like she was sure he did with every girl back home. But not her. She only needed him to father her children and nothing more. The less she had to see him the better.

Gulls called out as she reached the docks, seeming like they greeted her. She heard another call and saw a red throated crane flying over. The symbol of Yutuu swooped down low before gliding over The Winter Squall and making a turn to the west. She stared after it until it became a tiny bobbing dot in the sky. She'd never been one to believe in signs but this felt like a good one.

Umakaal jogged up to the ship, the sailors loading the last supplies saluting her. She nodded in return. "Did you need help with any of that?" she asked, used to pulling her weight.

"No, princess," one responded happily. "We have this."

She saluted them, jogging up the gang plank. The final preparations to set sail began with sailors calling out orders. The captain came up to her, saluting with a bow. "We should be ready in a few minutes, princess. The tide is at its best. At your say, we'll head out."

"Excellent," she said with an eager grin. "I'm ready to-" She stopped, looking across the deck. Coming from below, talking cheerfully with Ladawi, was Prince Mikhra. He laughed, voice carrying on the ocean breeze. "Excuse me, captain."

Her lover and fiancé didn't notice her approach and jumped at her presence. "What is he doing here?" Her voice had come out as a venomous hiss but was louder than she'd intended. She didn't dare look around to see if anyone else heard.

Prince Mikhra bowed shallowly. "Princess." Ladawi followed his gesture but far more respectful.

"What are you doing here?" Umakaal reiterated.

"I was ordered here by your brother," he answered. "He wished for me to be your bodyguard."

"He what?" she shrieked.

All work on the deck stopped and out of the corner of her eyes, Umakaal saw sailors staring. Ladawi leaned in close. "My princess," she started quietly, "you are being very *loud*. Perhaps we should continue this conversation below decks."

Umakaal gave the barest glance to her side, the slightest mortification gaining a foothold. Ladawi led the way below decks, the princess following and Mikhra bringing up the rear. They weaved their way past more sailors coming to a room near the captain's quarters. Ladawi closed the door behind them, listening for the retreat of other footsteps before rounding on Umakaal.

"This has to stop," she said, hands firmly on her hips.

Umakaal looked between the two. "What has to stop?"

"You are hating him for no reason."

The princess folded her arms. "I don't hate him for no reason."

"Then why is it that you hate me?" Mikhra asked, eyebrow quirked.

Umakaal faltered. She felt her face getting hot as he stared at her, expression firm. He wasn't the unsure man she'd met in the palace. Confidence wrapped around him now and it had more than her face feeling warm. She shook it off. "I hate you because my brother dumped you on me."

"So you hate me because of something I had no control over."

The princess struggled. He had her.

Mikhra hesitated. "I did not choose to come here, away from my home. I will never see my home again. I am my mother's least favorite son from her least favorite husband. I was born to be a…a…," he struggled for the word, "piece of a game. To be used to make her stronger." He tried to contain a frown but then let it spread across his face. "I have tried to be friendly to you. I have tried to be useful. I do not want to be miserable here so I tried. I understand that you do not want me. You and Ladawi have something together. But I cannot change that I am here. I cannot change that we are to be married. Can we not be enemies at the least?" He sighed, shoulders drooping, as if a great weight had been lifted from him.

Ladawi put a gentle hand on her shoulder. "Since you're both in the same situation," she said, looking at her firmly, "perhaps you can at least commiserate together? This was sprung on him too. He only had two days to pack up his entire life. No servants sent with him. No friendly faces. Just thrown here." She gave a piteous glance to the prince. "He and I have been talking, especially since you've been determined to avoid him. He's nice, my love."

Umakaal glanced between the two, Ladawi with her look that pleaded for peace and Mikhra who seemed defeated but unwilling to take any more abuse. She reluctantly admitted that she hadn't even thought about his side of the matter. She had good reason to be angry. But perhaps she'd been directing it at the wrong target.

Her lips twisted. She took a deep breath, exhaling in a huff. "I'm sorry," she said. She relaxed her posture, completely letting go of all of her anger over the situation. "I'm sorry. I've been very unfair to you. We're kind of in the same situation."

Mikhra's face lightened and he gave a small smile. "I accept your apology." He extended an arm.

Umakaal deliberated but clasped forearms with him. His palm was rough against her skin. She quirked a little grin at him.

"So, you are a bit of a warrior." She gave his arm a squeeze, just a bit too hard.

He looked surprised but returned the pressure just as firmly. "I have trained much to be one," he said with a smirk of his own.

Gods, he was…pretty. Those golden brown eyes and long eyelashes. Those perfect, bow-shaped lips. The cheekbones you could cut paper with. If he grew out his hair just a bit, he would be…beautiful. Umakaal let go of him with a strained chuckle. "Alright, Prince Warrior, I'll have to test out how much of a fighter you truly are on this trip."

He smiled, that gods damned pretty smile, and put his hand over his heart, bowing slightly. "I would be delighted to spar with you."

She looked to Ladawi before he could stare up at her through those long eyelashes. "I'm glad we had this talk," she said, backing toward the door. "I'll…I'll talk to you all again later." Umakaal fled the room, heading above deck, praying the sea breeze would clear her head.

What was wrong with her? He was pretty, prettier than most men she'd known. The image of his face with that smirk came to mind. Her stomach fluttered. He was so damned pretty. What was he doing to her?

"Princess?"

Umakaal's head snapped over to the captain who stood nearby, looking very concerned. The princess worked to fix her face before she spoke. "I'm sorry for the delay, Captain. I'm ready to depart when you are."

"Very good, princess."

Umakaal wiped her hand down her face, thankful for the feel of the wind spells swelling up to fill the sails. Warning calls were made and with a lurch, the ship moved forward. She adjusted herself to the sudden rocking of the vessel, thankful they were on their way. The sooner they got this trip over with the better.

***

Prince Yutuuan raced back to the palace, cleaned up, and

174

changed. He left Naret at the front to keep an eye on a certain person and make sure she wasn't trying to spy on him. Yes, he was rushing away from the front again but this time it was for very important business. Djelebe had arrived, apparently looking worse for wear. He gave them an evening to rest themselves but today he needed to speak to Wiluru's newest allies.

The delegation occupied the most luxurious accommodations Wiluru could offer. His mother had seen to that, gods bless her. And the emperor was stored a small side room to be cared for until they decided what to do with him. Yutuuan's mood soured slightly at the thought of that bastard. So much trouble just because of him and his blasphemy.

His conscious pricked him. *This war started mostly because of Izriamat.* If she'd just gone along with their plan of using her as a hostage, they could have bartered for Wiluru's freedom. But she had to go and provoke the man. He understood her hatred of him, but could she possibly have acted levelheaded? He let out a frustrated breath. It was no matter. The war was upon them now and the most important thing was to find a way to win it.

He turned a few corners and a pair of servants rushed to greet him. "Good morning, Prince Yutuuan," said one of them, an older woman with the dark gray of mourning still entwined in her hair. "The governor is right this way."

Yutuuan nodded, following the women to a room with high latticed windows on two sides. Its high ceiling made it seem light and airy. The governor paced slowly to the far side of a thick wooden table, stained a deep brown. He looked up with a smile as the prince entered. "Young Prince Yutuuan," he said jovially.

"Governor Mgobe," Yutuuan returned with a nod. This wasn't the same man he remembered from his brief years studying at Djelebe. That governor had seemed mousy and ill at ease around him, a prince come to his city for study. This man wore a haunted, hardened look in his eye. "How are you doing?"

Around them, servants scurried in to bring refreshments. "I am happy to be within the walls of Wiluru."

Yutuuan had to notice that Mgobe's smile didn't quite reach his eyes. "How was the trip through the pass?"

"It was enlightening," he responded, smile fading. "There were creatures in the path. Things I've never seen before. Nearly everyone had an injury at some point. One man, a guard..." He looked up toward the windows. "We tried to heal him but his wounds were just too much."

"I'm sorry," Yutuuan said horrified. "If there's anything we can do for you, let me know." Mgobe nodded his thanks. "What state is the emperor in?" He didn't want to ask about the man but he had to know.

The governor's face tightened. "He's alive and not falling toward death. My healers can keep him that way for as long as possible." Mgobe looked up to him. "So tell me, do you plan on executing him?"

"We haven't decided." *I haven't even spoken with the council yet*, he thought guiltily.

"He burned the university." Yutuuan's thoughts stopped cold. "It's gone, completely gone. Centuries of work are nothing but ash now. Some of our scholars were able to save a number of tomes, but it's one handful of water compared to a river. If you do execute him, I wish to watch." The governor's face was hard, pulling the slight wrinkles in his face taut. His eyes held a burning desire for vengeance.

Yutuuan wanted to sit down. The great university was gone. Its library had seemed endless when he first went there, a labyrinth of knowledge from countless authors across the ages, some even from his kingdom. The loss pained him almost as much as losing someone he knew. "I swear to you, when we do visit justice on that man, you will see it all."

Mgobe nodded again, the look of vengeance satiated. "How is the fight for the city? We could see smoke and spells as we approached."

The prince sucked in a breath. "The fighting is slow and arduous. It appears we're evenly matched." He gave a wry chuckle. "I have to give the Ega credit. They're far more capable warriors than I'd thought them to be."

"Have the Asfarans put their dragon's blood to use? I've always wondered what it looked like in battle."

Yutuuan stared at him. "Dragon's blood?" he asked slowly.

Mgobe tilted his head slightly, a tiny bit of the nervousness Yutuuan remembered coming through. "Yes," he began slowly. "Dragon's blood. The liquid from springs deep in the mines of Asfara."

Yutuuan searched his memory but came up blank. "I've never heard of anything of the sort."

"It was used against Wiluru in their last battle before they became part of the kingdom. The oath to never use it against the rest of the kingdom is in the treaty." Mgobe eyed him with concern. "Was this not taught in your history?"

Yutuuan felt off kilter. He didn't appreciate being caught off guard with information. Why was he not taught about this before? "I was told about the various treaties but never in depth. What is dragon's blood?"

Mgobe seemed to brighten up at the question, the eager scholar coming forth. "Dragon's blood is a substance of unknown origin. You do know the old tale of how the cliffs of Wiluru were formed, of the great dragon who's supposed to have died here?" Yutuuan nodded. "The Asfarans believe that this substance, this blood, is all that was left of it. Since it gathered beneath their city, they feel they were also chosen. Heirs of the great dragon, so to speak. That is why they were the last to bow to Wiluru. It's used in so many facets of their lives. From their hearths to their forges, anywhere they need a reliable, even fire."

Yutuuan remembered the odd, ghostly flames of Asfara from his visit. He'd assumed that they were magically formed. "Why would they withhold such a powerful tool from us?"

"That you'd have to ask them," the governor said, raising his hands in defense.

Yutuuan waved his hand to show he meant no offense but inside a rage was brewing. He could see Governor Begarmen's smug face as he'd extorted Yutuuan, trading the security of the kingdom for the chance to have his bloodline on the throne. All this time they held the secret to winning the war. Yutuuan pulled himself together. "It appears your arrival was a blessing indeed. Help yourself to the refreshments. I need to send a message."

"Of course, Prince Yutuuan," Mgobe said with a dip of his

head. "It was good to see you again."

Yutuuan left the room, letting his smile disintegrate. That piece of fetid bird shit. Begarmen wasn't just holding back forces. He was holding back the weapon that could crush the imperial forces. He found a palace scribe and had them send off an urgent message to Umakaal. He detailed the information about dragon's blood to her but he pressed one point. *Make Asfara remember who sits on the throne.*

Yutuuan returned to the front, still in a murderous mood. If Asfara wanted to play games, they were about to learn that they didn't hold all the cards.

* * *

Izriamat entered the palace through the side entrance again, not wanting to deal with her mother. She didn't have the strength or inclination to endure another futile argument. She didn't want to endure the distrustful stares of any of her family today or the uncertainty of the servants and staff. There was only one thing she'd come to the palace to do.

Djelebe had made good on their offer and arrived in the city a day ago with their precious cargo in tow. Thankfully, her brother had seen fit to send her a message about the emperor's return to the city. The moment she'd read it, her heart stopped. He was so near and completely at their mercy. They decided his fate now. She decided his fate now.

She briefly stopped one of the servants to ask where the "special guest" was being kept. The servant made a face at the mention of their guest but graciously gave her the location. Izriamat thanked them with a smile and worked her way quickly and quietly there. Guards stood at the door, looking displeased to be on such an assignment. They let her in without question, one even making a sympathetic expression as she passed. Izriamat ignored it. She didn't want their sympathy.

She stopped as she entered, taking in the scene before her. A trio of healers tended to the emperor, checking his vital signs and massaging his limbs to prevent complete atrophy. He lay on a soft cushion of a bed with a cushy pillow under his head. His body lay so still with only the barest movement of his breathing.

Izriamat had to make herself breath again. She never thought she'd see this man again, the beast from her nightmares. Now he was so close. She took a step forward. Close enough to touch.

"May we help you, my lady?" one of the healers asked cautiously.

Izriamat snapped back to herself. She took a moment to look at each one of the people. "I am Princess Izriamat, future High Priestess of Wiluru."

Realization of who she was crept into their eyes. They shared an uncomfortable glance. The one who'd spoken cleared his throat. "I'm sorry, princess. We didn't know your face. How may we be of service?"

"I just wanted to see him." They nodded and stepped out of the way so that she could come up to the bed.

Izriamat looked down at her former husband, a swirl of emotions in her chest. He had lost so much weight. His cheeks caved in and his collar bones stood out from his chest. The tendons of his hands seemed to be the only thing holding his skin up. She barely recognized the monster she'd been forced to marry.

"Please, leave us," she said quietly. The healers glanced at each other again. "I just want a moment." The lead healer nodded to the others and they filed out of the room.

Izriamat walked around the bed, taking in his nearly still body. "Can you hear me?" she said. She placed a hand on his chest, over the bandages crisscrossing his wound. Extending her powers, she could feel the depth of it, the severity of it, and how close to death he was. The healers were keeping him at a point that he certainly wouldn't die but so little would push him over the edge.

A smile stretched her lips as she healed him more. Bakari's breathing grew more even. She felt the wound knitting back together, his heart beginning to beat as it should. An unintelligible sound floated from his lips. "I know you can hear me now. I endured so much under your care. You took glee in defiling a priestess, one who was dedicated to her god. You couldn't even wait until we were married. I endured you taking your pleasures with me over and over and over again." Her last word echoed in the room. "Just when I thought I couldn't suffer any more, I had to bear your foul spawn, nurse him at my breast, then endure your defilement again."

She stepped back, taking a breath and lowering her voice. "Does it hurt?" she asked, close to his ear. She yanked his bandages back, jabbing a finger into the wound. Bakari groaned weakly. "That's what you asked me our first time then you laughed in my face. So you tell me, does it hurt?" She jabbed again. "Does it hurt to have someone take their pleasure with you? Does it hurt to be at someone else's mercy? Do you have nightmares of the arrow hitting you, bringing you so close to Death's embrace?"

She pulled her finger out of his chest, wiping the blood and puss off on a nearby cloth. The man who was her tormentor whimpered in pain, too weak to do much more. Her breath came in hot waves. "Your life rests in my hands now, Bakari. I could heal you. Your wound is no match for the power of Yutuu. But I could also let you die."

Or you could kill him yourself.

The thought came clear and unbidden to her. She stared at the thin body before her, too weak to do anything but take the care or abuse heaped on him. It would be so easy to kill him. The very idea caused a fluttering feeling in her heart. To watch him take his last breaths after all he'd done to her. She would savor that more than anything else in this life.

So just kill him.

She watched him, called his name, but there was no reaction. He wouldn't even know if she did it and did she ever want him to know it was her sending him to his judgment. Izriamat placed her hand over his wound, calling on the fullness of her power. She let herself be a full vessel of Yutuu, stitching flesh and bone back together, returning vitality to his body.

He began to breathe deeply and soon his eyes fluttered. Through thick lashes he took in her face, not recognizing her. "Hello, husband," she said with venomous sweetness.

He licked parched lips. "Izriamat?" he croaked, a barely audible whisper.

She gave him one last smile before snatching the pillow from beneath his head and forcing it against his face. Bakari gave a pathetic struggle. Izriamat forced the pillow down harder, her hands and arms tingling from the pleasure of his fight for life. For so long he moved in vain attempts to shudder free but it just made her push harder. Finally, after a lifetime of moments, he laid still.

Izriamat's panting was the only sound in the room. Her elbows ached from the force she was using and it took her painful seconds to unlock them. Slowly, she lifted the pillow, stepping back. She watched his face for any movement, even the subtle movement of eyes beneath eyelids. His chest was stone still as well. All of her hatred and exhilaration rushed out of her, leaving her weak. She took a few breaths to gather herself. It was over. Her long torment was over. She was free of him.

She took the time to replace the pillow under his head, making sure he appeared to be no more than asleep. She took a step back from the body, waiting for him to miraculously come back to life somehow. She took another few steps, inching towards the door. He didn't move. He was truly dead. Izriamat turned, leaving the room quickly but as calm as she could. She only nodded at the murmurs and gestures of respect the healers and guards gave her. She made it completely out of that wing of the palace before the shouts of alarm started.

Interlude

War stared over the walls of Wiluru, watching the tiny mortals churn in their struggle. Each side claimed to fight with honor. Each side was certain they were the right side. Each side would find their ends as easily as the other. It was utter, glorious chaos and she would drink in every drop.

"Why do you do this?" came Death's hoarse voice.

War sneered as she turned her head away from the battle. "Is it not my duty to stir up the hatred of the humans? To set them against each other?"

"Within reason," he roared.

War raised an eyebrow, lips pulled into a pursed smile. "Passionate, aren't we?"

Another presence approached with all of the force of a tsunami. "You. Get out of my lands." The voice of the Sea crashed down on them. He stood as large and imposing as ever, serrated spear held a little too menacing for her liking. His sea foam colored locs churned as if he were still underwater.

"Does not war come to all lands?" she asked plainly.

The sound of the ocean nearby grew and waves punished the shore. "You may play games with the mortals but do not seek to play them with me," The Sea rumbled. "You have touched my chosen."

"You go too far," Death said, eyes narrowed in disapproval.

"I always go too far as far as you're concerned," she drawled. Her attention turned back to The Sea and his churning waters behind his city. "Your chosen needed…motivation. Her little army has been pushed back. Her only influence is in the temple among the vagabonds, the poor, and the sickly. She needed something to renew her fight for your plan."

The Sea's voice rose and dark clouds began to gather. "If my chosen needed anything, I would have provided it for them." His spear raised slightly, the movement catching her attention.

"Now, now, my dear friend," she purred, "you wouldn't want to fight me and catch the attention of Sun and Moon. I don't think they'd want to see their charges fighting."

"Perhaps they should be alerted to your meddling," Death offered.

War wheeled around on him, hair aflame. "If they will be told about my meddling, then I'll have to tell them about both of yours."

The Sea stared her down, eyes swirling with the storm forming behind him. "My covenant with the people of this coast has been sealed since their arrival. I break no norms by choosing one for my own."

"I am only interested in restoring balance," Death said, an anger still behind his calm voice.

"Excuses, excuses," War snapped. "As plentiful and full of shit as spilled entrails on the battlefield. Am I supposed to sit idly by as the mortals go about their lives, behaving as if they tolerate each other? Like they are actually amicable to each other? That is not their nature. These cruel, hateful creatures love tearing each other's throats out, making a glorious bloody mess of their brothers, their sisters, even others they've never even seen before."

"But it is not your place to twist them toward that side of their nature," Death said. "Just as it is not my place to pull them toward my embrace. The mortals must make their own choices of what paths they will take."

"Did you ask your chosen if that was the path *she* wanted?" She scowled at him then turned to The Sea, her face holding the same question.

Death was quieted but The Sea snorted his disdain. He looked past her to Death. "There is no reasoning with her. She'll just have to be brought back down." Like the recession of a wave, his presence left.

War looked to Death who still hadn't answered her question. His face had gone blank and she couldn't even read any emotion from his eyes. "Well?" she asked tersely.

"Do what you will, War," he said at last. "You will get more than your fill of what you seek." With one last unreadable glance at the nearby battle, he retreated.

War turned her attention back to the glorious display before her. She was already more satisfied than she could have imagined.

Chapter Fifteen

Erenemo stared down at his priestly robes, laid out before him, the robes only reserved for major ceremonies. When was the last time he worn them? Ashaki's funeral? That felt like a lifetime ago. But it marked the start of a new era. He called for Unyemi to help him out of his current outfit. His personal sacred rooms felt cold once he'd disrobed, a chill that brought him focus. He had to be completely in tune with the gods today. He had to be the perfect conduit for their favor.

"The message to the warriors along Western Way has been sent?" he asked his acolyte.

"Yes, master. They should be assembling by now."

"Good." He stepped forward, saying a quick prayer over his robes before allowing Unyemi to dress him. They were gold with a red and purple sash that wrapped three times around his waist before laying over his left shoulder. Unyemi took the extra time to rub oil onto his hands and feet to ensure he looked presentable. His hair, which he'd been growing out to fit his more warrior dara style, was braided down close to his scalp. He placed his rings on in the order he'd learned in his first days studying at the main temple. Each ring represented the eight highest deities but he paused, contemplating the ring representing War.

Ngema. He'd never had much thought to her worship. He hadn't been a warrior so what need had he to invoke her except to bless their warriors before they set off to battle. It didn't seem that she was all that concerned with blessing them after how the war had turned out. Sure, Ashaki hadn't even given them the chance to see the true end to the war but the battle was harder and more costly than everyone expected. Perhaps she had finally seen fit to guide her people to victory.

Erenemo looked over his robes, straightening a few wrinkles. He let Unyemi inspect him and once his outfit met both of their approvals, he slipped on his sandals. The items he needed for this ceremony were already on the way to the front. He adjusted his rings again. Today was the day that would change everything. Today, he would seal his ascension to Great Dara. He stepped outside and caught the odd stillness of the city. A few clouds gathered to the south and he hoped that they didn't spoil today with rain.

When he reached the soldiers at the main encampment near the Ega district, they were assembled but none seemed particularly enthusiastic to see him. As they stood in neat lines, he could feel the disdain coming from their eyes. Efemu had infected them with his disrespect. That was about to change. He was a dara that commanded the attention of the gods. No better candidate existed for such a time as this.

Erenemo took his place at the front of the assembly, standing equidistant from each end. He heard a deep bellow and saw the bull he'd called for being led down the street. Now unsurety rippled through the warriors and he savored it. They were about to see how he worked his trade. The people of Nsongo were a fickle lot, indifferent about the gods until they needed them. He was even guilty of it. He paid them their proper respect with lip service for the most part and went about his day. It was time to give them their due in the most visceral way.

"Warriors of Nsongo," he called out in his booming voice. "I have assembled you here because I have received a sign." There were a few quiet grunts and a number of stifled comments. His anger sparked to life but he extinguished it. "The goddess Ngema has shown me that she wants blood spilt in her name. She wishes for the blood of our enemies to run down the streets of our city. I know it may have seemed as if she turned her eye away from Nsongo but she is watching. If we give her what she wants, we will finally eradicate the Egan infestation and be a free city again."

His impassioned declaration was met with silence, the warriors watching him with disinterested eyes. He extinguished his anger again. Ungrateful dogs. Keeping an aura of utter confidence, he motioned for the bull to be brought forward. The creature came dutifully but it seemed wary of him, its eyes roaming the crowd. It bleated again, the strength of its call echoing off the surrounding buildings. He smiled. Surely the Ega could hear that and wondered what they were up to. Let them wonder.

The bull's main handler unsheathed a large knife from his belt, handing it to Erenemo. The priest took it, studying the poor animal. Such strength. He hadn't done such a ceremony since his days as an initiate just to learn how it could be done. Most gods could be placated with simpler sacrifices. He placed a gentle hand on the bull's neck, feeling around for the main artery. The bull made to pull away from him, as if it could feel his intent, but its handlers kept it in place.

Erenemo felt the warriors' attention sharpen. He took a breath and began speaking. "O great Ngema, she of sharpened blades and spilled blood, she who sings the songs of battle and the cries of the wounded, the warriors of Nsongo wish for your eye to turn to us on this day and many days more. Move with every strike made against the enemy of your people. Drink in their blood until you are filled beyond measure. Let their cries of despair rise up until they terrorize their ancestors."

He raised up the knife to the bull's neck, angling to make one clean strike across throat and artery. "May this first bloodletting whet your appetite for the feast to come." The bull cried out as he sliced, the flesh splitting in a neat line. Blood sprayed forth, covering his robes and splashing across his face. It bucked for a moment, straining against its ropes. In one strong side movement, it threw itself sideways, shouldering into Erenemo and nearly knocking him to the ground. He steadied himself, wiping the blood from his face.

He watched, pleased as the animal's movement slowed until it collapsed. His acolyte gave him a large bowl and he knelt down to collect blood from the weakly pulsing wound. He pressed on the animal's neck, coaxing out as much blood as he could until the bowl was nearly full.

As he turned back toward the warriors, all eyes were on him. Most of them had probably never seen a bloodletting before. He knew he must be quite the sight, priestly robes splattered with the shining red of fresh blood. This was not what a priest should look like. It was more a sight associated with warriors. He soaked in their attention for a moment before standing in front of one of the assembly.

"Let all who see this mark know you fight under the eye of Ngema." He dipped his thumb into the bowl of blood, drawing a line from this young warrior's brow to the tip of his nose.

The man swallowed and dipped his head in reverence. Pleased, Erenemo moved down the line, anointing every warrior here with the blessing of Ngema. By the time he'd finished, all stood in awe. He took a few steps back so that all could see him. "Go," he said loudly. "Fight for your people."

The expected battle shout went up from the group and they eagerly went to join the front, no prompting needed. Erenemo resisted a chuckle as he watched them go. He turned to the bull's handlers. "See that the bull is butchered properly for the warriors." They lowered their heads and quickly went to gather help for the task. Erenemo turned and motioned for his acolyte to follow. He would do this again later for the warriors already at the front when they were relieved, but for now he needed a bath and change of clothes. He allowed himself to chuckle once he was far enough away. Praise Ngema.

***

The walls of Nsongo rose up in the distance and Efah had to contain her awe. While not as high as Ofolubaru, they seemed to go on forever, marking the capital of the south as its largest. Along the roads around it, farms spread in blankets of green and gold in the late afternoon sun. It made her think of her childhood home and the loving times she had there before her life turned to heartbreak.

"Welcome to Nsongo, the city of gold," Efemu said proudly from her right. "It is the greatest city in the world, but I am a bit biased."

She returned his small grin, chuckling lowly. "I didn't realize it was so big. I've only heard people talking about it."

"It's the largest city in the south," Kehesi said from behind them. "Only rivaled by Metkara."

She nodded, trailing her eyes along the walls. She couldn't imagine how many people lived inside. And the fact that there was a whole war going on inside the walls was mind boggling.

"Where are the enemy?" she asked.

Efemu pointed a long arm to a fork in the road and the side of the city it led to. "They dug in near the eastern gate which is where we're going to station ourselves."

Efah nodded, but a surprised, "What?" came from Kehesi. "Commander, we're not going to rejoin the main fight?"

"No," he said, face turning serious. "The Ega have changed their normal tactics so we have to as well. This isn't an honorable battle anymore, two forces meeting on the field. We have to rid this city of this cancer and we must do it by any means." He glanced back to his second. "With the eastern gate cut off, they'll have to truly fend for themselves and have to either surrender or die. We'll go through the gate in time, but for right now, we're going to make a point. With us and this wall at their back, they're completely surrounded."

"When you corner a wounded animal, they tend to get more vicious," Kehesi offered.

Efah nodded at the point but Efemu's lips twisted into a cruel grin. "I hope they do."

Beneath her Nesi yipped lowly. Efah put a hand on her companion's neck, patting her gently. She looked over to Usa who watched the city with intense focus. Her familiars were agitated, the fur on the nape of their necks starting to stand on end. Efah followed Usa's gaze to the eastern wall and felt unease creep into her. Something wasn't right. She couldn't put her finger on it but as they moved closer to that side of the city the feeling turned from a fleeting thought to a constant nagging at her mind.

"Is something the matter, Lady Efah?" Efemu asked. On this trip, even he had come to call her lady.

"I don't know," she answered slowly. "I'll see about it later."

Yet Efah couldn't shake the feeling of something greatly off from this city of gold, even as the day waned. Behind her, Efemu's force was settling in for the siege, lighting torches to make their numbers apparent to the guards protecting the tiny eastern gate. Many of them still watched her and her hyenas warily but it was of no consequence. Her purpose was higher than making everyone like her.

She clicked her tongue beginning to walk away from the

camp, keeping parallel to the wall. Nesi and Usa fell in step around her, keeping her nearly surrounded while not impeding her view of the city. She could sense death about this part of the city. While it was to be expected of a place where fighting was happening, it hung heavier than she thought it would.

Efah stopped, concentrating on the feeling. It wasn't that people were just dying. These were sharp deaths, brutal deaths. Something moved about the city. Skulking. Searching for another target. Another…victim.

She paused. Something was hunting. "Nesi. Usa. Call out," she said. Perhaps something that dealt in death so heavily would recognize a kindred spirit. Her hyenas' yips were sharp in the quiet of night, bouncing off the walls in eerie echoes. They waited, then called again and Efah realized they'd caught this force's attention.

She felt them, for there were a number of these death soaked beings approaching. It took a moment for her to see them moving in the dark. They climbed down the wall with ease, landing silently, before cautiously making their way over. Efah clasped her hands over her mouth to stifle her gasp. These creatures stood as tall as the tallest man she'd ever seen. Their teeth and claws caught the distant torchlight like polished metal. Nesi moved closer, rubbing her side against her for strength.

The closest one came within ten strides, regarding them with trepidation. "You smell of death but not blood," it said, head cocking to the side.

Its voice grated on her ears with the high notes of metal on metal hiding within the low tones. She swallowed, fear making her throat dry. She didn't know such horrors existed in the world. "I am the voice of Death," she said summoning her courage. "What are you? Where do you come from?"

The one who spoke regarded her for a moment then bowed, its companions doing the same. "We greet you, voice of Death, and pay all respects to you. We are the guardians of the Ibatu'bangi, sent here by the Batu'bangi, the people of the great forest."

Efah had heard of the people of the forest across the river before but only in stories. She knew they were the source of gold for the land but she never imagined them commanding such monsters. "Why are you here, guardians?"

"To seek revenge for the slaughter of one of the Batu'bangi. To convince the invaders to leave." It laughed, a high scraping sound. "But they are stubborn. They make for great sport."

"You don't attack the Nsongans, do you?" Her question ended a little more fearful than she'd hoped.

The leader cocked his head again. "For now. They have this chance to run these foreigners out of their city. If they cannot succeed then they will be considered in league with them. And the slaughter will expand."

Efah sucked in a breath. "You can't," she said.

"These Nsongans claimed to be allies but they allowed an ally to be killed on their soil and did nothing to make amends. The invaders have them on a leash like beasts. They cannot be trusted fully until they have shaken free of their master."

Their view of the situation was harsh and simple but she could understand. The people of the deep forest felt betrayed and, clearly, the price for betrayal was high amongst their people. She placed her chin in her hand as she thought. "Perhaps we can work together to gain revenge on the invaders for what they have done to both of our peoples?" she offered.

It angled its head the other way, clicking its massive teeth together. "We are listening, voice of Death."

She gestured to Efemu's forces, camped out behind her. "This force has come to cut off their supplies and its leader wants to kill all of the Ega and become the new dara of Nsongo. He wishes to bring the city back to how it used to be, the greatest city of the south and a true ally to the people of the forest. If they can get inside the city, the invaders will have a fight to their front and their back. They can't possibly hold up against that."

The leader studied her. "You wish for us to make a way inside the city for you. Kill the guards at the gate, maybe? That would be easy. We have done it before."

She looked past them to the small gate. It would take Efemu's force forever to push past that entrance. They could only march four at a time. Her eyes roamed over the tops of the wall then trailed down the walls themselves. She looked back to these creatures and their frightening, massive claws. "Do you think you could dig through the walls?"

The creature didn't speak at first. Its companions made small sounds that sounded strangely like the sucking of teeth. "You wish for us to become moles?" Efah didn't miss the disdain lurking in its voice.

"You want the invaders to pay for what they did, right?" She looked around at the creatures. "Help the army gain entrance to this side of the city and they will pay dearly. You will watch as they are slaughtered like cattle and if you wish to still take your own vengeance, the chaos will give you even more of a chance. Then we can restore Nsongo to its proper place and it can be your ally again." The creatures hesitated, clicking and grumbling among themselves. "Don't you want to see the invaders brought to the cold embrace of Death?"

More chatter, then the leader bowed his head. "We will do as you wish, Voice of Death. You will know when it is time for your people to strike."

Efah nodded to them all. "Thank you."

Without a sound, they all turned as one and began their swift entrance back into Nsongo, climbing the high walls as if it were nothing. Efah let out a breath, scratching her hyenas' shoulders. They nuzzled up to her, making tiny yips as if to reassure her.

"That was scary, huh?" Usa laughed and she couldn't help bursting out into giggles as well. Of course they weren't frightened. They were sent here by Death himself. She was sure they could bite those creatures in half. She gave them another affectionate rub and headed back to camp. The commander had to be informed about their new path into the city

Chapter Sixteen

Sept'ha found Hetsaf sitting up in bed, looking over a map when she returned to his bedchamber. "You're supposed to be resting," she said, trying to keep the worry out of her voice.

"I've been thinking," he said. His voice was still scratchy but had lost some of the weakness from when he'd first come to. She was glad that he seemed to be improving but that didn't mean he had to throw off the healer's order for bed rest.

She glanced at the map when she came to the side of the bed. "Did you get that map by yourself?"

He slid his eyes to her for a second and she swore she could see the tiniest bit of guilt. His attention caught on her hands. "What have you been doing?"

Sept'ha brought up her hands for inspection. She found nothing until seeing one last smear of red along the back of her left hand. She thought she'd wiped all of it off. "I was talking with the woman who poisoned you," she said with a shrug. "I found out who sent her."

Hetsaf rolled up the map, giving her his full attention. "Who?"

"The empress Arkole."

Sept'ha expected a burst of anger, incredulity at the least. Hetsaf merely looked down, nodding with a pensive expression. "I didn't think she would ever go this far," he said lowly. "Then I was right." He unrolled the scroll again.

"Did you want something done about this?" she asked, confused by his uncharacteristic calmness. "She tried to kill you."

"I am going to do something about this." A bit of his usual snark crept into his voice, bringing her a little relief. "As I said, I've been thinking. About this whole affair, you and I and our plan. We can't do it with the empresses in the way. I want to send them away." He looked up to her with a conspiratorial smile. "For their own safety."

A bark of a laugh escaped her. "You'll have to drag the empress kicking and screaming out of the palace."

"But not if the lives of her children are threatened."

Sept'ha stared at him, amused. "How can you be sure?"

"If there is one thing that I know, as much as they feared not having a male heir and as much time as she dotes on the

newborn, my brother and his wife love their daughters. If the palace seemed like too much of a danger for them, she would be more than willing to leave it."

The certainty in his voice piqued her interest. She'd never seen him in a true scheming mode. "A poisoning?" She suggested. "It would be like something out of a poem. She finds the same method she tried to use turned on her loved one. But surely, you're not thinking of killing one of the princesses? They're your nieces."

He waved his hand. "Even I don't want to kill children. An attempted assassination would do nicely. Arkole's not smart enough to realize that there's no reason to try to kill her or her daughters. They're inconsequential to everyone but their parents."

Sept'ha nodded, liking the plan. "Did you want to use the Arakgu'un again?"

Hetsaf shook his head, swallowing in pain. Sept'ha retrieved a cup of water from the room's table. He took a few gulps then cleared his throat. "A paid servant would do. Perhaps the one that you won't let me know where she is."

Sept'ha glanced aside without any remorse. "She's going to be too obvious. Too many bruises."

"Then we'll find someone else," he said after a small chuckle.

She stared at him again. "Where in the world has this calm and clarity come from? You're suddenly acting as if we're equal partners."

His gaze dropped, falling on the map but not looking truly at it. "I almost died, Sept'ha. I felt it, the cold abyss of death closing in on me. But you kept me from it. Just when I thought I was going to succumb, I felt your power. I felt Met's power flowing through you, keeping me here, giving me the strength to fight off this poison until the healers could arrive."

He took a breath. "I've…I've never felt a god's power before. I know for sure now that I am supposed to rule the empire." He glanced up at her with slight embarrassment. "With you by my side."

She barely managed to hold in her laugh. Acknowledging that he needed her must have been like pulling teeth. "Of course, with me by your side. I'd love to be your chief adviser. I'd still love to be chancellor."

"That's not what I mean." He took another quick sip of his water. His lips pulled into a tight line as if his next words tasted sour. "If I am going to be emperor, I'm going to need an empress and," he paused, swallowing, "I've chosen you."

Sept'ha gasped so hard she inhaled her own saliva and fell into a coughing fit. She wheezed in her next breaths, trying to get a grip on herself. "What?" she croaked.

"I need a wife," he grumbled, sounding more like an angry boy than the man who kept the empire going. "I don't want to search and I know I can trust you."

She stared. He was serious. It pained him to ask this. He wouldn't even look her in the eyes for more than a second. She swallowed. Marriage. Just the word sent a shiver through her. And to Hetsaf. It sounded like a nightmare. It had been hard enough working with him. To have to be shackled to him…and maybe even do *that* with him. "No. Absolutely not. I'll look for a wife for you."

"I want you." He saw the revulsion on her face and scowled at her. "No, not like that. I'd rather swallow poison. Again."

She regarded him like a pile of dung she had to clean up. "Why on earth would you choose me?"

"You understand me." Every word was a battle. "And we have the same goals in mind. I even accepted that you serve a god after the emperor forbid their worship. I serve that god now." His face twitched in its scowl. "There's no one else I want to be my empress. Please."

The last word sounded like it was torn from his throat. Such a rare and weighty word, that single please. "You've missed a very important fact," she said. "I am a servant. Your servant."

"I'm already usurping the throne. Who cares who my wife is?"

"Choosing wives from noble families would lend you some credibility."

"I don't want wives. One is more than enough."

Sept'ha narrowed her eyes. "What about heirs?"

This time he was the one to shudder. But he quickly recovered, his face settled into resolution. "I can promise you; I would never set myself upon you like my brother did his wives."

A laugh bubbled up from Sept'ha. That was the most awkward phrasing to avoid saying sex that she'd ever heard, a perfect addition to this entire ridiculous conversation. "But I would have to have them," she said, returning to seriousness.

"And you would literally be in charge of guiding the emperor, present and future. Isn't that what you were sent to do?"

Sept'ha's mouth snapped shut. Her mind ran back to her first meeting with Met in her ruined temple. It felt so long ago that she'd been called. She thought that her mission had changed with the emperor, the *current* emperor, so near death. Sept'ha swallowed, a lump in her throat. She was sent here for another emperor entirely.

***

Arkole stifled a yawn as she nursed her son. He was putting on weight little by little and getting hungrier as he did so. The evening breeze wafting in from her room's balcony was warm and inviting and she struggled to stay awake. Her servants waited patiently for the little prince to finish feeding so they could bathe him and put him to bed. Arkole hummed a tune her own mother sang to her as a child, watching him grow sleepy as well. He looked more and more like his father with each passing day.

Her smile faltered. Still no word about Bakari's condition. With their fastest riders her message should have been there by now. Perhaps the message back had been delayed somehow. Perhaps it was still on its way and she would get something in a day or two. But the complete lack of updates remained puzzling. And worrying.

Arkole suppressed another yawn, trying her best to keep her thoughts from her face. "Don't worry, little one," she whispered. "Your father will return to us before you know it. He will be overjoyed to see you. My little Atelmet." She whispered the name like it was a secret between them. It was the name they'd chosen during her second pregnancy but that turned out to be their eldest daughter. It was the name of his great great grandfather and it was time for it to return to use.

She couldn't help the little feeling of relief when he finished and she could turn him over to his nursemaids. She saw him off and then went to her own washroom where her servants waited. The ceramic tub was filled with warm but not quite hot water, just what she needed. Arkole slipped off her dress, handing it off to one of her handmaidens, before stepping in. She shuddered in relief at the change in temperature. The nights were starting to cool off so relaxing in the warm hug of her bath was a welcome end to her day.

She sighed, putting a hand to her forehead. Her entire life was nothing but problems. No one respected her. Her messages weren't being replied to. She was getting no news from the fronts of the empire directly. And that damned Hetsaf had lived. She'd been assured that the poison would be swift and he'd die soon after eating. She didn't know how he'd survived but he did, sending all of her hopes of ruling the empire without interference up in smoke. She had time to put things in place with him taken to his bed but who knew how long that would last? Arkole bathed and let herself be dressed for bed, her mind swirling with troubles.

"My lady," said her most senior handmaid. "Would you like me to bring you something to drink to ease your sleep?"

"Yes, Jahada. A northern wine will do."

Her servant went off immediately while she returned to her sleeping chamber. She sat down heavily on her bed. Poison hadn't worked on the chancellor and she doubted he'd be so careless again. Perhaps she could find an assassin to hire. Perhaps those priests would be willing to do this if she said it was a command from the emperor himself. She was sure she could forge Bakari's signature on a mandate. She had one of his seals.

That alone would make it official. If they were as good as everyone thought they were, taking care of one self-important man would be nothing.

She chuckled to herself as Jahada brought her a cup of the requested wine. Arkole sipped from it, letting the smooth, lightly sweet liquid coat her tongue and throat. She felt the alcohol take its effect after a few sips, her body and mind beginning to relax. "Thank you Jahada. You may put out the lights."

"Of course, empress."

Arkole settled into her bed as her servants scurried around to blow out the many lights of the room. As she closed her eyes, the image of Hetsaf choking and pleading on his knees for her to spare his life formed in her mind's eye. She smiled as it turned into dreams of him dying, horribly, over and over again. The idea of his smug face contorted in unimaginable pain became the best sight of her life, more welcome than seeing her husband return.

She groaned as she registered a sharp noise. A bang? No, something dropped. Someone screamed but it was cut off. Arkole's eyes opened heavily and she blinked a few times before registering the dark shape looming over her. Her attention locked on the slight glint of the person's eyes, catching the hint of light from the moon outside. They moved slightly and she saw the light catch on the blade of a knife. She screamed, hurling herself over the far side of her bed.

Arkole shuffled away from the attacker, half tangled in her bed covers. The person, the assassin, moved slowly around the bed, coming at her knife raised. "For the gods," he croaked and lunged for her.

Arkole shrieked at the top of her lungs, throwing herself aside. She scrambled to her hands and knees trying to get away but the fabric twisted around her tripped her up. She realized she heard a baby's cry and her heart thundered against her chest. No, not her only son. She couldn't let them take another son from her.

She tried to stand but the assassin caught the bed coverings, pulling her back. She tried yanking her feet free, kicking at the assailant in a pitiful attempt to defend herself. He stabbed for her but she rolled to the side to avoid it. She struck out, panicked. Her blow caught the man solidly across the face just as her flailing legs came free of the covers. Arkole got to her feet quicker than she ever had in life and started to run. The assassin reached out, catching her wrist this time. She screamed again as she saw him raise the knife.

Then the sound of footsteps came down the hallway accompanied by the voices of guards calling for her. The assassin faltered, looking toward the entrance. Arkole struggled against his grasp and he let her go. She fell to the floor roughly, her elbow taking the brunt of her weight. She curled in on herself as the pain exploded up her arm.

Guards exploded into the room, swords already in hand. The assassin paused for a moment, then ran towards the balcony. Half of the guards sprinted after him but he jumped over the railing and into the courtyard below. Calls of alarm carried across the space, the palace starting to come alive.

Two guards came to her side, helping her to her feet. Arkole pushed them aside. Her son was crying. She held her arm as she ran to the side room her son lay in. His nursemaid lay on the floor, unconscious. The babe lay crying on the floor, his small bed overturned. Arkole dropped to her knees, cooing to him as she worked to pick him up with only one arm. She cried, half from pain, half from fear.

A servant came into the room, helping her up. Another tried to wake the nursemaid who made unintelligible noises. She looked to one of the guards as she came back to her room. "The princesses. Make sure the princesses are all right," he commanded.

He bowed and rushed off. Arkole held her son tighter, trying to calm her crying long enough to calm him down. They could have been dead. The thought began to sink in fully and her heart wouldn't stop racing. Her son, the future of the empire, could have been killed before he even had a name. Greater measures had to be taken. Her son had to be safe.

***

Hetsaf relished the feel of sitting at his desk, parchment and papers in his hands. The near week it took him to recover from the poisoning had been torture. Sitting in bed, having to rest and be tended to like an invalid or child. He was sure that the physicians would chide him for going back to his office to work but damn them. He had an entire empire to run.

He was pleased to see that Sept'ha had kept things as tidy and orderly as ever in his absence. The items he needed to look over were placed in a neat stack to one side but he was sure she'd already informed him of the subjects. It was… nice having her to help. An assistant made things easier. It was foolish to think that he'd never considered getting one before. She'd cut his work in half, taking care of all the annoying tiny tasks that he hated with a passion. It's a shame she wasn't a man. She'd would have made a fine choice of chancellor when he took the throne.

He paused, swallowing hard. He would marry her, however. The idea still seemed sound. She was the only woman he could stand being around on such a regular basis. Other women would want affection, attention, everything he hadn't to give. Sept'ha understood that this was a partnership, no more. He could deal with that. Maybe even respect it.

His mouth twisted at the thought. He hadn't met a woman yet that commanded respect, not even his mother. Not that he'd known her. The northern princess had seen fit to throw herself off of a balcony when he was two. He couldn't even remember her face. But Sept'ha was unlike any woman he'd ever met. Smart and cunning, but there was that defiant streak that he hated. If any woman came close to getting his respect, it would be her.

She'd saved him from his poisoning, saved his very life. And poisoning by that rat Arkole. Sept'ha deserved much. Even he wasn't so cold hearted to deny her a reward for her service. That's why he'd given her today off and a future as the empress and his right hand. She deserved it.

"Excuse me, Chancellor Hetsaf?" came a meek voice.

He looked up from the first paper he'd started reading to see an unfamiliar servant at his door. "Yes?" he asked curtly. "What is it?"

"The second wife is here to speak with you."

He set the paper down, staring with confusion. "Send her in."

The servant stepped back into the hallway and soon enough, his brother's new second wife entered the room. Hetsaf frowned. He didn't have time for the antics of these women. She walked toward his desk meekly, hands clasped together tightly as if to stop them from fidgeting. She glanced at him then made effort to meet his eyes. "Good day, chancellor. I would like to speak with you."

He raised an eyebrow. "Concerning what?" Perhaps she'd finally come to her senses and parted ways with that fool Arkole.

"I wish to leave the palace."

Hetsaf blinked slowly. "Do you mean leave your position or leave this place?"

Her hands went to wrinkle up her dress but she stopped them. "I'm sure that you know we were attacked the other night. Assassins came in but the guards were able to chase them away. The empress told me that she barely made it. I can't put my children in any more danger. They are princes. They must be safe at all times."

He leaned against his desk, intertwining his fingers in front of him. He couldn't possibly be this lucky. To get one of the wives to leave the palace *voluntarily*? It was too good to be true. His mind went to Sept'ha and her goddess. *His* goddess. Perhaps it was more than luck. "I was informed of the attack the night it happened. Unfortunately, the attempted assassins couldn't be found so they're still out and free. You are right to think of my brother's sons. As princes of the empire, they have to be kept in complete safety and it appears the palace is no longer completely safe."

He paused, feigning deep thought. He went to one of his shelves and selected a scroll listing out the cities where royal palaces had been built. Pretending to study it, he sat back at his desk. He'd had a place chosen for her and her spawn since he'd constructed this plan. It was far enough away that she could be forgotten and close enough to her home city that she'd be satisfied. "Here," he said laying the scroll down and pointing to the city for her to see. "There is a royal abode here that you can take your sons to. I'll send a number of guards with you. You may remain there until the danger has been dealt with and the palace is safe again."

Her eyes widened as she read the name of the city. "This is near the city I where I was born. My family will be overjoyed to see the boys."

"I do have a question," he asked and her happiness dimmed. "Have you spoken to the empress about leaving?"

The young woman frowned. "I did but she was adamant about staying. I asked her to at least send the children away and she said she would consider it." Her voice dropped and he strained to hear her. "I didn't tell her that I was coming to you. I know you don't care for us but you would be the one able to see my sons and myself to a safe spot."

So the girl had some sense. "You were right to come directly to me. I'll see that your way is made as soon as possible." He leaned over the desk. "And if the empress gives you any problems with it, tell her to speak with me."

She nodded, quickly. "Thank you. I will make sure we are packed and ready to leave immediately."

She walked out, leaving Hetsaf to marvel at the way his plan was falling into place. One game piece was out of the way. Now, he just had to get that stubborn Arkole to leave and everything would be set. He tapped his finger on his desk. If getting the second wife out was so easy, he knew he could find a way for the first. He chuckled to himself. Praise be to Met.

Chapter Seventeen

Tekhamun dreamed of better days. Of a time when everywhere he walked people regarded him with respect and they were fervent followers of the gods. Those who wished to lord over the less fortunate had been cut down and made public examples of, their stories used as cautionary tales for children. The tale of his exploits, of how he saved the empire from heretic ways, was told the most and spread farther and farther across the land. He lived in the warm favor Gu'un every single day.

But something was pulling him away from such blessed peace.

He groaned quietly, blinking against the shock of light when he opened his eyes. It took a moment for him to remember where he was. A few more blinks and his room came into view, Moon resting on the small bed beside him. One of his hands rested on her breast and he put his head back down to bury his face into the back of her neck. A sound came from outside and he gave Moon a squeeze, pulling himself closer to her, refusing to wake up from such a wonderful dream.

Another moment and he realized someone called for him. Tekhamun's mind jerked awake. He climbed over Moon as quickly and gently as he could, not wanting to wake her. Perhaps if he took care of this quickly enough, he could return to lay beside her for a little longer. Perhaps, they could do other things too.

He threw on his robes, wishing he could wash first, and hurried downstairs. He met Nurmet at the bottom of the stairs, an unusual focus on his normally cloudy face. "Master, we have a problem."

Alarm made Tekhamun's heart skip a beat. "What sort of problem?" he asked.

Nurmet motioned for him to follow and he hurried to keep up with the man's long strides. "I think we may be running out of food. When I realized no one was keeping up with our stores, I decided to look into it. We still have a lot but it won't last forever."

Tekhamun ground his back teeth together, grimacing. "Is it truly that dire? Surely we can feed everyone for a little bit longer?"

They reached one of the merchant storehouses, Nurmet holding the door open for him. It was dark inside with only a few heavily latticed windows. He swore he heard more than one thing scurry away from them in the gloom. Nurmet took the waiting lamp from the wall, lighting it with its nearby flint. The wick at the top of the small clay pot caught flame easily, giving them a better view of the room. Tekhamun took in all of the contents, frowning. There were plenty of large, sealed containers of food and the sacks of grains were plenty but quite a few spilled their contents on the floor as if they'd been opened hastily. Such spills had surely attracted vermin. He would have to get a cat for the room.

"Have people been coming in and out of here as they please?" he asked, looking at the mess to be cleaned up.

"Yes, master." Nurmet hesitated for a moment. "You didn't see that anyone was in charge to make sure that wouldn't happen."

Tekhamun felt injured. He thought that people would have been honest enough to take no more than their share. But, it appeared, even amongst the faithful there were those who couldn't resist their greed and selfishness. "I will have Moon see to it." He looked around again. "But it seems as if we still have more than enough. Do not worry when there's no reason to." He put a hand on Nurmet's thick shoulder, trying to look cheerful.

Nurmet's face went blank. "Master, we haven't had any merchants or farmers come in with their stock. This food can't stay good forever. And we had even more people arrive at the gate this morning."

"How many?" the priest asked, suddenly eager. More people drawn to his cause. This was time to celebrate.

"Twenty-five."

"That's wonderful. Don't you see, Nurmet? The news of our

cause grows. More people are turning from the netkoleh's evil ways. We should greet them." He turned to exit the storeroom, but Nurmet put a hand on his shoulder.

"Master, more people mean the food has to be split up even more. People get…mean when they don't have enough to eat." He took a step to be in Tekhamun's full view. "We have to get more."

The priest bristled at being told what to do. Karatel thought he could tell him what to do and he betrayed him in the end. "Fine then," he spat out. "We will have to take more of the city. We'll gather our best fighters and attack tonight. Whatever the rest of the nobles of the city have will be ours."

He took to the street, heading back towards the home he'd made his own. Perhaps Moon wasn't awake just yet and he could slip back into bed. Nurmet caught up to him in no time. "Master," starting in a tone Tekhamun wasn't sure if he liked, "many of our best fighters were killed in the last conflict. I'm more than happy to kill more nobles but we need more people."

"Then get more," he snapped loudly. The few people around him looked up, surprised at his tone. "Find people. Make them fight. If they won't listen to you then I'll get them."

Nurmet's face went slack with surprise. "If that is your will, master."

"Master!" came Moon's hoarse shout.

Tekhamun's eyes shot to her at the panic in her voice. She ran, sandals slapping the bricks of the road. "What is it?" he asked, alarm returning.

"Narjet and Mjobe are gone," she gasped. "I went to check in on them and all of their things were gone." Her bad eye teared up and she wiped it away. "Half of our weapons are gone too. I wish I could say that they didn't steal them, but it was something we would have done easily before."

All of Tekhamun's breath left him. He gripped his chest, mind reeling at the news. First Karatel and his blasphemy, now Narjet and Mjobe with their abandonment. He forced a breath into his lungs. No, no, no. This couldn't be happening. All of his most fervent followers had left him. Just like his family. Just like those dirty, heathen townspeople back home. He would not be betrayed again.

He looked up to her. "Moon," he said with a smile. "Sweet, faithful Moon, you and Nurmet are all I have left." Tekhamun took a moment to compose himself, running his hands over his coarse curls. Gu'un would guide him, would guide them. He, as the blade of his god, would lead these people to the right path if they chose it or not.

"Nurmet, get people rounded up. As many as you think we need to attack the rest of the city and bring them to the main square for training. Moon, gather weapons and bring them to the square as well. If these people want to be a part of our holy cause, then they will have to earn it."

***

The main square was full of the sounds of training, of people shouting and calling out after getting struck and of Tekhamun's meticulous instructions. He stalked the square, watching, hands behind his back like his own master, looking for any mistakes. And there were many.

This group had been roused from their sleep early this morning and shocked to find out that they were going to be part of a hastily assembled warrior group this very evening. They'd only been permitted a hearty breakfast before being herded to today's task. On the other side of the square, Nurmet showed a group of young men the basics of fighting with knives. At another side, Moon assigned weapons to a group that Tekhamun had determined were ready for such. He truly wished they had better armaments to give out but it appeared those traitorous bastards had stolen the best of the weapons in their desertion.

He calmed his anger. He couldn't let this bring him to complete unbridled rage. But if he ever saw Mgobe and Narjet again, they would pay dearly for their sins. He would bleed them until they confessed every unholy act they'd ever committed and cried out to the gods for forgiveness. He smiled in malicious glee at the thought. They would learn to fear the gods and him before he sent them to the other side of life.

"Master Tekhamun," a follower said meekly.

He snapped out of his reverie, pulling the smile from his face.

He looked to the group he was near. They all stared at him, concerned. "Go through the form again," he said firmly. "We must be ready for tonight."

"Yes, master," several of them said in unison.

He moved on, looking over the next group when a scene caught his attention. Hamena stood at a street corner speaking with three men. He hadn't seen them before, not even casually, so they had to be part of the newcomers. They talked familiarly but when she looked directly at him, she seemed caught and turned away. Tekhamun frowned and began making his way over there. It heightened his suspicions when the men moved away as a group once he made it halfway.

Hamena finally turned her full attention to him with a pretty smile. "Master Tekhamun," she said happily. "Good morning. Your training seems to be going well."

"Who were those men?" he asked. She startled and he was surprised at his sharp tone as well.

"They are some of the new people who arrived this morning. I was just explaining how things worked here. They were very curious about the fighting. I told them they could join in but they didn't want to for now."

"And what are you doing today?"

She stammered for an answer, blinking rapidly. "I'm making myself useful where I can. I always want to be useful to you." Her last statement had turned sultry, her smile recovering.

He scowled at her. She was nothing more than a temptress, taking advantage of him and his weakness. Trying to worm her way into getting his favor. "Moon will be seeing to the distribution of food. You will help her."

"But master," she began, a tiny pout forming.

"You will do it. I am your leader and you will do it." He hadn't realized that he'd shouted until the echo of his own voice reached his ears. He glanced over his shoulder and several people stared. Tekhamun shot a full scowl at them sending everyone back to their training.

Hamena stood before him, stunned. She gave him a nod, lips pursed. "As you wish, master."

He watched her go, trying to cool his anger. Why wouldn't

people just obey? He turned around to find Moon standing in front of him. She looked him over, concern in her eye. "Master, perhaps you should take a moment to rest," she said quietly.

He looked about at the raggedy group of fighters he'd put together. "No, no," he said absently. "We have to be in the best shape we can be for tonight." He walked off and continued forcing his students to be better.

The sky was just starting to darken when he released them for the evening meal. There were grumbles and side eyes as he passed but he didn't care. Training was hard. It was uncomfortable, but the results were worth it. Moon brought him a light dinner and he ate with the rest of the group. He didn't care if they disliked him now. They would understand the reasons for his harshness in time and tonight they would see the fruits of their labor.

As the sun set and the city was plunged into darkness, Tekhamun returned to his home, washed up and changed. He took a moment to pray before returning to the square. He prayed for tonight's attack to go well, but he also prayed for the increase in faith in his followers. They would need it.

All eyes were on him when he returned to the square. There were those who hadn't left but many had taken this opportunity to rest and wash as well. They trailed in and he was glad to see they hadn't abandoned the mission. He was also glad to see a few familiar faces coming up to join the attack, people who had fought in their last battle with the army and made it out alive. They would be vital. They waited a little longer for people to show up and then, with a gesture of his hook sword, he led them toward the unoccupied city.

All was quiet as they left their part of town, the buildings closest to them obviously left empty in fear of the uprising. He sent a few people inside but there was nothing of value that they could use. Everything had been stripped clean. Frustrated, Tekhamun pressed on. He knew people still lived in this city. He could hear them at times, shouting and still going about their lives. Enjoying the ill-gotten gains of their greed while others suffered. They would pay.

He stopped the group when he smelled fowl roasting. He

looked down a street and could make out the faint lights coming from several homes. The sounds of chatter drifted to him and while he couldn't make out conversations, he definitely heard the merriment in them. Tekhamun's face pulled into a deep lined frown. There was the excess. There were the people living fat and happy as sacrificial pigs while their lessers suffered and toiled. He took out his sickle knife, heading into the street. Sacrificial pigs indeed.

He turned to his group once they were in the midst of the residential area. "No mercy for heretics," he said, only loud enough for them to hear. He motioned for his people to take to different houses and they did so without question. There were looks of hesitation and he made sure to remember the faces of those who didn't hold absolute faith in their mission. He couldn't tolerate waverers anymore.

Tekhamun entered a house, skulking along until he encountered the occupants. They were around a long table on the second floor roof, eating and talking about the state of things while two servants scrambled to fulfill their needs. No one even noticed him until he was behind what must have been the eldest son. The wife screamed the moment his knife slid across the son's throat. Blood sprayed across the table, inciting more screams. Tekhamun couldn't help a macabre grin as he hurried to execute the rest of the family. They shrieked and squealed their horror as he sent them to the judgment of the gods. The father didn't even beg for mercy. He knelt on the floor, looking on at the bodies of his slain wife and children.

Tekhamun grabbed the man by his hair, forcing his head back so he had no choice but to look him in the eyes. "In the name of Gu'un, I condemn you and your family to death for your decadence and irreverence to the gods." The man's protest was silenced as his throat was cut and Tekhamun left him to bleed on the floor.

The two servants huddled by the small rooftop kitchen. He aimed his knife at them. "You may join us. Become fervent worshipers of the gods again and reject the netkoleh's heresy or join your masters in death."

One of the women sunk to her knees. "I have always been a

faithful follower of the gods. I never went along with the heresy in my heart." The other woman looked to her, then at him, and slowly sunk to her knees as well. She nodded, tears in her eyes.

Satisfied, he motioned for them to follow him and they left the house. He could hear other screams from other houses. A couple ran out from the home across the street. He intercepted them, slicing on of the men across the stomach. When the other turned in horror, Tekhamun finished him off with two well placed attacks. The man on the ground had his throat slit a moment after.

The priest of Gu'un looked around, noting the homes he'd sent people in. Some of his followers were already coming out, ready to head to their next targets. Yet one of the homes was silent. Tekhamun walked to it, fearful that his people had lost their nerve or, worse yet, been killed. He stepped inside, eyes adjusting to the lamplight just in time to see one of his followers getting his throat cut open.

It was such a casual move as if the attacker was savoring the severing of every bit of flesh. It took Tekhamun a moment more to register that this man carried a knife just like his own. His eyes shot up to the man's face and in the lamplight, he recognized one of the newcomers. They stared at him with mild curiosity, dropping the dying man on the floor. With a flick of the wrist, they flung the blood from their knife on the floor, taking unhurried steps toward him.

Tekhamun backed out of the house, glancing about for his other followers. The screams had ceased, leaving him alone in the quiet night. He exchanged his knife for his twin swords. More of his brothers in the order were here, obviously sent by the wretched netkoleh to squash his rebellion. He took his fighting stance. He wouldn't let them stop his holy cause. Gu'un was on his side.

The other Arakgu'un took his time coming outside, languidly stepping over the threshold. He took out another knife, twirling the curved blade in his hand. Tekhamun glanced around again. None of his followers were coming back into the street. His heart began to race. A door opened and his attention shot to it. Two figures came out but it wasn't any of his people. It wasn't even Nurmet. The curved blades they carried were black with blood in the dark of night.

This was all wrong. They were blessed of Gu'un. His god wouldn't let his true follower fall so easily. He backed up, swords at the ready, to keep all of these false priests in sight. "You would follow that heretic, the netkoleh?" he snarled at them.

The three men paused. One of them shook his head. "To think we've come all this way for some country zealot."

The man who he'd seen kill his follower shrugged. "It's a shame that it's one of our own but our mission is clear. Deal with him and his followers."

"Can't wait to get back to the capital," the last man grumbled.

Tekhamun strengthened his stance as they began approaching. They had been sent from the viper's nest itself to try and destroy his rebellion. He was the last true priest of Gu'un left in this land. He took in their weapons, shiny and extremely well made. He'd never even met a priest from the capital before. What if they were better fighters than he was? He shook away the doubt. Gu'un was with him. He repeated the phrase in his head until his fear was manageable. He couldn't let them destroy this; all he'd built. He couldn't let them kill any more of his followers. They couldn't kill Moon.

The fear came back. It must have shown on his face because the first man smiled cruelly at him. He took a step back in spite of himself. Then the fight began.

The first attacker raced toward him and began a punishing array of slices. Tekhamun could barely keep his larger and less agile swords in place to block the attacks. He found himself quickly treading back. As the fight moved, he saw that the other two members hadn't even moved from their places. They didn't consider him a threat in the slightest. Tekhamun's back foot slid, hitting a wall. He had nowhere left to retreat and his attacker smiled smugly.

A needle of panic pierced him. He couldn't die here. He couldn't let them kill Moon and his other followers. He prayed to Gu'un for strength and did his best to fight back. He launched heavy blows back at the other priest, surprising him and setting him on the defensive. His wild, hard attacks left him open for quick jabs and he received cuts along his arms in return. The injuries burned fiercely but he wouldn't be deterred. He kept swinging, finally making contact with the man's forearm. His blade cut deep, making the other priest drop his blade and dance back away from Tekhamun.

Tekhamun didn't pursue him, holding his ground. His breath came raggedly, his swords starting to feel heavy in his injured arms. The other Arakgu'un looked to their freely bleeding comrade who stared daggers at Tekhamun. The man clutched his arm and nodded his head toward him. The other two priests took out their weapons, making their way carefully his way.

Tekhamun couldn't catch his breath. His heart threw itself against his rib cage with each beat. Fear ran cold through his body. He couldn't beat them. He'd barely fought off one, now two were approaching and they were ready to kill him cruelly by the look in their eyes. He felt himself about to dry heave from the terror of the moment. If he died right here, his movement was over. They would kill all of his followers and there would be no one to fight against the netkoleh's evil decree.

He turned and ran. The surprised shouts of his enemies sounded behind him. He put his swords up, putting all of his strength into his escape. He had to escape. Gu'un had chosen him. If he died the cause died. If he died, Moon died. The thought made something crack within him.

He burst into his makeshift home, gulping in a breath. "Moon," he shouted.

She came out of her room at the far side of the first floor nearly immediately. She gasped as the light from her room flooded the hall and rushed over. "Master, are you all right? You're bleeding."

"We have to go. We have to go now."

She nodded and hurried to put on her shoes. Without a word, they hurried to the back of the house, slipping through a servants' entrance into the street. He grabbed her hand, leading her through the darkest streets toward the main gate of the city. His chest burned from the running; his heart strained from fear.

They crept through the shadows at the edge of the main wall as they neared the gate. His gaze darted in every direction looking out for the men he knew were surely on their trail. Seeing no one around, he clutched her hand tighter and made a run for the gate. They took to the road, letting the light of the moon guide them, Tekhamun praying for forgiveness for the people they'd just abandoned.

Chapter Eighteen

Umakaal smoothed out a few errant wrinkles in her tunic. The meeting with Asfara's governor was now and she had to look perfect. It was her first diplomatic mission after all. She couldn't let her brother or the kingdom down. She turned to Ladawi and Mikhra. "How do I look?"

He studied her from his seat on her plush bed. Ladawi looked her over then straightened her gold medallion belt. She stepped back then looked to Mikhra for his opinion. He rose, walking around her, chin in hand. "You need something."

Umakaal rolled her eyes playfully. "What do you know of how a warrior princess should dress?"

"I was a throwaway prince. I know of clothing. My mother kept me in the best fashions like the prize horse at market." He snapped his fingers, untied his knife belt from his waist, tying it around hers. She tried her best to lean away from him. He smelled of oranges and honey. Did he bring his own soap? "Your ancestor, the great queen Henateer, wore her sword everywhere she went, even to bed." She raised an eyebrow. He caught her expression and shrugged. "When you would not talk to me, I did some reading."

Umakaal snorted, adjusting the knife until its weight felt natural. "Well, what about now?"

Her lover and her fiancée both nodded. "You look like a true representative of the throne," Ladawi said with a smile that melted Umakaal's heart.

"Thank you, love." She grinned roguishly at them both. "Wish me luck."

She took a quick breath and left the room before she could hesitate more. Guards waited for her outside, escorting her down the proper hallways. These halls had no windows and were lit by the same eerie green torches Yutuuan had mentioned from his first trip to Asfara. The palace was half built into the cliffs of the city, a fortress of stone that deterred attackers. The long hallways were a maze and Umakaal found them stifling and dizzying. She didn't understand how people could be fine living underground like an ant. She needed the sun and the smell of the sea wafting through her window.

The guards opened the door to the meeting room. She entered, giving them a nod of thanks. It was a long room with one window that let in the light of the late afternoon. An equally long table, obviously meant for many guests, sat in the middle of the room with refreshments gathered to one end. At that end stood the governor of Asfara, hands behind his back as if he'd been patiently waiting.

He wasn't as old as she'd expected. His curly hair only had white at his temples and his face bore far fewer lines than her father had. He looked to be only in his fifties and she found it odd that her brother's future father-in-law was so young. But her father had been much older when she was born so she guessed this was probably normal. He wore a long tunic, belted at the waist with a thin silver colored braided belt. On his wrists were golden cuffs decorated with purple jewels. Governor Bergarmen may not have been a large man or a well-muscled one, but he had the air of a man with authority.

"Princess, I'm so glad that we could go ahead and have this meeting," he said in smooth tones. He gestured to the refreshments on the table. "Please, sit, and we can discuss the matter that your brother seems to find so urgent."

Bergarmen sat at the head of the table, as it was his house, and she took one to his right. After the governor poured them drinks, she took a small sip, smiling. The wine was exceptionally good. "I've never tasted wine like this," she said, surprised.

"It's an Asfaran specialty. We do have to save something for ourselves," he said, chuckling. "I can send a couple of jars back with you if you'd like."

"That would be wonderful." She schooled her delight and set her glass down. It was time for her to do her job. "Governor Bergarmen," she said, trying her best to mimic her mother's firm tones, "as I'm sure you know by now, the empire has attacked Wiluru in earnest, breaching the gates for the first time in many centuries. You made a pact with my brother to lend the full might of Asfara in exchange for marrying your daughter. He has kept his part of the bargain. Now, he wishes to know why you haven't."

The governor considered her for a moment, drink in hand. He placed it down, interlacing his fingers before him. "Princess," he began in a tone that exuded patience, "I fully understand the agreement your brother and I made. However, amassing a force such as ours takes time. We provide the second largest fleet, the second largest contingent of magicians, and nearly a third of the sailors for the navy. We've sent messages out for the fleet to return but, as I said before, it takes time. Your brother will have his reinforcements as soon as possible."

He gave her a kind smile. "We also need to make sure that we keep the city safe. As the western most hold of the kingdom, we must be prepared in case the empire attempts to launch an attack by sea."

Umakaal felt her patience crack. She knew the tone of someone who didn't want to be bothered. He spoke to her like a parent dealing with an annoying child. The insult to her intelligence stung. "Governor, I am aware of the might of Asfara and all it has to offer. But I'm not so foolish to truly consider the Ega an oceanic threat. All of their might lie in their army, which is at our doors, may I remind you. They don't even have warships. Any attack they may mount would have to be in commandeered fishing or merchant vessels and I fully believe Asfara can defend against that even without the full might of its fleet." She tilted her head, this time being the patient one.

"Well then, it seems you've given this great thought," he said, swirling his drink around in his cup absently. "I can sacrifice half of the rest of the fleet for the effort."

"Two-thirds," she countered.

He chuckled. "Very well, princess. Two-thirds. I'll have that done very soon."

She was growing tired of his condescending nature. "You know, it doesn't sound like you're in much of a hurry to obey your king," she said tersely.

This time he looked at her directly but that patronizing smile hadn't left. "I will be happy to obey my new king. I look forward to the day that he becomes it. My daughter will be his queen after all. Now, I understand your eagerness to add to the warriors at the battle, but my fleet will be gathered in time."

Her jaw clenched and she had to make herself relax it. "Governor, I have studied the ways of running a kingdom just as my brother has, including running the navy. In time is not an answer. What is your timetable? I need to know specifics when I return to report to my brother."

"As soon as I can figure that out, I will send word."

Umakaal closed her eyes for a moment, trying to hold back her temper. Her brother sent her here to be diplomatic. They needed these warriors and magicians. However, they had Djelebe assisting them magically now. And if Asfara wanted to act like a rebellious city then she would treat them like one. She released the reins on her anger.

"Governor Bergarmen," she snapped. "The accord between you and my brother was made months ago, plenty of time for you to gather the bulk of your fleet. You must think I'm a complete fool. If you don't think I see through you dragging your feet to get what you want with the least cost to you, you are the fool. I understand the chip on Asfara's shoulder toward Wiluru. I understand that your ruling class still holds threads of animosity toward the throne that conquered you.

"But these are not the old days. You are part of the Wiluruan kingdom now. You have a duty to obey the throne and you are behaving like you are separate from it." She sat back in her seat, a deadly calm coming over her. "If you want to behave like you are not part of the kingdom, that's fine. We'll treat you like you're not part of the kingdom. With everything that comes with it. We will treat you like the rebellious city that you are. You will have no trade with us. *I* will be in charge of the kingdom's fleet and *I* will see that you are cut off from the shipping routes. You will be on your own. Is that what you want for your people?"

Bergarmen frowned, seeming to finally take her seriously. "You don't have the authority to make such threats."

"When my brother sent me in his place he sent me with the full authority of the throne. Every word I speak carries the weight of it. And I don't make threats. I promise you that if you don't perform your half of the bargain immediately, Asfara will be a pariah."

"Your brother wouldn't agree to such harsh measures."

Umakaal barked out a laugh. "You don't understand the trust my brother has in me. I was sent on this mission because he wanted you to understand the weight of his displeasure, of our displeasure as the future king and the future naval commander. You should realize who you're dealing with."

The governor was quiet for a moment then gave a single nod. "Very well, Princess Umakaal. I will see that members of the fleet arrive with you in Wiluru and the rest arrive shortly after."

"Thank you. You've made a wise decision." She paused, waiting to bring up her last demand. "I also look forward to seeing what you and your forces can do with this dragon's blood of yours."

His face dropped. "Who told you of that?"

"So you've been keeping secrets as well."

He took a deep breath, eyes smoldering. "Asfara has kept this a secret for ages. Who told you of it?"

"Someone very knowledgeable about the old days." She took a casual sip of her wine. It tasted even sweeter. "What does it do?"

"It burns," he said. "It is a liquid that bubbles up in the deepest parts of inner Asfara. It burns hotter than any other fire ever produced. In its purest form, it can only be extinguished by magic. We dilute it to produce the inakrafire that lights the palace and warms the rooms." His lips pulled into a thin line. "I will see that some is transported for the attack. But that is the last concession I'll make."

"That's perfectly fine. I appreciate it." She pushed away from the table, standing and giving a nod to the governor. "I'll be leaving the morning after the next. I'm glad we could come to an agreement so quickly." She turned and began walking out.

"Your brother should have sent you the first time," he said, a reluctant humor in his voice. "You have far more fire in your spine. He came to me like a begging prince. You handle yourself like a queen."

Umakaal paused, the compliment sitting uneasy on her shoulders. She nodded, uneasy, and left the room.

***

Umakaal returned to her guest room, head swimming with pride. She'd done it. Her first diplomatic mission and she'd done it. They'd gotten everything they wanted, even the dragon's blood. She had no idea Asfara was holding such a valuable weapon to themselves. If they'd had that at the beginning of aggression this fight could have been over ages ago. They might have won by now and people wouldn't have gotten hurt. Asfara had been playing games while warriors were dying. She smiled, smugly. Well, they'd lost this game.

She entered her rooms, eager to tell Ladawi what had happened. Grinning brightly, she pushed open the bedroom door and froze at the sight of Ladawi and Mikhra sitting on the bed. Nude. Kissing passionately. Her heart beat an odd, painful rhythm at the sight of their hands roaming over each other's bodies. She'd never seen a naked man before. She'd only ever seen Ladawi nude. But her eyes took him in, his lean muscled body, his beautiful face with its long eyelashes. She watched his fingers cup Ladawi's rear and part of her wanted to get angry but couldn't muster the feeling. Instead, a heat rose up her neck to her cheeks.

"What is going on here?" she asked, closing the door behind her. She tried to sound insulted but her voice cracked. They startled, looking over surprised at her. Surprised but not ashamed.

Ladawi gave her a sheepish grin. "Well, you weren't using him," she said in that playful tone Umakaal loved.

"You don't like men," she protested.

"I never said that," Ladawi said, holding up a finger pointedly. "You assumed I didn't like men."

Umakaal looked to Mikhra, sitting on her bed—*her bed!* — and her eyes began to trail down his flat stomach to his- She jerked her gaze up. Her lover and fiancée glanced to each other and Ladawi smiled, getting up from the bed. "My love," she began, walking seductively toward her, "why don't you join us?"

"What?" the princess squeaked.

Ladawi took her hand, intertwining their fingers. "Why don't you join us?"

She leaned up and kissed Umakaal deeply and the heated feeling grew. She closed her eyes, sinking into the sensation, and when she opened them Mikhra was standing beside her. Umakaal was acutely aware of his scent, that mix of oranges, honey, and something unknown that marked him as foreign and alluring. He stepped closer, Ladawi moving aside to give him room. Umakaal was caught in his eyes. She hadn't realized what a beautiful shade of brown they were. He gently cupped her cheek, tipped her chin up, and kissed her.

His lips were full and soft like Ladawi's. They gently pressed against hers before moving sensually, coaxing her into reciprocating. He pulled back after a moment, still a breath away from her. "I have found myself pulled to you from the moment I saw you."

Ladawi turned her chin back to her, kissing her again. Mikhra kissed her neck, the touch igniting a fire within her. Then they pulled her toward the bed and she didn't resist. She was freed from her clothing, piece by piece. More kisses found her now exposed skin before trailing back to her lips. Umakaal tingled with desire. Hands moved in light caresses across her body, cupping her breasts and finding her most intimate areas. She didn't know who caused what sensation. She was caught between them and drowning in her own pleasure.

Ladawi laid down at the edge of the bed, pulling her to crouch on top. Umakaal leaned down to kiss her, her lips pressing hungrily against her lover. She moaned in ecstasy as Mikhra's tongue licked up her spine. He ended with a wanton bite on her neck. She could feel him against her, hard and insistent. Ladawi's fingers reached between her legs, teasing her, and he entered.

They were a tangle of mouths, hands, and bodies, finding pleasure in each other. Umakaal couldn't think. She could only react to what was being done to her and try her best to reciprocate. All she could hear were their mingled moans and grunts and, finally, cries of completion. She reached hers violently, biting her lip hard and tasting her own blood. Ladawi arched under her as she came to ecstasy, rubbing their bodies together. Umakaal rode the waves of pleasure coursing through her until Mikhra grabbed onto her hips, giving one last thrust.

They stayed entangled for what seemed like an eternity to the princess before finally pulling away from each other and collapsing, spent, onto the bed. Umakaal curled on her side, turned toward Ladawi. Her lover gave her a languid, satisfied smile before moving closer to give her one last kiss. "Was that not amazing?" Ladawi whispered.

Before she could answer, she felt Mikhra slip his arm around her waist. The heat of his body pressed against her back and he brushed his lips against her neck again. The sensation sent a tingle through her body, causing her lust to rise again. She put her hand over Mikhra's and moved her other arm so she could caress Ladawi's face. She took in the moment, pressed between the affections of her *two* lovers. She swallowed and nodded to answer Ladawi's question. It was amazing. If this was going to be her life after marriage, she could get used to it.

***

When Yutuuan returned to the commandeered headquarters for a well needed rest, one of the vice captains cornered him immediately. He passed a message to him. "My prince, this arrived just a few minutes ago." Yutuuan opened it and smiled as he read. Umakaal had succeeded in her mission to Asfara. She'd be arriving with the forces in just a few days. The commander hesitated. "Also, the queen is here to speak with you. She's waiting in your room."

Yutuuan glanced back at Naret, who was on his heels, with a grimace. Naret's only show of emotion was the slightest raise of his eyebrows. "Thank you," he said to the man and proceeded to head upstairs.

His bodyguard whispered, "Good luck," before finding something to occupy himself with on the main floor.

The prince took a breath and jogged up the stairs. Another

breath and he pushed open the door to find his mother sitting demurely at the table in the room. Her hair still haloed her head in a soft gray cloud and it seemed the lines in her face had grown in number since the last time he'd seen her. Her gown was still the color of storm clouds but while she was obviously still observing her mourning period, her face was hard.

"Mother," he said, crossing the room to embrace her. "What had brought you to the battle front?"

"I have kept this secret for the last day but I wanted to tell you myself." She took a deep breath and Yutuuan prepared himself for the grave news she must be bringing. "The emperor is dead."

It took a moment for her words to sink in. "What?"

"He was found dead shortly after your sister visited him. She is out of control, Yutu."

He slumped into the chair opposite her. The emperor, dead. Their possible bargaining chip was gone. He shook his head. "Surely, he succumbed to his injury. She couldn't have killed him. She's a priestess of Yutuu. It's not in her nature."

His mother looked away, sadly. "I think we have underestimated the hurt and pain that she's gone through. She's not the daughter I remember. How can she be after we had to send her off to the heart of that terrible place?" They sat in silence for a moment, his mother wringing her hands together and he shaking his head every few moments.

His sister, a killer. He couldn't believe it. No, he refused to believe it. "I'll talk to her. There must be some other explanation."

His mother's face pinched, painfully. "There is something else. I think…" She took a breath. "I think she's trying to take your crown."

"Mother, please."

"She called the council together to decide the fate of the emperor. I wouldn't have even known if a servant hadn't rushed to inform me." Her face morphed from sorrow to anger. "She made it seem like she'd already spoken to you."

"She did, but I hadn't made a firm decision."

His mother reached out, putting her hand on her son's. "She's trying to take the throne."

He breathed out, exasperated. "You sound like Umakaal now."

"What do you mean?" his mother asked.

"She said that one night she saw Izri sit on the throne. Tried to warn me about her."

"It seems the youngest has proved to be the wisest among us," his mother said lowly, looking off. "I wish I had known. It would have put so much in perspective."

Yutuuan thought of all of the interactions he'd had with his older sister lately. How obstinate she'd been to the point of being disobedient to him, the man who'd be her king. "I'll…I'll talk to her."

"Yutu, you may have to see that she's put away," his mother said, pain lurking in the back of her voice. "Perhaps sent somewhere else, somewhere far from the throne. It's clear she has too much influence here."

He swallowed, not wanting to think of it. Izriamat was his sister. She'd told him stories and played soldier with him when she wasn't training for the temple. He loved her. How could he send her away? "I'll make sure she's not a problem, mother."

"Good." She rose from her seat, coming over to hug him tightly. "A ruler must make hard decisions, my son. Sometimes even those that hurt our family if it's best for our people."

Like how you and father sent her away the first time. "Yes, mother." He hugged her back and led her to the door of the building. He quickly assigned two warriors to join her guards in taking her back to the palace. Once she was gone, he had a runner go and fetch his sister.

Naret looked up from where he ate a quick meal, raising his chin in an unspoken question. Yutuuan shook his head and waved the man off. He couldn't speak right now. He retreated to his room, pacing while he waited for his sister. Izriamat had killed the emperor. Once again, she'd ruined their carefully laid plans in her quest for revenge. He felt for her. She'd suffered through being married to that beast for seven years, even had to endure bearing his spawn. But surely there was enough of the sister he remembered left to reason with. There had to be.

After some time, there was a polite knock at his door. "Enter," he commanded.

The door was opened by Naret and Izriamat entered. She wore that same content look she always had now. He was beginning to hate it. "Brother," she said with the smallest smile.

He gave Naret a sharp nod and his bodyguard left the room. He knew the man would stand guard outside and prevent anyone from bothering him right now. It was for the best. No one could know what they were about to talk of until it was time. "Mother told me that the emperor was found dead soon after you visited him."

He watched her face but it didn't change. Not even the faintest betrayal of guilt or shame. "Yes, I killed him. There's no need to deny it."

"How could . . ." He stopped, lowering his voice. "Why would you do that? We talked about this Izri. We were going to decide this together."

"It was my right," she said firmly. "No one has suffered more at his hand—at the hand of the empire—than me. I deserved to see him take his last breaths and I did. He fought for his life with no more strength than a babe."

Yutuuan paused. "I thought he wasn't conscious."

Izriamat blinked slowly and the coldness in her eyes sent a shiver down his spine. "I healed him enough that he woke up."

He stared in shock at his sister. Never, in all his days, had he expected such cruelty from her. To heal a man just so he could know that he was being murdered. "This kind of vengefulness isn't you. Is this what you think Yutuu wants you to do?"

"If it is by my hand then it is the will of Yutuu."

"Is it also the will of Yutuu that you hold secret council meetings?"

Once again, her face remained impassive. She took a breath, releasing it slowly. "Is that what this is really about? You and mother feel your power is threatened so you must chastise me? Yes, I called a council meeting. You have yet to do so and someone had to inform them of the emperor's pending arrival."

"I don't like you implying that I'm neglecting my duties," he said slowly. It was he who felt a pang of guilt. He hadn't paid even the barest attention to the council. But how was he supposed to? There was a war going on. The force was his to control. Once he could conclude this, then he would be able to draw full attention to his duties as ruler. "I have a war to tend to," he concluded.

"I'm very aware," she said. "This is your element, brother. Perhaps you should stay in it."

Her comment needled him. He would get to the governing side of his responsibilities when the time was right. Did no one understand that he couldn't do both? "Sister, I'm going to give you one last chance to do your duty to the throne by resuming your place as the next high priest. Uncle Munabis isn't going to be with us much longer. I need you there. Please."

"I will be wherever Yutuu needs me to be," she said, colder than an errant northern storm.

His heart tore at her stubbornness. It hurt him to have to command her. He hated making people do what they didn't want to do. "If you don't return and stay at the temple, I'll have to make sure you stay. Please don't make me do that." He looked down at his older sister searching for any of the familial love he'd seen in her before. There was none.

"Do what you feel you must, Yutuuan, and I will do what needs to be done. We are finished here." She turned on her heel and headed for the door.

"Izri," he called after her. "Izri!" He hurried out of the room, calling for his sister to come back, but she continued on until she shut the door behind her. Yutuuan stopped at the foot of the stairs, acutely aware that everyone was watching the future king lose control of his own family.

Chapter Nineteen

Tutahmen ran a hand down his face, trying to clear away the sleepiness. A full night's rest seemed like something that he would never find again. He stood on a roof overlooking the sunset lit city. It was calm but the kind of calm that set his nerves on edge. The air was heavy, weighed with the promise of change. He couldn't stand it and with night falling, there was always their ever present threat of the monsters. They'd been quiet for the past few nights and no new bodies were discovered in the morning. That made him even more worried.

Some streets away were the Nsongans, probably readying themselves for another push against the Egan defenses. He didn't understand what had gotten into them as of late. They treated this war carefully until now, planning their attacks only when it was clear they had a chance to gain an advantage. All of a sudden, they threw themselves against the defenses. They were suddenly trying to force an advantage, taking risks to try to pry open the barricades and make a crack in their walls.

The first morning that they changed started with one of their damned war songs. It filled the streets around the main barricade, rising into the air like a cloud of Nsongan pride. It was soon copied by the forces at the riverside and before long it sounded like the whole city was flooded with the song. It woke him from his last fitful sleep. He'd jerked awake, thinking he was still on the battlefield years ago. It took him long, panic ridden moments to remember where he was and what was happening. He made his way outside to find most of the soldiers standing in the street, caught by the noise.

Worse yet, as he started to make his way to take up his usual post to oversee the battle, he heard another group join the song. It was the force just outside the gate. The song, usually just to announce their arrival to the battlefield, was a sharp warning to the enemy that they were surrounded. It took everything in him not to give in to the unease growing in his stomach.

Now another day was ending and he could see no way out. The thought terrified him. He'd always been the soldier with a plan even when it seemed his superiors lacked one. He was always able to find a way around the southerners' battle plans. Yes, they suffered some losses in the war but never more than was necessary. He'd whittled the southerners down until the only choice they'd had was to surrender. The shoe was on the other foot now.

A Nsongan command cut the air and then he heard the distinct sound of their new war machine. A large flaming ball rose into the air, sailing neatly over the barricades and smashing into a street. His soldiers' shouts went up as they scrambled to keep it from setting the surrounding buildings on fire. If he could just get a look at whatever this new machine was, he was sure they could engineer a better one. But they kept it hidden and his soldiers only caught glances of the infernal thing.

Another flaming ball was launched from a different location and he cursed. They'd built another one. How had they done it so quickly? He shouted orders down to the men inside and they scrambled into action. Every soldier on the battle line would have to be a firefighter now. There was no telling where an attack would come from. This was an escalation of battle that he'd not foreseen. A string of curses grumbled out of him. Fine, then. If the Nsongans were willing to set their own city aflame then they would have to become just as ruthless.

Night fell as he watched, his mind churning with thoughts of retaliation. More flaming balls were launched but luckily only one building caught on fire. He was growing annoyed at this new machine when shouts of alarm sounded in the streets behind him.

He turned, panicked, thinking that the monsters were killing their way through his soldiers again. They couldn't take much more of this. Their numbers already grew close to desperately thin. His heart pounded as his eyes searched the dark. But there were no shadows running along the roofs. And the shouts were growing louder, closer, and starting to mingle with the sounds of fighting. He turned in the direction of the gate. Those battle hungry southerners couldn't have tried it. The narrowness made it impossible to launch a viable attack. He followed his ears to the sounds of fighting. No, it wasn't the gate. It was spread out along the edge of their territory and it was getting louder.

Tutahmen hurried from his lookout point on the roof, running to the gathering of commanders either trying to get some rest or waking for their turn. "Rouse the men," he shouted. "We're under attack from the rear. The Nsongans are here in mass."

The other commanders scrambled into action, some heading outside immediately and shouting orders. Discarded armor was quickly put back on and weapons retrieved. Tutahmen took to the street himself, heading to the nearest building to call the men to battle. Getting ready would take precious moments and he hoped the Nsongans wouldn't be on them by then. A small contingent at his back, he led them towards the back wall.

An alarm came up from the front on the great fairway between their forces, the alarm that the defenses had been breached. The general cursed repeatedly as he sprinted along but didn't let himself stop and turn. The other commanders would take care of that. But someone must take care of the battle ahead of him.

The street they were on took a curve and they rounded it to find the far end filled with their enemy. The Nsongans called out as they charged a mass of battle clubs, short spears, and swords. Tutahmen took out his sword, heart beating in the excited yet fearful rhythm before meeting an oncoming force. "For the empire," he yelled over the thunderous noise and led his men forward.

He was surprised by the strength of the first woman he encountered, a stocky thing that snarled in his face. He countered her sword attack and threw his weight forward to stab her in the stomach. The look of surprise on her face was satisfying, the moment of realization that she would more than likely die here something he would savor. He ripped his sword back out and moved onto the next opponent.

He managed to put down three more before a mountain of a man hit him with a shield, knocking him into a wall and knocking all the air out of him. He worked despite the panic of his lungs and brought his sword up. The man began to approach but glanced up and smiled. Before Tutahmen could look up, he was being jerked off of the ground.

He found enough breath to shout as he was dragged vertically, lifted like a child under the arms and pulled to the roof. He was deposited on his back for just a second before being caught and dragged along again. That second was all he needed to register the monsters that had been plaguing his men for weeks. He screamed as one pulled him along by a shoulder, two others running behind them. They jumped across from roof to roof, not caring of how their rough handling treated him. The edge of one roof caught him in the hip sparking a burst of pain.

Tutahmen tried to fight the creature. He slashed futilely with his sword but the blade barely made a scratch when he did connect with its hide. In the jostling, he eventually lost his grip on it and it clattered to a street below them. He kicked and punched with all of his might to the same result. He would not die by these creatures. He would not end up an eviscerated pile of organs and shredded skin, head propped up like a grotesque souvenir. After all he'd been through, all the battles he'd fought and won, this couldn't be his end.

The beasts jumped down from a roof near the wall, only using enough strength to keep him from completely slamming into the ground. Tutahmen grabbed the creature's arm in a vain attempt to wrench himself free but it laughed— it laughed! —and continued dragging him along violently. He thought they would drag him through the city until he died or they decided to finally dismember him, but they came to a stop and he was tossed several feet ahead of them. He blinked, eyes adjusting to the sudden torchlight. Nsongans surrounded him, one in particular standing just before him.

Tutahmen struggled to get to his feet, injuries screaming. Several warriors grabbed him, forcing him back to his knees. The man, one he recognized from the war, looked him up and down with disgust. This was one of their higher commanders, related to the line of daras somehow. The commander looked to his left and Tutahmen finally noticed the woman standing beside him. She stepped forward and stooped down in front of the general, looking him in the eyes.

He thought his heart had stopped. This girl wasn't natural. Something in her resonated with power. She tilted her head. "Is this their commander?" she asked in a southern accent so strong he could barely understand her.

"Yes," the man said.

She nodded gravely and placed a gentle hand on his chest. He choked on the cry that tried to form in his throat as every harmful act he'd ever perpetrated in his life flashed through his head. The girl pulled her hand away, tears in her eyes. "By the gods," she whispered, taking a step back. She looked to the commander. "I've never seen someone so evil. What will you do with him?"

Tutahmen couldn't stop himself from struggling desperately in the grasp of the warriors. The commander looked down at him and a feral smile stretched his lips. "He deserves death, don't you think?"

Her face pulled into neutrality. "Yes." Somewhere nearby, he heard the gleeful laugh of hyenas.

***

Efemu watched the vultures gather at the top of the wall as they cautiously moved closer to the head of the Egan general. It made a gruesome decoration just above the gate, with the last drips of blood trailing down from below his slack jaw. He would have given anything to have had this moment during the war but even with years of delay it was still satisfying. He and his forces, his new and old contingent, brought down the Ega inside of Nsongo. Songs would be sung of his leadership. Not that he needed the flattery but it would be nice.

Quiet footsteps approached him and he glanced over his shoulder to see the Lady of Death approaching. She stared up at the general's head with disgust. Not disgust at the sight but at the man. "I thought about placing it at the main gate of the city," he said casually. "But the gate that the battle happened at seemed more appropriate."

Efah nodded. "There is still one more vile root that needs to be pulled up here," she said gravely.

Efemu grunted. His father would probably try to take responsibility for this victory even though not one drop of the enemies' blood had stained his clothes. "I will take care of him soon. I promise."

"I'm not rushing you," she said. She put a hand on his arm in genuine kindness. "I know this must be hard to have to remove your father from his position."

"It's not his position. I just know this is going to be a difficult task."

Efah nodded again. "You could borrow Usa and Nesi." She shrugged. "To make a point."

Efemu looked down to her in surprise at the tiny smile pulling at her lips then laughed. "I thank you for your generous offer, but I can handle my father. I should have a long time ago."

She looked toward the gate, catching notice of something, and when he followed her line of sight, his heart leaped. Barabi walked toward them. Every moment that brought him closer became a struggle for Efemu to keep his composure. Barabi, on his part, had a pleasantly neutral face. He was always so much better at keeping in control. He held Efemu's gaze for a heartbeat before saluting. "Grand Commander Efemu, greetings on this morning."

Efemu couldn't help his smile being a bit too bright. "Greetings to you as well." Barabi gave a half glance towards Efah, raising an eyebrow for a moment. "Ah, Vice Commander Barabi, this is Efah, the Lady of Death, chosen by Death himself."

Barabi looked at her fully then his eyes slid beyond to her hyenas playing in the distance. He bowed deeply. "It is an honor to meet you. I suppose your god was the one who brought us victory last night."

Efah gave a friendly nod. "We were able to enlist some help."

"The monsters of the forest," he said, stiffening for a moment. "You truly are sent by Death if you could sway them to help us. Thank you." He turned to Efemu with a small, familiar smile pulling his lips. "War Minister Ngali wants to see you."

"Of course." He nodded to Efah. "Excuse me."

She smiled. "It's okay. I'll have Nesi and Usa help *clean up* while you're away."

Barabi bowed lowly to her one more time and began to lead Efemu into the city. They entered the gate in silence, walking past dead Egan soldiers that hadn't been collected yet. Vultures already started to collect in unnatural numbers to pick at the bodies. Efemu looked around and at the first narrow alley between buildings, he pulled Barabi in.

He put his hands to his love's cheeks, feeling the light beard that had grown, and kissed him deeply. Barabi groaned slightly. His arms snaked around Efemu's waist, pulling him closer. Barabi smelled of sweat and dust but Efemu couldn't care less. To be near the man he loved with all his heart after being separated was bliss. He'd make love to him in this alley, among all of the carnage, if he knew they wouldn't be discovered.

Barabi pulled away, gasping in a breath. "I missed you too," he said, brushing his lips against Efemu's. "But Ngali's waiting."

Efemu sighed with the weight of duty. "Do you always have to be so responsible?" he grumbled as they continued on their way.

"One of us has to be."

Efemu resisted a hearty chuckle and the urge to put an arm around the man. It was getting harder and harder to be *on duty* around him. He stole a glance at Barabi who gifted him with a smirk. He couldn't wait to be married to this man, tradition be damned.

They made their way through the streets of eastern Nsongo. Other warriors saluted or greeted them as they passed, many of them especially eager to see him. As they neared the place of battle by the river, the cleanup had begun in earnest and piles of Egan soldiers were already loaded up on carts to be taken outside of the city. Efemu noticed the bodies born signs of vicious attacks, some being savagely torn apart. He looked to Barabi in question. The grim look on his face told Efemu everything he needed to know. The monsters happily joined the battle here as well.

He'd only gotten a glimpse of them during the fighting but

what he did see turned even his stomach. It was no wonder they'd worked on behalf of the Lady of Death. They were death itself. He looked out over the river to the thick forest beyond. He wondered if they had retreated to their home for good. He prayed they had. Perhaps they could finally resume their trade with the Batu'bangi again. Nsongo couldn't survive in its present state without it.

War Minister Ngali stood near the docks, barking out orders in her harsh voice. She nodded when she saw them approaching, motioning for them to follow her inside a nearby building. She gave her last instructions to a few nearby warriors and pushed open the door. "Barabi, you may stay," she said as he went to bow and close the door behind Efemu.

Efemu didn't glance back at his lover but saluted to the leader of the Nsongan forces with the greatest respect. "I am at your service, War Minister."

She opened her mouth to speak, then paused. Efemu was surprised. Ngali was never at a loss for words. "Efemu, how did your force gain the advantage at the eastern gate? I know the warriors sent with you were less than ideal."

It was Efemu's turn to hesitate. How did he explain Efah? His commander had never been a particularly religious woman. "The witch I was sent to crush in Olofubaru wasn't a witch at all. She is the chosen one of Death." He paused at the look of utter incredulity on his superior's face. "I didn't believe it either but she looked into my soul. She saw everything that troubled me here in Nsongo. She walks with two great hyenas and commands flocks of vultures. She came back with me because she said it was her mission to rid the south of the rot that had taken hold of it. She spoke to the monsters from the forest and they dug tunnels into the wall so that we could break through and overwhelm the Ega."

Ngali stared at him, face gone neutral. "So that is why those…creatures joined us." She gave a shudder. "I'm willing to believe your tale but I still want to meet this chosen of Death. You won the battle for us, Efemu. Between commissioning those new war machines and enlisting the monsters you made all the difference. Thank you." She clapped him on the shoulder and Efemu felt his heart swell with pride.

Barabi took a step forward. "War Minister, since Commander Efemu has made such a difference and, once again, shown his leadership abilities and prudent decision making, perhaps you'll support his bid to become Great Dara?"

They both looked at the man, stunned. Ngali grumbled something under her breath. "You're as stubborn as your father, you know," she said to Efemu.

"When the Lady of Death read my soul, she saw my father," he replied. "She told me that if the old trees won't fall then they need to be uprooted. She didn't even have to meet him to know he's unfit to lead us. Support me and I will see that the south is once again free."

She took a long, deep breath, releasing it slowly. She looked to Barabi. "I assume you'll be there as his chief advisor."

"I will," he answered, slightly flustered.

"I fully intend to make Barabi my spouse," Efemu said, chin stuck out defiantly. "He will be my partner in everything."

Ngali shook her head and chuckled. "This is why I separated you two. People in Wiluru could see how much you were enamored with each other."

"I thought my father separated us," Efemu said slowly.

"He suggested it and, for once, I agreed with him." Her lips pulled into a line. "Even as Great Dara, you know people will talk."

"Let them talk," Efemu said. "I love Barabi and I'd rather die than be with someone else."

Barabi caught Efemu's gaze. "There is no one else in this world my heart desires."

Ngali looked over the two younger men again and nodded, obviously approving of what she saw. "Very well, High Commander Efemu, savior of Nsongo, I will speak to the council on your behalf to see that you are installed as Great Dara." Her lips twisted. "Maybe that will silence my mother about me taking the title," she grumbled.

Efemu saluted her so hard he hurt his chest. "Thank you, War Minister."

Barabi saluted beside him. "For everything," he said, taking

Efemu's hand.

"You're welcome. Dismissed."

They saluted again and left. Once Efemu reached outside, with the sun shining brightly and the river before them flowing so peacefully, it truly felt like a new day. He grabbed Barabi, pulling him into a kiss and not caring who saw.

Chapter Twenty

Sept'ha looked down at her wrists, heavy with a dozen be-jeweled bangles each and frowned. They rested on her lap, slightly creasing the fabric of her new gown. Behind her a trio of servants braided her hair. She hadn't realized that it had grown so long and as one braid swung over her shoulder it reached down to her chest, golden beads threaded into it. She held in the weary sigh she felt in her heart.

This was foolishness. She didn't know why she agreed to this ridiculous marriage. Being stuck to Hetsaf for the rest of her life and afterlife sounded like torture. Her face twisted sourly. She had planned on working with him anyway so was it so much of a difference?

Yes!

At least she wouldn't have to sleep with him….often. She nearly gagged at the thought. One of the servants asked if she was alright and she muttered that she was. The last thing she wanted was some man on top of her, rutting and breathing hard into her face. She couldn't even imagine Hetsaf touching her in a way that wasn't him trying to be authoritative. She did release that sigh. She was a fool. This was a terrible idea and she was a fool.

Another servant came and applied her makeup, taking expert care to paint her eyes. Once she was done all of the servants stepped back while one brought up a copper mirror. Sept'ha nearly recoiled at the sight. She didn't recognize herself. The woman staring back at her was some noble woman. She touched the elaborate necklace she wore, a gift from her husband-to-be. She felt like she was in someone else's body.

Sept'ha nodded her approval, feeling sick from the sight. One of the servants brought up her sandals, elaborate affairs for her dutifully oiled feet. She even had jewelry for her toes. She stood, the feel of the fabric on her smoother than anything she'd ever worn. She walked out of the room they'd been preparing her in and another set of servants led her to where her future husband waited.

Hetsaf stood in the main courtyard of the palace watching as horses were saddled with heavy loads. There would be gifts of fine fabrics, silver, and perhaps even gold all going to her family as a present for their marriage. Hetsaf wore a finer outfit than she'd ever seen him in and as he looked over, she could finally see the resemblance between him and his emperor brother. He was actually wearing jewelry. He looked more out of place than she felt.

He walked over, stopping before her awkwardly. "Good, you're here." He dismissed her servants with a look.

"Let's get this over with," she sighed.

"You did send word to your family that we're coming?"

"Of course. I didn't tell them why though." The truth was she couldn't bring herself to write the word marriage so she left it out completely. They would enjoy the surprise.

He nodded, looked around unsure, then offered his hand to her. Sept'ha stared at it for a second. Exasperated, he snatched up her hand, leading her to the palanquin waiting at the front of the procession. A host of palace guards surrounded it, ensuring their safety on the journey through the city. It was an almost gaudy thing, with scenes of royal leisure painted along its sup-ports. Gauzy curtains would hide them from the view of onlook-ers. She rolled her eyes. This would be the most elaborate event to ever happen to her dusty little section of the city.

Hetsaf helped her in and she settled against the cushions in the low space. Once he had entered, he gave the command and they departed. Sept'ha relaxed her posture and let the swaying rhythm carry them away. She watched through the veils as they exited the courtyard, stepping into the busy streets of Metkara. People parted quickly for the procession and she could barely make out the looks of confusion or contempt on their faces.

"You seem unhappy," Hetsaf said at last. "Don't you want to see your family?"

"My family and I aren't on the best terms." She threw him a sarcastic smile. "But at least they'll be ecstatic about this. All they ever wanted was for me to find a wealthy husband."

He seemed to run this over in his mind. "At least they saw to your schooling."

"Only to make me more desirable. My brother was always the favorite. He could do no wrong." She snapped her mouth shut. This line of conversation was ruining her mood even more. "Can we not talk about it?" Hetsaf seemed surprised but nodded.

Sept'ha returned to looking out of the window. The scenes of the city quickly changed from the elaborate buildings near the palace to more modest structures. They'd given the directions to her familial home and she had to give their carriers credit for not getting lost in the maze of streets. A dreary resolution fell on her as lanes she recognized came into view. Before she knew it, they were coming to a stop.

Sept'ha looked up at the two story dwelling when she was helped out of the palanquin. She'd spent nearly her whole life here and after nearly a year it felt like the most distant place on earth. She took a deep breath. *Met strengthen me.* Hetsaf offered his hand with a pointed look and she took it this time, allowing him to lead her to the door.

It flew open before they could knock, her mother looking shocked at them and the procession filling the small street. Sept'ha resisted rolling her eyes. She'd probably been spying from one of the windows upstairs. Her mother's gaze fell on her, eyes growing even bigger. "Sept'ha?" she stammered. "Gods, I didn't recognize you." She looked at Hetsaf, taking in his finery and dropped into the lowest bow Sept'ha had ever seen her perform. "My lord."

"Rise," Hetsaf said, his usual snide tone sounding appropriate in this instance.

"Is father home?" Sept'ha asked.

"Yes, he is," her mother stammered. "Come in. Come in." She stepped aside, showing the utmost deference. She hurried to another room as they entered, coming back with her father who didn't seem like he was expecting company at all. He snapped to attention at the sight of the couple, mouth working like a fish.

"Mother, father," Sept'ha began, cutting off this foolishness. "I have come home to inform you that I am marrying the chancellor of the empire, Hetsaf."

Hetsaf nodded to them and her parents nearly tripped over themselves trying to bow lower. "Mother, father, I bring you gifts as a thank you for raising a glorious woman to be my partner in life."

The traditional lines crawled down her spine. He gestured sharply behind them and guards started bringing in the various chests, filling up the front room of the house. She watched her parents' greedy eyes take in the wealth of marriage gifts as they were opened, her father obviously tallying the sum. When the pile of riches was complete her parents still stood there, staring at it for a moment. Sept'ha cleared her throat, looking at her father sharply.

"Thank you for your gifts, great chancellor. May you have a long, happy, and fruitful marriage," he said. They promptly fell into a puddle of bows. "Let us drink to this moment. I honestly didn't think it would come."

"I didn't either," Sept'ha replied, forcing a smile on her face. "But we can't stay. Hetsaf has much to do being the chancellor and all." She looked to her future husband with theatrical admiration.

"Yes," he said sharply. "I have to return to the palace. I hope these gifts can ease the pain of your daughter leaving."

"Why is the street blocked?" yelled a voice from the rear of the house. "I had to come in through the kitchen." Sept'ha's attention snapped to the entrance of the next room, all pretending gone. That was a voice that she'd hoped to never hear again. Her brother grumpily stomped into the room, took one look around at all the boxes of treasure, then settled on her. "Sept'ha?" he said.

Her brother was thinner than she'd remembered and his hands and feet were dirty. His brow shined with sweat, something she thought she'd never see on him. It was about time he did some work. "Imhoten," she ground out.

"What is all this?"

Their mother glowed with excitement. "Your sister is marrying the chancellor. He's brought us gifts."

Imhoten sneered at Sept'ha. "About time you made yourself

worth something to this family." Their father called his name sharply and he ignored him. "You run off and now I have to work to help put food on the table. The least you could do is fool a wealthy man into marrying you. And the chancellor?" He laughed heartily. "Sure. And I'm fucking the empress. How much did you suck this man's dick to get him to lie for you?"

Hetsaf crossed the room before Sept'ha realized what he was doing. The sound of his blow filled the room and was followed by the thump of her brother hitting the floor. Her parents looked horrified. Sept'ha stared, shocked. Hetsaf's face was actually enraged. "Speak of the wife of the chancellor again and I will see you die slowly and painfully."

He turned and came back to her side, offering his hand. She timidly took it, following him out. He still looked ready to strike as they reentered the palanquin. "You are too good for that family," he said lowly. "Your parents are greedy and your brother is a piece of shit." He paused, some of the anger abating. "I see why you left."

She nodded, looking out the curtains at her parents' home one last time. She would truly never have to see this place again. She would never have to suffer being talked down to by any of them again. She sat back as the palanquin began moving. Hetsaf had defended her. He only cared about things that were important to him. She stole a glance. He watched the city as well, face still moody. Perhaps he actually did value her. She shook her head. That man was truly an enigma.

The sight of him striking her brother stayed with her all the way back to the palace. It made her feel a bit better about the whole day until they returned to his section of the palace. Her legs froze as they came to the hall that led to his room. "What's wrong?" he asked.

Everything was wrong, she wanted to tell him. She'd slept in his room for months but the idea of going in there now terrified her. They would be united as husband and wife, the last act to seal their partnership. "Nothing," she said quickly. "Nothing."

She nodded as servants took her to another room, what would be her own room to use as she pleased. She stood passively as the servants undressed her and removed her jewelry and makeup. They put her in a simple shift dress, one easier to take off. The fabric was exceedingly sheer and clung to her in ways she didn't like. She hoped her preparation would take longer but it was over quickly and the servants left her to go to the room of her husband to be.

Sept'ha swallowed difficultly as she made her way down that hall. Was this truly the path Met sent her on? Would she have to endure everything she hated to serve her goddess? She prayed for her deity to send her some sign, some disruption that would save her from this.

Did you not want to be a powerful woman?

Yes, she answered.

Then this is the way you will wield true power. You will hold the future of this land in your hands. There was a pause. *Or you can return home to cook and clean for your parents and brother until they die. I leave this choice to you.*

Sept'ha felt tears starting to well in her eyes and blinked them away. She wouldn't be her family's servant for the rest of her days. She'd rather die. She took a deep breath and entered Hetsaf's room.

Hetsaf stood at the foot of his bed in something simple, looking like he'd rather be anywhere else. Lamps were already lit for the coming evening casting the simple room in a golden hue. He took her in and looked away, uncomfortable. His jaw tightened and he forcibly turned his head back to her. It was almost comical how he refused to look at her body. "Should we start?" he asked.

Sept'ha rubbed an arm. "I've never *been* with a man," she said looking aside.

"I've never been with a woman either." He crossed the distance between them, put his hands on her shoulders, and darted in to give her a kiss.

The time their lips touched wasn't even a breath. Sept'ha looked at him in disbelief. "I don't think that's how this starts."

"Well, then how?" The question was almost a challenge.

Sept'ha resisted groaning in defeat. She was going to have to lead him into this. She took a breath. She'd seen people do this. Her heart beating nervously, she tiptoed up and pressed her lips gently to his. After a moment, she began moving her lips and thankfully, he reciprocated. It felt wet and weird. Disgust roiled in her stomach and she pulled back.

"Take off your clothes," she said. He nodded, stiffly, and did so. She pulled her dress over her head and blushed at the sight of him. She looked away quickly. The thought that she couldn't do this started to come up again but she banished it. Casting her gown to the floor, she shyly made her way to him. He was pointedly looking away from her, embarrassment coloring his face.

She took a few quick breaths and pressed against him. She moved her hand slowly down and grabbed his manhood. He gasped, looking at her in surprise. With her other hand she took his and placed it at the point between her legs she'd explored herself. As she coaxed him to arousal, he caught on, massaging her until she felt the first lightning strikes of her completion.

She pulled away from him, leading him to the bed. She climbed in trying to not let the mixture of her fear, revulsion, and nervousness kill her arousal. She looked away as he moved into position on top of her. She guided him to her and with thrust he entered. Sept'ha curled in pain. "Not so hard," she hissed at him, tears forming.

"Sorry," he grunted.

He began again, softer. She looked aside, enduring every jolt to her body until it didn't hurt anymore. Anger built in her as her body betrayed her and enjoyed it until she strangled down a cry of ecstasy. Hetsaf built in speed and force until he finished, grunting in her ear like an animal. Bile rose in the back of her throat as he stiffened and groaned.

The thought of his seed entering her, maybe even taking root, made her want to vomit. *I will be the most powerful woman in the empire,* she thought to herself as he collapsed on top of her. *No one will be able to order me about again.* Hetsaf freed himself and rolled over, leaving her to stare at the wall aware of the possibilities that this act may have. *I will be the most powerful woman in the empire,* she thought to herself over and over as she held in her bile.

***

Arkole stalked the halls of the palace, an accountant with a slate tablet in her wake. Servants scurried to get out of her way after one look at her face. Today was not a good day to cross the empress. Changes had to be made in this palace and urgently. Hetsaf would not get the upper hand on her.

Her one ally left the palace, gone to some summer residence near her home city. Arkole knew in her heart and soul that the chancellor had convinced her to leave. That girl knew they had work to do in Bakari's absence. Now the ruling of the empire lay at Arkole's feet and she would have to carry that weight alone.

She turned down corridor after corridor until coming to a section of the palace she'd only been to one time since becoming Bakari's wife. The Hall of Treasure held several rooms running along it with guards by each door. These men, exceptionally broad shouldered and hard faced, bore a terrifying aura to deter any would be thieves. Failure of duty meant immediate execution in the most horrible ways.

"Open one of the chambers," she snapped at the accountant. The scrawny man took out his ring of keys, sliding them along until he found the one for the first door. Arkole waited impatiently as he opened the series of locks. With a grunt, he pushed the door open, revealing the mountain of treasure inside.

The smell of stale air rushed out to her and she was instantly transported to a simpler time. She was a new wife and her husband, the Great Royal Prince, brought her here to show the riches that now belonged to her as well. They'd walked the rows of containers of gold and jewels, him opening up each one to watch the delight in her face. They'd even copulated on the largest of the chests. She smiled sadly. By the gods, she missed him.

She entered the room, opening the chests to give an estimate of the amount held inside. "Write this down," she snapped over her shoulder. "I'll be taking six of the smaller ones. Make a note of the exact worth and be sure that it's deducted from the treasury." She looked around again, calculating. Taking this made just a dent in the crown's riches. There were seven more rooms exactly like this one. "Make it seven of these chests. Have them delivered to my rooms by this evening."

The accountant looked confused for a moment but changed his expression with one glare from her. "Yes, of course, empress."

Arkole swept from the room, heading back to her rooms. She had funds, now she had to find the right people to give them to too. Arkole needed guards. Her personal force had been increased since the assassination attempt but she needed to know the people around her and her girls were truly loyal. She wouldn't have men who wouldn't listen to her commands if it came to a choice between her and Hetsaf. She would—had to—come out on top.

And she knew Hetsaf was up to something. His servant girl hadn't come to her rooms with information for days and now she was hearing rumors that he'd married the girl. A servant! Was he so desperate for companionship that he'd take anything? Surely Bakari would let him have one of his concubines on his return or even arrange for a proper marriage. He didn't have to settle for his…What was she exactly to him? Secretary? Scribe?

Arkole pushed the thought from her mind. It didn't matter. She just needed to secure her own loyal group of guards among the palace guards and she would be safe from Hetsaf's machinations. Then he would see who really wielded the power of the empire.

She slowed her pace as she neared her apartments. There was far too much noise coming from them. She halted in her tracks when she saw the first servants walking down the hall, carrying her personal items. She watched, stunned for a moment, as her furniture and statuettes were taken away. Arkole picked up her skirt and hurried to her rooms. She passed room after room as her things were starting to be packed away, a host of servants and guards attending to the task.

"What is going on here?" she shouted. All movement around her stopped. The servants that were in the midst of carrying out items paused, all of them pointedly looking away from her. Arkole stormed up to one of the guards. "Who has ordered this?"

He swallowed. "The chancellor, my empress," he stammered.

"You will put it all back immediately," she shrieked. No one moved, unsure glances passing between them. Arkole came to one woman who carried a large tied up bundle. She started shoving her back into the room she'd come from. "Put it all back. I am your empress. You will obey me."

"No," came another voice. "Keep doing as you were commanded."

Arkole looked over toward the voice, venom in her gaze. She blinked as she saw Hetsaf's servant turned wife standing in the doorway to her private rooms. She was dressed in a fashion befitting of her new station, jewelry tinkling as she moved. The woman gave Arkole a disinterested glance and went back into the room. Arkole tore into the room after her. Here another army of servants quickly packed things up. Sept'ha began giving commands as to what needed to be put away next. Her son's nursemaid stood in the corner, holding him and watching the events in shock.

Arkole reached for this upstart's arm, jerking her around to face her. "What do you think you're doing?"

This woman dared look down at Arkole's hand and jerked her arm out of her grip. "I have been tasked with overseeing that you're packed up for your trip." There was no servant's humility in this woman's demeanor any longer.

It enraged Arkole. "I don't care what that bastard has in his plans. I am still the empress of this empire. The emperor has said that my word is law."

"What is the law if no one respects it?" She had the nerve to look down her nose at Arkole. "You and your children will retire to the manor outside of Ux. For your safety. I'm sure the girls will love island living. It is where your husband often spent his summers as a child."

Arkole grew so incised words failed her. "Bakari will never stand for this."

Sept'ha blinked slowly at her, seeming to consider something. "The emperor," she said leaning forward, "is dead."

Arkole slapped her, her own hand stinging from the force. Sept'ha's head turned and she stumbled a step sideways. Both of them looked on, surprised, as she wiped blood away from her split lip. Then Arkole's face shattered into a thousand shards of pain and she hit the floor. The room spun. She made out feet in front of her and looked up to see Sept'ha, hand balled as if she meant to punch her again. The other woman forcibly relaxed her posture. "The emperor is dead," she said again. "That is the only reason for the lack of messages, even a response to your little missive to Djelebe."

She straightened up and signaled for two guards. They came and helped Arkole to her feet. "Hetsaf is trying to steal the throne," she cried, speech slurring. "I know it. You were his willing accomplice in this the entire time."

The other woman said nothing for a moment, regarding her with disgust. "When your son comes of age, you may return with him to assume the throne. Until then, enjoy the seaside. You'll be safe there."

The guards began taking her out. "This will not stand," she screamed. "I will have your life for this. Do you hear me? I will see you and Hetsaf executed for this treachery." Her cries echoed down the hallway as she was pulled away from her rooms and no one came to her aid.

Chapter Twenty-One

Tekhamun waited patiently while Moon threw up their meager breakfast. She hunched over the side of the road, back arching with each forceful heave. Tekhamun nervously watched the road behind them. His hand twitched, a breath away from his weapons and ready to take them up at any moment. Three days. They'd spent three nerve wracking days on the road, barely getting any sleep, with Moon's new ailment slowing them down in the morning. There hadn't been any sign of the other Arakgu'un. But he knew they were there. He flexed his hands again, glancing to Moon nervously. Thankfully, she wiped her mouth on a sleeve and came back to the road.

"We have to go," he said quickly.

She nodded, face still sour. "I'm sorry I'm slowing us down."

Guilt hit him in the chest. "No, no," he said. You can't help that you're sick. We'll have to find better food." He thought to the lizards they'd managed to cook on the road and grimaced. "At the next town we'll see about getting something good."

His anxiety abated slightly as they continued walking. He couldn't believe it was just he and Moon now. He had a mission with a host of followers. He was rallying people together to fight against vice and heresy. Their numbers were growing as news spread of the uprising. He'd weeded out the betrayers in his midst and found his true close companions. He swallowed, throat dry. He'd abandoned one of those companions to the members of his brotherhood. Tekhamun prayed that Nurmet made it out of the city. His gut told him that it was a fruitless prayer.

Was his god even listening?

He tried to abandon the thought, but it persisted. How could his deity raise him up so high just to cast him down so low? He licked his dry cracked lips, struggling to bring what little moisture he had in his parched mouth to them. He was so, so low. A struggling, thirsty chosen whose stomach cried out louder than his prayers. Surely, they looked like a pair all the gods had abandoned.

Tekhamun shook his head vigorously. No, no, he wasn't abandoned. Gu'un would never abandon him. When no one else believed in him, believed that he would amount to anything, he found his purpose in service to the god of the blade of justice. Being part of something greater than himself sustained him in a way that nothing else had. Now, he felt empty. He tried to summon the surety that always accompanied him but there was nothing.

Anger started to rise and he tried to fight it to little success. Where was Gu'un's guidance? His left hand flexed, anxious to take up and use his blade. Something to cut. He needed to strike something down to rid him of this anger. He couldn't let his frustration consume him. Gu'un would lead him on the right path. Soon. It would happen soon. He would finally have another dream and everything would be clear. He'd know what to do then. No more confusion.

Tekhamun closed his eyes, taking a deep breath. He released it slowly, blowing out all of his doubt, all of the feelings that had no place in a true, faithful follower of the gods. He rebuilt his surety, piece by piece until he felt nothing else but fortified by Gu'un. When he opened his eyes, he noticed a dark smear on the horizon.

"Master, are you okay?" Moon asked timidly.

He pointed an arm out. "There's a town up ahead. We can rest and eat when we get there." He looked over to her. She'd regained some of her color and didn't look as sick as she had this morning. His heart was pricked. Gently, he took her hand, giving it a firm squeeze. "Everything will be alright," he said. "I promise."

She looked down for a moment, lost in thought. Then she smiled and nodded at him. Her belief filled him with even more strength than his faith.

***

Newa resisted the urge to scratch his stomach. Never had a wound itched so much. He knew that traveling like this, in the hot sun with his robe rubbing against it, was the source of its irritation. He should be resting somewhere, eating plenty of food, and making sure it didn't get infected. He resisted the urge to scratch again. At least he knew it was healing.

Unfortunately, stopping wasn't an option. He shaded his eyes against the midday sun, sighting the town just in the distance. They could make it there in about an hour and then he could sit down for a little bit. Just a little bit. The tug of his mission was growing stronger with each day, with each step, until his feet felt like they moved of their own accord. His target loomed closer than he'd imagined. A mixture of churned inside of him. Anxiety, hope, and satisfaction tumbled over each other, gaining prominence in his mind until the next knocked it aside.

He was so close to the end of his journey. Then he could return to Efah. He sighed, prompting a glance from Masola but he kept his eyes on the road. The thought of seeing her again brought hope to the forefront. This mission would be completed, his god satisfied, and he could spend the rest of his days in her presence.

But only after he defeated this false priest. Anxiety rose up. What was this heretic like? A swarm of images formed in his mind of his future opponent. He pushed the thoughts away of a large man that might be able to overpower him in his current state. Tikiri favored the slender. His foe would probably be like him. Maybe they'd even tried to become Arakgu'un and been turned away. Honestly, he'd far prefer if it were a wayward member of his sect. At least he'd get a good fight.

"Don't scratch it," Masola scolded.

Newa frowned at her but lowered his hand. "Thank you, nursemaid."

"You're welcome," she said with a smug smile.

He snorted a little laugh. Efah would adore her. It would do the girl good to have someone else to look up to. Someone far more nurturing than him. Having a killer as your only role model couldn't be good for a young person. He thought of his own upbringing and grimaced. No, it *definitely* wasn't good for a young person.

"Can we stop at the town and eat?" Masola asked.

He looked to the wavering mass, judging their travel time again. "Sure. We can see if we can even find something better than travel provisions."

"Good. Don't scratch it."

"Damn it." He jerked his hand down to a snicker from his teen student.

They traveled on, the sun reaching its zenith and baking the land. This dry season on the plains was looking to be a brutal one. He couldn't believe he looked forward to the wet heat of the deep south. At least it was an even heat. Even if it felt like a man could drown from just breathing some days. And the insects were the size of horses. Almost. But it was home now and he couldn't wait to return.

A few people came from the town as they approached. He hurried along, beads of sweat collecting on their faces, eyes wide with terror. They weren't even laden with packs for travel either. They took in Newa's robes and shied away, giving them a wide berth and avoiding eye contact. Once they were past, they increased their speed to nearly a run. Newa, stared after them for a moment then turned his attention to the town. The tug of his mission nearly jerked him forward. His pace quickened out of his control.

"What's wrong?' Masola asked, jogging to catch up with him.

"I think he's here." Newa's eyebrows knitted in confusion. The pull was stronger than it had ever been.

"The priest you're supposed to kill?"

Newa nodded absently. They stepped past the town's barrier and he stopped midstride. A shiver ran up his body, setting all of his nerves on edge. His mind replayed his vision of the false priest robed in shadow and lies. He knew with every fiber of his being that this was the final destination of his mission. The man, his enemy, was in this town and this was where he'd meet his end.

Newa slowed his pace as they walked into town. There was

the expected quiet of midday as people took refuge inside but a certain tension electrified the air. He caught sight of a face staring out of a window, but by the time he looked, they ducked away. He signed to Masola for silence. Something was dangerously amiss here.

They made their way slowly toward the center of town. That was where they found the first body. A man lay on the ground, fresh blood soaking the dirt around his neck. A trail lay in drops behind him, leading up to the steps of the town's travel house. Another body sprawled down the pair of steps leading up to the door, blood running to the ground. Newa motioned for Masola to stay put but be alert and the girl placed a hand on her knife.

He came close to the first body, examining the cut to the man's neck. It was clean, severing the artery and windpipe in one level slice. He turned back to the travel house, his tug pulling him towards it. The man he was searching for was a killer of innocents. He'd have no regrets sending him on to the gods.

"False priest of Gu'un," he yelled. "You have made a mockery of our purpose and have committed sins against our god. Come out and face the judgment of his blade."

Silence surrounded him for a number of heartbeats. He fixed his eyes on that doorway, ignoring the feeling of more and more eyes watching him from other buildings. The faint sound of footsteps shuffled inside, coming toward the door. A few moments later a figure emerged from the darkness. He wasn't an impressive man. Robes just as road worn as Newa's hung from a lithe frame. The sharp angles of his face made his head seem oddly boxy. The sunlight reflected from the growing bald spot in his tight curls. He was a ragged, pathetic looking man and Newa couldn't believe this was who his deity sent him to deal with.

The man squinted, concentrating on Newa's face. "I know you," he said, deep country drawl dragging his words out. "You came from the capital to spread the lie of the emperor. You were trying to get me to go along with the heresy."

Newa squinted, taking this man in again. No, he didn't recognize him. He'd talked to a dozen or more priests on his journey before heading south. It felt like ages ago. "I'm sorry, but I don't remember you."

The false priest barked out a choking laugh. "Of course you wouldn't. A corrupted vessel of the netkoleh's heresy would never think to remember the men he'd led astray." He took out his twin swords, leveling one at Newa. "Well, I didn't fall for your lies. Gu'un showed me the true path and I will be the one that leads this empire back to the gods."

"Does that path involve killing innocent people?" Newa asked glancing down at the body on the stairs.

"If they will not aide in my mission, they aren't innocent," he snapped. "People who would interfere in the work of the gods deserve to be cleaved."

Newa took a small breath. So this man was a fanatic. He looked over his shoulder to Masola, motioning for her to back away some. He took out his blades, the movement making him cover a wince as a twinge of pain hit part of his injury. Behind the false priest, a woman came to the doorway, large with one bad, milky eye. She looked on concerned. A follower. He hoped she wouldn't try to get involved. He didn't want to spill any more blood than necessary. "What is your name?" he called to his enemy.

"I am Tekhamun," he said proudly. "Chosen of Gu'un."

Newa lowered his head in acknowledgment. "I am Newa, chosen by Tikiri, known here as Gu'un, and I have been sent by him to kill you." He brought his swords up. "Come and meet your fate."

"Heresy," Tekhamun shrieked. He came down the stairs, stepping over the body. "I am his chosen one." He rushed forward, bringing both swords down in a heavy downward strike.

Newa brought one of his swords up to block. He swung his other blade across to try to catch this Tekhamun across the stomach. The man flipped one of his swords, stopping Newa's attack just in time. Newa used this moment to push back against the first attack, knocking his opponent off balance.

But the wide swing pulled his healing wound taut and he barely restrained the recoil from the pain. The glint of sunlight alerted him to Tekhamun's next attack and he swung up to meet it.

This was foolish. He was injured. His training told him that he should have ambushed this man. However, his heart told him to meet him in an honorable duel. This man was fighting desperately, understandably so. His life was on the line. At his normal strength, Newa could have made short work of him. This priest was a true Arakgu'un but he wasn't a capital trained member. His strikes lacked the finesse Newa was used to seeing. This could have been easier. But perhaps fate saw fit to have this fight happen now and spare any more death by his hand. Newa thought of the bodies in the street and the horrors that were probably waiting inside the travel house.

So be it.

He pushed his attacks, setting this man on the defensive. If he wanted to be a monster, out here killing in the name of Gu'un for his own gain, then Newa would show him a true monster. Tekhamun would meet the man who walked the path to become the next Hand of Gu'un.

He matched his opponent blow for blow, ignoring the itching that turned to pain across his stomach. Tekhamun punished him with strikes, each clash of their blades ringing down Newa's arms. The other priest's eyes burned with conviction. He grunted and snarled as he fought like a cornered animal. Newa switched techniques, moving to a more flowing style, working not to overpower the man but just meet his ferocity. He had to wait this fight out until just the right moment.

Tekhamun attempted a cut at Newa's chest and he jumped back in time to avoid it. Newa twisted in a lunge forward to pay back the blow. He realized his mistake a moment too late. He felt the rip of his wound so acutely, he swore he heard it. He stumbled forward, his blow trailing off uselessly. He managed to bring one of his swords up to deflect Tekhamun's next strike but not in time to fend off the second. The blade bit into his gut, deep and clean.

He had a moment, just one moment, before he went down. His mind cleared and he saw the opening. Newa swung a sword up, heavily, cutting the other man's throat open from side to side. Tekhamun recoiled as blood sprayed out. He clutched his throat futilely trying to stem the flow.

Newa took a couple of shaky steps back, arm across his

midsection, as he watched his opponent fall. His robe was already soaked and the bulge of his organs pressed against his arm. The sharp tang of excrement caught in his nostrils. His lips pressed together, grimly. He didn't have long. He fell down, legs giving way.

Across from him, Tekhamun dropped to his knees, slumping to his side as his life pumped away in a puddle of red. The woman with the bad eye rushed forward, scrambling to his side. A deep, strangled wail crawled up from her throat, tumbling out of her mouth until it spilled into the air. Her hands trembled as she touched his face, tears streaming in thick rivulets. She touched her forehead to his, whispering to his vacant expression.

Newa began falling back and fell against the waiting arms of Masola. "Master," she said, panic causing a tremble in her voice. "Master, let me get the needle and thread. I can fix it."

He smiled, half of it a grimace. "No," he struggled against the pain. "No fixing." His arm lowered from his stomach as his strength fell away. He saw the horror on Masola's face as she saw the extent of his injury. She started gasping in breath, tears welling in her eyes. "Go south. Olofubaru."

His mind wandered to his Lady of Death waiting for him to return. She would be so sad. He drew in a breath. "Find Efah. Tell her…I'm sorry I didn't keep my promise."

Masola dissolved into tears. Newa blinked, the effort to open his eyes again was monumental. He couldn't hear Masola's words, couldn't hear anything. He looked up as another figure approached, backlit by the noon sun. They were dark, a deep brown he'd only seen twice before. He couldn't make out their features but he was filled with a sense of contentment

Well done. Now rest.

Newa smiled as the last of his strength left his body and allowed his eyes to close.

Chapter Twenty-Two

The ships prepared to dock at Wiluru's harbor and Umakaal found herself praying. She held onto the railing, watching the city rise up before them. She felt odd calling out to the gods. She rarely went to temple. They never seemed a factor in her life but today, right here, right now, felt like the perfect time. *Please Yutuu,* she thought. *Let us turn the tide of this war and push the Ega out of our kingdom once and for all. Please let me be a good commander. Let me prove myself today.* She sat with the prayer for a moment hoping her conviction would sway their patron deity. She didn't know what to expect from such a prayer. Was she supposed to feel overconfident or perhaps have the chilling surety her sister did? She frowned. She didn't need to be *touched* by Yutuu to know that they would win this fight. She looked behind her at the group of mages and dragon's blood handlers from Asfara ready to depart the ship and join the battle. They would carve their own path to victory and Yutuu could help them along the way.

Her excitement barely masked her nervousness as the ship made its preparations to dock. She tapped her fingers on her sword hilt. She'd never used it in actual battle before, only practice sessions. She'd never actually been in an *actual* battle before. Umakaal took a breath as the ship came to a stop. That was the prayer she should have prayed. Don't let this battle be her first and last.

She turned to the people gathered above deck, trying her best to pull up all of her authority. Her protective group of warriors, Asfara's warriors and mages, and the dragon's blood handlers with their mysterious sacks at their sides all looked at her expectantly. Mikhra stood with her protectors, looking serious and ready. She resisted giving him a smile.

The gang plank lowered to the dock. Umakaal took a deep breath and puffed it out. "Set out to the gate," she commanded, glad her voice sounded sure. "We're going to show those Ega bastards the wrath of the people of Wiluru."

A shout of acknowledgment went up along the various ships as the command to set out spread. Umakaal rushed down to the dock, setting a quick pace to make it through the city. The sound of so many people, marching in time behind her, all ready to destroy their hated enemy made an excited spark run down her spine. The noise echoed around the quiet city and soon there were people peeking through latticed windows to see the commotion. Doors began to open, Wiluruans crowding to watch the approaching force and calling out in praises to them and to the gods. Umakaal hoped the smile on her face didn't look too smug.

The sounds of heated battle reached them by the time they passed the palace. Umakaal focused on the great walls rising up in the distance. Before them lay the chance to catch the Ega by surprise. Her mind ran over the number of mages she'd brought back with her and the dragon's blood bearers. Even with knowing the nature of the substance, the Asfarans were still secretive about its application. If they didn't want to spell it out to her, fine. She had her own ideas for it.

She glanced behind her and motioned for the leader of the Asfaran forces to walk with her. She was a tall woman with an imposing spirit, a no-nonsense kind of person that the princess hoped to be one day. "These dragon's blood bearers of yours, can they fight as well?"

"Of course, your majesty," she responded. "We would never send anyone off to a conflict that wasn't prepared to fight."

If this was a slight at the princess, the commander hid it well. Umakaal nodded. "Then I have an idea that may change the trajectory of the war. But we have to retake the wall first."

"Whatever you command, princess. We are here to save Wiluru."

The princess didn't like that statement but let her feeling go. She would just have to trust that the Asfarans would remember that this battle was for their sake too. "Good. Then I need a group of twelve mages and twelve dragon's blood bearers to come with me. I'll lead them through the side streets to the edge of the battle. If we can fight our way up to the top of the wall, we can rain down fire on the troops outside."

The commander looked to her, surprised. "You would lead this yourself? Are you sure you're ready for it?"

"I have been ready to defend my people—all of my people— my entire life. It's what I was raised for. I'll take those people and the rest of you can report to my brother just ahead."

The woman looked her over as if reassessing her and nodded. They called a stop to the procession, the fighters Umakaal wanted filing their way up front. Anxiousness ran through her as they looked to her for their next command. This was it. She was really doing it, leading troops into battle. She took a shallow breath, trying to expel the nervousness. "Follow me," she commanded. The fighters did so without question.

The side streets near the wall were just as dead as the rest of the city. She took her small group on a circuitous route hoping to avoid any possible Egan warriors. The enemy had taken all four of the guard houses along the wall but the main Wiluruan force couldn't focus on those for the push of the main battle. There weren't any forces to spare. Umakaal just needed to take back one. They would gain access to the wall and then things would truly change. She would end the full on war her sister started and then she could finally take her proper place as leader of the warriors of Wiluru.

She stopped them as they came up to the last corner before arriving at the guard house to the farthest left of the gate. Umakaal peeked around to see a small group of Egan warriors standing guard at the entrance to the small building. There couldn't be too many more inside. Each guardhouse only held enough space for a quartet of guards to eat and a couple of beds. She glanced up to the wall and saw more milling about, most watching the battle far below them.

She motioned for them to follow her and they rushed in. Only one guard saw their approach, crying out a warning. A fireball flew past Umakaal's head, hitting him in the face with such force that it knocked him down. The other guards turned, beginning to ready their weapons, but not before a handful of spells took them out.

Umakaal ran into the guardhouse, hopping over the injured

men. She surprised a guard inside, slashing him from face to stomach. It was a shock to feel the resistance of a real body under her blade. It was more solid than she'd imagined and the jolt of connecting made her pause for half a breath. Another warrior scrambled to get his sword but she kicked her first opponent into him, sending them into a tangle of limbs. She brought her sword up to block the blow of a third man. The force of his attack brought her sword dangerously close to biting into her shoulder. She felt panic lurking in the back of her mind. With a roar of determination, she pushed against him with all her might, knocking him back. Realizing her opening, she stabbed forward.

Her sword sunk into his torso, just below his ribcage. She looked up to him in surprise, and saw her expression mirrored on his face. He grabbed her sword hand, a limp grasp, but she wrenched her blade free, allowing his blood to gush forth. She watched, stunned as he staggered, then fell. The life left his eyes and they stared, soullessly, back at her.

A spell flew past her to take care of the other two men in the guard house but she couldn't move. Her eyes refused to look at anything other than the man she'd killed. Umakaal jumped when a hand was placed on her shoulder. "Is this your first kill?" a mage asked quietly. She swallowed and nodded. "It's never easy for anyone, but it gets easier. Don't let them see you're rattled."

The princess nodded again and led them up the long flight of stairs to the top of the wall. She did her best to keep the image of the dead man out of her head, his lifeless body, his staring eyes. A cold sea wind slapped her as she took her first step on the wall, making her stumble but focus. She caught the sharp sting of salty air and cooking fires. The faint notes of the flowering vineyards to the east mingled with the musky scents of the warriors below. She smelled Wiluru and everything that made it great. She looked out to the sea and saw a great storm gathering on the horizon, lightning streaking across the wrathful gray clouds. She felt an anger come over her. These people were here fouling her city. For that, they had to die.

Umakaal's grip tightened on her sword and she made her way along the high walkway to the first of the Egan soldiers. He noticed their approach, calling out the alarm and fumbling to unsheathe his sword. She could see the fear in his eyes, a wild animalistic energy. He was young, perhaps a few years older than her. But she felt no pity towards him. Her sword plunged into his stomach just as he managed to get his blade free. She jerked it out, pushing him toward the outer side of the wall. He stumbled and fell and she didn't give him a second look.

She pointed her blood stained sword forward and the mages rushed to battle. Spells flew expertly, hitting their targets with deadly precision. Several more warriors flew off the wall, usually burning on the way down, while others lay pierced with ice shards. As the other Egan warriors advanced toward them, wind spells kept their arrows from finding targets.

Umakaal looked down over the side, at the great morphing cluster of the Egan army below. They looked like a swarm of ants trying to invade through a crack in a building. Her lips pulled tight. That was going to change today. A glance to her left showed that her force had nearly taken this side of the wall. She looked around to find one of the dragon's blood bearers. Motioning him over, she tried to judge the distance between them and the far end of the army.

"Yes, princess," the bearer said.

"What do you have in those sacks?"

He reached in and pulled out a curious orb. It was clay and large enough to fit into a hand with a strip of cloth coming out of its sealed top. "Dragon's tears. Light it and throw it at the enemy. It will burn until it runs out of fuel."

Umakaal looked back over the side. "Show me."

The bearer raised his eyebrows, then smiled. He closed his eyes momentarily, a small flame springing to life at the tip of a finger. He lit the strip of cloth, then threw it. The orb sailed far out before arcing downward into the midst of the Ega. It exploded in an eerie splash of blue-green flame. A moment later Umakaal heard the rush of the explosion chased by the blood chilling screams of the Ega. The strong breeze brought the stench of burning flesh up in a rush. Her stomach lurched, but a growing sense of satisfaction kept the nausea in check.

"Dragon's blood bearers," she called out over the wind, "attack!"

The bearers fell into line along the wall as if they were waiting for this moment. A shower of dragon's tears were launched over the side, falling into the still chaotic force below. The explosions looked like fat raindrops from this height and the fire spread as aflame Egan fighters ran about. Umakaal smiled as the shrieks and yells of pain, panic, and confusion landed on her ears. She called for another volley and more of the Ega lit up with blue-green flames.

The thunder rolled behind her and the wind brought the strong scent of the sea strengthening the grimly satisfied feeling within her. She looked over the other side of the wall to where the Egan fighters congregated near the gate. She grinned, feeling feral. She didn't want anything in the city to be set ablaze by the dragon's blood but the utter confusion that would be caused by a well-placed attack would be glorious. She called for the bearers to come to the wall near the gate. "Aim away from the buildings and cause as much carnage as you can."

"Yes, princess," they called in unison.

She watched their new tactic in action again savoring the screams now inside the city. She hoped her brother was taking note of this. She was going to win this battle for him.

***

Umakaal walked over the bodies of fallen Ega fighters, taking in the carnage, soaking it into her memory. Battle and overseeing the aftermath would be her domain soon enough. She had to familiarize herself with the brutality of it until she accepted its place in warfare. Seeing so many of the fallen enemies satisfied her. The invaders deserved to take their last breaths so far away from home and the embrace of their loved ones. Let the empire learn the price of attacking Wiluru. They would never lay down for them again.

A hand clutched at her leg and she stumbled. Umakaal looked down, pulling out her sword, ready. One of the Ega wasn't quite dead, his grip on her ankle limp. She paused. The Egan fighter couldn't have been older than her. Blood pooled out from a wound in his side. His lips moved in near incoherent words but she could make out the word mother. A stab of pity pricked her heart. Even here, dying among the bodies of his companions, he called for his mother.

Umakaal placed her sword over his chest and stabbed down with all her heart. The babbling stopped. She pulled her sword out, wiping it on his uniform. Perhaps there was room for at least a small bit of mercy.

"That was kind of you," Mikhra said close by. He'd resumed his unofficial duty of bodyguard since she'd returned from the wall, even accompanying her into the main battle. If one could have called it that. After they'd dropped the dragon's tears among the inner Egan forces, all attempts at forming a defense dissolved. Wiluru's forces managed to push them back all the way to the gate.

Umakaal glanced at her fiancée, now splattered with blood, both of them now truly battle tested. "I suppose I can't be completely heartless."

"No one should be heartless," he said. "Only the truly evil are completely heartless. You are not."

"Thank you." She gave him a little smirk which he returned.

A young Wiluruan fighter hurriedly picked her way over. "Princess," they said, out of breath. "The commanders are meeting."

She glanced to Mikhra, motioning with her head for him to come. They followed the fighter back to the planning house. Inside was crowded with nearly all of the commanders in attendance. The only ones missing were those holding the line at the gate. Umakaal tried her best to hide her excitement as she entered. It could finally happen today. She could finally take her place as high commander of Wiluru's forces. With these experienced commanders as her advisers, she knew her time as their leader would be a rousing success.

Her brother entered the room from upstairs and everyone saluted. Something about him was off. There was a weariness that hung on him like a weight from his neck. He straightened his spine, saluting them back. "We have two decisions to make in this meeting," he began without preamble. "The first is how to conduct this war now that we've taken back the gates." He gestured to the crowd for their input.

"We have to continue the assault," Umakaal said. It wasn't even a question in her mind. "They're in chaos. They're having to regroup after the dragon's tears attack. Now is the perfect time."

"I must say I agree with the princess," chimed in another captain. Around them, the majority of the commanders nodded their agreement.

Yutuuan nodded, but Umakaal could see the slight reluctance. "With this break in the heavy fighting, we could use this time to regroup, rest our soldiers for a heavy push."

"With all due respect," began the top commander of the Asfaran fleet, "my people came here to see battle. We are fresh and ready to deal with the southern invaders. Not wait around."

Umakaal liked her but that was brushing the line of disrespect. "I think what the commander is saying is that we have the advantage now," she said. Passion and eagerness had slipped into her voice and she prayed it didn't make her sound childish. "We have fresh forces, a new weapon, and the Ega are backpedaling. Now is the time to strike, brother. Break them. Send them running back to Metkara. Pay them back for all the years that they made us bow down to them. Isn't that what we all want?"

She looked around the room and all eyes stared at her. It was a mixture of surprise and pride but agreement played on everyone's face. She had them. She turned her attention to her brother. He saw the shift in the room as well and caught her gaze for a moment before turning his attention back to the rest of the room.

"Then we will push our advantage," he said. "My sister is right. Now is the time to break the Ega threat once and for all."

He began giving orders for the fighter organizations but Umakaal could tell his heart wasn't in it. He put up a good facade but the weariness still clung to him. "The second decision we need to make is what to do about...," he trailed off, frowning in anger. "What steps should we take now that the emperor is dead."

"The emperor is dead?" gasped the Tiirazan captain.
"When? How did this happen?"

Her brother laid out the tale of the emperor's arrival in the city and how someone murdered him but they hadn't figured out who. Umakaal saw Naret across the room and by his utterly blank face she could tell that was a lie. "Now," he said after his explanation, "what do we do with his body and the news of his death?"

A small chuckle of disbelief escaped Umakaal. "Is that really a question? Hang that goat fucker's body from the wall and let the fear of death run through his people."

There were a few who agreed with her but most were still contemplating. An older captain spoke up. "I think we should send his body back to Metkara once this conflict is over with a message warning them to never return to Wiluru under the banners of war ever again." More people agreed with that.

"Why bother with his whole body?" the Asfaran captain shrugged. "Just send his head. It can still go with the message and is gruesome enough to say that we mean every word of our warning."

Umakaal knew she was right to like this woman. "I agree with that plan." The majority nodded along.

Yutuuan stared at her for a second as if he were trying to figure something out. "Then, yes, once the conflict is over, we'll send the emperor's head back with a warning. That is all I called you for today. See that the attack is carried out as soon as possible. Let's put an end to this."

Everyone saluted him and began to leave. Umakaal waited to the side of the room as the other captains filed out, ready to restart the fight. Several of them nodded to her, the Asfaran taking a moment to look her fully in the eyes before nodding. Mikhra tilted his head toward the door, eyebrow raised in question. She nodded and he left. With everyone gone, the only people remaining were her, Naret, and her brother. The bodyguard looked less than pleased.

"Naret," she said, not taking her eyes off of her brother, "could you give us the room?"

"I would rather stay, princess. I think your words are going to reflect many of my own thoughts."

Yutuuan closed his eyes and sighed heavily, leaning against a table. "What is it?" he said. Weary. Annoyed.

Umakaal marched her way in front of him. "What is wrong with you?" she asked, exasperated.

"What are you talking about?" He still wouldn't look at her. He rubbed the bridge of his nose.

"It's like your heart isn't in this anymore. I shouldn't have to take the lead like that in front of the captains." She made frustrated growl. "What is going on with you?"

"I'm tired. That's all." He finally looked her way and for the first time, she noticed the dark circles around his eyes.

"Yes, you look like a shipwreck, but this is more than that. It's like you don't want to do this anymore."

There was a moment of hesitation that was more confirmation than if he'd answered the question outright. "I'm fine. I just need some rest. This has been a long conflict."

"Then turn it over to me," she ground out. She couldn't understand why he was being so stubborn about this. He was going to be king now. He didn't have to worry about running the force anymore. "I'm going to be taking over anyway. Or do you think I can't do it?"

"It's not that I think you can't do it. But you are young."

"You were only a year older than me when you took command."

He sighed again. "You're right. You're right. I should give you command. It's just…." He ran his hand down his face but didn't continue.

Umakaal straightened as a thought occurred to her. "You don't want to be king," she breathed. "But you act like you don't want to be here either. Where did your conviction go, brother?"

"It's gone," he said. "It's been almost a year of this. I went from one battle straight into another. I'm tired. I just want to-" He stopped himself, pressing his lips together.

Naret finally moved from his spot near the wall. "Luunja pressured you into something, didn't she?"

Umakaal had never seen her brother so pained. "She said I can never see Talekh again. How can I do that, Naret?"

Umakaal closed her eyes and prayed to all the gods for patience. "I understand you're upset. I understand that you care about that woman…and your child. But you have to pull yourself together. You are going to be king whether you like it or not. You can't be in both positions. Especially if you've lost the conviction to do either wholeheartedly." She took a breath, not wanting to just speak in anger. There had to be a solution to this. Why was she the one to fix her siblings' messes?

"May I make a suggestion?" Naret said at last. She and Yutuuan nodded. "If you would rather stay in your current position, let the princess take the throne."

Umakaal blinked, shaking her head in disbelief. "Me?"

Naret continued. "One of you has to assume leadership. And honestly, one of you has." The prince looked hurt. "I'm not saying that you were or are a bad commander but things have changed. You have changed."

Yutuuan looked down, thinking. "I don't know."

"Then I'm going to put it this way, brother," Umakaal snapped. "A leader can't be indecisive. Either let me assume the throne or let me assume leadership of Wiluru's fighters. If you won't make the decision, I'll make it for you." She turned, heading to the door. "Now, I'm going to the front to make sure our forces are victorious. Again."

***

Yutuuan pulled himself up, step by step, to the palace. The battle against the Ega was turning into a rout and Umakaal and the other commanders seemed to have everything firmly in hand. He'd left Naret at the front, to protect Umakaal along with her new fiancée who didn't want to leave her side now. He had to admit his sister was falling into the role of high commander even more eagerly than he did. Perhaps he did need to just turn it over to her. But that meant taking up the throne and the idea of the entire kingdom's future resting on his shoulders terrified him.

He entered the palace through the private entrances, the evening shift of guards surprised to see him. He walked along slowly through the familiar halls until he reached the quarters of his parents. He hoped his mother was nearby. He'd never wanted her council more than he did now.

He finally found her in the inner courtyard of the area, sitting on the bench that she would often occupy with his father as they watched him and his sisters play. The one tree here, a willow that was a gift from a distant island kingdom, drooped its branches down nearby, framing her. She still hadn't braided her hair back and the idea of having to come to his still mourning mother with such a heavy topic made him feel like a sorry excuse for a son.

He considered leaving but she noticed him before he could. "My son," she said with a smile. Her face changed to concern at his expression. "What is it?"

He came nearer and she patted the bench beside her. Yutuuan hesitated, not wanting to take his father's place. He gave in and sat beside her. "I need your council, mother."

"I am here for you, just as I was there for your father," she said patting his hand.

Yutuuan bit his lip for a moment. "Mother, you think I've been a good commander all of these years, don't you?"

"Of course, my son," she said slowly.

"I...I have never had a conflict like this. It just seems to keep going and going. I want it to stop."

His mother didn't say anything for a moment and his heart cracked. "May I remind you that this is what you and your siblings conspired to do?"

"I didn't want to start a war," he countered. "We hoped to avoid one. We planned to use Izriamat as a hostage to keep the emperor from attacking."

"But I know you were hoping for one."

His protests—his excuses, really—stopped. "Yes, I was."

"And now are you trying to run away from the conflict you all caused?"

"No, mother." He dropped his head. "There's so much. In order to secure Asfara's help, I was forced into marrying Luunja. She's been twisting my arm, holding their support as a bargaining chip to make this deal more favorable. And she knows my greatest secret." He took a breath. "I...I have a son."

His mother went very still. She could have been a statue until he saw her take a deep breath. Her face didn't change, didn't show the barest amount of anger or disappointment. "A son?"

she asked, voice barely even.

"Yes. He wasn't named when I saw him." Yutuuan couldn't keep the smile from his face. "I'm sure he has a name by-"

"Who is the mother?"

He was thrown off by his mother's sharp tone. She hadn't spoken to him like that since he was a child. "She was a priestess of Koleh. She's one of the emperor's lesser half-sisters."

"By Yutuu," his mother wailed, burying her face in her hands. "How could you be so reckless?"

"Mother, I love her. She loves me. I would give anything to be with them. It's all I want." His thoughts stopped for a moment. That was all he wanted. If he weren't the prince, this would all be so easy. He could be with Talekh and their son and they could live happily. Together. He looked to his mother. "They are all that I want in this world."

"But you've made a promise to marry the daughter of Governor Bergarmen. You must honor your promises."

He nodded, sadly. "I know. Mother, I don't know what to do. We're stuck in a war that I would give anything to have over. I'm stuck in a marriage with a wife that I despise and I'll never see my son or his mother ever again if I go through with it. Izriamat is trying to take my throne and Umakaal threatened to take command of the forces if I don't give it to her."

His mother sighed, clasping her hands together in her lap. "So many of your problems would be fixed if you would just assume the throne now instead of later."

"It wouldn't solve the problem of my family," he said hanging his head.

She didn't respond immediately. After a moment, she reached out and lifted his chin, turning his face towards her. "Look me in the eyes," she said gently but firmly. He did so and she searched his face. "Do you truly love this woman and your son?"

"With all my heart."

"And you would do anything for them, even sacrificing your life?"

Without hesitation, he said, "I would give my life in a heartbeat for them."

She searched his eyes again then released him with weary sigh. "Breaking the oath you made with Bergarmen is something only an honorless cretin would do. The kind of honorless cretin who would turn his back on his family. Perhaps even desert them to cavort with the enemy." Her expression hardened. "Do you understand me?"

He stared at her hard glare until he did. He nodded slowly. "Yes, mother."

She pulled him into a fierce hug, then kissed him on the forehead and cheeks so many times he was sure he'd never forget. She held him at arm's length looking him over. "You look so much like your father," she said, voice nearly cracking. She took a breath, composing herself. "Take care of your responsibilities."

He went to hug her, realizing the seriousness of the moment, but she pushed him away. Yutuuan stood, numb, wanting to carve her face into his memory. "Goodbye, mother." She nodded once and he left the courtyard.

Chapter Twenty-Three

Erenemo readied himself for the council meeting he'd called, taking a peaceful moment to have a snack. He didn't want his stomach growling as he was permanently installed as Great Dara. His servants were about the city, informing the members. He should be at the council chambers before any of them. He wanted to look each one of them in the eye as they entered. Despite their feelings about him, he was the one who had brought them this victory. He invoked the gods to set the downfall of the Ega in place.

The niggling reminder of his son's forces gaining the upper hand in the conflict needled him. He sucked his teeth. His son was lucky. No. Blessed. He had called down a great blessing on all of Nsongo's warriors, his wayward son included. Once again, his efforts won the day.

The sound of sprinting feet came down the hallway toward him. He turned, annoyed by the repetitious slapping of sandals. One of his messengers skidded into the room, holding onto the entryway to keep from falling. He bent over, gasping for breath. "My priest, the council is already meeting."

Erenemo's blood ran cold. "What do you mean?" he asked slowly.

The man gulped in another breath. "I went to Councilmember Hafulo's compound as you told me and his servant said that he'd already gone to a council meeting. He left some time ago."

Erenemo dropped the morsel he'd been about to eat in a bowl and hurried to put on his sandals. He rushed past his servant, nearly running towards the entrance of the compound. *This couldn't be*, he thought as he burst onto the streets. There was no council meeting without him. This was a full-fledged conspiracy. His worry morphed with each step until it rolled itself into a tight ball of anger. He was dara. There wasn't a step this city could take without him.

He shoved open the outer doors to the council building, nearly knocking over the servants who'd tried to open them for him. He stalked the hallways until he reached the main chambers. He could already hear their voices in discussion. It sounded like every member was in attendance. Without him. Conspiring. Erenemo placed a hand on the carved wooden door, closing his eyes for a moment to pray to the gods for calm. Then he pushed it open.

Conversation withered like a sapling in the sun. He looked around, taking in each of the conspiring members, then rested on a face he hadn't expected to see. War Minister Ngali sat comfortably among the assembly, staring back at him with calmly narrowed eyes. He glanced back at some of the others, panic flaring. Surely, they weren't thinking of installing her instead of him. He looked to Oshala. This was all her idea. The old bat.

"Acting Great Dara Erenemo," said the eldest, Okepeli, cooly. "Good morning."

The purposeful use of *acting* chaffed him. "Good morning, esteemed council members. I thought to convene a meeting this morning but I heard you all were already here so I thought I would come."

"Ran all the way here too," Oshala muttered.

Erenemo resisted cutting his eyes her way. He worked even harder to slow his breathing. "I have to wonder what matter would be so pressing that the council would meet without their leader. And with the War Minister as well."

The council shared glances in a way he didn't like at all. Oshala finally slapped her hands on her knees. "I'll say it since all of you have forgotten your bravery today." She looked Erenemo in the eyes, a more serious face than he'd seen her in years. "I called the meeting to discuss choosing a permanent dara because my daughter has new considerations for us."

Erenemo's temper flared. "I should have known you'd try to get your daughter in the seat," he snapped before he could stop himself.

"Priest Erenemo," Ngali said firmly. "I have no desire to become dara. You couldn't force me into the position, despite what my mother might want. I have come to the council to present the case for Efemu to fill the position."

Erenemo felt as if all the air fled his lungs. His knees threatened to fail him. "You can't be serious."

She turned her attention back to the group. "As I was saying before, it was Efemu and his forces that turned the tide of the battle."

"It was my efforts," Erenemo interrupted. "I was the one who blessed the warriors with Ngema's favor."

"Yes, yes. I remember your little ceremony. But Efemu has the favor of the Lady of Death. She commanded the monsters that were harrying the Ega to break their defenses and allow our forces inside. It speaks to his strength as a leader that he was able to take the rather unexperienced force he'd been assigned and make them into the heroes of the battle."

"Tell us of this Lady of Death," said the old commander Embalu. "Have you met her?"

Ngali continued, completely ignoring Erenemo. "I have. She's unlike anyone I've met before. She's young, yes, but she carries herself with power and authority. I have no doubts as to her claim. I mean, her companions are two great hyenas that act as puppies by her side. If anyone was ever truly touched by a god, it's her. And she chooses Efemu as the new Great Dara. I support him too."

Fear and insult consumed Erenemo. A few eyes turned to him. "You would listen to the words of a witch over your high priest?" he said, reclaiming his indignation. "I am of the line of Yundasha. I have been high priest for decades. No one is more fitting candidate for Great Dara than I."

There was a moment of silence and he felt his words fall limp. Embalu cleared his throat. "It appears that there is," he said solemnly. "If you are so fit for the stool of Great Dara, where were you during the battles with the Ega? Any of them?"

Now all attention fell on him. He was a mouse in a trap and had never felt so small in his life. Half a breath of panic clamped around his heart and he struggled for an answer. "I was communing with the gods and ancestors to ensure our victory."

Looks of disapproval spread around the room. Panic's teeth began piercing him. "We need a leader," Ngali said to the room after a pointed glance at him. "Efemu may not have been our first choice but he has proven himself, turning a humiliation into an honor. That is something worthy of the great line of Yundasha."

"Then we should put it to a vote," Oshala said with a sagely nod. "Who here supports Efemu, son of Erenemo, of the line of Yundasha, to be the dara of Nsongo and Great Dara of the Great Cities?"

Erenemo watched in horror as all hands went up across the room. He stared at the elder Oshala whose hand still rested in her lap. She locked eyes with him and a slight smirk pulled at her lips. With exaggerated slowness, she raised it. Erenemo suddenly found it hard to breath. He stepped back, shaking his head in disbelief.

"So shall it be," Embalu rumbled in his deep voice. "In a harmonious decision, this council has appointed Efemu as Great Dara."

"So shall it be," echoed the other council members.

The priest took another step back, heart racing. They had unanimously rejected him. Even old Embalu, who hadn't had any particular love for his son, voted for him. The attention of the other council members slowly started to focus on him as if waiting for his response, some looking at him as if wondering why he was still here. Erenemo sputtered for an answer but words failed him. Defeated, he turned and hurried from the room.

***

A maelstrom of indignation consumed Erenemo by the time he returned home. The council had removed him from the rulership of Nsongo. After all he had done, the knots he'd twisted himself into to show them that he was the proper choice to lead the entire south. How could they choose his son over him? One great battle and suddenly he was god chosen. Or witch chosen. They'd voted for a boy only useful in battle who'd aligned himself with the witch who'd stolen Ofolubaru. Madness. Absolute, petty, vindictive madness.

He stalked the halls of his compound until he came to

Efemu's wing. "Is my son at home?" he said, snatching up the nearest servant.

"Y-yes," the small man answered. "He's in his courtyard."

Erenemo released the man and continued his march. Other servants scrambled to get out of his way, his aura of anger repelling them. When he came to the entryway to Efemu's small courtyard, he stopped, sneering at the scene. His son lounged on a bench as his lover sat in the low grass, the head of a giant hyena in his lap. The other animal lounged behind Barabi, leaning against him. He petted the both of them, a childlike smile on his face.

"I have always wanted a hyena," he heard the strategist say. "Ever since a troop of performers came to the city when I was ten."

"Enjoy it now," Efemu chuckled, "because we are not keeping hyenas."

Erenemo's eyes slid over to the last person sitting in the courtyard, a young woman with a low afro crowning her head. He didn't get a chance to assess her. Her attention was already focused on him. He felt his heart stop, his breathing halted. Authority pressed down on him. A part of him grew afraid, the raw, naked, animalistic sort of terror. The witch. He worked to pull himself out of the well of fear. No witch would overpower him. He was the highest spiritual authority in Nsongo.

"What conspiracy did you craft to sway the council?" he snarled at his son, entering the courtyard. Efemu sat up surprised. The hyenas started to come to attention but Barabi soothed them with whispers. The witch never took her eyes off of him.

"Father," Efemu said with the barest of nods. "What are you talking about?"

His son looked neither guilty nor pleased, a true curiosity painted his face as if he truly knew nothing about today's event. "You know damn well what I'm talking about. The council voted you in as Great Dara. How did you persuade Ngali to speak on your behalf?"

"High Priest Erenemo," came Barabi's even tone. "You're shouting and you wouldn't want to upset our rather large guests, would you?"

His attention turned sharply to the hyenas. They stared back at him, eyes focused and threatening even from their lounging position. Erenemo swallowed some of his anger, turning it into a smoldering heat. "How did you do it?" he hissed. "Was it the witch?"

Only then did his son look angry. "She is not a witch. Father. Allow me to introduce Efah, the chosen one of Death. And no, she didn't influence Ngali. That was a decision the War Minister made on her own." He paused, chin in hand to think, a childish habit he'd never dropped. He looked to Barabi. "I'm Great Dara," he said elated.

Barabi smiled. "I would get up to congratulate you, but I'm buried under affectionate beasts."

Erenemo watched incensed as Efemu came down from his seat to kiss his lover. Completely ignoring him. Celebrating as if this were a happy occasion instead of a tragedy. He started to storm his way over to yank his son to his feet but the witch was in front of him before he could cross half the distance.

She had a hand up, a finger's length from his chest, and it was enough to stop him cold. "You will not interrupt this happy moment," she said coolly.

This girl even carried herself with authority and it clawed against his spirit. "Get out of my way, child. This is a family matter and you have no place within it."

"I have every right to see that the right person sits in the seat of the dara."

"I am the right person," he roared.

"I don't think that you are."

Then she touched him.

Erenemo gasped as he felt her spirit touch his, no, clutch his. He tried to fight her off and pull back from her invasion but she moved his efforts aside like a bothersome fly. He felt his jealousy of his brother rise up, festering and rank. It was replaced by his smoldering hate of Ashaki, a deep blue-purple miasma that sat about his spirit. He saw himself give the poison to Masola, heard his words to her before and after she'd done the horrible, horrible deed. It echoed in his mind over and over again.

Until it stopped, Efah gasping. She looked up to him, shocked, tears forming in her eyes and he found them forming in his as well. Erenemo forced his lungs to take in a breath, to start working again. She backed up, shaking her head and looking more like the young woman she was than this so-called Lady of Death.

"What's the matter?" Efemu asked, but his voice came distantly to his father.

The girl looked horrified and he realized that she saw everything. Everything. He lunged for her, reaching for her throat. She would not ruin everything. He'd worked too hard for far too long for everything to come crashing down.

A strong hand slapped him in the chest, pushing him back violently. Erenemo stumbled, falling down to the bricked path. His son stood by the Lady of Death protectively. Efemu stared at him, face set in anger, but his eyes held the sorrow of disbelief. "What did you see, Efah?" Efemu asked slowly.

"He killed his niece, your cousin," she said, voice trembling. "He sent her daughter to do it, made her think it wasn't poison. He had that girl kill her own mother then told her to run away."

All anger drained from Efemu's face and he stood shaking his head. "You killed Ashaki?" he asked, voice suddenly hoarse. "You killed your own blood?"

Erenemo struggled for a response. His heart still beat erratically from whatever that witch had done to him. His normal lies failed him. "She needed to go," he said at last. "She wasn't worthy. We both agreed on that. Half the city agreed."

"But you murdered her." He looked aside but the feeling of heartbreak was plain on his face. "This is unforgivable."

Erenemo's heart cracked under his son's disappointment. "Son," he pleaded, "I did what needed to be done."

That Efah girl dared to speak up. "This is serious. Kin killers should die."

Panic filled Erenemo as Efemu looked to Barabi. "He's your father. It's your decision, my love," Barabi said sadly.

Erenemo struggled to get to his feet, cursing his age. Efemu stared at him, sorrowful at first but then a grim determination settled over him. For the first time, Erenemo was frightened of his son. "Kill him," Efemu said firmly. "We'll say his heart was attacked and it was too strong for the healers to save him."

The priest couldn't move, his feet planted in shock. He watched as the girl approached him, disgust painted across her face. He struggled as she held his eyes with hers, wanting to escape. He could run to one of the other cities, tell them of this betrayal by the council. Surely he could get someone on his side. He could always make a plan to come out of any situation better.

Efah touched his chest and this time she grasped his very spirit. She pulled with her hand and he felt it jerk just outside of him. The pulling maw of the other side of life began tugging at his back. He held hands grasping at him, latching onto him for a moment before losing their grip. Tears formed in his eyes. Efah looked back to Efemu and he gave a confirming nod. She pulled her hand as if plucking an errant thread and he felt the moment his soul's connection to his body snapped. He was falling. And then there was nothing.

Chapter Twenty-Four

Sept'ha did not like the swell of her breasts or the fact that her stomach was catching up to them. She ran a hand along the slight rise of her belly, uncomfortable with the fact that something grew within her. Servants scurried around her as she stood wrapped in a blanket after her bath, fetching her clothing and jewelry for the day. Having so many people around her annoyed her in profound ways but she tried her best to stay reasonably pleasant. They were eagerly helping her after all. They could have been trying their best to sabotage her but it seemed like they were glad their prior mistress was gone. She smirked. So was she.

"How is your stomach this morning, mistress?" one of the servants asked. The older woman and head of her handmaids seemed to have appointed herself Sept'ha's new mother as well.

"Fine," Sept'ha answered. "I think the sickness is passing. Finally."

The woman's face lit up. "Wonderful. I'll have your breakfasts increased. We have to make sure both of you are fed properly."

Sept'ha pushed a small smile onto her face, nodding. When she'd first started feeling nauseous in the morning, she'd panicked, thinking someone had tried to poison her. Then as the days passed with the same routine, she grew worried. Hetsaf actually showed concern about her health in his usual cold demeanor. She assured him it was nothing, but then her breasts began to swell noticeably just as her menses stopped. She hadn't wanted to tell him. The idea of carrying his child—any child— was a disgusting prospect. But this was what they'd agreed to do. It made her laugh when she realized what was finally wrong with her. It was just her luck to get pregnant after her first and only time having sex. She was sure Met was pleased. She felt the unpleasant fluttering in her stomach and frowned. *Please just stay still so I can ignore you.*

The flurry of activity drew to a close and her maids had her dressed, face painted, and hair done in incredible time. One held up the large copper mirror that used to belong to the empress— the old empress— for her to examine their work. Sept'ha had them raise it so she could only see from her shoulders up. She was still not used to this. She looked like a completely different woman. A bauble. An empty headed companion.

Not the powerful woman she was promised from her vision.

Sept'ha worked hard to banish the feelings of sadness and the tiniest thread of betrayal that washed over her. She allowed her servants to lead her down the hallways to where Hetsaf waited for her. He paced in the hallway just inside of the doorway to the balcony that overlooked the main plaza of the city. Sept'ha remembered standing in that plaza, listening to the netkoleh as he denounced the gods and proclaimed himself emperor. Now, here they were, about to undo all of his work.

"You look nervous," she said in lieu of a greeting.

His head jerked toward her as if he hadn't noticed her arrival. "I am going over my address. You look…well." His eyes darted uncomfortably to her stomach and back.

She wished he hadn't. "I am. When do we begin?"

"Soon. People are still arriving in the plaza." He closed his eyes for a moment, taking a long, deep breath. The nervous energy fell away from him and his face set in a focused calm. He turned and studied her face. "You don't seem happy."

Sept'ha stiffened, not realizing her many concerns were playing across her face. She glanced over her shoulder and her attendants retreated to the end of the hall. "I'm…not," she said lowly. She wanted to lay out all of her feelings on the turn of events. How, once again, she felt used and dragged along by the whims of her goddess. How, if one thought about it on the surface, she'd gotten exactly what she'd wanted, but once you delved into the complexities of the matter, had she really? Hetsaf waited on her to elaborate. She sighed. "I am not enjoying this," she said gesturing to her rounding belly.

He nodded, looking down and away from her. "You do know we'll have to do this again. In case something happens."

"Yes, I know." Bile threatened to invade her mouth and she

swallowed sourly. They may have to produce at least three children to ensure they make it to take the crown. Her hand went to her stomach. If she had the misfortune of producing girl after girl like Arkole, who knew how many times she'd have to endure this invasion of her body.

Hetsaf shook her firmly. "Sept'ha, it's time to speak to the crowd."

She snapped out of her horror and focused on him. "Yes, I'm ready."

"All you have to do is stand there. Don't be a disappointment to me now of all times."

She almost swore he'd insulted her on purpose. "I would never be a disappointment to you, husband." She lovingly took his hand, enjoying the little shiver of revulsion from him. Turning toward the balcony, he set his face back to neutral and led her outside.

Seeing so many people gathered all around made for a dizzying sight. Sept'ha was half tempted to turn and flee back inside. She could barely stand the thought of the servants seeing her in such a state. Now half the city would see her. She focused to keep her breathing steady, concentrating on the feel of Hetsaf's too tight grip around hers and trying to ignore the sounds of the chattering crowd below.

Hetsaf raised his hands, taking a step forward. The crowd silenced their conversation almost immediately.

"People of Metkara, the heart of the empire, I come to you today with a heavy heart." His voice was sure and steady, carrying over the plaza with the aid of magicians so even the very edges of the crowd could hear. "The emperor has fallen in the war and after a long battle against his injuries, he succumbed to death."

The gasp that rose from the crowd surely could be heard across the city. Sept'ha watched the crowd carefully, trying to discern expressions and how people were reacting to the news. Shock showed the most on many faces. Yet, there were a few that she could see that didn't seem too concerned with the news of the late emperor's demise. She knew that most of the priests would feel vindicated that he'd been struck down. Many of the faithful as well might feel glad that he was dead. It made the next words that they'd worked many, many nights to perfect all the more important.

"I know that the emperor, my brother, wanted to take the empire on a different route than our ancestors. I know that his hand was heavy on many of you. He struck at the very core of what makes this empire so strong. Our reverence to the gods. He chose to abandon them, to dishonor their temples and their ways. His blasphemy thrust us into a war in the north, conflict again with the south, and rebellions to our west. The empire will not hold if we continue on in this manner."

He paused and she looked to him, hoping he wasn't losing his nerve. His posture changed as he stood straighter. "That is why I will take up the mantle of emperor to ensure that the future of empire of the Ega will be strong again." He took a planned pause as murmurs started in the crowd and he let the words sink in.

Isn't it beautiful? She heard as Hetsaf continued, extolling his virtues as the new emperor and laying out his plans. *They hang on his every word already.*

They don't have much of a choice, she shot back. She truly didn't want to talk to her absentee deity at the moment. *And I just get to stand here, a swollen, silent trinket.*

Met chuckled. *Ah, but the words he says are yours as well. And so will be all of the decrees, plans, and orders that the empire follows. You will lay the foundation for generations of this empire.* Sept'ha felt Met's hand on her stomach, caressing gently. *Isn't that what you wanted?*

She stopped herself from jerking away. *You promised me that I would be a powerful woman. A woman who would direct armies.*

"I will bring our forces back from Wiluru and the southern cities."

And for now, you will direct them home. Ebb and flow, push and pull. That is War. We have pushed, now we must pull back. But it is only for a little while. We will push again soon enough.

Sept'ha's temper flared, the only reaction she could dredge up for the abject betrayal she felt. *You tricked me.*

The god sucked her teeth. *You wanted power. You wanted to*

rule over your own life. You have more power than any woman in this entire land from north to south. If you didn't think you would have to make a few sacrifices then you tricked yourself.

"I will restore the gods to their proper place of reverence and restore the priests to their posts."

Sept'ha felt hot, fat tears gathering in her eyes. *But I didn't want this.*

My dear chosen, Met said in a truly pitying tone, *we don't always get what we want.*

"And when everything has been set back to its right path, I and my empress will guide this empire to its grand and glorious future."

The crowd cheered, the sound deafening, surrounding them in the adoration of their new subjects. The tears that had been threatening to fall finally streamed down Sept'ha's cheeks as she felt the first kicks of the future of the empire.

***

The sea churned beautiful, blue, and noisily at the shoreline. The princesses of the empire ran barefoot through the sand, the youngest chasing after gulls who protested their disturbance in loud calls. A servant held the tiny prince's hands as he tottered his way after his sisters. He would be walking on his own soon and eager to chase after them.

Arkole watched the scene from beneath a large canopy held aloft by a quartet of servants. She kept her stroll to the dry parts of the beach to not lose another sandal to the sand. It amazed her at how her children had taken to this new life, ignorant of their banishment. It was their first time seeing the sea—Arkole's as well—and every day brought them new wonder. They ran through the halls of their new home, finding hiding places for their games and being a minor disruption to the servants.

She sighed heavily, the weight of carrying the truth drooping her shoulders. Surely, her Bakari was dead. Hetsaf wouldn't make such a bold move without knowing for certain. Tears pricked her eyes and she struggled to blink them away. Never in all her days did she think she'd lose her Bakari so soon. They were supposed to watch their children grow together, grow old together.

Her hand clutched onto her dress over her heart, the pain growing. Now she was alone. Alone and banished to a seaside palace that hadn't been occupied since his father's days, doomed to live out the rest of her life in obscurity and exile.

She quickly wiped her tears away when she saw her eldest daughter break away from the group and make her way over. Arkole smiled through her heartache. She hadn't had the heart to tell them about their father. She didn't want to give them too many shocks at once.

"Tired of playing?" she asked. Her eldest was nearing womanhood, starting to grow lean and tall like her father.

The girl wore a serious face as she approached, looking so much like Bakari that it almost broke Arkole's heart again. "Mother," she began, falling in step beside her, "when are we going home?"

Arkole nearly stopped, voice catching in her throat. "We're not," she answered gently. "This is our home now."

To her credit, her daughter didn't fall into hysterics or even show shock. "It was the chancellor, wasn't it?"

"Yes." Why should she lie? They should know who their enemy was.

"Isn't he our uncle?" she asked thoughtfully. "Why would he do this to us?"

Arkole took her daughter's hand, giving it a squeeze. "Power, my heart. Some men will do terrible, evil things for power. Even betray their own family. Never forget that. Your uncle is evil and despite what anyone in the future may say about him you must remember that he is our enemy." She stopped so she could look her in the eyes. "Do you understand?"

The girl frowned slightly, thinking, then nodded. "I understand, mother."

They continued on, walking hand in hand. She should have known her eldest would know something was wrong, the wonderful, perceptive girl. Arkole wouldn't be able to keep the severity of their situation from her or the others for much longer. She had to make sure they were strong for the days ahead. Their enemies could come for them at any time.

A now familiar rage resurfaced at the thought of the two usurpers occupying the palace in Metkara. She could imagine Hetsaf's smug face as he took the crown of the empire. She was sure that becoming the emperor was his ultimate plan. Being regent until her son came of age wouldn't be enough for that evil, vile bastard. Now he had that woman as his co-conspirator. Arkole couldn't believe she'd been fooled so completely by her. Sept'ha's façade as a simple servant was an amazing act. Now she probably sat in Arkole's rooms enjoying the comforts that a woman so low born had no right to have.

"Mother, are you alright?" her daughter asked.

Arkole released the hard scowl from her face and smiled down at her daughter. "I'm fine, my heart. Why don't you go back to playing with your sisters? Perhaps you could encourage your brother to walk on his own. He does adore you so."

Her daughter looked concerned but dipped her head. "Yes, mother."

Arkole watched as the girl jogged back to her siblings, taking the servant's place leading her brother around the beach. This was no life for the princess of the empire to live and certainly no life for the future ruler. In the capital, they would have fine betrothals that would ensure they lived in comfort for the rest of their days. Now what sort of matches could she find for them if any at all. She watched, sorrowfully, as her eldest daughter tried to get her brother to release her hands and walk but he clutched onto her even harder. Her laughter broke Arkole's heart.

Her son had a throne he may never see. She took a breath, shoring up her resolve. No, her son had a throne and one day he would have it. She would cast Hetsaf and the betrayer Sept'ha from the palace and let them live in exile. She scowled harder. She would have them executed as traitors to the crown. It could be her son's first decree as emperor. But first, she must make sure he grew strong and proud of the lineage he came from. She'd make sure he understood his rightful place in this world. Then, she would help him seize it.

Chapter Twenty-Five

Izriamat disrobed, set her sandals by the antechamber's single seat, and descended the stairs to the inner temple. The stone was cool beneath her bare feet, causing a tiny shiver to run up her body. The waves gently lapped at the sand at the cave's opening. The sound echoed off the rough walls, creating a quiet blanket of rhythm to which one could meditate. She walked across the sand to where the sea waited, coming to where the depth of the water was just at her ankles. Light began peeking in through the low, narrow entrance. The sun had finally come out this morning. A wonderful sign that it was a new day in Wiluru.

Izriamat lay down in the sand, feet toward the opening. The water ran up her body in cold waves and she had to stop herself from gasping each time until she acclimated to the temperature. She let her mind lose focus, letting her spirit be open to Yutuu's presence. She was his vessel on earth and she wanted to express her utter gratitude.

The battle for Wiluru died down even as she lay here. The Ega were being destroyed or held as prisoners from what her people told her. Her people grew in number and there were fewer and fewer sick by the day. She may not have been able to find her way to the battlefield herself or stop her people from being barred from it, but she initiated this fight for her people's freedom. She had disposed of the evil heretic and, with Yutuu's blessing, she would clean this city from all of the blasphemous influences the Ega had placed on them.

She felt the calming presence of her god surround her and whispered praises to him for all that he had allowed her to do. She waited to hear from him like she had before. She knew what she had to do for her kingdom but the priest in her still wanted to hear from her deity first.

And she waited.

Silence.

Izriamat took a deep breath and moved down so that the water could cover her face. Yutuu was there. She could feel him but he wouldn't speak. She remained under the water until her lungs burned. Still not a single word from the kingdom's patron. She broke the surface, gasping in a breath. Why couldn't she hear him?

"Princess," came a distant voice. Sami.

Everything told her to ignore it but it came again, more insistent, and she could no longer focus on her connection. Annoyed at the disturbance, she rose from the sand and returned to the antechamber. She heard Sami call again as she used the waiting bucket of fresh water to rinse off the sand before dressing. Izriamat didn't respond until she was clothed and out of the temple's most sacred space.

She found her follower just outside the entrance to the inner sanctuary. She bowed the instant she saw Izriamat. "Yes, Sami?"

"There's a message from the palace, princess," Sami said urgently. "You're being called for a council meeting."

Izriamat grinned, surprised. Perhaps the council and her mother had seen the light. "Very well. Accompany me there."

She stopped by her rooms to change into better robes and happily began the walk to the palace. Many people greeted her as she walked the streets of Wiluru, several making signs of Yutuu in reverence. Each gesture filled her with pride. These were truly her people. The others who didn't believe would come to with time. They would see their god's blessing on her and know that it was her divine right to lead this city into a new future.

Izriamat started to go to one of the side entrances to the palace but stopped herself and continued on her way to the front. The guards there, several more than she remembered, hesitated before letting her and Sami pass. It felt wonderful to not have to sneak into her own home.

The guards protecting the council chamber didn't even hesitate and opened the doors for her immediately. She thanked them and Izriamat walked inside to a waiting council. And her sister standing before the driftwood throne.

She stopped, looking about the room in confusion. All eyes focused on her with the same disapproval they had when her father ruled. Her mother sat to Umakaal's side, in her usual head councilor's seat. Her sister regarded her coolly and was clearly waiting for her to come closer.

"What is happening?" Izriamat asked cautiously, coming in the room.

Umakaal's eyes flicked behind her. "Your servant can wait outside."

Izriamat looked back to Sami who seemed slightly panicked. "Wait outside," she told her calmly. "I'm sure we'll be finished in no time." Sami hesitated but retreated out of the council room. She turned back to her sister. "Where is Yutuuan?" She asked.

"Yutuuan has proven himself a coward and a traitor. He shirked his duties and fled," her sister said.

Izriamat took a step back. Yutuuan would never be a deserter. Not with how much he loved his position. "That can't be."

"He left me a note this morning," their mother chimed in. "He fled the city with his Egan lover."

"Let me see this note," Izriamat said.

"I think you should be more concerned about yourself."

"Izriamat, first daughter of Taagreb," Umakaal started. "I have brought you here today to inform you of your banishment."

The word nearly knocked her to her knees. This couldn't be. Her sister couldn't be looking to get rid of her. This had to be her mother's plan. It had to be. "You can't banish-"

"I am still speaking," her sister said in a voice that echoed through the room. "You have made it clear that you were trying to take the throne from our brother, the former, rightful heir. I and this council believe that, as long as you remain in Wiluru, you will always be a threat to it. Therefore, before the sight of this council and Yutuu, I banish you from this kingdom. Effective immediately. A ship is waiting for you."

Izriamat looked around the room. She found not an ounce of sympathy or remorse in any of their faces. "I have been chosen by Yutuu," she said, voice pitching high. "He has chosen me to lead his people."

"Perhaps he changed his mind," Umakaal said. "You led people who couldn't fight into battle while you stayed safe at the temple. You tried to betray family to gain the crown. That doesn't seem like the actions of a priest."

Izriamat breathed hard, the rage in her building. "I will show you all that I am his chosen. He has given me powers, abilities beyond any that you've ever seen. If you don't submit to my place as his chosen-"

"Let me guess, you'll heal me to death?" her sister drawled. A snicker sounded toward the back of the council.

"I won't go!" Izriamat shouted. "I won't. Wiluru is where I'm meant to be."

Her sister motioned and a pair of guards came in toward her. Izriamat panicked. There was nowhere to run to, no escape except through those doors. She turned to her mother. "Mother," she called, tears starting to form in her eyes. "Mother, don't let them do this to me. Don't send me away again." Her mother stiffened and turned her head.

Strong hands grabbed onto Izriamat's arms, pulling her toward the door. She struggled against them, screaming not to be banished. Tears burned her cheeks as they dragged her, kicking and shrieking into the halls and away from her home.

***

The morning blew in unusually cold as Umakaal made her way through the dark toward the docks. The first pinks of dawn started to lighten the eastern sky but sailors were already up and preparing their ships. These were the first trading ships to visit the port since the war began and they were eager to take advantage of the day's first tide.

She stopped near a small vessel resting at the end of the dock. She pulled the hood of her cloak around her more securely, making sure she couldn't be recognized. She glanced about, searching in the dark. A moment later, a duo came, also cloaked, from another street, rushing along with several packs. Umakaal made her way over.

"Late as usual," she said quietly.

Yutuuan looked down at her with that cheerful grin of his.

"We had to get Talgreb to stay asleep."

Umakaal felt tears starting to form but blinked them away. "You named him after father?" She looked over to Talekh who held the bundle in her arms.

"We thought he should have some connection to his heritage," her brother explained.

She looked between Talekh and her brother's son. Her nephew. "Can I hold him?" she asked.

Talekh came over and settled the tiny baby into Umakaal's arms. She moved the fabric aside just enough to look at his face. She could already see that he was going to be the image of his father. "We love you," she whispered to him, giving him one gentle kiss on a chubby cheek. Reluctantly, she handed him back to his mother.

"Where is the ship taking us?" Yutuuan said, looking over her at the vessel.

"Ujali," she answered. "My brother, before he turned deserter, told me that they don't ask too many questions there."

"You brother sounds wise," he chuckled.

Then he crushed her into a hug. Umakaal threw her arms around him, holding him as tightly as she could. She wanted this moment to last as long as possible. If this was the last time, it had to count. Her tears came a moment later and she fought not to dissolve into bawling. She buried her face into his shoulder as she felt a couple of tears fall on hers.

"I think I'm going to miss you most of all," he said, voice wavering.

Umakaal pushed away from him, wiping her eyes on the edge of her cloak. "Shut up. I won't miss you at all."

He chuckled, wiping his own eyes, then playfully pulling her hood over her eyes. Talekh came over and actually gave her a hug. "Thank you for this."

Umakaal could only nod and watch them board the ship, explaining that they were the arranged *special passengers*. She stayed at the dock until the first rays of the sun lit the sky and the ship set sail. She stayed even longer, watching the ship fade into the distance until it was just a dot on the horizon, and then until it was gone. She took a long, soul aching breath, then turned on her heel and headed back to the palace.

The city was truly awakening by the time she returned home, with the streets starting to fill with people. The last of the Ega that hadn't been taken prisoner fled back south in a barely held together mass. The delegation from Djelebe readied themselves to return home with a number of Wiluruan workers to help them rebuild the great library. It was the least they could do for the newest ally of the kingdom.

The official story of the crown prince deserting the war effort hadn't gone over well. However, the captains and council seemed to sense that there was more to the story and Umakaal wasn't inclined to squash any rumors. Luunja had been furious but what was there to do? Their support had already been given and she made it clear to the woman to tell her father that the threat still stood. The alarmed confusion on Luunja's face was the greatest satisfaction.

Umakaal slipped in a servant's entrance, making her way along quickly and taking off her cloak the moment she reached the main halls. She jogged her way to her private rooms, making her way in as quietly as she could.

"You're late," Mikhra chided her the moment she entered.

She gave him a sheepish smile then turned to see Ladawi staring at her disapprovingly. Her lover picked up her clothes to help her change quickly. "You watched the ship leave, didn't you?" she asked after giving her a quick kiss.

"I did," she answered sadly. "But I got to see the baby."

"That is wonderful," Mikhra said. "Good morning, by the way." He tipped her chin up to give her a kiss as well.

"Good morning. Sorry. I forgot I left before you all woke up."

"It is fine. I am only heartbroken." He passed her a handful of grapes. "Because I know you did not eat."

Umakaal muttered a thanks as she popped one in her mouth. She hurried to finish getting dressed—and eat—and let Ladawi work her braids into some kind of style, then they all left quickly for the council room.

She paused before the great double doors, running her hand along the carved wood. She took a breath and closed her eyes.

She could do this. With everything she'd done since the war began, she was more than ready. She opened her eyes, releasing the breath. It was time.

The council came to their feet as she entered, all of them bowing as she walked down the ancient carpet leading up to the throne. She paused briefly to pay respects to her mother who sat at the closest council seat. Mikhra took his seat to her right as would be his place when they could finally have the wedding. She looked to the newest seat she'd had placed to the left of the throne and it was empty.

Umakaal searched the room until she saw Ladawi standing off to the side with the other waiting servants. She smiled and gestured for her to come over. Ladawi looked confused but came to her princess' beckoning. Umakaal motioned toward the newest chair. "I refuse to choose." Ladawi looked as if she were about to cry but shyly took the seat.

Umakaal settled herself into the throne, still getting used to looking out at the council instead of just watching the proceedings. The council took their chairs a moment later. She inhaled deeply, letting it out in a long breath. She looked around at the waiting council, lastly looking at her mother who gave a nod of approval.

"Let us begin," she started in a clear, strong voice. "We have much work to do to carve a new path for a free Wiluru."

Chapter Twenty-Six

So much fighting still had to be done. So much of the outside influences, of the rot of that had taken root here had to be burned out. Death walked the lands of the south collecting souls as he wandered. He was thankful to be bringing the elderly or sick with him instead of so many lives cut short by a blade. This was the way he preferred, the way it should be.

This new Great Dara in Nsongo would be an interesting one to watch. A man who would lead during the first time of peace in nearly a generation. Working to route the last of the outsiders from his lands, yet ready for any conflict the empire might try again. He was a good choice.

Death walked the streets of Olofubaru watching the people of his chosen. They were happy now and the children grew fat, the lines of their lives extending by years. His chosen had done an excellent job. He was so very proud of her but the cost to her was immeasurable.

He took to the walls where she waited day by day, looking to the northern road from the city. Today proved no different. Her dress flowed behind her in the soft breeze. Death felt a deep sorrow as he approached. It pained him to do this. He placed a gentle hand on her shoulder.

"I know," she whispered as tears began to trail down her cheeks.

***

War sat atop the highest roof of the palace of Metkara, of the ancient place of Met-Khara, of her city. Soldiers limped back from north and south, maimed and broken souled men who would be a burden to their families and communities in one way or another. The scars on their bodies and souls were beautiful. The scent of the blood on their hands sent ecstasy through her very being. The sight of the hauntedness in their eyes quenched her thirst more than any libation ever could. She was more than satisfied at the worship these mortals gave her.

And it would be just as satisfying the next time.

ABOUT THE AUTHOR

Sarah A. Macklin is a writer and artist from just outside of Columbia, SC. She is the author of the Royal Heretic series, Bride of the River God, and her short fiction has been published in FI-YAH literary magazine, Fantasy and Science Fiction, and more. She is also a graphic novelist, debuting with her first book, The Violent Vixens Ride Again, in 2023. When not creating new worlds, you can find her at her sewing machine adding to her wardrobe or in the kitchen testing out new recipes. She still lives in the midlands of South Carolina with her family who are her biggest cheerleaders.

Acknowledgements

This moment has been a long time coming and there are so many people who I'd like to thank for their support. I'm going to try to catch everyone, but if I forget you "charge it to my head and not my heart," as we say in my neck of the woods.

First and foremost, thank you to my family. My parents who've always supported my creative endeavors from childhood to today, I love you to the moon and back. To my husband, who is my first reader, your excitement has kept me going when I thought I was writing absolute crap. My daughters, y'all are a trip! I'm so glad I make you proud. And to the rest of my family—my in-laws, my aunts and uncles, my horde of cousins—I thank you all for supporting my dream of becoming an author. The Bowman family rides hard for each other!

To the CIIP Lunchtime Book Club, I'm glad that I could brighten up your lunch hour… except for the days I forgot to bring over my manuscript. Ms. Becky, Graham, you two are among my first fans and I'll never forget you. The rest of the CIIP crew, I sold out of every copy I had on hand thanks to you all. Isaiah, I hope you got your books back!

My dearest friends, Charise and Jennifer, thank you for understanding the times I couldn't hang out because I was writing and for celebrating every win with me. With friends like y'all, I can do it all.

I can't pass up thanking all the great folks of my writing group in that secret space station. This has been a space of some of the best writers I know and it has been a joy to be in communion with you. Y'all inspire and encourage me to do my best. I pray for only the best for each and every one of you.

To the man who made all of this possible, my publisher, Milton J. Davis. You believed in this story before it was even a story. I'm grateful for your faith in my writing and your mentorship, whether you knew it or not.

Most of all, I want to thank God for gifting me with my place as a storyteller. I do not take this gift lightly and pray that I can bring joy, a little escapement, and maybe even change some thinking one day.

And to those who are reading this, thank you. What is a writer without readers.

SARAH MACKLIN

Visit MVmedia, LLC for more exciting action
packed Sword and Soul adventures.
Sword and Soul Forever!